<u>Did I Read This Already?</u>
Place your initials or unique symbol in
square as a reminder to you that you have
read this title.

464					

THE MISTLETOE
MATCHMAKER

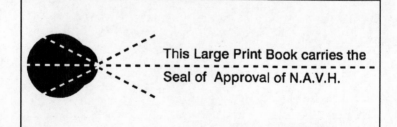

This Large Print Book carries the
Seal of Approval of N.A.V.H.

THE MISTLETOE
MATCHMAKER

FELICITY HAYES-MCCOY

THORNDIKE PRESS
A part of Gale, a Cengage Company

GALE
A Cengage Company

Farmington Hills, Mich • San Francisco • New York • Waterville, Maine
Meriden, Conn • Mason, Ohio • Chicago

Rb 32

Copyright © 2019 by Felicity Hayes-McCoy.
Finfarran Penisula.
Thorndike Press, a part of Gale, a Cengage Company.

ALL RIGHTS RESERVED
Thorndike Press® Large Print Women's Fiction.
The text of this Large Print edition is unabridged.
Other aspects of the book may vary from the original edition.
Set in 16 pt. Plantin.

LIBRARY OF CONGRESS CIP DATA ON FILE.
CATALOGUING IN PUBLICATION FOR THIS BOOK
IS AVAILABLE FROM THE LIBRARY OF CONGRESS

ISBN-13: 978-1-4328-7088-1 (hardcover alk. paper)

Published in 2019 by arrangement with Harper Perennial, an imprint of
HarperCollins Publishers

Printed in Mexico
1 2 3 4 5 6 7 23 22 21 20 19

For Carmel, who was
poised to save the day

PROLOGUE

Each year, the post office printed a leaflet that gave you the last dates for sending Christmas parcels overseas. You could find the same information on the internet, and that was far more convenient, but Pat Fitz liked having the leaflets as well. They were part of a thrilling countdown that she looked forward to every year.

You'd get the first real nip in the air around the end of October or the beginning of November. There'd be a tang of wood smoke curling from garden bonfires, and sea salt blown by Atlantic winds. As the bracken and wildflowers died back on the mountains, the grey shapes of the stone walls would stand out between the fields. In the town, the lights would glow in the shops as the evenings began to get foggy. And if you went for a walk on the beach you'd need a scarf.

Then, as November went on, you'd start

to get in the fruits and spices to make the cake and the pudding. And the deli down the way from the butcher's would start selling Christmas treats. There'd be long boxes of sticky black dates preserved in honey, and old-fashioned sweets that Pat's husband ate, like Hadji Bey's Turkish Delight, and things she liked herself, like Amaretti. And chocolate Bath Oliver biscuits in tall tins.

Then, come December, you'd be looking for lifts into Carrick, to start choosing presents to send to the grandkids. And you'd drop round the corner to Lissbeg post office to get your stamps and your airmail stickers, and see if the leaflets were out. Pat always tucked hers up on the mantelpiece over the range. The truth was that she knew well what the postal dates were for Canada. They hardly changed at all from year to year. But the sight of the leaflet lifted her heart — and, anyway, there were different dates for posting cards and parcels. She always sent hers early, but you'd want to be sure all the same.

One year, at a Christmas fête, she'd found cards that were photographs of Broad Street. You could see the shops on one side, and the old convent on the other, and the horse trough in the centre covered in snow, like sugar icing, and bright stars above in the night sky. And there was a glittery bunch of mistletoe in the top right-hand corner, with glittery writing underneath that said 'Across the Miles . . .'.

Her kitchen was on the first floor, at the front of the house, above the butcher's shop. It was a fierce busy time of year and a great season for business. Ger would be below at the counter, trussing up Christmas turkeys. And Pat would be above in the firelight, with the kettle singing on the range and the tea made.

And each year, as the excitement built, the coloured lights strung out across Broad Street would shine onto the table where she'd sit writing her cards.

1

Cassie Fitzgerald's family was upwardly mobile. Thirty-five years ago her dad, Sonny, had come to Canada from a rugged little peninsula on the west coast of Ireland and within five years had become a citizen, found a job, achieved promotion, and married Cassie's mom, a go-getter who'd started a business at her kitchen table and turned it into an empire. Well, maybe not exactly an empire but certainly Toronto's fastest-growing office-employment agency.

Five years later, having built up an impressive portfolio of contacts, Sonny had branched out on his own and, armed with Irish charm and a reputation for innovation, established a computer company that came to employ eighty people. So, having started married life in a cramped apartment, he and his wife, Annette, now owned a house in a leafy suburb, complete with a three-car garage, a landscaped garden, and an open-plan kitchen with a made-to-measure breakfast island.

Along the way they'd produced Cassie and her two siblings. And, in proper Fitzgerald fashion, the older kids were now building empires of their own. Cathleen had her own knitwear label and a growing list of contracts with high-end stores. And Norah, who was a bit low on academic qualifications but high on social ambition, had married the heir to a chain of motels, so no problem there.

It was Cassie, the youngest, who was the problem, at least in the eyes of her parents. With top grades at school and all the advantages of the family's hard-won position, she could have done anything — she could have had her pick of university places, been an intern in any firm she liked — but instead she'd announced at the age of sixteen that she planned to work as a hairdresser. On cruise ships. She wasn't interested in upward mobility, she told them. She was going to see life.

There was no arguing with her. Before making the announcement to her parents, she'd found and signed up for a hairdressing course, and established when and how to join a waiting list for placements with liner companies. And by the time she'd finished her course and been through a local apprenticeship, a job had come up on a short cruise from Vancouver to Alaska.

Her mom was horrified. 'Alaska! You'll freeze and there's nothing to see there.'

Cassie told her she was crazy. 'There's glaciers and grizzly bears and acres of rain forest. And it's in September so we'll see the Northern Lights.'

'But you've got to get all the way to Vancouver first.'

'Well, yes, that's part of the fun. Dad can donate his air miles and call it my birthday present.'

'And what happens when you're back?'

'Who knows? If I like the first trip I might sign on for another. Or if I feel like a change of climate I'll head for the Bahamas. Or somewhere. That's the point, Mom. I'm going to hang loose and take it as it comes.'

The cruise had turned out to be fun. There were occasions when she groaned at the thought of yet another middle-aged woman wanting her hair set in rollers. And there were some dodgy moments when one of the stewards decided he fancied her, and kept going on about her Irish eyes. Still, lots of the people she met were really interesting. She wasn't supposed to socialise with the passengers but, on the other hand, it

13

was part of her job to be pleasant. So, taking care to keep things appropriate, she made friends wherever she found them. On a long hike across the tundra, a bearded travel writer from Chicago told her all about his book. The following night she lay on deck and watched the Northern Lights with a Swedish girl who turned out to be an astronomer. And on a shining day, surrounded by miles of white saxifrage and pink fireweed, she celebrated her nineteenth birthday with whale blubber and dried caribou.

On that first cruise Cassie realised that, if she wanted to up her game, she'd need more experience as a stylist. Never one to do things by halves, she spent seven solid months on land improving her CV. As a result her next cruise took her farther from home and paid better. It was three balmy summer months on a classier ship for richer, more standoffish people, but the girls who shared her cabin were easy to get along with, and some of her clients actually wanted a proper cut and colour. On the Alaskan job she'd kept her own hair pretty nondescript — classic and obviously cared-for, but not really her style. This time her boss was out to encourage the wealthy passengers to experiment with expensive cuts and treatments, so Cassie cheerfully had her smooth bob chopped into an asymmetrical crop with a long, feathery fringe tipped with peacock blue streaks. The effect on the ship's salon's takings was remarkable, and several elderly ladies disembarked looking nothing like the photos in their passports.

When she got home she was tanned by sea air and tropical sunshine, her fringe was tipped with purple and gold, and she'd plaited a row of tiny seashells close to her zigzag parting.

Her mom blinked at her appearance as she hugged her at the door. Then she held her away and shook her head. 'You didn't text me your arrival time. I might have been at the office.'

Cassie dumped her case on the kitchen floor and dug in it for presents. 'I wasn't expecting a welcome party. You would have turned up sometime. Look, I got this for you in Bathsheba, in Barbados.' It was a little heart-shaped crystal pendant on a silver chain. 'One of the ladies at a stall in the food market had a tray of bric-a-brac among the fish. I'd say it's Victorian, wouldn't you? God knows where she got it. I didn't ask!'

Her mom picked up the pendant doubtfully. 'Well, it's lovely, sweetie, but do you really think you should have bought it?'

'Oh, Mom! I don't mean she snatched it from the neck of a passing tourist. She just had a tray full of bits and pieces. Old postcards and stuff. I spotted that in a corner and spent ages cleaning it up.'

As Annette crossed to the sink and washed her hands fastidiously, Cassie's lips tightened. 'Maybe I should have lied and said I got it from an antique store.'

Annette thrust the towel away and reached crossly for the coffee cups. 'Oh, for heaven's sake, Cassie, you've just come in the door! Don't start trying to be provocative.'

Meekly sipping her coffee, Cassie told herself that that was the problem. She never tried to be provocative. She didn't even want to be. But that was how the family always seemed to see her. Provocative, meddling, and far too fond of asking questions. And disgracefully unwilling to settle down and get rich.

Probably it had been really dumb to bring Mom a gift she'd picked up at a roadside market. She'd felt such a thrill when she'd spotted the little pendant, though. It was tarnished and grubby but she'd seen at once that the workmanship was beautiful, and she'd known how well it would look around her mother's elegant neck.

16

It had taken several hours to clean it, working in her cabin in the evenings with cotton buds and a tin of silver polish borrowed from the purser, then a drop of gin followed by soapy water to shine the crystal heart. And now that Mom knew where it had come from, the chances were she'd never wear it. She probably even saw it as proof that her daughter was a cheapskate, whereas, in fact, Cassie had paid almost as much as it would have cost in a store: it hadn't seemed fair to cheat the poor fish lady in the market, who clearly hadn't known what the pendant was worth.

Out of the corner of her eye she could see Mom looking rueful. Ever since Cassie could remember, the two of them had been this way. They'd set off down the wrong track and struggle to find a way back. Neither of them ever meant it to happen but somehow it always did.

Pulling herself together, she set down her coffee cup, tossed back her fringe, and asked how the family was doing. 'Did Cathleen get that contract she was hoping for? And how are Norah's kids?'

Mom took the olive branch gracefully enough, and for a while she kept up a smooth flow of talk while Cassie sipped and listened. Norah had found the perfect

17

playgroup for her twins. Cathleen had got the contract and everything was fine; she was thinking of upsizing to a new apartment and changing her personal assistant. 'The truth is that they're so busy I haven't seen them in weeks.'

'And how's your own work? And Dad's?'

'Couldn't be better. Exhausting, you know, but things are really expanding. I suppose it's just as well that you kids are busy, too, or I'd feel like a bad mother!'

This seemed so unlikely that Cassie glanced up sharply. The others had upped sticks long ago — it was only she who still treated the family house as home. Anyway, even when they were kids, they'd spent most of their time with au pairs. If Mom was coming down with Guilty Mother Syndrome it was definitely late-onset.

Catching Cassie's eye, Mom twisted her wedding ring. 'I mean, in a way it's a bit difficult that we're all so busy right now.'

'Why?'

'But, of course, *you*'re not, are you? Busy. I mean, you're home for a while?'

'I don't know. I haven't made plans.'

'Well, that's what I mean. You probably need a rest after all those long hours and hair nets.'

Cassie grinned. 'More like silver streaks

and razor cuts but, yes, I could do with a break. Maybe a month or so. I've plenty of savings so I might take a road trip.'

'The thing is . . . Dad got a call from Lissbeg the other day.'

'From Ireland?' Cassie swivelled round on her stool but Mom had turned away to fetch more coffee, so she couldn't read her face. 'Is everything okay?'

'Fine. Fine. It sounds like Frankie's shouldering more of the business now the parents are getting older.'

Frankie was Dad's elder brother. Cassie had never met him, though he and his wife regularly sent birthday and Christmas cards.

'And are Gran and Grandad okay too?'

She'd never met them either. Grandad ran some kind of retail enterprise he'd set up a million years ago and, according to Dad, he was so focused on work that he never took a vacation. Which, given that he was a Fitzgerald, sounded par for the course. Gran made the odd Skype call and kept in touch a bit on Facebook. Mostly she put up shots of Finfarran — the peninsula where Lissbeg was — and eager requests for news of the family, which usually went unanswered until Mom stuck up a photo.

Now and then, when yet another handknit sweater the wrong size arrived in the

19

post as a birthday present, Cassie had felt bad about the lack of real contact with her grandparents. But whenever she'd tried to ask Dad about Ireland, he'd always seemed determined to change the subject. To be honest, she hardly even knew what Granny and Grandad looked like.

Now Mom turned round, holding the coffee pot. 'They're both fine. Fighting fit, by the sound of it. In fact, that's why it's really great that you're hanging loose again. The call was about their arrival time. You can pick them up at the airport next Tuesday.'

2

Pat Fitz tapped the poker against the bars and, bending down, peered at the flames, like a doctor inspecting a patient. She'd been coping with this range for thirty years and a tap on the bars at the right moment could make all the difference in the mornings. That or a lot of coaxing with a bit of rag and some paraffin. Thirty years was a long time to put up with its sulks and temperaments, though Ger still screwed his face up and referred to it as 'that new yoke'. It didn't matter, though. Having tiptoed round it all that time, Pat had the measure of it. And, having coped with Ger for fifty years and more, a sulky range was no bother to her.

It was a damp Irish day with an autumnal nip in the air, which was why she'd lit the range. Mind you, the sun had been splitting the stones yesterday. You never knew what the weather might do in Finfarran. People were always telling each other you could get the four seasons of the year in a single day, and that was true. Especially since you wouldn't get winters with snow and ice, like you'd see on a Christmas card.

Of course, most years there'd be white caps on the mountains that reared up in the west, dividing the little fishing port of Ballyfin, at the end of the peninsula, from the rest of Finfarran's farmland, cliffs, and villages. And Knockinver, the highest peak in the mountain range, was often silver-white from Christmas to Easter. But here in Lissbeg the worst of the winter howled in as gales from the ocean. Usually accompanied by weeks of mist and rain. Not snow. Pat could almost count on her fingers the times in her life when the town had had a white Christmas.

And, God knew, her memory went way back. She'd grown up in a nearby village and attended Lissbeg's convent school for girls. Ger had gone to the Christian Brothers' school down the way, where Brother Hugh sounded just as bad as crazy Sister Benignus. That was how it was back in those days, boys in one school, girls in another, and no place for them to get to know each other, the way kids did these days. Instead, they'd just hung round after school, cracking jokes and taking dares round the stone horse trough in Broad Street.

Neither Pat nor Ger had much time to themselves back then. Pat got a lift home after school from a friend's dad, who collected them sharp at four in his blue Morris Minor; and Ger was always getting roared at from his dad's shop across the road. And by the time Ger was fourteen his schooldays were well over. But Pat and her friend Mary, Ger and his mate Tom had made up a foursome by then and, in the end, when Tom had married Mary, Pat had married Ger.

Frankie, who was born a year later, was the apple of his father's eye. Even when the lads were still at school, Ger had his mind made up to leave him the business. Whatever else you might say about Ger, he was a close man with a nose for a deal, and by the time the lads were in their teens he'd trebled the size of the family farm. He'd bought sites, too, that developers from Carrick came round later and gave him a fortune for.

In fact, if you could believe the gossips, he'd enough banked now to buy and sell half of Finfarran.

Pat herself wasn't sure that she did believe them, because Ger was a great one to puff himself up and look canny. Half the time you couldn't be sure that he wasn't just striking attitudes. But plenty of money went into the till, and she and the lads were always taken proper care of. It was one thing to have a reputation for being a close man, but another to let yourself down in front of the neighbours. Ger wouldn't do that. And if he wasn't quite as rich as people said, sure it made him feel good to act like it. He'd always been a little short fella, with a kind of a wizened face on him, and even at school he'd been bullied.

With the fire aflame, Pat closed the range door and glanced round the kitchen. It was strange how big it seemed now, with the flat empty except for the two of them. When she'd married she'd thought it a poor poky place to be rearing children, but the shop and the flat were what they'd been left with and Ger's brother Miyah had fallen in for the farm. A while back, after Miyah had died, Frankie had built himself a fine new place next to the farmhouse. He and his wife had never had kids, though. And Jim and Sonny were away off in Toronto.

It was Ger who made that happen. He hadn't worked all his life, he'd said, to see a grand, growing business broken up by his sons. So he'd sent Jim and Sonny to college in Cork and then, with nothing for them at home, they'd gone off as soon as they'd graduated. And, what with work and commitments and the price of fares, neither of them had been back.

Of course, it was easier to keep in touch these days, with Skype and emails. And there was a Fitzgerald Family Facebook page, set up by one of the grandkids over in Canada. But each time Pat posted a photo on that she told herself that the damage was done: her sons were gone and she might never meet her grandkids or Sonny's daughter's dotey little twins.

Then she'd take heart again and keep trying. She took photos round the town, or if she went walking, and found out how to get them from her phone onto Facebook. And she tried to put up things that would interest the grandchildren. But sometimes they'd be up there for weeks and nothing would happen. And there were nights when she'd dream that the lads had come home and wake up in tears because they hadn't.

Now, though, as she put on her coat, she could hardly breathe for excitement. Descending the stairs, she passed through the shop, where Ger was selling rashers to Ann Flood from the pharmacy. There were plenty of tourists walking the pavements of Broad Street in spite of the rain. Plenty of

25

hire cars, too, and the odd tour bus, though in a week or so you'd see few enough of them.

Pat waited for a gap in the traffic and crossed to where the old horse trough now stood on an island of grey flagstones, flanked by council benches and planted with scarlet geraniums. Then she ventured into the next stream of traffic and reached the far pavement. She'd already checked her flight details three times this morning, once on her phone and twice on her laptop. Both the phone and the laptop had said exactly the same thing: Patricia Concepta and John Gerard Fitzgerald were checked in on a flight to Toronto next Tuesday. Still, God alone knew what kind of viruses a yoke might have when you'd got it in a place called PhoneMart. Lissbeg Library's computers were proper, official desktops, installed by the county council. So she'd just drop in there kind of casually, log onto the airline's website, and take another look at her booking.

3

LOUISAS HERE IVE SET JAZZ A PLACE2 U GET SAGE4 LIVER

In the midst of checking out a pile of books, Hanna Casey's eyes flicked sideways to her phone. It was possible that one day her mother might issue an invitation without following it up with an endless stream of texts, but it didn't seem likely. So if Hanna had any sense, she told herself crossly, she'd have paid attention to her own neatly printed notices and kept her mobile turned off in the library.

Mary Casey, who was well into her seventies, was born giving orders. The peremptory commands that in Hanna's childhood were bawled up the stairs or hurled across the kitchen now appeared in a series of gnomic texts, always in uppercase and seldom, if ever, punctuated. And Hanna wasn't the only recipient. Having lost a loving and attentive husband, Mary now transmitted her demands and requirements at random, expecting the instant reactions that she'd had from her beloved Tom.

Hanna squinted sideways again, aware that the young man in front of her was beginning to look aggrieved. Originally she'd been invited to drop over for supper, but now it seemed that her daughter, Jazz, was going to be there as well. And with the appearance of the signature liver casserole, and the addition of Louisa, her ex-mother-in-law, to the invitation list, the casual supper was obviously turning into a family party.

Flustered, she shot back *OK,* smiled apologetically at the young man, and told him to enjoy his weekend reading. Then she realised that each book she had just swiped out dealt with diseases in fish.

A second text appeared on her phone with a ping:

BRING THAT ARCHITECT AND A DROP OF CREAM 4THETART

Hanna's teeth clicked together in annoyance, and the young man took his books and left, obviously making mental comments on inattentive librarians. As he opened the door he stood back politely and, looking up as she turned off her phone, Hanna saw Pat Fitzgerald. 'How's it going, Pat? All set for your trip?'

'Well, yes . . . more or less. Just a few last bits and pieces.' Pat reached into her bag and produced a library book. 'This is due back before we come home so I thought I'd bring it over.'

'You shouldn't have bothered. You could have renewed it online.'

'Yes, well . . . I was passing anyway.'

'Anything else I can do for you?'

'No. Well, yes. Could I have a quick look on a computer?'

'They're all booked for the class at ten but you can if it's just for a minute.'

'I've the laptop packed, you see, and my phone wants charging.'

'No problem. Work away.' Hanna smiled. The chances were that Pat's luggage had been packed for at least a week. The whole town was aware of her upcoming trip, and most people were delighted for her. Everyone knew how she'd missed her sons and wanted to meet her grandkids, and it was clear that if things had been left to Ger, the trip would never have been booked. His reputation for meanness was legendary.

But then there'd been a breakthrough. At

29

sixty-nine, Pat had learned how to use the internet. The idea had been to improve her contact with her family, but in a year or so she was teaching a computer class in the library. And one day, in the midst of a session on search engines, she'd seen an unbeatable deal on flights to Toronto.

Hanna suspected that if Pat had been alone she'd never have made the booking. But her class of pensioners had egged her on, and before she knew it, she'd bought the flights on her credit card. Not only that, but the class knew how little the trip had cost her. So if Ger Fitz had made a fuss, the whole town would have despised him.

Recently, as Pat's planning for her trip had become more intense, she'd arranged for Hanna's library assistant to take over her class. Now Pat looked up from the computer and said she hoped it was going smoothly.

'It's going grand and you're not to worry. Conor has them eating out of his hand.'

Pat beamed and said that her own last-minute arrangements were coming together perfectly. 'I've a cousin in Dublin with a house on the north side, where Ger and I can stay on Monday night. So we're all set at this end, and I heard today that Cassie's going to meet us in Toronto.'

'Is she one of the grandchildren?'

'Sonny's youngest. Cassandra. She'd be about a year younger than your Jazz. Cassandra Mary Margaret Fitzgerald. Isn't that a dreadful name to go wishing on some poor baby?'

'Why did they choose it?'

'God knows! It won't have been Sonny's choice, I know that.'

Hanna's lips twitched. 'Maybe his wife enjoys Jane Austen.'

'Didn't Jane Austen write *Emma*? We had to read it in school.'

'Yes, but she also wrote a novel called *The Beautifull Cassandra*. In her teens, I think. The heroine goes off into the world to find adventure. She's named after Austen's elder sister.'

'Well, that sounds like Cassie. She goes off on cruise ships.'

'But she'll be around when you're over there?'

'She will, and isn't it great timing? Because she's only just come back from somewhere. I'm telling you, Hanna, this trip is blessed. We're going to have a great time altogether.'

Her pleasure was so palpable that Hanna felt a twinge of anxiety. Pat asked so little from life that to see her disappointed would be awful.

Leaving the eager figure crouched over the

computer, Hanna went to the little kitchen at the end of the room. With the door ajar, she could keep an eye on the library, but this was a phone call she wanted to make without being interrupted.

Brian picked up at once. 'Hi there. How're you doing?'

'It's me. Hanna.'

'I know. I've got caller ID.'

'Oh. Yes, of course you do. Look, I'm sorry to call you at the office.'

'You haven't. I'm out on a site visit.'

'Okay. Well, look, are you free tonight?'

'Yes, sure. What's the story?'

'Well, I've just had a text from my mother. Who seems to be throwing a dinner party.'

'And?'

'And she says, "Bring that architect." '

'No! Really? In capital letters?'

'Yes, indeed. Also some cream for the tart. With four expressed as a numeral.'

Brian gave a snort of appreciation. 'Is the second instruction intended for you or for me?'

'Me, I think.'

'Right, then. That's no problem. Tell her I'll be delighted to accept her kind invitation.'

Through the crack in the door Hanna could see the pensioners gathering for their

32

computer class. Pat was being hugged and kissed as she left the library. 'I've got to get back. But, Brian, listen, are you sure? It could be hell on wheels.'

'Nonsense, it'll be brilliant. I just hope the tart is apple.'

'Don't you know it is? With six cloves, shop-bought pastry and half a pound of white sugar.'

'In that case, I sincerely hope that the cream you bring will be squirty.'

4

Mary Casey's bungalow had been built long
before the main road became a class of a
motorway. You got a fierce rush of traffic
past her front door now, charging from Carrick to Ballyfin. But there was no harm in
that. It added interest.

Tom had had the bungalow built to her
exact specifications as soon as they retired.
By then Mary had had enough of slaving
behind the bacon-slicer and pushing stamps
and postal orders under a wire grille. Mind
you, they'd had a fine little business between
them — a village shop always did well on a
crossroads, and having the post office there
as well meant the world and his wife depended on them.

But Hanna had gone off to London and
they'd known she'd no plans to come back.
So they'd sold up and made a decent
whack, and that was the end of living over a
shop, like poor, put-upon Pat Fitzgerald.

There was no poky range in Mary Casey's kitchen, and no slit of a bathroom with condensation running down the walls. The bungalow had a proper wide hallway. It had a cloakroom, the utility room and a grand big kitchen at the front of it, and bedrooms round the back overlooking the garden. There was a separate loo and a bathroom, and the master had its own ensuite in avocado. No detail was forgotten. All her windows were double-glazed and each room had a storage heater, and a light in the middle of the ceiling that took a proper-strength bulb. There were no dark corners where dirt could gather, and no stairs to be brushed down, or banisters holding dust.

The garden had always been Tom's province and, as far as Mary was concerned, he could do what he liked with it. But the house was her pride and her palace, from its die-straight roof to its pebble-dashed walls to the stained-glass door of her porch.

After Tom died she'd changed the garden. She couldn't be doing with all that digging and weeding. There was a plain square of grass out there now and a narrow hedge. Johnny Hennessy, her neighbour, came in with his mower and kept it all cut back. She'd left Tom's pots of night-scented stocks and evening primroses on the patio, though. They'd always been his favourite and, besides, they smelt nice in the summertime under the bedroom windows. Not that she opened her own window too often. You'd be driven mad with the bees that you'd have to go flicking out with a towel.

Sweeping crumbs from the kitchen table into her cupped hand, Mary told herself she was glad in a way that Tom had been gone by the time things went wrong for Hanna. He was stone mad about that girl, and if he'd known the kind of man her pup of a husband was, he'd have gone over and killed him.

Well, not really, because Tom Casey was the gentlest man in creation. He would have gone over to England, though, and tracked down that Malcolm Turner. And Tom had a way of looking at you when you'd done wrong that would leave you naked and bleeding. He'd never turned that look on Mary herself, but she'd seen grown men crushed by it.

Anyway, Tom was dead by the time Hanna came knocking on the bungalow door with Jazz, who was only a schoolgirl then, and a hastily packed suitcase, saying she'd left yer man in London and needed a place to stay. Twenty years that Malcolm of hers had been off sleeping with a floozie! You could nearly call him a bigamist.

It had started long before Jazz was born, and Hanna had only hit on the truth when she'd found them there in her own bedroom. The thought of it still made Mary want to spit. At the time she'd berated Hanna for not digging her heels in and making him pay. Any wife with a tither of sense would have stayed put and taken him to the cleaners. Especially since Malcolm was loaded. All the same, Mary had had a sneaking sense of pride in Hanna's reaction. It must have felt great to tell the pup where to stick his money.

And wasn't it funny the way things had worked out eventually? Look at the lot of them now. Jazz, who'd been born and raised in London, had moved into a bedsit, put down roots, and was planning to stay in Finfarran. Hanna had found a new man, her own house, and the job in Lissbeg Library. God alone knew what the man would turn out like, and as for the house, there was no knowing why Hanna would want to live there. It was nothing but a little place out in the wilds of nowhere — two rooms that you couldn't swing a cat in, and one of them just a kitchen you walked into from a muddy field. But apparently Hanna was happier living there than with her own mother.

Pushing open the window, Mary threw out the handful of crumbs for the birds. The truth was that she and Hanna had never got on great anyway and, with Jazz off in a place of her own, they'd been at each other's throats till Hanna had flounced off, announcing that she wanted her independence. Mary had her pride, too, and she'd be beholden to no one, not even family. But the fact was that, with Jazz and Hanna gone, the bungalow felt fierce lonely. So here she was about to share her home with Malcolm 'The Ratfink' Turner's widowed mother.

No one was more surprised than she was herself when she'd had the idea. When you thought it through, though, it wasn't that daft. Malcolm might be a low-down cheat but the fact remained that Louisa was Jazz's granny. Not only that, but she was a quiet woman who knew how to keep a spotless kitchen.

After Hanna had left, when Louisa used to be to and fro to visit Jazz, Mary had put her up. At first, of course, she'd worried a bit about breakfast. What would an Englishwoman know about frying rashers? But it turned out that Louisa knew lots about pigs. She'd had a neighbour near her house in

Kent who bred Gloucestershire Old Spots. As soon as Mary had heard that she'd slipped into Lissbeg for Ger Fitz's opinion, and he'd told her the Old Spots were mighty. According to him, a woman who appreciated them lads could be trusted with anyone's rashers. Ger was a damn good butcher, so Mary took notice. Besides, Louisa had a great way with the frying pan and she'd baste you a lovely egg. Mind you, she hadn't had a clue when it came to the black and white pudding. But she picked things up quickly and was happy enough to be told.

It had taken them a while to get used to each other. At first they'd eaten breakfast at the kitchen table, but one morning Mary came down to find it set on the patio. That was the class of thing Hanna had wanted when she and Jazz lived in the bungalow, and, back then, Mary had put her foot down. But Louisa had cushions on the chairs and the table laid properly and, with the sun shining, it all looked very nice.

And, with Louisa around, the meal could go on for ages. They'd be sitting there in their dressing gowns, popping in to make more tea, and even reading the papers. Mary hadn't read a paper over breakfast for years — and why would she with no one there to discuss the bit of news? But Louisa was always interested if you offered a remark or an opinion, or if she wasn't, she never let on. And, of course, they'd be properly dressed in time to wave at the postman. Showered and decent, too, which was only right.

So, after that, the thought of ending up living alone had been kind of bleak. Then Louisa had dropped a bombshell. She was selling up her home in Kent and investing in a business in Finfarran. Jazz was going to be working with her, doing some class of marketing. And, while Louisa would keep a foothold in England, she'd need a local base. Somewhere small and quiet that would be a home from home.

That was when Mary had come up with the notion of the two of them sharing the bungalow. And now, only a few weeks later, the plans were drawn up and work was about to begin. The changes might feel strange to start with, but Mary was certain that things would work out. She'd agonised over them in bed for many a night before making her offer to Louisa, and more than once she'd turned to her wedding photo and asked Tom what to do. But the photo in its silver frame told her nothing. Tom just stood there laughing in the sun, with his head thrown back in triumph and his arm around her waist. She had no one to hold her firm now, or to pet and reassure her. So she'd turned the bedside light off and made her mind up for herself.

Now, hearing a footstep in the hall, she went to switch on the kettle. Louisa had flown in from London last night, delighted with the completion of her house sale. She'd said she was very touched by the thought of a celebration dinner, which was just as well because, for the sake of the night that was in it, Mary had washed the good ware. Louisa called it china, but whatever name you put on it, you couldn't beat the look of a decent plate on a table.

She'd ironed a tablecloth, too, and it was folded and waiting. They'd have a great meal and, at the same time, a chance to see Hanna's Brian. Not that Louisa seemed any way curious about him, but then, of course, she wouldn't be. An ex-mother-in-law wouldn't feel the tremors of a mother's heart.

With the tea made and the cosy on, they sat down at the table. Louisa was tired after her flight, of course, but her eyes had a glint in them. Mary threw her a bit of a wink. They were both widows whose lives had

41

seemed to be over, but look at them now with a new future ahead.

5

Cassie arrived at Pearson airport with a bunch of flowers, feeling goofy. As soon as she'd heard about her grandparents' visit she'd called her sister Norah.

'I wondered if you and the twins would come to the airport. We could make a Welcome banner and the kids could hold it.'

The moment she'd asked, she'd known that it wasn't going to happen. The twins were in the background throughout the call and most of Norah's attention was focused on keeping them quiet.

'Shona, sweetheart, put down the kitty. We don't hold kitties so tightly. Sorry, Cassie, what did you say?'

'I said it'd be good to have a family welcome at the airport.'

'But aren't we doing a huge get-together at the weekend?'

'Yes, but I want to do a welcome at the

43

airport as well.'

'Oh, stop it, Cass, you're just being Min the Match.'

'Being Min the Match' was a family expression derived from the name of some ancient Irish relation who'd apparently been famous for meddling.

'I am not!'

'Yes, you are. Everything's already fixed, so just leave it. Anyway, the last thing they'll want after flights and coping with a transfer is a jamboree at the airport.'

So Cassie had accepted that the welcome party would just consist of herself and, at the last minute, as she'd headed out for the airport, she'd grabbed a bunch of roses from the hall table. They'd end up coming home in the car and back in the vase they'd been taken from. But at least the grand-parents would be greeted with a splash of colour.

It proved easy to spot them, even though Gran turned out to be smaller than she'd seemed in the photos she'd posted on Facebook, and Grandad looked nothing at all like Dad or Uncle Jim. They emerged from the sliding doors at Arrivals, pushing a trolley piled with bags and suitcases, all secured by monogrammed straps, with red ribbon tied to the handles. They both

looked tired and strained. Gran's eyes
flicked anxiously from side to side while
Grandad marched doggedly forward, clearly
embarrassed by the squeaky wheel on his
trolley.

'Hey! Hi, over here!' Cassie caught their
attention and pushed through the crowd,
waving her bunch of red roses. She could
see Gran's anxiety turn to relief. Sweeping
them both into a hug, Cassie took over the
trolley. Gran linked her arm and smiled up
at her, though she could feel Grandad
resenting the loss of control over the luggage.

Later, in the car, he sat rigid and uncom-
municative in the rear while Gran sat up
front next to Cassie and chattered. When
she saw the first sign for Leaside, she gave a
gasp of delight. 'I've written your address
on so many letters and parcels and look at
it there, up on a sign by the road!'

A few minutes later, as the car swung off
the highway, Cassie saw Gran's hands
tighten in her lap. 'You okay, Gran? We're
nearly there.'

'I'm fine, love, just tired. And I'm not used
to this side of the road.'

'I guess if you've spent a lifetime driving
on the left it must feel kind of weird.'

'Well, it is. Not that I was driving all that

long. But your uncle Frankie bought me a car a while back and I had a great time for a fair few years before I had to give it up.' Her hands had been getting a bit stiff, she explained, and her eyes weren't as good as they used to be. 'Anyway, I've got everything I need around me in Lissbeg. It's great to be bang in the middle of town, where you can step out your own front door and find all you want within a spit of it. I can walk out into the countryside in no time, too, can't I, Ger?' There was no response from behind her and she smiled across at Cassie. 'Ger does be busy all the time, so I'm lucky not to need lifts.'

When Cassie pulled into the driveway, Gran gasped again. 'Oh, Holy God, isn't that a gorgeous house? Isn't it, Ger? Look at it!'

Inside, as Gran exclaimed about the spaciousness of the hallway, Cassie picked up the two smallest bags and announced firmly that the rest could be carried up later. Then she led the way upstairs and ushered them into their bedroom.

Vanya, Mom's help, had made up the room with fresh flowers on the dresser and crisply ironed linen on the beds. Cassie opened the door to the walk-in closet, demonstrated how to operate the shower in

46

the bathroom, and how to control the TV and the central heating in the bedroom. 'Mom and Dad will be home about six but I'm not going anywhere. Come down and have a look round the house as soon as you'd like to, but I guess you'd like time to freshen up first.'

Grandad stumped across the room and settled himself in an armchair. Gran smiled at Cassie. 'It's been a long trip and you're a dote to have come and collected us. I'd say we might have a rest now and see you later on.'

With her duty done for the time being, Cassie went to her own bedroom, changed into a bathrobe and slippers and padded down the hall to the family bathroom. Three girls sharing one small shower had led to a certain amount of annoyance on the ship, particularly during the last leg of the cruise, when people were tired and tempers were fraying. Sweating the small stuff wasn't her thing, so Cassie had breezed through the tensions. Still, it was heaven to soak in a huge tub for as long as she liked.

Lying back, she closed her eyes and let her thoughts drift to the future. Everything in her lovely unplanned life was going exactly to plan: she'd completed this last cruise with more than enough savings to take a few months' break or a road trip before going back to sea. Maybe she'd stay in the city and do some volunteer work. Or take off to Prince Edward Island and admire the fall foliage. Anyway, there was plenty of time to decide, because she'd have to stay home for at least a few weeks to avoid being rude to the grandparents.

Vanya had gone, leaving the house immaculate, so, having rearranged the roses in their vase on the hall table, Cassie took a glass of milk and some cookies and wandered into the family room. Two hours later, flipping lazily between rolling news and episodes of *Judge Judy,* she looked up to see Gran standing in the doorway. Cassie smiled at her. 'Did you get some sleep?'

'Well, I had a bit of a rest anyway. Ger's above in the bed, dead to the world.'

Cassie sat up, swinging her legs off the chesterfield. 'Would you like a coffee? Or something to eat?'

'Do you know what it is, if that's milk you've been drinking I wouldn't mind a drop myself.'

She still looked awfully tired, and her voice was a thread. So, having tacitly agreed to leave the tour of the house until later, they settled down to another episode of *Judge Judy* with glasses of milk and a plate of Vanya's brownies. Gran, who said she'd never seen the show before, watched with great attention. Then, when the closing credits appeared, she clicked her tongue in amazement. 'God, you'd think there wasn't a woman going these days with a tither of wit or a mother! To be putting their trust in men who'd only make fools of them!' She bit into a brownie and shook her head at Cassie. 'And old fellows that are just as bad, being led a dance by the young ones!'

'Would your mom have stopped you making a fool of yourself?'

'You may be sure she would! Mind you, she wouldn't have let me go moving in with some wastrel pup in the first place. Times have changed, though, and I know that's what girls do nowadays. And, fair play to them, haven't they a right to be making their own choices?' She shook her head disparagingly. 'No one has a right to be bone stupid, though. Could that old fellow not see that that young one was trouble?'

The girl had been the kind of mercenary predator that always produced Judge Judy's most scathing comments. 'Maybe the danger was what attracted him in the first place?'

Gran's voice was emphatic: 'I wouldn't doubt you. And, by the sound of it, he

49

wasn't the first poor woman's husband she'd made a fool of. What a woman needs is a steady man, and to keep a good eye on him.'

Looking at the trim little figure sitting beside her, Cassie smiled. Gran might be tired, but clearly she was feisty. It was going to be good to get to know her.

6

As Bríd Carney put her key into the front door of number eight St Finian's Close, she told herself how lucky she was to have this place to come home to. Finding an affordable place in Lissbeg wasn't easy. The property in the town centre was almost all shops, pubs, and businesses, where the owners either lived upstairs or let out their upper floors as commercial spaces. And people could spend years waiting for a council house. They were designed as family dwellings, too, so it was families that got priority. The result was that if you were young and single your chances of renting were practically zero. But Bríd's cousin Aideen owned number eight outright.

Their aunt Bridge had bought it years ago, through a scheme that had briefly driven council policy. Whoever Aideen's dad was he'd never been round at all, and her mum had died in Carrick hospital having her. It

51

was Aunt Bridge who had brought her up. Actually, she wasn't an aunt, really: she was some kind of cousin of Bríd and Aideen's granny. So, basically, Aideen had spent her childhood with two elderly ladies.

Then, a few years after their granny died, Aunt Bridge had had a massive stroke in the chemist's and was dead before the ambulance could get there. They found out later that she'd been going to the doctor for a good while, but Aideen, who was in the middle of her Leaving Cert, hadn't even known she was ill. The rest of the family organised the funeral, and Bríd's mum offered to take Aideen in till she'd see what she'd do. No one seemed to have a better idea, and Bríd was off doing a culinary-science course in Dublin, so Aideen had had her room for the next few months.

It must have been pretty awful. By all accounts, she'd sleepwalked through the rest of her exams, and her results weren't all that brilliant. But then it turned out that Aunt Bridge had left her the house in St Finian's Close and a bit of money. So when Bríd came home, they'd opened a deli in Broad Street, and decided to live together at number eight.

It was Bríd who had done most of the organising. Aideen had kept her old bedroom and Bríd had the big one. Aunt Bridge's room became a little office where they set up the computer and had meetings with their accountant. There was hardly any room in the deli, which they'd called HabberDashery, so they'd turned the dining room at number eight into a storage space for things like takeaway cups and paper napkins. The house had a kitchen big enough for a dining table, and a sitting room with plenty of space for a sofa and chairs and a telly, so it all worked out. They split the utility bills down the middle and Bríd paid a fair rent.

Now, as she came in the door, she found Aideen and Conor McCarthy in the sitting room. They were drinking tea, curled up together in an armchair and, by the look of them, they'd recently been curled up in Aideen's bed.

Conor looked up at Bríd. 'How's it going? Will you have a cup of tea?'

'Well, I wouldn't like to break up the idyll.'

As Conor went to put the kettle on, Aideen wriggled round to look at Bríd. 'How was your swim?'

Bríd dumped her bag on the floor and pushed her hair back from her forehead. 'Lovely. Chilly, though. I wouldn't say I'll be having many more this year. Not in the sea, anyway. I suppose I could join the gym in Carrick and use their pool.'

'God, I wouldn't fancy driving to Carrick each day after work.'

'Um. Me neither, really. And the gym costs a fortune.' She flashed her eyebrows at Aideen. 'Maybe I'll be like you and find an alternative way of keeping fit.' She laughed, seeing Aideen blush. 'Oh, don't go all coy on me! I think it's lovely that Conor and you are so happy.'

Aideen laughed. 'I know you do. And how are things going these days with you and Dan?'

'I don't suppose it'll work if I tell you to mind your own business?'

'Damn right, it won't. I'm dying to know.'

Conor came in with the tea at that point, so Bríd didn't have to answer. Which was just as well.

She and Dan Cafferky fancied each other — that much she definitely knew. What she didn't know yet was how far she wanted to let him into her life. It was one thing to fall into bed with him after a party. That could happen to anyone, especially when they'd been going out together for months when they were at school. But a lot had happened since their schooldays. She'd spent a couple of years studying and working in Dublin and he'd been off to Australia. Stuff like that changed people, and just because they were both back in Lissbeg didn't mean that they had to get together.

Admittedly, they'd gone on a couple of dates together after the night of the party. A meal with friends. A trip on his boat, which was actually pretty cool. And, okay, he'd come back to St Finian's Close a few times. And stayed the night. But they definitely weren't a couple. With Conor and Aideen all starry-eyed and saving up for their wedding, there was far too much talk going on about people settling down.

Anyway, Dan's life was kind of messy. He lived with his parents in Couneen, a clifftop village on the southern side of the peninsula. The family kept the local shop and internet café, and he'd always had notions about running marine eco-tours from the little pier in the inlet below the cliff. But the business had sort of started and then foundered, which was why he'd gone off on his travels to Australia.

Then, recently, he'd arrived home, bringing a guy called Dekko, whom he'd met on some beach. Dekko apparently had money to invest, and the idea was that he and Dan would run the marine tours in partnership. He was a Dubliner, a kind of nondescript, bland bloke that Bríd couldn't quite get a handle on. Dan was almost the opposite — tall, good-looking, and impetuous, with a lot of chips on his shoulder and a bit insecure underneath.

Bríd herself was clear-minded and determined, and never one to hold back when it came to speaking her mind. So it was a bit odd to find herself wriggling now as Aideen questioned her. The bottom line, she supposed, was that she didn't fancy being quizzed when, uncharacteristically, she wasn't quite sure of her ground.

Still, Aideen was easily diverted. You only had to mention her engagement ring and she was off on a riff about Conor. Now Bríd murmured something about the setting and Aideen turned to her eagerly, displaying the ring. Wasn't Conor amazing? Hadn't he spent hours trawling the internet in search of the perfect stone for her? Who'd have thought that he'd find it there in a jeweller's shop in Carrick?

It was hard to see Conor, with his farmer's hands and unruly hair, as a diehard romantic. But he really had gone looking for a stone that would perfectly match the colour of Aideen's eyes and tracked down a beautiful oval of lapis lazuli set in a red-gold band. He'd also proposed in front of a crowd of astonished spectators in the middle of Lissbeg Library, a romantic gesture that was the talk of the town for weeks.

Now Conor nudged Aideen affectionately and told her to shut up. But, clearly, he was amused, rather than embarrassed, by her fervour. Aideen took her mug of tea from the tray he'd brought in from the kitchen, and their conversation turned to the future. As usual, it was a litany of aspiration and anxiety.

Like Dan, Conor had been raised in the countryside. His family had lived on the same farm for generations, and he and his brother, Joe, were struggling to keep the place going in the face of rising costs, falling prices, and the fact that their dad, Paddy, had recently injured his back. Conor also worked three days a week as an assistant in Lissbeg Library.

Aideen had already explained it repeatedly to Bríd. 'If it wasn't for his job at the library, the farm would have to be sold. Honestly, Bríd, they're only just holding things together. And I don't know what's going to happen because he loves the farm, I know he does, but the truth is he really wants to go off and become a proper librarian.'

'So why doesn't he?'

'Well, that's what I'm saying. How can he? Running the farm is a three-man job and Paddy can't do any heavy work. So Conor and Joe are killing themselves to keep going. But the place doesn't yield a proper wage for the three of them. So the money Conor makes from the library job is basically what he lives on.'

'But that's peanuts.'

'That's what I'm *saying*!'

She was saying it again now, curled up in the armchair with Conor, her face creased with anxiety.

'It's a matter of working out what we're going to do when we're married. I mean, where we're going to live . . . what we're going to do.'

The other day, when the two of them were eating dinner, Bríd had given her an answer. 'Oh, for God's sake, Aideen, can you not see the bloody elephant?'

'The what?'

'The elephant in the room. It's Paddy. What kind of father sits watching this and doesn't step in and do something?'

'But what can he do?'

'Retire. Make the place over to Joe. Let Joe do what he likes with it, and let Conor feck off if he wants to.'

'But he doesn't want to.'

'No. What he doesn't want is to be the person who precipitates the crisis. Look, Conor's the kind of person who has to fix everything for everyone. But in this instance he can't. He can't simultaneously save the farm for his family, gain a career for himself, and carry you over some perfect romantic threshold. It's not possible. And you shouldn't let him think that it is.'

Aideen's face had crumpled. 'Conor does love the farm. The McCarthys have farmed that land for ages. You've never seen him there. You haven't been to the farmhouse. It's gorgeous. You haven't sat in his mam's kitchen. There's a big range, and a cat that eats Marmite, and a flower garden outside the window.'

'A cat that eats Marmite?'

'Oh, *stop* it, you're just being cynical. Yes, there's a cat. And they've got dogs and cattle and hens and sheep, and Conor loves the lot of them. He's brilliant with animals. And farm machinery. And . . . growing stuff. And he loves his dad too. And Paddy's not well — he's on all kinds of medication. And not just for his back, he's got depression. And you'd have depression, too, if you felt useless. And if you knew that people were sitting round calling you a bad father!' She'd stormed out at that point, leaving

Bríd to do the dishes.

They hadn't mentioned the row since, but now, as Conor rehearsed alternatives, Bríd saw Aideen glance at her as if she were an unexploded bomb. It seemed unkind to hang around, so she finished her tea and said she'd take a shower. But as she left them deep in anxious conversation, she found herself stabbed by a flash of pity for Conor. Clearly this engagement was about to add to the sum of his life's complications. Because it was pretty evident that Aideen had visions of wedded bliss in a farmhouse.

7

The Fitzgerald family get-together was held
on Pat and Ger's first weekend in Canada.
Cassie watched as everyone arrived full of
bonhomie, carrying flowers and eager to
show affection. People laughed a lot and
exclaimed. Cathleen brought a huge bunch
of lilies that shed orange pollen on the back
of Gran's cardigan as she lifted her up in a
bear hug; Norah appeared with a monster
basket of hyacinths; and the twins were carrying posies to present during the photographs.

There were lots of photographs. As soon
as Grandad saw the phones and cameras he
retired to drink beer in Dad's den with
Norah's husband, the motel mogul. Gran
posed gamely in front of Vanya's beautifully
laid buffet, smiled for selfies with the
cousins, and allowed herself to be enthroned
on a satin loveseat for a full family portrait.
When Grandad refused to appear, she

laughed it off. 'Isn't he far happier inside there, chatting over a beer? I've never known a Fitzgerald man that wasn't!'

Everyone joined in the laughter, and the hired photographer sat the twins on either side of Gran, holding their posies. Cassie saw Dad exchanging glances with Uncle Jim, who shrugged and pulled a face.

Shortly afterwards, when the professional photographer had left, Grandad emerged from the den and stood at the back of a group shot lined up by Cassie, who reckoned he'd needed the couple of beers to give him the courage to come and face the lens. She smiled at him encouragingly but he dived back into the den as soon as she'd taken the shot.

The twins, meanwhile, were sticking to Gran like glue. Even at the buffet they stood on either side of her, holding her skirt. Then, when Cassie offered to carry her plate to a table in the corner, they trotted across the room with her and squatted on the floor with their elbows on Gran's knees. Norah spotted them and bustled over, trying to lure them away. 'Ice cream! Anyone for ice cream? Let's leave poor Granny to eat her food in peace!'

Immediately the twins crawled under the table, while Gran looked pleadingly at

Norah. 'Let them stay here with me and we'll make friends.'

But Norah assured her they had to learn obedience. The woman who ran their playgroup had been very clear about that. 'We establish boundaries and we stick to them. And, Simon and Shona, if you need to speak to me, you can stop that screaming and use your words.' Then she hauled the protesting twins from under the table, knocking it over in the process.

No amount of ice cream could control the resultant hysterics and, after a while, Norah gave up and said that perhaps they should go. There was a general checking of watches and Uncle Jim's wife squeaked and said she'd a meeting to go to that evening. She flitted over and kissed Gran, said she wouldn't disturb Grandad's beer fest, and made it to the door in time to leave with Norah, the mogul, and the twins.

The party staggered on for another hour before Cathleen, who'd been checking her phone again, suddenly announced that the grandparents must be exhausted. 'OMG, people, we need to go!' She thrust her phone into her pocket and went to hug Gran. 'We'll have to have lunch next week, or maybe the week after. I'll fix something really nice and we'll do it in style. We'll be ladies who lunch!'

She led the general exodus and, a week or so later, her assistant called to say that she'd booked a restaurant table, and ordered a car to take Gran there and back.

Gran returned from the lunch looking slightly startled and, when Cassie asked, said she'd had mascarpone-filled crackers with a white balsamic reduction. 'The menu said they were truffled, dear, and I suppose that was what gave them the taste they had. We had a grand table, anyway, right by a big window looking out on a lovely patio. And Cathleen had calamari in a cone.'

That was how it was throughout the rest of the stay. There were other outings with other family members: Mom brought Gran to the theatre, and Uncle Jim and Dad took Grandad off to play golf. But no one ever had quite enough time to spend with them, so a lot of their days were spent in their room, resting up. In fact, Grandad hardly emerged from it at all.

Cassie spent a lot of time catching up with friends in the city, doing a few cover shifts at her old salon and, occasionally, driving Gran to the nearby park or the mall. Whenever they went out together Gran was full of enthusiasm. But she seemed equally happy to hang round at home, watching celebrity-chef shows and *Judge Judy.*

One afternoon, Cassie knocked on the guest-bedroom door and suggested a cup of coffee. By that stage she'd realised that Grandad didn't do small talk, but Gran always seemed happy to come downstairs and chat. They settled down on the chesterfield in the family room again, with coffee and cake. Grandad had agreed to go for a beer that night with Dad and Uncle Jim, and Gran told Cassie confidingly that she was hoping to persuade him to wear a new sweater she'd bought him at the mall. 'It's a lovely colour, you know, and it really suits him.'

'Do you think he's enjoying his stay?'

'He is, of course, love, only he's a dreadful man for not showing his feelings. And he never was a talker, so you mustn't mind that. But look at the lovely place your dad has here, and your uncle Jim's house. And the lovely healthy families they have. Sure, Ger's like a dog with two tails, seeing how they've got on.'

Suddenly it struck Cassie that, while Gran was a great listener, all she really talked about was shops and programmes on TV. Turning, she looked at her thoughtfully over the rim of her coffee cup. 'Was it weird raising sons and having them emigrate?'

Gran said nothing for a moment, then shrugged. 'I suppose, back in those days, that's what we all did. People used to call it raising them for export. It was a terrible thing to think about, though, when they were growing up. The truth was that you didn't think about it, really. You'd only go breaking your heart.'

'But you never came to visit?'

'Ah, child dear, it's an awful long way to be coming. Flying's got cheaper now, but it's still a big thing.'

It occurred to Cassie that there could have been a family trip to Ireland too. But there never had been.

Gran looked troubled. 'It wasn't that we didn't want to visit. I was dying to see the lads, and so was your grandfather. And I'd always wanted grandkids. Especially girls. I felt really bad not seeing you growing up.' Putting down her coffee cup, she clasped her hands in her lap. 'That's why I was always trying to choose the right presents. Well, I still am. The thing is, though, that I hadn't realised how fast the time is passing. I don't know do I send you the right things at all.'

Cassie had a sudden vision of books and games, glanced at and discarded, and hand-knitted sweaters, unwrapped and never worn. She hoped she didn't look guilty. But Gran didn't seem to notice. Instead she turned her head and smiled. 'Do you remember *The Turf-Cutter's Donkey?*'

For a moment Cassie thought she was crazy. Then she remembered a book that had come in the mail on her thirteenth birthday. That had been the year that her best birthday gift had been a trip to Niagara Falls. Mom and Dad had invited her three best friends from school and they'd stayed at the Americana Waterpark. 'Yes, of course I remember it.'

As far as she could recall, she hadn't even turned the pages. Like everything else that came from Lissbeg, it had looked boring and seemed much too young for her age.

Gran smiled. 'I hoped you'd like it. That was my copy, you know. I had it at your age. I mean, I got it as a birthday present when I was thirteen. It's a grand story altogether. I'm glad you liked it.'

Cassie groped for a reply and found inspiration. 'That was the year you sent us a really cool Christmas card. Do you remember?'

Gran shook her head. Astonished that she'd remembered it herself, Cassie grabbed at the chance to avoid talking about the book. 'It was a street scene. I think it was

Lissbeg — with snow on the houses. A photo that had been made into a card. There was a Christmas greeting inside and writing on the front in glitter, saying "Across the Miles . . ." and there was a kind of glittery bunch of mistletoe hanging over the houses.'

Gran smiled. 'Do you know what it is, I do remember. I got it at the Christmas Fête. Some fellow on the committee had a lot of them made up and they sold them in packs for charity. I got one for your family and one for Jim's.'

'Yeah. Well, I really loved it. I kept it as a bookmark in *The Turf-Cutter's Donkey* for years.'

The flush of pleasure on Gran's face seemed to justify the lie but, later on, as she washed up the coffee cups, Cassie hoped it wouldn't come back to bite her. The bit about the card was true, though. The street surmounted by its glittery mistletoe really had taken her fancy, and she'd sneaked the Christmas card up to her room when Mom's back was turned. For ages afterwards she'd fantasised about walking into the picture and being over in Ireland.

But she'd never mentioned the fantasy to Dad. Somehow, Ireland had always been forbidden territory, and conversations about his childhood were out of bounds. Nothing explicit, just a sense that the past was over and done with, and the present was all about making plans for the future.

None of the rest of the family seemed to find that weird, but she did. And now that she'd met Gran it seemed even stranger. Gran was sweet. It was clear that she'd have loved it if they'd all come over to visit. So why, in all these years, had Dad and Uncle Jim never wanted to go home?

Cassie grinned, imagining a family chorus telling her not to be Min the Match. Which was fair enough. The rest of them had their own lives to live, and if Ireland wasn't important to them, that was their own business. But, as a child, it had always seemed to her to be the perfect destination. A place that was utterly foreign and yet a part of who she was.

Suddenly her eyes widened and the stream of water from the faucet ran unheeded into the sink. Why not just do it? Gran and Grandad were going home to Ireland in a couple of weeks. Why not take the plane with them and go visit Lissbeg?

8

So many things had added to Hanna's sense of disorientation when she'd left her cheating husband and moved home to Ireland with her daughter. Not the least of them was her decision to revert to her maiden name. Having spent thirty years as Mrs Malcolm Turner, the supportive wife of a successful London barrister, it was strange to be plain Hanna Casey again.

But the name change was only the tip of the iceberg. It felt weird to be working as a local librarian, having spent so long facilitating her husband's stellar career. And, after years of hosting dinner parties in an elegant London home and weekend jaunts to a stylish Norfolk cottage, living in her mother's bungalow was bizarre. Not only that, but trying to decide what, and how much, to tell Jazz about Malcolm's affair had tortured many of her waking hours and invaded her nights' sleep.

Yet, perversely, the strangest thing of all was the fact that Lissbeg Library was housed in the old convent building where she herself had gone to school. It was unnerving to enter her workplace through a gate in the high, grey wall she remembered from childhood, and to work among trolleys of books and steel shelving in the panelled hall where she'd giggled and whispered through boring school assemblies. And, in the beginning, this strangeness had added to her dislike of a job that she'd applied for simply because she'd had no option.

Mary Casey hadn't hesitated to open her home when they'd turned up on her doorstep. But neither had she hesitated to point out that, if Hanna was planning to stay in Finfarran, she'd better go out and find work. And underlying that purely practical statement was a hint of spiteful triumph. It was Tom, Hanna's dad, who'd supported her decision to spread her wings and take off to London in the first place. Mary had always resented her ambition, and said it would come to no good. More to the point, she'd always resented Tom and Hanna's closeness. No one — not even their daughter — was allowed to take Tom's attention from his wife.

It had never been Hanna's plan to end up

in a local lending library. She'd gone to London with her sights set on becoming an art librarian and building a stellar career of her own. So to find that the man for whom she'd given up her dream had been cheating on her for years had hit her hard. And, having reappeared ignominiously in Finfarran, she'd have done anything to avoid meeting the neighbours with whom she'd grown up and gone to school. But, having refused to accept a penny from Malcolm, she'd had no option but to brush up her only qualifications and apply for the vacant position in Lissbeg. As Mary Casey had repeatedly told her, she was damn lucky the job had happened to come up. So perhaps it was inevitable that her first years back home had been dogged by the fear that her failed marriage had made her a focus of gossip. Looking back, Hanna knew she'd been prickly and standoffish, the sort of petty tyrant you'd find in Wodehouse or an Agatha Christie, with a ramrod back and a sour look on her face.

But that was all behind her now, largely thanks to her relationship with Brian. And in the last year her work had increasingly become a source of pleasure. Now, though you entered the library through the same paved courtyard that had once been the school entrance, the wall had been breached to give access from Broad Street to the former nuns' garden, while the school and convent buildings, which bounded the garden, had become the Old Convent Centre, accommodating council offices, a pensioners' daycare facility, and airy, modern studios and workshop spaces for rent.

Best of all, the library had been modernised, extending the original beautifully proportioned panelled hall to include a state-of-the-art exhibition space for the Carrick Psalter, an illuminated medieval manuscript that had been gifted to the county. Knowing herself to be the custodian of such a treasure brought Hanna endless delight, and the new relationships she'd forged with her neighbours were a source of daily pleasure. But, even so, she found herself subject to sudden losses of confidence. It was more than seven years since she'd left Malcolm, five since the divorce, yet she was still in the process of absorbing the fact that she'd never really known her husband.

And now that her relationship with Brian had become established, she was facing new moments of strangeness, generally more comic than painful, but occasionally disconcerting. Like the moment a couple of months ago when they'd first arrived as a couple at Mary's bright pink bungalow. 'So — my daughter, my ex-mother-in-law, and my mother's liver casserole, are you sure you'll cope?'

Brian had laughed. 'I love when you do that.'

'What?'

'Ask me if I can cope with things when it's actually you who's worried.' Irritated, she'd pulled away, but he'd put his arm around her shoulders. 'I'll be fine and you'll be fine and there's nothing at all to worry about. So long as you've brought the sage and the squirty cream.'

'You don't love it at all, do you? You think I'm just being neurotic.'

He'd looked down at her quizzically, pressing the bell on Mary's hall door with its stained-glass inset of poppies. 'No, I don't love it. It's bloody annoying. But I do love you, so let's not argue semantics.'

As her mother's figure loomed down the hall, Hanna had hissed crossly that semantics meant shades of meaning, not contradictions.

'Now that really is just semantics.'

Torn between annoyance and amusement, she'd introduced him to her mother, who was all benevolent charm.

'So you're Hanna's architect? And isn't it

high time I met you? Come through to the patio, won't you? We're out there having a drink.'

In the garden, Louisa and Jazz were sitting with glasses of wine in their hands and a bowl of Tayto on the table between them. You knew the occasion was a formal one when Mary Casey produced her Belleek bowl, which was pale yellow porcelain embossed with wreaths of green shamrock.

In a weird way, the dinner had been successful. Brian, in his crumpled, well-cut linen suit, looked totally unlike Malcolm in his trademark Armani. But beneath his laid-back manner, he had all of Malcolm's assurance. There was a difference, though. Brian's attention was on the world around him, while Malcolm's, despite his brains and charm, was essentially focused on himself.

After their drinks they'd proceeded to the kitchen from the patio, where Tom Casey's night-scented stocks still perfumed the air. As they sat at the table, Brian had admired Mary's bone-handled cutlery. Nothing could have endeared him to her more.

'Well, now, do you like them? I'm glad to hear that. They were a wedding present, weren't they, Hanna? My late husband Tom sent over to London for them, Brian. I'd seen a lovely canteen in a picture in a magazine. And, can you believe it, he got on to a shop in London and they sent him over the best.'

Brian had turned a fork in his hand and balanced its weight on his forefinger. 'They're beautiful. I hope you keep them in their box.'

'I do, of course, and it's beautiful too. Lined with velvet. And, do you know what it is, Brian? Those handles have never seen a drop of hot water. Not a single drop. Though, God knows, if Hanna had her way, she'd probably have left them soaking in it. Isn't hot water the one thing that'll turn a bone handle yellow? I don't know how many times I had to tell her that when she was small. God, she was a child that needed telling — you always had to keep your eye on her.'

'And look at her now. A credit to you.'

Mary had beamed and, seeing Jazz and Louisa's faces, Hanna could well imagine the colour of her own.

But the blush had receded in a wave of amusement when Brian glanced at her wickedly. And later, as he'd driven her home, she'd turned and smiled. 'Thanks for making an effort.'

'It wasn't an effort. I really did enjoy

myself. I adore apple tart and squirty cream.'

'Oh, shut up. You know what I mean.'

'No, seriously. It was good to meet them properly. Jazz is such a bright kid. You must be proud of her.'

That night, watching the trees by the road leap up as the headlights caught them, Hanna had felt a renewed rush of gratitude toward Louisa. Jazz had been bewildered by the precipitous break-up with Malcolm but, with the resilience of youth and Louisa's support, she was now focused on the future. Over dinner she'd been full of excitement.

'It's such a simple, brilliant idea. We're developing and producing organic cosmetics made from herbs grown here in Finfarran. "Edge of the World Essentials". That's our name. I mean, it's really early days so, right now, it's more about development than production. But we've found the perfect manager. And I'm the creative marketing director. Louisa's the brains of the outfit, and I'm the brawn.'

It had been strange to hear Jazz, who until recently had called Louisa 'Granny Lou', refer to her as a business partner.

There had been several similar occasions since at which Mary had monopolised Brian, who'd been vastly amused, and

Hanna had observed her daughter's shrewd interest in the unfolding relationships between the lot of them. In the car on the way home on that first evening, Brian had glanced at her. 'Was that really why Louisa set up the business? Just to give Jazz a job?'

'Well, her house in Kent was far too large, and she's getting old. Malcolm loves her but he never could be bothered to entertain her, so if she'd sold up and moved to London she would have been awfully lonely. Anyway, under the genteel veneer, she's always been a formidable woman. I think she's just been waiting for a chance to spread her wings.'

Brian said nothing and, after a moment, Hanna laughed. 'Okay, I reckon it had a lot to do with Jazz as well. Louisa's given her a reason to put down roots.'

'What does Malcolm think?'

'I gather he was slightly shocked to find that his mum had sold his childhood home without seeking his permission. But this way he escapes a weight of responsibility. If she's mostly here in Finfarran she won't be needing attention in London. And that was where she could have ended up.'

'You're really fond of her, aren't you?'

'Yes, I am. I always was. Well . . . I suppose there was a while there when I felt she

78

was to blame for raising Malcolm as a rat-fink. But she didn't, of course. That's just the way he turned out. Anyway, this venture is going to move us all forward.'

'All of us?'

'Even you and me.'

'And how do you work that out?'

'Well, maybe I've spent too much of my time worrying about Jazz's future. Now I can claim my life back.' Seeing the look on Brian's face, she laughed. 'What?'

'I was just wondering how often I've heard you make that statement.'

'That's nonsense!'

'I've a special notebook in which I keep a tally.'

'Yeah? Well, I'm going to start keeping a list of your shameless compliments to my mother.'

'She does sort of command them. Still, every word was true.'

'Oh, please!'

Brian had chuckled. 'Well, okay, maybe not the bit about loving her Padre Pio altar. But it does have a kitsch appeal, so it wasn't exactly a lie.'

Now, walking from her car to the entrance to the library, Hanna felt buoyant. In the weeks since the dinner party, Jazz and Louisa had forged ahead with their business, and the work at Mary Casey's place was very nearly complete. Louisa would soon have her own section of the bungalow to live in, and Jazz had found herself a matchbox-sized flat in Lissbeg.

The fact that Mary would have company was going to make life much easier. If nothing else, there'd be fewer demanding texts.

9

As if to celebrate Cassie's arrival, Finfarran
had produced a glorious morning after a
night of rain. Peering through the window
of her bedroom over the butcher's shop,
Cassie could see smoke rising from chim-
neys into a cloudless sky. When she leaned
out and breathed the air it was clean and
slightly chilly, touched with salt and mixed
with the scent of smoke from a garden
bonfire. Craning her neck, she could see
that the wide street beneath her window was
bright in the wintry sunshine, and the scurrying figures below were muffled in scarves
and gloves.

Everything in Lissbeg was smaller than
she'd expected, perhaps because the sur-
rounding landscape dominated the view.
Out beyond the town's grey streets, with
their painted timber shopfronts, the low hills
rolled away, dappled in green and brown;
and, away to the west, a mountain range

reared up on the horizon in a series of jagged blue peaks and crags.

Cassie and Pat had both overslept, still suffering from the effects of jetlag, so it was eleven o'clock when they crossed the road from the butcher's shop and paused by an old horse trough on a traffic island, where scarlet geraniums were shedding their petals onto the flagstones. At the far side of the road, in some kind of park beyond the traffic, Cassie could see the tips of tall fir trees and masses of late autumnal foliage.

Pat took her elbow, waiting for a break in the traffic. Then, raising her hand to a van driver who'd paused to accommodate them, she piloted Cassie across to the other side. You'd have to take your chance when you got it in Broad Street, these days, she explained earnestly. The traffic was always woeful this time of the morning.

To city-born Cassie, the single stream of traffic had looked easily negotiable and the courteous gesture from the driver felt rather sweet. The raise of Pat's hand had been accompanied by a dignified nod, and they'd swept across the road like a couple of galleons in full sail. But while the rest of the traffic had taken its lead from the battered, red van, a stocky guy in the car behind it had sounded his horn.

Glancing back, Cassie saw the van driver deliberately take his time starting up again. He was a rangy looking man in his late sixties, with a small dog on the passenger seat beside him, and the way he ignored the guy in the car was superb. 'That was kind.'

'No more than I'd expect from Fury, pet.'

Apparently Fury was the rangy man's name. Cassie was already getting used to Finfarran's penchant for nicknames. They'd been given a lift from the train station last night by an elderly man called Horse.

Over breakfast in the flat above the butcher's shop, she and Pat had sorted out a few ground rules. 'You'll have to call us Pat and Ger now we're here in Lissbeg, love. We've never been anything else in this town, so you might as well follow the fashion.'

'Deal. Provided you don't start introducing me round the town as Cassandra.'

Pat had shot a smile at her and said that she'd remember. Then Cassie had explained that she was planning to find her own place. 'It's nice of you to offer me a room but I really don't think it would work out. You guys are used to your own lifestyle. And I want to be free to come and go as I choose.'

Afterwards she'd thought that it might have been better to say she wouldn't like to disturb them. But there was never any point in beating about the bush. Anyway, Pat had nodded, as if she'd expected it.

Later, as she'd brushed her teeth, Cassie had thought that, while calling Gran 'Pat' felt perfectly natural, hailing Grandad as 'Ger' would feel weird. She hadn't got to know him at all. In Canada he'd hardly spoken to her or Mom, and she'd had the impression that his outings with Dad and Uncle Jim had been taciturn as well. He'd slept most of the time on the journey to Ireland, when she and Pat had chatted. And when they'd arrived in Lissbeg his first action was to call Frankie for an update on the turkeys their supplier was fattening for Christmas. Then, with the call over, he'd retired to bed. This morning he'd got up at the crack of dawn and gone out to some appointment.

Now, as Cassie and Pat reached the pavement, a tall girl emerged from a car park down the street. She was walking with her head bent, putting her keys in her handbag, when, looking up, she saw Pat. With her dark hair flying, she ran up and hugged her. 'You're back! How lovely! Did you have a great holiday?'

The girl was about Cassie's age, maybe a year or so older. She kissed Pat and, turning to Cassie, waited to be introduced.

84

'This is Cassie. My granddaughter. Can you believe she's come over on a visit? I'm taking her into the library to say hello to your mam.'

The girl held out her hand and said that her name was Jazz Turner. 'My mum's the librarian here, but I guess Pat said. Are you going to be round for long?'

'Could be. I'm not really sure. Most likely till after Christmas.'

Pat beamed at the two of them. 'Would we have a cup of coffee in the Garden Café before we go into the library? Hanna's always up to her ears at this time of a morning.'

Jazz shook her head. 'I'm really sorry, Pat, I can't. I've got a meeting. Did you know we're renting space in the Old Convent Centre? I'm on my way to check it out.' She smiled again, and walked away, her well-cut hair and expensive handbag swinging. Clearly this was someone else who was into empire-building. She seemed nice enough, though.

Pat took Cassie's arm. 'It's probably too soon to be thinking of coffee anyway. Come and look at the garden.'

They walked to a gate through which Jazz had disappeared. This was the public space that Cassie had glimpsed from across the road. There was a little café, which, Pat explained, sold cakes and sandwiches made in the local deli. 'You can sit indoors looking out if you want and, if the weather's nice, the café has tables by the fountain.'

The tables were set out today, looking inviting in the sunshine. Trees bordered the garden's wide herb beds, which were separated by narrow gravelled paths. Where four paths met, a statue of St Francis, with his arms extended, stood on a plinth. Water gushing from stone flowers at the saint's feet made ripples in a shallow granite basin with a broad rim.

Cassie looked around. On two sides the garden was enclosed by high, grey buildings at right angles to each other, and the third side was bounded by a wall.

Pat explained that one of the buildings had been the school and the other a convent. She'd been to the school herself. 'The council has it all joined up inside now, and they're doing the redevelopment bit by bit.'

At the far side of the garden the sun shone on a row of stained-glass windows. 'That was the nuns' refectory. There's big kitchens in there as well. I heard some crowd was interested in renting them for a cookery school.'

'What's Jazz going to use her space for?'

'I'm not sure, love. Something to do with soap. There's a grand set-up for the pensioners in there as well. A big lounge and space for yoga and dancing. And a room for a chiropodist. Isn't it mad to think I get my feet done now in the room where I used to do my lessons?'

The October sun falling through evergreens touched the crimson leaves of a Virginia creeper that grew against the wall. As Cassie watched, there was a flutter of wings in the dark branches and a tiny bird swooped across the herb beds to the fountain, to land on the statue's hand. The bird's gold crest and olive plumage echoed the colours of the stained-glass framed in its stone arches. Turning to look at the windows again, Cassie noticed rows of grey headstones beneath them, enclosed by cast-iron railings. According to Pat, this was the nuns' graveyard, now cared for by volunteers who looked after the herb garden. 'That's the way the whole thing began, really. People got together to clear up the garden and they started planting new herbs. Most of the school was boarded up, and only a couple of old nuns were left living in the convent. Sister Michael and Sister Consuelo. They're both dead now. Sister Michael was a lay sister who used to work in the garden. She knew every bit of planting here and remembered the lot.'

As they walked down a path between the herb beds, Cassie brushed her hand across a rosemary bush, releasing its spicy fragrance. 'You mean she helped in the restoration?'

'Well, there was a book inside in the library. Hanna's assistant found it stuck in some cupboard. And it had drawings of all the herb beds, and the flowers and bushes. The nuns here used them to make medicines. And they made beeswax polish and candles for the altars. God, there used to be a fierce smell of polish when I was at school. Furniture polish and the smell of cabbage from the kitchens.'

They paused at a sunny bench and, by tacit consent, sat down.

'Anyway, between what was inside in the herb book and what Sister Michael could remember, we got the garden looking mighty. And, in the heel of the hunt, the council bought the whole site from the Church. Mind you, they wouldn't have lifted a finger if the volunteers hadn't gone at the garden first.' Pat beamed at Cassie. 'You'll have to ask Hanna. She'll tell you all about it.'

Cassie wasn't sure that a visit to the local

library was right at the top of her bucket list. But Pat and the librarian were obviously really close.

'Her mam, Mary, and I were in the same class here at the convent. I knew Hanna's father well too. Himself and Ger were great friends at the Brothers'. You didn't have boys and girls going to the same schools in those days. God, the changes I've seen in my life, love, you wouldn't believe them.'

'For better or worse?'

Pat straightened her shoulders and looked at her directly. 'For better. That's what I'd say. And I know well that there's many going that wouldn't agree with me. But look at this place that was once shut up so nobody could get into it. And look at the newcomers now in the town, bringing life and new ideas. It don't do to have small lives and few choices, Cassie. It breeds a quare lot of jealousy and spite.'

10

Conor was under Miss Casey's desk, looking for a rogue pencil sharpener, when Phil, the manager of the Convent Centre, stuck her head around the library door. As Conor wriggled out backwards with the sharpener in his hand, she laid a poster on the desk. 'Could you hang these for me, please, Hanna? Somewhere prominent.'

Phil's posters always had to be hung somewhere prominent. They were always laminated too. The word was that she'd recently marched into some council committee and come away with a pile of money for the centre's admin office. So her desk was now jammed with hi-tech gizmos. Half of which, according to Ferdia, who worked with her, would be obsolete by next Tuesday.

Conor squinted sideways and read the top line of the lettering, which was printed in bright red: 'RISE to the CHALLENGE of YOUR FUTURE in an EDGE OF THE

WORLD WORKSPACE!!'

It was Ferdia who'd come up with the idea of calling the peninsula 'The Edge of the World'. Back when the volunteers were working on the nuns' garden, they'd created a community website that he'd put together for free. It had taken off big-time, and the council reckoned it was a great tool for promoting local tourism.

Conor remembered the day they'd announced the plan to develop the Old Convent Centre. Someone had kicked Ferdia on the ankle, saying the next thing he'd know would be that they'd claim the website as their own. They'd tried it, too, but Ferdia was too fly for them. Which was why he was now running the website from Phil's office, and drawing a council salary with a pension down the way.

Phil had always been one to get carried away by a project. And with the Old Convent Centre going from strength to strength, and tourists flocking to the psalter exhibition, she was charging round these days, like a bull on speed, on a mission to sell Lissbeg. Now she pushed her specs onto her head and burbled brightly at Miss Casey, 'That's eight small businesses we've accommodated so far. And three of them start-up! Isn't it just the greatest thing for the town?'

When Phil had left, and Conor was about to hang the poster, Miss Casey called him over to her desk. 'Sit down for a minute, Conor. I've a proposition for you.'

Conor sat down with the poster between his knees and his toes curling apprehensively. Propositions meant change and, right now, his life was complicated enough.

'I've been wondering if you'd consider doing the mobile library run this winter.'

'What — taking it over from you?' Miss Casey, who lived a few miles out of town, had always done the mobile run herself. Two days a week Conor was in charge in Lissbeg while she drove to the county library in Carrick where the library van was kept. Then she'd do the regular route down the peninsula, taking the north side on one day, the south on the other, and dropping the van back to Carrick before going home in her car.

Now she put her elbows on the desk. 'What with opening up here and then driving to Carrick, I never pick the van up before half eleven. So that'd be your shift on mobile days — eleven thirty to five.'

'You'd be cutting down my hours?'

'Look, it's only a change of schedule. It wouldn't affect your pay. And if it doesn't suit you, there's no problem. But this way, on those two days, you'd have more daylight hours on the farm.'

As the logic began to dawn on him, Conor felt his toes uncurl. It'd make a hell of a difference to his workload at home if, two days a week, his work for the library didn't begin at nine. 'Are you sure that's okay? I mean, shifting the schedule.'

'You'll be doing me a favour. Driving the back roads of Finfarran in winter isn't always a picnic. There'll be plenty of days when I'll be here in a nice warm library and you'll be battling with storms.'

That was only her being nice. But Conor decided not to argue. If you wasted time, she tended to get impatient, and he wasn't going to risk having the offer revoked. 'Right so. Right, that's what we'll do then.'

It was brilliant and, come lunchtime, he'd nip over to the deli and tell Aideen. Meanwhile, he climbed onto a chair and stuck up the poster, his mind reorganising his workload for the winter weeks ahead.

At about ten to one Pat Fitz came in, full of her Canadian holiday. There was a girl with her that Conor hadn't seen before. She was short, with a wide mouth and a snub nose and a peacock-blue fringe, like a feather, falling over one eye. Pat dragged her up to the desk like she'd won her on the Lotto. 'Now, this is Cassandra! I want her to meet the two of you.'

It turned out that the girl, who was Pat's granddaughter, had heard about the nuns' herb book.

'I told her she'd see it if she came in. Go on back with Conor, love, and he'll show it to you.'

Conor led the way to the end of the room and opened the glass-fronted bookcase where the nuns' books were kept. 'These aren't part of the library's collection. They were here when this was a school hall, so Miss Casey left them in their case.' He opened it and took out the herb book. 'Are you interested in herbs?'

The girl wrinkled her nose. 'Nope, not in the least. And I'm not much of a library freak either. I mean, I don't read much.' She leaned against the wall and took the book from Conor. 'But I suppose, with the garden outside, having this in here is kind of interesting.' She flipped through the book's pages and handed it back to him. 'On the other hand, maybe not.' Then she saw his expression. 'Oh, shit, was that totally rude?'

Conor laughed and put the book back in the bookcase. 'Are you really called

94

Cassandra?'

'I really am. And I swore Pat to secrecy about it but that hasn't done much good.' The girl dug her hands into her pockets and looked around her. 'This is a nice room, though. And it is a lovely garden. I think I'm going to like Lissbeg.'

'Are you here for long?'

'Everyone keeps asking me that! I'm not sure. I need to find a place to stay. And don't ask if I couldn't stay with my grandparents. I could. I just don't think it would work.' What she wanted, she said, was somewhere small and fairly basic, where she could come and go as she pleased. She asked Conor if he lived in Lissbeg.

'Nope. I just work here. Part-time.'

'So you're a bookworm?'

'Actually I don't get a lot of time for reading. But, yeah, I like books. And libraries.' One thing he loved was the feel of old books in his hands. Their bindings had tooled edges and rubbed gilt decoration and the endpapers had feathery patterns on them, like you'd get on a cream slice. He didn't fancy telling her that, but she was looking kind of disparaging so he felt he had to say something. 'There's masses more to libraries than borrowing books. We have a computer class and a quilting group and an art club, and we lend films and CDs. And you can get help filling in forms and stuff, and free online database access. And adult literacy and kids' storytelling. It's a real focus for the community, and there's a mobile service as well.' He stopped, realising he was sounding like a mad evangelist.

The girl raised an eyebrow at him and shook back her peacock-blue fringe. 'I'm called Cassie, by the way. Thanks for showing me the herb book.'

'Which doesn't interest you.'

'No, but the fact that I've seen it has pleased Pat.' She shook his hand cheerfully and went back to join her gran at the desk.

Seeing that they all had their backs to him, Conor dodged into the Biography section and risked a quick call to Aideen. Then, as the phone rang, he found himself having a eureka moment. It was like he was in a cartoon and a lightbulb had flashed above his head.

But when Aideen answered she sounded kind of flustered. 'Conor? What's the story? We've got a queue out the door for lunch.'

'Sorry, I know, but I've had a proposition from Miss Casey.'

'Miss Casey's *propositioned* you?'

'What? No. Of course not. She's told me she's changing the schedule.'

'Okay. Well, can you fill me in later? I've got six salad boxes to do, and the coffee machine's playing up.'

'Yeah. But listen, there's more, I've had an idea.'

'Good for you. But I've really got to go.'

The phone went dead and Conor leaned back against the shelving. Okay, that might have been a classic case of bad timing. But when Aideen heard his brilliant idea she was going to be over the moon.

11

The Royal Victoria Hotel in Carrick had a bar where you could sit and get a proper sandwich at lunchtime. None of your guacamole and alfalfa sprouts. Just a decent slice of ham or chicken in white bread spread with real butter, and Colman's mustard served in a pot. Neither Pat nor Mary could be doing with mustard in a sachet. Or mayonnaise, for that matter. You couldn't open it, to begin with, and then it got all over the cuff of your blouse.

The Royal Vic was an institution. It had a ladies' lounge with writing tables, embossed notepaper and brass inkstands; loos with real towels; a grill room much frequented by bank managers; and the bar, where Pat and Mary had a favourite table in the corner. And PJ, the head barman, who had worked there for donkey's years, always wore a spotless white jacket and a tartan bow tie.

Pat ordered a sandwich and tea, which came in an EPNS pot with a bit of weight to it, not a flimsy bit of tin that would flood the saucer when you tried to pour a cup. Mary, who'd arrived before her, had already told PJ that she'd have her usual chicken without any lettuce. And a latte with a chocolate stirrer. Because, as she said to Pat, why wouldn't she? At their age, they deserved a bit of a treat.

It was the first time they'd met since Pat had come home from Canada. Mary tucked her shopping bags under the leather banquette and inspected her. 'You're looking well, I'll give you that. Were the lads good to you? God knows they owed you some attention, so I hope they shaped up.'

Pat was about to say that it wasn't the lads' fault that they'd left home in the first place. But that would be handing out ammunition. She knew well that Tom's devotion to Hanna had often had Mary spitting with jealousy, but it always appeared in conversation as proof of his superior virtue. So any talk about why Sonny and Jim had gone to Canada would only produce a sniff about Ger's failings as a father.

Besides, PJ was arriving with the sandwiches, which looked lovely, and it was grand to be sitting chatting with Mary again. 'I haven't seen you for ages and I hear you've had great work done in the bungalow.'

'We have and I'm delighted with it. You'll have to come round and see.' Mary nodded at Pat's handbag. 'Come on, then. Show me your photos.'

Pat produced her phone and swiped through shots of the house in Toronto, the big family party on the first weekend, and the mall and the park where Cassie had taken her shopping and walking.

Mary peered at the screen and demanded to know who she was looking at. 'Is that Sonny's wife? My God, there isn't a pick on her. Doesn't she have great taste in clothes, though? I'd say that suit is Chanel.' She reached over to the phone and enlarged a photo. 'Is it Norah has the twins? Isn't she fierce like Ger's mother? And tell me this, is the husband foreign?'

Pat explained that Norah's husband was French Canadian.

'Would he have English?'

'He would, of course.'

'Well, fair dos now, Pat, they laid out a great spread for you. Who's the girl behind the table?'

'That's Vanya. She helps in the house.' Vanya was a dote, she said, and so obliging.

100

'I told her we liked liquorice and she'd always bring us a packet when we ran out.'

Mary looked at her sharply. 'Wouldn't you think your own flesh and blood would do that, and not leave it to the maid?' She swiped through a few more shots and sat back, stirring her latte. 'I thought Canada was a great place for mountains and lovely scenery.'

'Well, it is. But Toronto's a city.'

'And did they never take you out into the countryside on a drive?'

'Well, they would have, but you know, Mary, they're awfully busy. The lads took Ger out golfing a few times.'

'Ah, Holy God, girl, weren't you gone for weeks?'

'I know. And we did get out lots of times. Cathleen took me to lunch, and Cassie was always driving me off to the mall.'

'You must have been eating a quare lot of liquorice in that case, if you couldn't buy it yourself and you out at the shops.'

Pat bit into her sandwich. There was no point in rising to that remark, so she re-claimed her phone and found a photo of their bedroom. 'They have a guest suite that they put us in, with a big window overlooking the garden. And a balcony outside.'

Mary looked at the photo. 'Not much of a

balcony.'

'Well, it was only a little railed place, you wouldn't go walking round on it. Ger used to step out, though, for a breath of air.' Feeling she was letting the family down, Pat closed her phone and put it away in her handbag. There was a pause in which she could see Mary's eyes slanting sideways. It was a look she recognised. Having pushed things just a bit too far, Mary was feeling bad. Now she'd either come up with some gesture to try to make things better, or she'd get in a huff and go into a massive sulk.

As if responding to a cue, PJ the barman shimmered up beside them and, inclining his head at an angle, asked if he could bring them anything else. Pat could see the liver spots on his head between the strands of his heavily oiled comb-over. It occurred to her that the three of them were much the same age. When she and Mary had been sitting in Sister Benignus's class at the convent in Lissbeg, the chances were that PJ had been keeping his head down at the Brothers' place here in Carrick. You had to keep your head down in those days if you didn't want a belt.

She'd never really asked Ger about how bad it was at the Brothers', but she'd always had a feeling that it was worse for him than for the rest. Well, worse than for Tom Casey, anyway. The big, tall lads who were great on a football field had the best of it. And if you had a bit of a way with you, you probably did better than most.

Ger was always small and kind of gawky-looking, and he'd never had Tom's charm. If you cornered him he'd go for you, but he'd sooner avoid trouble. That was probably the rock he perished on. By the sound of the Brothers that used to be in Lissbeg, you'd have been targeted like a shot if you looked like a coward.

Mary told PJ they might have a pudding. 'What would you say, Pat, would we chance a bit of flan?'

It came with flaked almonds on the frangipane topping, and squiggles of chocolate sauce. PJ put the two plates down with a flourish and made a pass over each with a silver sugar sifter. As the white icing sugar settled like snow, Pat told Mary that Norah's twins had been sweet. 'Imagine me with great-grandchildren! I only wish I'd had a chance to get to know them better.'

'Sure, you might go back another time.'

'I suppose we might. I don't think so, though. We're not getting any younger. That's why it's great to have Cassie here now. Sure, you know yourself. You must be made up to have Jazz settled down in Lissbeg.'

'If she does settle! You're right, though, it's great to have her.' Mary took a sip of latte. 'So Cassie's not staying with you and Ger?'

'No. Well, she's young. They want their own place these days, don't they? Take your Hanna. Not that she's just out of her teens but . . . Well, no one likes to feel they're being looked at judgementally.'

There was another pause in which Pat watched Mary absorb the hit.

They sat in silence for a while, eating the flan. The Royal Vic gave you pastry forks where most places gave you soup spoons — but most places gave you cake in a soup bowl now, so you wouldn't be that surprised.

Pat described the lunch in Toronto. 'In fairness now, it's a lovely place. Your man who owns it has a big show over there on the television, and Ger says, by the look of his steaks, that he'd use only the best. But, glory be to God, I'm telling you, girl, the meal I had was a fright. Calamari in a cone! That's what Cathleen had. I was expecting it to turn up with a chocolate flake in it. And the money they charged — ah, Mary!'

'Terrible?'

'Woeful.'

'Sure, that's the way the young ones are these days. More money than sense.'

'Mind you, Cathleen's doing well. I'd say they all are.'

'Did you ever think they'd be eating calamari in a cone?'

Pat snorted with her fork to her lips, and the powdered sugar went up her nose. That set Mary off giggling and the two of them were there like eejits, groping in their bags for tissues and dabbing the tears off their cheeks.

Then, as soon as they'd calmed down, Mary set them off again. 'Ah, Holy God, Pat — Jasmine and Cassandra! 'Tis far from that my Hanna and your poor Sonny were reared!'

12

A gust of wind snatched Hanna's hat and bowled it along the clifftop. As Brian loped after it, Hanna struggled with her hair: the wind had tugged it from the loose plait into which she'd braided it, and the long tendrils were whipping across her cheeks.

Brian returned with the hat thrust into the pocket of his anorak. Turning her back to the wind, Hanna managed to bundle her hair up under it, pulling the knitted band down over her ears. Already blinded by flying spray, she now felt deafened as well. With his legs straddled, and his feet braced in the short clifftop grass, Brian leaned in to speak to her. 'Shall we keep going? Or call it a day?'

It wasn't an easy decision. Though the weather was shaping up for a proper Atlantic gale, the sun was shining and the air on the clifftop was like wine. They'd started their walk from the field behind Hanna's house, climbing the stile that took them over her boundary wall and onto the broad ledge with its narrow path fifty feet above the churning ocean. Tonight, heavy rain and gusts of salt spray would batter her seaward windows and, having seen the forecast, Hanna knew that the next few days wouldn't bring walking weather. So to turn back now would be a shame.

The cliff path, curving westwards towards the dunes and beaches on the outskirts of Lissbeg, was a constant delight to her so, having driven home from her Saturday morning's work at the library, she'd called Brian and suggested he come over. 'I'll do dinner for the two of us, and we can work up an appetite with a walk.'

An hour later his car had pulled up at her gate, and she'd heard his footsteps as he'd appeared round the gable end, swinging a carrier bag from HabberDashery. He'd nipped into Lissbeg and bought pudding, he said, leaning on the half door and looking into the kitchen. Two slices of Bríd Carney's super-sinful chocolate cake.

'When did you start calling food sinful? It's fuel, that's what it is, and by the time we're back from our walk, I promise you we'll be needing it.'

'Don't start on me! I was quoting the label.'

'Maybe people are prepared to pay more if they reckon it's sinful.'

'It certainly costs a fortune, but it's well worth it.'

As they'd climbed the stile, she'd asked him if the price of the cake had gone up.

'I don't think so. Why?'

'Well, Conor and Aideen have been worrying about money.'

Standing on the step on the cliff side, Brian had laughed up at her. 'And now you've decided to do their worrying for them!'

'I haven't. It just occurred to me.'

As she jumped down beside him he threw an arm round her shoulders. 'Everyone their age worries about money. They're planning a wedding, aren't they?'

'Yes, and that's another thing. They're going to have problems . . .'

'Which are theirs, not yours. Now, are we going for a walk or aren't we?'

Striding along against the wind, Hanna had told herself he was right. Jazz was in her element in her new job and her mother seemed to be getting on fine with Louisa. Finding a new reason to fret was just ridiculous. Now she smiled and suggested they keep walking. Another half hour against the wind would be exhilarating, and when they turned round it would be at their backs, blowing them home.

Later, in the kitchen, she lit the fire while Brian went down the field to dig some potatoes. He returned with a bucket of Kerr's Pinks, his hands black and muddy. Hanna could remember trudging up the garden herself as a child, carrying spuds in a copper milk pan with a broken handle. The house had belonged to her great-aunt Maggie then, and no receptacle, however damaged, was ever thrown out if Maggie could still find a use for it.

One of Hanna's most vivid childhood memories was of sitting at Maggie's kitchen table sharing a meal of boiled potatoes, dipped in salt and served with yellow, home-made butter. Her own table was in the same place now, under the kitchen window, and Maggie's dresser still stood by the fire, with its shelves of crockery and dim green glasses.

Having eaten dinner, they savoured their cake by the fire, listening to the storm outside and the occasional black spot sizzling on the hearth as raindrops blew down the chimney. Their relationship had passed the stage of wondering whether or not he'd stay the night, though they both still meticulously avoided leaving belongings in each other's territory.

Brian's flat, high in a modern block on the outskirts of Carrick, was very different from her stone house with its two original rooms and tiny extension, but he and Hanna shared a fastidious sense of privacy, both physical and emotional. It was what had drawn them together in the first place but now, to a certain extent, it was what stood in the way of them taking their relationship to what Jazz called 'the next level'.

Delighted with the developments in her own life, Jazz had quizzed Hanna about that only the other morning — and received a pretty sharp set-down.

'Don't use that foul expression. And mind your own business!'

'Oh, come on, Mum, he's lovely. You don't want to lose him.'

Hanna had ended that phone call with a laugh, which she'd later identified as camouflage. Brian had always wanted to take things faster than she did. But lately, at the back of her mind, she'd acknowledged that she'd hate to lose him. It was extraordinary to find herself able to trust again, after what she'd been through with Malcolm. But that was what had happened. And, as she'd asked herself crossly after her phone call with Jazz, what was 'the next level' anyway?

Now, she turned her head, Brian smiled at her.

'You're thinking again.'

Hanna laughed. 'Last time I looked it was legal.'

'What's on your mind?'

'Nothing. Well . . .' she improvised hastily '. . . I was thinking about the psalter exhibition.'

Brian hunkered forward and threw another log on the fire. As County Architect, it was he who'd designed the modern space within the old school hall that housed the psalter exhibition, separating it from the library with a soaring glass wall. 'It must be getting fewer visitors at this time of year.'

Hanna nodded. 'Well, you certainly don't get many tourists. I'd thought we might have more locals coming through in the off-season. But I guess, since I only turn one page a month —' She stopped suddenly, no longer wanting to put Brian off track, but focusing on the new thought. 'Actually, that's a point. Maybe we should do something specifically aimed at local people. Not tied into the tourist thing. Just for us.'

'Like what?'

'I don't know. Something for the run-up to Christmas?'

Brian sat back, brushing bark off his hands. 'How about Advent? Turn one page a week for each of the four weeks, and tie it in to the festive excitement. Anticipation. Colour. A countdown-to-Christmas thing.'

'That's genius.'

'I aim to please.'

'No, seriously, I think I should do it. It's a lovely idea. We could spread the word on the Edge of the World website. And just via people who'd normally come to the library. Pat Fitz is back teaching her computer class. And I've been planning a creative-writing group. People have lots more free time in the winter. And all the coming and going at the Convent Centre means we get more footfall now than we did before.'

'Well, good. I think you should do it too. Just don't decide to turn the last page on Christmas Eve, will you? Or, if you do, hand the job over to Conor.'

'Why?'

'Because we've got plans for Christmas Eve.'

'Have we?'

'I hope so.'

'What are you on about?'

'You know the way kids dream of going to

Lapland to see Santa Claus? Well, there's a sort of architect's equivalent. The ice hotel in Jukkasjärvi.'

'An *ice* hotel?'

'Right up in the Arctic Circle, in Swedish Lapland.'

'Literally made of ice?'

'Literally. It's bonkers, but I've always wanted to stay there. Pure fantasy.'

'But . . .'

He wriggled his eyebrows at her. 'You know, I've never confessed this to anyone else.'

'Okay, I'm touched. But what are you saying?'

'That I want us to go there for Christmas.'

Hanna blinked.

'Just think of it, Hanna. Everything, including the beds, made of ice.'

She sat back, seeking words and finding none. This was taking it to the next level with a vengeance.

13

Cassie turned left off what everyone seemed to call 'the motorway' and meandered through a network of narrow country roads. The motorway, which was actually just a dual carriageway, took you straight to Ballyfin, where all the tourists went. In the other direction it led to Carrick, which Pat had said was Finfarran's county town. At some point Cassie intended to explore them, too, but right now she was looking for a road less travelled.

That was a concept she liked. Ages ago, her mom had been lent a book by a woman who worked for her. It was called *The Road Less Travelled.* Cassie had picked it up one day, thinking it would be about going on safari, but it turned out to be a religious self-help thing she hadn't read it. It was a good title, though, so it had stuck in her mind.

This side of the peninsula seemed less

populated than the countryside round Liss-beg. She drove between a patchwork of small fields separated by low stone walls, where groups of grey-black, squawking crows rose up at the sight of the car. Miles away to the west there was a mountain range. Not exactly huge if you compared it to the Rockies, but pretty impressive all the same. Probably because the scale of everything here was smaller than in Canada. The fields were mostly pasture, and sombre-looking cattle looked up as she approached, turning their heavy heads to watch as she passed.

The car was on loan from Pat. It was the one she'd talked about in Toronto, a gift from Uncle Frankie that Pat didn't use any more. Yesterday Ger had driven Pat and Cassie to collect it from Uncle Frankie's place, where it had been garaged. He'd needed to pick up something at the farm, so he'd dropped them off at the house for tea and announced that Cassie could drive them back.

The tea party had explained a lot that Cassie hadn't quite understood. Having grown up with the idea that Ger had a big retail business, it had been weird to find that he and Pat lived over a little shop. The flat was really poky, too, and had fairly shabby furniture. And on the first night, when Pat had filled a hot-water bottle for Cassie's bed, she'd been led up a narrow staircase to a room that was basically a garret. It would have been nice for her to sleep in her dad and uncle Jim's old room, Pat said, but it was full of Ger's filing cabinets, with a desk in the corner where, these days, he did his accounts.

The garret, which had once been Uncle Frankie's room, was actually quite lovely. It had a sloping ceiling and a roof-light, and a comfortable bed with a patchwork quilt, under which Cassie found a hi-tog duvet and four feather pillows. Pat explained that she'd made the quilt herself.

'It's beautiful.'

'Well, it's nice, and it's a grand bit of colour. And I had a new mattress put on the bed when I painted and put the new carpet down to make it a spare room.'

On the way over to Uncle Frankie's place, Cassie had gathered that his house was built on a site on the family farm. The old farmhouse was lived in by a manager, employed to look after the land. Pat had explained that Ger had bought more fields since his dad died. And, as Ger drove west through rich farmland, Cassie had begun to realise that what was involved was a serious amount of real estate.

Uncle Frankie's house was a revelation too. It was built on a height, set back from the road, and surrounded by a wide concrete plinth and green lawns. Ger swung the car through an entrance between concrete gateposts topped with plaster pineapples, and up a curved gravel drive to a double door topped by a fancy portico.

Uncle Frankie and his wife, Fran, were on the step to meet them. He was a short guy, older than Dad and Uncle Jim but easily recognisable as their brother. Fran kissed Pat, hugged Cassie, and led them into a big, comfortable living room with a view of the garden, while Uncle Frankie and Ger went off to talk to the farm manager.

Over tea it became increasingly clear that the family on this side of the ocean were empire-builders too. The farm didn't just supply Ger's shop: stock was bought and sold all the time, and meat provided to retail outlets across the county. And the Lissbeg Fitzgeralds seemed to have branched out into commercial property.

But, despite Uncle Frankie's grandiose house and the fact that he seemed to be central in running the business, it seemed that Ger still had hold of the reins. Later, Cassie had asked Pat why they'd never moved out of the flat over the shop. 'Ger never wanted to, love' was all she'd got for an answer.

The peaks of the mountains up ahead were lost in mist while, lower down, the wintry light picked out the curves of valleys and the courses of streams, where bronze bracken was dying back between outcrops of grey rock. On Cassie's left, the road began to run alongside woodland — tall deciduous trees that she couldn't name. Oak, probably, and other trees, with silver trunks, that might be ash or elm.

Then, up ahead and to the right, the pale sky was suddenly full of seagulls. She turned a corner and found herself driving along a clifftop road between the forest and the ocean. The gulls were wheeling and tossing in shrieking f locks, their white wings and pale gold beaks glinting in the low sunlight. Pulling in, Cassie went to lean on the hood of the car, her camera in her hand. She tried to focus on a single seagull. It was no use, though. The birds were moving at speed, lifted and tossed by gusts of wind from the ocean and, anyway, the light wasn't right for photography.

After a few botched shots, she gave herself up to the spectacle, and the counterpoint between the gulls' cries and the deep notes of the waves sounding in the distance. There was a low stone wall between the road and the fields beyond it that appeared to slope down to the edge of the cliff. Sheep were grazing in the field nearest to the point where she'd pulled the car in; at times the swooping seagulls' claws seemed to rake their woolly backs.

Back in the car, she travelled on, aware that the clouds that had hung on the mountains were drifting down to creep through the forest beside her. Tiny droplets formed on her windshield and the mist began to obscure the road ahead.

Cassie switched on her headlights and slowed down to read a signpost. Apparently there was a village not far ahead, so she idled along till she came to it: a couple of houses and a shop with woodland behind them, and a fingerpost, on the seaward side, indicating a steep slope that led down to a pier. She parked in front of the shop, which had a table and benches outside it, and a sign saying it was also an internet café.

Once inside, she could see it was a general grocery with three tables just inside the door and shelves of supplies and the shop counter beyond them. Cassie smiled at the middle-aged woman behind it. 'Hi. Could I get a coffee?'

'You can, of course.' The woman, who had dark curls and a broad smile, nodded at the tables. 'Sit down there and I'll go through and make it for you. Were you looking for something to eat as well?'

'Maybe a sandwich?'

'No problem. Or a scone? I wouldn't have a full menu this time of the year, but I made some scones this morning.'

Cassie sat at a table by the window, decided on a tuna sandwich and said she'd have a scone as well. On Pat's recommendation, she'd eaten a homemade scone with black currant jam at the Garden Café in Lissbeg, and the basketful she could see on the counter promised to be just as good.

'Are you on holiday yourself?'

Cassie had learned that it was easier to offer information than to have it extracted bit by bit. 'I'm Pat and Ger Fitzgerald's granddaughter. I'm staying in Lissbeg.'

'No! Are you really? I knew they'd come back from Canada but I didn't know they'd brought a granddaughter with them. Are you Sonny's youngest or Jim's eldest?'

Obligingly, Cassie gave her the whole story, ending with her decision to visit Finfarran because she'd never been there before.

'And isn't it great to have the freedom to

take the time off like that when you want to? I suppose the hairdressing's a wonderful thing. You can come and go as you please and, so long as you have your scissors, you can work anywhere.'

It was never worthwhile trying to explain the freelance life, so Cassie didn't argue.

The woman held out her hand and said that her name was Fidelma Cafferky. 'And look at me, standing here when I should be making your coffee! I won't be a minute. Would you like cream with your scone?'

Cassie said she would, and took out her phone. Fidelma looked over her shoulder as she went to go through to the kitchen. 'You'll need a password for the Wi-Fi. It's dantheman1. All one word and lower case for the letters, then the number one. No fear of me forgetting it — it's my son's nickname.'

Cassie keyed in the password and checked her messages. When talking to Fidelma she hadn't mentioned that she was looking for lodgings in Lissbeg. In the last week she'd found that produced one of two reactions — either slight disapproval, as if she were disparaging Pat's hospitality, or lengthy assurances that she'd never find a place that was half as good. Now, as she scrolled through her inbox, she found a message headed 'Room' that made her eyes light up. Triumphantly, she hit Reply and shot off a response arranging an appointment in Lissbeg at eight p.m. Then, for the next half hour, as the mist swirled by the window, she sat back happily, uploading botched shots of seagulls to Instagram, drinking coffee, and savouring Fidelma's homemade jam.

By the time she was back on the road, the worst of the mist had lifted. Fidelma had waved her off, saying that if she kept going she'd find her way back to the main road. 'You don't want to be retracing your tracks and there's grand views of the coastline for the next few miles if you just keep going. Any road to the right will get you to the motorway eventually, but the one you want is about five miles on, by a field with a five-barred gate. It's not signed but you can't miss it.'

After twenty minutes Cassie knew that she'd missed it. The twists and turns of the road kept revealing new dramatic cliffs and headlands and, with her attention constantly drawn to the unfolding panorama on her left, it had been hard to look for an unmarked turn on the right.

She was about to reverse when a four-wheel drive appeared up ahead, driven at speed. Pulling in, Cassie opened her window and leaned out, waving.

The guy who slowed down and stopped beside her was about her own age. He was dark and tanned, in a not very Irish way, but his accent sounded local. As he leaned out of his own window Cassie could see another guy beyond him, in the passenger seat. The same age, or maybe a year or so older, he was short and stocky and wearing a khaki parka. The driver wore a thick polo-neck sweater under a quilted body warmer. He grinned at her. 'You okay?'

'Fine. But I think I've missed my turn. If I keep going can I make a right up ahead and get back onto the motorway?'

'The motorway? And you've a Finfarran number plate. But you're not from round here, are you?'

'No, Sherlock, I'm not. Are you going to answer my question?'

He laughed. 'Well, that's me put back in me box. Yeah, if you drive on you can turn right but you could get lost if you try it. Better to turn back and drive for a couple of miles, till you see a —'

'Five-barred gate. I know. I shouldn't have missed it. I just wasn't looking.'

'Mind you, half the farm gates round here have five bars to them. The one you want has a pallet in the ditch beside it.'

'Oh, that's helpful. What's a pallet?'

'Tell you what. Do a U-turn and follow me. I'll stick my hand out and wave when we get to the turning.'

Cassie smiled, said thanks, and they set off in convoy. The four-wheel drive, which was a bit battered, had a tow-bar at the back and a workmanlike roof rack on top. When they came to the turn, the driver slowed and gesticulated and, leaning out of the window, pointed to a wooden frame filled in with planks that was stuck in a gap beside the galvanised gate.

'That's a pallet! And there's your turn.'

She opened her own window and shouted, 'Thanks, Sherlock!' before turning onto the side road. It was narrow and even more winding and, in some places, the trees that lined the fields on either side almost met overhead.

As she negotiated the potholes, Cassie tried to remember where she'd seen the guy who'd been sitting beside the driver. She couldn't think where she might have encountered him, and she was sure that they'd never spoken to each other, but somehow she knew the set of his short, stocky body. It wasn't until she reached the main road that she finally managed to place him. He was the impatient guy who'd honked his horn when the van driver with the little dog beside him had stopped the traffic on Broad Street to allow Pat and herself to cross.

14

Hanna opened the glass case and looked down at the psalter. The little book that stood open on its stand was hardly bigger than the paperback she'd been reading in bed last night. The double-page spread it was opened at was largely taken up with text: clean strokes of black ink on soft creamy-yellow goatskin, with an illuminated capital letter on the left-hand page, where the margin was decorated with a flourish of cross-looking rabbits playing hand bells, running along a gilded flowering branch.

Since the opening of the exhibition Hanna had turned over a new page each month, sometimes revealing dense text with minimal decoration, and sometimes pages on which glowing illustrations took up most of the space. But now, as Brian had suggested, she planned to turn a new page for each of the four weeks of Advent.

The idea, which had been flagged on the

Edge of The World website, had become a talking point in the town. As Conor said, it felt kind of Christmassy. And today, as she'd arrived at the library gate, a couple of women on their way to the shops had stopped and told her it was great. You'd hardly get a chance to see the psalter in summer with all the tourists. But you'd like to come by in your own time and take a proper look.

The entire book had been digitised for the exhibition and, as well as interactive images of every page that allowed visitors to zoom in on detail, translations of the text in different languages could be accessed via wall-mounted screens. But, for Hanna, the real pleasure lay in these solitary moments when the book lay between her hands like a jewel, its vibrant colours gleaming in the low light.

It had been given to the library by Charles Aukin, an American banker who'd married the last living member of the Anglo-Norman de Lancy family, once landlords of Finfarran. According to family records, they'd acquired the psalter during the Reformation, when the monks who had made it were driven out of their monastery in Carrick.

Charles, who lived alone in his late wife's slightly dilapidated family castle, had made a stipulation with his bequest: the book was to remain on the peninsula and be housed in Lissbeg Library. And — clearly used to the labyrinthine procedures of rural local authorities — he'd avoided argument by commissioning and paying for its exhibition space himself.

The religious connotations of the psalter meant little to Hanna. By the time she was growing up in the 1970s, the traditional stranglehold that the clergy had held on Irish life had loosened; and, once in England, she had seldom gone to church. All the same, she never approached the psalter without reverence. Whenever she saw the flowing images that had emerged from the scribes' deft pen strokes, she was shaken by an exuberant sense of their power. Each page was a glorious balance of symmetry and aberration, simultaneously reflecting divine authority, human weirdness, and the bizarre complexity of the natural world.

That the monks had been responding to places she knew and loved added to her pleasure. Wandering the back roads of Finfarran, she too had admired the fall of the cliffs on the southern side of the peninsula, the sunlight filtering through leaves at the margins of the forest, and the shape of Knockinver burning against a winter sky at dusk.

Now, with infinite care, she turned a page and revealed a new illustration. The psalm, on the right-hand page, was numbered thirty-three, and the beginning of each verse was marked by a star in the margin, trailing shining tails made of minuscule dots of paint. The facing picture showed busy figures on a deep blue background. At the top of each page, emerging from a pair of pursed, disembodied lips, were spirals of white, suggestive of wind, and more whirling stars.

The figures, who were little monks in dark habits, were working on a yellow beach where white-topped waves reared above them, streaked and flecked with foam. Two monks, whose robes were girded above their knees, were catching a falling wave in a pottery jar. Others were loading full jars into oxcarts — one cart had tipped over, and a stream of water from a jar's gaping mouth had knocked a portly monk to the ground with his naked rear in the air.

There was a great sense of energetic organised chaos. In the middle distance, a row of carts was disappearing into a barn, with wide doors and a curved roof. The heaving oxen's muscles stood out like hawsers, and other monks with girded-up robes were dragging more jars towards the beach on a kind of wooden sleigh.

The picture was framed with a frieze of stars and seaweed, through which the faces of grotesques and animals peered out at the toiling monks.

Hanna bent closer to look at it. Each star was as bright as the day on which it had been painted and the seaweed was rendered as accurately as if in a scientific reference book. She recognised bladderwrack and the kind that her great-aunt Maggie used to call dead men's bootlaces. And horsetail and what she thought was called beadweed. Then, as she stood upright, the detail was no longer evident and the frieze resolved into glittering abstract scrolls.

Crossing to one of the screens on the wall, she looked up the translation of Psalm Thirty-three. Two verses had been conflated in the illustration, one of which declared that 'the starry multitude of the skies had been made by the breath of God's mouth', and the other that he had 'gathered the ocean waters into a heap and put the deep seas into jars'. Hanna smiled, imagining the psalmist who'd conjured up those images. What would he have said if he could have seen them realised hundreds of years later by a monk in a cell on a western Atlantic shore?

Locking the case, she went to open the library. Turning the pages of the psalter was a reminder that time was passing and, so far, she still hadn't been able to make up her mind about Brian's invitation. Christmas in Sweden was a tempting prospect, but ought she to indulge in it? After all, this was Louisa's first Christmas with Mary Casey. And how would Jazz deal with Christmas dinner at the bungalow? She might not fancy a day spent solely in the company of her grandmothers, and it wasn't as if she had anywhere else to go.

15

Bríd scowled and flopped onto the sofa. Aideen was being infuriating, and Conor had no bloody business to be putting his oar in at all.

It was seven forty-five and the argument had been going on for an hour. Aideen, who was sitting opposite Bríd, clasped her hands round her knee. She looked as if she was trying to stop herself throwing something. Except that Aideen was never violent — only, as Bríd had just told her, really, *really* sneaky.

'I am not sneaky! How can you say that?'

'Oh, please! Making plans behind my back and not even bothering to consult me!'

'I didn't make them behind your back. And I'm talking to you now.'

'Five minutes before it's a fait accompli!' Seeing Aideen's reaction, Bríd rushed on to safer ground. 'Okay, all right, so you told me in the deli this morning, with half the town in the queue so I couldn't say anything. And you've been soft-soaping me ever since we got home. But the bottom line is you dreamed up a plan — *and* went and discussed it with Conor! — when it's *my* life and *my* home that are going to be affected.'

Conor, who was sitting on the arm of Aideen's chair, reached down and took her hand. 'It wasn't Aideen's idea, it was mine.'

'Oh, this just gets better and better! *You* came up with a plan for what should happen in *our* house?'

Aideen glared at her. 'Don't you dare start on Conor! Yes, it was his idea. And, yes, I discussed it with him. Why wouldn't I? I'll talk to anyone I want, Bríd, about anything I like. And, in case you've forgotten, the house is mine, not ours.'

There was a pause in which they all absorbed the fact that Aideen had just said the unsayable. Then Conor charged into the breach. 'I'm sorry, Bríd. Honest. And nothing's actually been fixed. It just seemed like a good plan, since Aideen and I are desperate to up our savings. But if it doesn't work for the both of you, that's no problem at all.'

Aideen shook her head vehemently. 'It's not us who need to apologise. I'm sorry too,

Bríd, if we've upset you, but we haven't done anything wrong. And I've told you already that Cassie's only coming for a chat. We mightn't like her at all, or she might hate the place.'

Bríd opened her mouth to speak but Aideen went on regardless: 'And if you've made up your mind to dislike her without even seeing her, then *you're* the one who's being sneaky. And plain mean!'

Sitting on the sofa, which was lower than the chair, felt wrong so Bríd stood up abruptly. The whole notion of turning the dining room into a bedroom and renting it out to some girl that Conor had met in the library was daft. Okay, they didn't need the dining room to eat in, but they did use it as a store room. Was this stranger supposed to sleep on a pile of boxes? She snapped the question at Aideen, who shrugged her shoulders.

'We'd move the boxes out of there. Naturally. And don't start fussing, I've worked out where they'd go. There's plenty of room at the Garden Café, and they'd be far better there anyway. Much easier for deliveries, and far more convenient with the deli across the road.'

The trouble was that she was right about that. When they'd set up the deli, the Old

Convent Centre hadn't been opened. But now, as well as running HabberDashery, they provided food for the café in the nuns' garden, so Phil could hardly object if they stored stuff there. Actually, it was an efficiency that Bríd should have thought of herself.

There was no point in asking about furniture either. That was all sorted. According to Aideen, Conor's mum had a single bed, a wardrobe and a chest of drawers going begging, and Conor could give them a fresh coat of paint. They'd have to buy a new mattress, but the blanket box on the landing was full of linen and a spare duvet, still faintly scented with lavender sachets made by Aunt Bridge. 'I'll pay for the mattress and we'll do all the shifting. You won't have to be involved, though if you had any bit of decency you'd help.'

Bríd glanced at her watch and saw that this Cassie person was due in a couple of minutes. She glared at Aideen. 'Three people in the bathroom in the mornings? Someone else sitting here at night? What if Dan's round and he and I just want to hang out? I mean, we're not like you and Conor, always disappearing up to the bedroom.'

As soon as she'd said it, she wished she hadn't. Aideen looked like a stricken deer and, anyway, it was nonsense. Dan hardly ever came round, and when he did they always disappeared upstairs themselves.

Conor gave a hoot of laughter. 'Ah, for God's sake, Bríd, would you cop on to yourself? I've known a few times when Dan and I have been fighting over the bathroom. Not to mention the TV remote. And haven't we all managed so far with no bones broken? You're behaving as if Cassie's the last straw, but the fact is that she'll only be round for a matter of months. Or maybe weeks. Only till after Christmas, anyway.'

The doorbell rang before Bríd could reply, and Aideen got up to answer it. On her way to the door she shot Bríd a look. Biting her lip, Bríd went and stared pointlessly out of the window. She knew perfectly well that the real issue wasn't the bathroom. Or the bedroom furniture. It was the fact that Aideen, who'd always deferred to her advice, had moved on and was focused on Conor.

The girl who was ushered in a few minutes later appeared to Bríd to have what Gran always called 'a great welcome for herself'. She was short and wide-eyed, with blond hair that was razor-cut at the back and a feathery fringe dyed a daft shade of blue. As Conor offered her a chair she slipped out of

136

a puffy metallic coat that looked both rugged and stylish, as if she were about to trek to a party at the North Pole. Bríd noticed a tiny tattoo at the nape of her neck, where the razor-cut ended in a couple of curls of dyed hair, like a duck's tail.

Aideen introduced her as Cassie Fitzgerald, and Cassie smiled at Bríd. 'Pat and Ger Fitz from the butcher's granddaughter. I'm beginning to feel I need to say so each time I meet someone new.'

Bríd had an insane urge to look blank and say that she'd no idea who Pat and Ger Fitz were. Just to wipe the confident look off the snub-nosed face. Instead she escaped to the kitchen, saying she'd put the kettle on.

By the time she came back with the tray the others had shown Cassie the dining room, and Cassie was back in the armchair, all enthusiasm. 'Really, it couldn't be better. I've practically no luggage, so don't even bother with the wardrobe. Maybe we could find a rail, or stick a few hooks on the door.'

Aideen asked if she was certain the room would be big enough.

'Hey, I've shared cabins that were smaller — it's perfect, really. And, just so you know, I'm not saying a word against Pat and Ger's place. It's nice and they're really hospitable. I just don't want to have to tiptoe past their bedroom each time I come in late at night.'

Bríd heard herself announcing that there wasn't much nightlife in Lissbeg. Cassie shot her a surprised look. 'Well, I wasn't expecting Las Vegas. Still, there must be something to do in Carrick.' She picked up a coffee mug and smiled at Bríd over the rim. 'It's not just about nightlife, anyway. Pat's sweet, and if I stayed with her she'd feel she had to entertain me. Whereas I'm far happier entertaining myself.'

The mug she'd picked up was the one that Bríd herself always drank from. Irritated by Aideen's look of concern, and a flicker of amusement from Conor, Bríd held out a plate and announced that the biscuits were Bourbons. Cassie smiled again and took one, saying she'd had a cookie at the Garden Café that Pat had said was made by a girl from the deli.

Aideen beamed. 'Bríd does all our baking. She's brilliant at it.'

'Yes, well, these are from the supermarket, I'm afraid.'

Bríd's tone was brittle but Cassie didn't seem to notice. Instead she smiled again and said thanks.

Aware that she'd sounded priggish, Bríd was groping for something to say when Dan's face suddenly appeared at the window. She went to the door to let him in, as Conor explained to Cassie that this was her boyfriend, Dan Cafferky. 'His mum and dad keep the shop in Couneen and Dan does eco-tours.'

'Oh, right.'

As Bríd led Dan into the room and began to introduce him, Cassie interrupted her and gave him a big wink. 'How's it going, Sherlock?'

To Bríd's horror, Dan winked back at her. 'Never better. How're you doing yourself?'

Throwing a quick glance at Aideen, Conor turned to Cassie. 'So you two know each other?'

'Oh, Dan the Man and I are old friends, aren't we?' Cassie bit into her Bourbon. 'Seems like, since we found each other, we just can't keep apart.'

16

The mobile library served the north side of
the peninsula on Tuesdays and the south
side on Thursdays; and the northern route
continued westwards round the foothills of
Knockinver to Ballyfin. On both days it was
a straight run back up the motorway to Carrick once Conor's work was done.

Miss Casey had given him strict instructions about where to park, and how he
wasn't supposed to pull in anywhere other
than his designated halting places. Then
she'd relaxed and said some of the people
who lived along the route were devils for
standing by their gates, waving books at
you. It was okay to stop if they looked a bit
flustered or were elderly. But you'd have to
take a view. 'People like Darina Kelly just
try it on, so you can ignore her. She's only
down the way from Couneen and she's
perfectly capable of getting there just like
anyone else. There's a few more like her as

well, but you'll get used to them. You just want to make sure that no one takes advantage of your good nature. Trying to flag you down is only the half of it — you'll have to start as you mean to go on.'

The pull-in at Couneen was in front of Cafferky's shop. When Conor got there, Mrs Kelly was among the little group of locals sitting in the window drinking coffee and waiting for the van. Dan's mum waved at Conor from the doorway, and the group came out and lined up while he opened up the van. Finfarran wasn't part of the new national libraries management system yet, so if a book wasn't available in the county you still needed to order it by inter-library loan. Most people were happy to stick to the system they knew, anyway — there were even some who refused to renew a book online, preferring to pay a fine if they couldn't return it on time.

But now Darina Kelly, who dressed like some class of a hippie and was forty-five if she was a day, was suddenly getting ratty. The new management system was brilliant, she said, so why couldn't she use it?

'I'm afraid it hasn't been rolled out to Finfarran yet.'

Conor could see the rest of the queue getting cross about being kept waiting. It was dry enough today, after several days of rain, but the wind was chilly and everyone's coffee was cooling inside on the tables. No one was actually complaining, but he could feel them thinking that, when it came to the library, Miss Casey was the real engine driver, and he was no more than the oily rag.

Deciding he had about a minute and a half to get things under control, he took a deep breath and asked Mrs Kelly if she'd put in an online request.

'No. I mean, what's the point? You've just said that Finfarran isn't part of the new scheme.'

'The old system's not quite as quick as the new one, but we can still order a book for you from any library in the country.' He paused, playing to the queue and registering world-weary patience. 'And if you'd done an online request a week ago I could have had it here today.' Sensing the queue's approval, he moved in for the kill. 'Unless you find using the online facilities difficult?' The suggestion that she was computer-challenged freaked Mrs Kelly, as he'd known it would. Her face went red and she hitched her Afghan coat up around her ears.

Then, before she could open her beak again, Conor turned to the man who was standing behind her. Without your woman noticing, they gave each other a wink. 'How're you doing, Jack? Did you like the read?'

The man fished in a supermarket carrier bag and produced a copy of Sebastian Faulks's James Bond novel, *Devil May Care.* 'Do you know what it is, Conor? I kind of liked it. Faulks is no Ian Fleming, mind, and you'd notice the quirks in his style. Only now and then, of course, but I'm an aficionado. I'd have Fleming's nuances in my ear.'

He handed the book to Conor, who, aware of the queue's eyes on him, reached round and produced William Boyd's *Solo.* 'Well, see what you think of that.'

Jack took it and shook his head thoughtfully. 'I thought I'd give it a go but, you know, I'm not all that sure about these "continuations". But I've started so I'll finish, as the fella said.' He tapped Mrs Kelly on the shoulder. 'All the way from Kilkenny, Darina, and only a click or two to get it. You can't beat ordering books online.'

Darina began to gobble like a prize turkey. 'I'm perfectly well acquainted with online ordering! What I was complaining about was the fact that the service isn't cutting-edge.'

Jack shook his head again, this time in

mock interest. 'Is that so? Well, you've come a long way on a cold day to stand and complain about that.'

By this point the whole queue was hiding smirks and giggles. Conor felt a pang of remorse as Darina Kelly stepped away with a huge show of dignity, and crossed the road to get into her Deux Chevaux. On the other hand, though, he knew he'd laid down a marker. When it came to the mobile library route, Miss Casey would always be the engine driver, but after today, no one would say that he was the oily rag.

Back on the road, he found himself thinking about liver fluke. Joe had been worried about the sheep for a while, and the other day they'd found a couple of dead ones. The results of the tests on the carcasses should be back shortly, but their dad reckoned it was liver fluke, and he was seldom wrong. Swinging the wheel, Conor told himself that stuff like that, and having to go through soil sampling and sending things off for analysis, weren't part of Aideen's vision of farm life at all. She'd come over for tea last week and hung out in the kitchen while he and Joe were working. After they'd eaten, he'd taken her up for the cows on the back of the Vespa, and all the way she'd been shouting over his shoulder, saying how gorgeous everything looked, and telling him how she'd helped his mam feed the hens.

Up to a while back the winter had been so mild that there was still growth in the grass, and the trees had leaves on them. Then, last weekend, the wind had stripped them naked, and the rainy nights had pounded the fallen leaves so hard that the queue in Couneen today had stood in soggy mulch waiting for their library books. But when he and Aideen had gone for the cows the air had been full of thistledown, and curled leaves, the colour of her hair, were falling like flames from the chestnut trees.

Later on, when he'd taken her home, she'd told him that, when she'd been out in the yard, the hens had gone mad for her wellington boots and stood in a circle, pecking them. She'd wanted to know why. And why did they lay fewer eggs in winter, and how did you teach dogs to herd cattle, and when would the lambs be born, and would they be cold up in the fields if it was snowing?

So he'd told her that hens needed sunlight to lay eggs, that the dogs taught each other, and that the lambs would have to be found on the hill and carried down to the farm if the weather got bad. He didn't tell her that ewes could go blind in the snow and the

145

wind, and be out there bleating for their frozen babies. And he said nothing at all about liver fluke.

As he turned the van off the coast road and began the climb towards his next halting place, Dan Cafferky's four-wheel drive came towards him. It slowed down but, with his eye on the time, Conor just waved and kept going. One good thing, anyway, was that the fuss about Dan and Cassie had blown over. It turned out that Cassie had been messing and they didn't know each other really — Dan had only given her directions when she'd stopped him on the road.

In fairness to Bríd, she'd obviously known she'd gone way over the top with her first reaction. Anyway, she'd simmered down, and Cassie seemed to have settled in fine at number eight. Which was great, because Aideen was happy. Of course, the next row with Bríd would be when Cassie left, and Aideen wanted to get a replacement lodger. The bit of extra money each week would make a difference to their savings, so anyone could see it was going to be hard to go back to doing without.

Maybe he should have thought the whole thing through better when he'd first come up with the idea. But even if he had, he didn't suppose he'd have managed to keep his mouth shut. The look on Aideen's face when he'd suggested it had been magic. She'd kind of glowed, as if he was the one who could solve all her problems. And, really, that was all he ever wanted. Just to make her happy. Whatever it took.

17

Pat's range had decided it would behave itself. For three days in a row it had lit without coaxing, which was lucky because the chilly weather had definitely set in. The kitchen was grand and warm, though, with the range lit, and there were heaters up in the bedrooms if they were needed. Pat didn't believe in waste any more than Ger did. Fine to turn up a radiator if you needed to, but no point going round heating empty rooms.

When Cassie had gone off and rented a room from Aideen Carney, Ger had snorted and said he supposed the flat was far too cold. Pat was sure he was wrong. Cassie was the kind who'd have held her ground and said if she'd wanted more heat. Not like Sonny and Jim at the same age, who'd grown up knowing it wasn't wise to cross Ger.

It was sad the way Ger had made a white-headed boy out of Frankie, letting the other lads feel as if he didn't rate them as high. You couldn't exactly put your finger on it, back when they were growing up. Oftentimes Frankie got things before the others just because he was older. And he knew more about running the farm because Ger would take him there more often, and set him to work.

It was little use that Frankie got from his big shoulders nowadays. As soon as the manager was put into the farm, he'd sat himself down behind a desk and hardly lifted a shovel since. And putting the manager in was a case in point. It was Frankie's idea and Ger had been all for it. Though if Sonny or Jim had been in charge and suggested it, Ger would probably have cursed them for a couple of lazy tykes.

So that was how it was, and there was no help for it. But Pat had always thought it was a shame that the younger lads had grown up with no love of the land. Maybe if they'd been out in the fields in all seasons they'd have felt the pull of Finfarran after they'd left it. Instead, as far as she could gather from Cassie, they never spoke of it at all.

Cassie herself seemed to be loving the place. She'd settled in with the girls from

HabberDashery and, as far as Pat could see, she was off skiting day and night. And why wouldn't she be? At her age, she was better off with her own generation than hanging round here of an evening. Half the time, Ger did nothing but fall asleep in front of the telly and you'd be torn between keeping the sound low so it didn't wake him, and turning it up so you'd hear it over his snores.

Having said that, Cassie appeared to get on well with anyone, regardless of their age. And she wasn't just out for a good time. After a couple of weeks of exploring she'd turned up at the flat and asked Pat about the Old Convent Centre. 'Did you say there's a pensioners' club there or something?'

Pat explained that several rooms had been turned into a day-care space.

'Does anyone do haircuts?'

'No, love. You'd get your nails cut but not your hair done.'

Cassie had nodded thoughtfully and said no more. But a couple of days later, when Pat was in the centre, there was a poster offering free consultation and cuts by Hairdresser Cassie Fitzgerald. A few moments later Cassie herself had emerged from Phil's office swinging a little backpack, like the kids had these days instead of a handbag.

Questioned, she'd said she'd been telling Phil what she'd need to set up the haircuts. 'Nothing fancy, just a chair and a mirror, really, and a shelf or a little table. And access to a washbasin. I'm coming in once a week.'

'How did this all happen?'

'Well, I can't spend my whole time here behaving like a tourist. I'd always planned to do some volunteering before my next job. So why not here in Lissbeg?'

And, according to everyone at the day-care facility, she was brilliant. Pat had been bowled over by the compliments. Cassie took her time, they said, and was full of suggestions. She could do a straight wash and set as good as any salon in Carrick, but she also had great ideas.

Nell Reily, who'd worn her hair scraped up on the back of her head in a tortoiseshell clip, now had a short bob with a side parting, and the clip transferred to the other side, to keep the hair out of her eyes. It took years off her.

Ann Flood from the pharmacy, who'd experimented with the dyes on her own shelves for ages and ended with hair like a scouring pad, had submitted to a deep conditioning process that had left her silky and smug as a cocker spaniel. And even a couple of the men who dropped in for the district nurse's exercise sessions were sporting well-trimmed nose hair and short back and sides.

These days, you couldn't walk down Broad Street with Cassie without someone giving her a wave or shouting a greeting. It'd make you burst with pride.

And she even seemed to have made friends in Carrick. A while back, when she'd taken Pat to a matinée at the cinema, they'd been pulling into a car park when a young fellow in a guard's uniform had slowed down beside them and given her a thumbs-up.

Pat was dying to ask questions but she didn't want to be inquisitive. Cassie didn't seem bothered, though. As she parked the car she said that she'd met the guard at a nightclub inside in Carrick called Fly-By-Night. She hadn't known he was a guard then, because he hadn't been wearing his uniform.

'And when did you find out?'

'Just now.'

'You mean he never said?'

'Well, nightclubs are a bit noisy. You don't tend to get much conversation.'

Pat supposed that was true enough. He looked a nice respectable fellow anyway, and he'd had a big smile for them.

Now, as she settled the poker by the range, she wondered how different things might have been if Sonny had gone off to Carrick and met himself a nice girl. The lads had gone to school dances all right, and a few parties, but most of the time they'd be up in their rooms doing lessons. Or, in Frankie's case, charging round a field playing rugby. Sonny and Jim were more like Ger, small-built and not great on a playing field, and Jim didn't even play tennis because of his glasses.

Of course, for all Pat knew, they might have gone out with dozens of girls at college. But, if they did, they'd left them there in Cork and never brought one of them home.

Opening the local paper, she glanced at the cinema listings. There wasn't much on that you'd want to see, what with blockbusters and kids' cartoons and horror movies. Anyway, Cassie had suggested that, this week, they might take a day trip to Cork. And, actually, Pat had been wanting a chance to do a bit of Christmas shopping.

A week or so after coming back from Toronto, Ger had said he needed to go down to Cork on business, and she'd said she'd go with him and take a look around the shops. But that hadn't suited Ger, who'd got all agitated. He needed to set out at the crack of dawn, he'd said, and he couldn't be waiting round for her. And he didn't want her sending him texts all the time, demanding to be taken home. All nonsense, of course, because she was always ready and waiting whenever they'd fixed to go somewhere, and never made a demand on him in her life.

Thinking about it later, she'd been at a loss to make head or tail of it. Still, it didn't do to be questioning Ger, who'd only go getting irritable. And the chances were he was meeting some fellow who'd taken him off to the dogs.

18

Most of the peninsula's piers stood unused now, with tags of rope flapping at rusty moorings and piles of abandoned fish boxes stacked against the walls. A combination of emigration and EU quotas had reduced Finfarran's fishing communities from a dozen down to two. A few boats still worked out of Reesagh, near Lissbeg. And there was still a fleet in Ballyfin, where local fishermen had to fight off attempts by the town's hoteliers to move the working boats because of the smell. But it was a good thirty years since a fishing fleet had used the little pier at Couneen.

Dan, whose grandfather had fished out of Couneen with six neighbours, was always raging at Bríd about the Ballyfin hotels. 'People go there expecting to find a fishing port, not to sit on a flashy veranda taking selfies with a dead pier!' His grandad would turn in his grave, he said, if he saw the way the village was now. And as Bríd approached Cafferky's internet café, she thought he was probably right.

There were several abandoned houses on the road above the little pier, their thatched roofs gone and their stone walls gradually returning to the earth. Dan's parents had built their shop on the piece of land that had once belonged to his grandfather, and the old house, behind the new building, had been roughly reroofed for use as a shed. At one time, this had been a thriving village. Now it was a coffee break on the road to someplace else.

Bríd drove her car down the sloping descent by the shop, and parked on the grassy turning point above the path to the pier. The steep path, cobbled with wave-smoothed stones, was wet with spray. The pier below, which was far smaller than those at Ballyfin and Reesagh, had been built in a sheltered inlet with high cliffs on either side. Part of an energetic scheme initiated in the nineteenth century, it was constructed of huge blocks of dressed stone, which, according to Dan, had been brought round by sea, using local manpower. 'The de Lancy crowd that lived in the castle were all for progress in those days. They organised some kind of an agricultural co-op thing that was meant to improve farming. And they had local men building the piers under a foreman over from England. Or some guy that was cracking the whip for them anyway.'

'But wasn't it good for the people?'

'Maybe so. They lent them money for nets. I know that, because my grandad said so. His own grandad got nets and enough to buy a boat. It all had to be paid back, though, and the castle wanted to buy the fish at a special price.'

Bríd had shrugged. 'Well, I suppose it was a regular order. We do that at the deli. Say a business is willing to commit to a platter of sandwiches every Tuesday, we'll give them a price.'

'Yeah, well, you don't charge them rack rent for the houses they live in. And you didn't turn up with an army in the first place and steal their land.'

The de Lancys had arrived in Finfarran with the Norman invasion, so he was going back a bit. But that was Dan all over. He was always going round with a chip on his shoulder and blaming the world for his woes. Bríd herself just liked to get on with stuff. On that occasion, though, it hadn't seemed wise to say so. The fact was that HabberDashery's business was slowly but steadily improving, while Dan's tours from

Couneen pier had disappeared down the drain.

Still, things were looking up. According to Dan, he'd picked up a lot of great ideas in Australia and, with Dekko's investment, he was all set to relaunch his business in the spring.

The tour boat had been rented to a guy in Ballyfin while Dan had been away and was out of the water now, in dry dock for the winter. So, as Bríd walked along the pier it was deserted, except for the dinghy pulled up behind the little shed that Dan had built against the wall. The shed was part store, part workshop, and Dan was sitting outside it on an upturned box, disembowelling an outboard motor. His face lit up when he saw Bríd, and he reached out an oily hand.

Eyeing it askance, Bríd hunkered down beside him with her back to the wall. It was chilly enough but, at this time of day, the sheltered inlet was a sun trap, so the smooth, dressed stone felt warm, even through her thick coat.

Dan nodded at the kettle on its camping stove in the shed. 'I'll make us a cup of tea in a minute. What's the story in Lissbeg?'

'Nothing much to tell.'

'World War Three not broken out yet at number eight?'

Bríd made a face at him. 'Just drop it, okay?'

'Fair enough. I see your woman's volunteered to work in the Old Convent Centre.'

Giving him an old-fashioned look, Bríd refused to rise to the bait. The fact was that Cassie's self-confident air continued to be irritating, though everyone else seemed to think she was marvellous. Yesterday she had arrived home with the news that she was joining a creative-writing group in the library. And Aideen had gushed. Wasn't she clever? Wasn't that a great thing altogether? Aideen herself had thought of joining but couldn't get up the nerve.

Bríd had been about to say that it didn't sound all that hazardous, when Cassie got her say in first: 'Nothing clever about it. I just thought it might be fun. You should have a go, Aideen. You could always leave if you don't like it.'

No thought at all of what joining up and then just dropping out might do to the group. And that, Bríd had thought, was typical of bloody Cassie. She sailed smugly through life, thinking only of herself.

But her own thought had hardly been formulated when Cassie piped up again, as if just to annoy her: 'Actually, I'm not all that interested. But Pat is. Big-time. I could tell by the look on her face when she told me about it. You could see she was dying to sign up, but felt that maybe it wasn't for her. So I said that I would if she would, and that did the trick.'

So, of course, Bríd was left feeling like a bitch.

Now, eager to change the subject, she asked Dan where Dekko was. He was usually hanging around somewhere, but it turned out he'd gone up to Dublin today. 'Is that where his family are?'

'It's where he comes from but I dunno if he's still got family there. He never said.'

'When's he coming back?'

'God, Bríd, what is this? The Spanish Inquisition? He'll be back whenever he's ready, I suppose. It's not like there's anything to do round here in winter.'

Looking at Dan's oily hands, it struck Bríd that there was quite a lot to do before the business could reopen. And not just physical stuff. There was advertising and organising, and things like finding an accountant, and networking with other people in tourism on the peninsula. But, apparently, Dekko was an investor and nothing else, so that would all be down to Dan, who just didn't seem to get it.

Now he wiped his hands on a rag and

hauled her to her feet. 'C'mon, let's have a cup of tea and I'll take you out in the dinghy.'

'In this weather?'

'There's nothing wrong with the weather. I'd say we mightn't get another day like this for a long time, though. Come on, don't be a wuss. You might see a dolphin.'

'Or a flying pig!'

'Okay, probably not a dolphin. But you'll get a bit of wind in your hair. And if you don't like the effect you can always go to Cassie for a makeover.'

Later, drinking tea out of chipped mugs, she listened as he talked about his marine tours. 'I dunno how much it has to do with climate change, but the seas are definitely warming. We're getting all classes of fellas out there you'd never see before. Not just the dolphins and the humpback whales and the minkes. I saw them when I was a kid. And the seals and the basking sharks. But back just before I went off to Australia, I saw a pod of killer whales only a mile or two offshore. You see, the water temperature's rising and that brings a lot of feed. That's bad for fishing because the fish have less interest in bait. They can eat all they want out there in the ocean. But it's great for bringing in the big fellas, and they're

161

amazing to see.'

Tourists wanted to get out and take photos and videos, he said. And plenty would want to go diving. 'If I grow the business properly I'll be hiring out diving gear on the side. But the great thing would be to get a glass-bottomed boat. God, Bríd, you should see the Great Barrier Reef. I went on one of them out of Cairns and you wouldn't believe it.'

'Was that when you met Dekko?'

'Yeah, we met in a bar and we got talking. God, you wouldn't believe the coral they've got over there. And the turtles. They've got six of the world's seven species.'

Once Dan started talking about the ocean, you could never shut him up. As he leaned forward, Bríd found herself focusing on his eyelashes. How come guys so often had long, curling black ones, while women were stuck with mascara? When Dan went swimming he emerged from the waves with his hair and lashes sleek as a seal's back, while she was left struggling with tangles and so-called waterproof eye makeup.

'You know what, though? There's stuff here that beats Australia hollow. Maybe less spectacular but so cool.' His eyes widened, like a child's. 'There's a beach a mile or so round to the west with no way down from

162

the cliffs to it. Just a little horseshoe shape, with sloping sand and flat rocks round the edges. You can only approach it by boat and that's why the seals use it for breeding. I'm telling you, you should see the photos I took round there last year. There was one cow had a white pup — oftentimes the mother rejects an albino, but this guy was playing there on the sand with his brothers. And they'd no fear at all. As far as they were concerned, I was just passing by on the sea, like I might have been one of themselves. God, if I'd only had a really decent camera, I could have been winning prizes.'

His eyes focused on Bríd again, and he slugged back a mouthful of tea. 'The thing is, though, that you'd want to leave them their privacy. I think that's the core of what I want to do. Show people all the incredible stuff that's here, but make them see that other species, and all the marine landscape, have to be given space to thrive.'

It was at times like this that Bríd feared she was actually losing her heart to him. Despite his wheeler-dealer airs, Dan wasn't all about making money. He really cared about what he was trying to achieve. And, the way things had been, the odds had been stacked against him. It didn't seem fair. She and Aideen had started off with money in the bank and number eight as an asset. So, hard as it was making payments on a loan, at least they'd been able to get one.

Compared to them, and to people like Jazz Turner, whose start-up company was financed by family money, Dan was facing a far dodgier future. And having messed up his first attempt at setting up a business, he hadn't just felt humiliated, he'd been left with a hopeless credit rating. No wonder he was over the moon now, having found himself an investor. Bríd just hoped that Dekko hadn't gone off and left him in the lurch.

The meeting

19

As Conor came into the big room in the
Old Convent Centre he could see several
hairdos in front of him that had yet to face
the weather. Clearly some of the old ones
had stayed on to attend the meeting after a
session in Cassie's chair.

The day-care facility was warm and well-
lit, the blinds were down, and someone had
the tea urns heating in the kitchen. Even
though the night was shaping up for a
storm, there was a good crowd in the room,
including a solid sprinkling of the town's
retailers. Timing the meeting for six fifteen
had brought in plenty of people who, if
they'd had a chance to go home first, probably wouldn't have come out again.

The posters had said 'FREE
REFRESHMENTS' in massive letters, too,
and that always made a difference. And
above that, printed in the largest font that
Phil's printer could cope with, was a line

that read:

!!TIME TO GET CLUED-UP AND READY FOR FINFARRAN'S WINTER FEST!!

Ferdia was up at the top of the room, fiddling with a computer. Phil was dodging round beside him, trying to set up a shiny new projection screen. It was packed into a tubular case and came out in endless numbered bits that had to be screwed together. Conor could tell from Ferdia's face that it wasn't the one he'd have chosen if he'd been asked.

The meeting actually didn't interest Conor. But the girls from number eight were coming so he'd tagged along, intending to go for a drink with Aideen afterwards. Dan, who must have been working on the same principle, had sloped in behind him and was leaning against the doorframe at the back.

Cassie arrived a few moments later, carrying a mug of coffee, and strolled casually up to a seat near the front. She'd obviously jumped the gun when it came to accessing the free refreshments, and you might have expected the rest of the crowd to look peeved. But, instead, they all seemed delighted to see her, and half the old fellows were falling over themselves to find her a place to sit down.

Phil tapped on the microphone till the chat in the room died away. She was wearing big glasses with black-and-white patterned frames, like an owl disguised as a zebra. Conor could see Miss Casey up at the front, with Brian Morton. He had a sudden, irreverent vision of most of the men in the room being there on a promise, and only dying for the meeting to start and be over so they could get home.

One way or the other, the chances were that, whatever Finfarran's Winter Fest turned out to be, Phil would find it more exciting than the rest of them.

'Now! *Tá fáilte romhaibh go léir, a dhaoine uaisle,* you're all very welcome! And isn't it great to see such a grand crowd on such a wet evening? But we're here now, and I guarantee that what I have to say will make you feel that your journey was worth it. A couple of health and safety notices first — the emergency exits are at the back of the hall and here behind me, and the collection point, in case of fire, is outside, in front of the Garden Café.'

Conor tuned out and looked at the back of Aideen's head up in front of him. Her red hair was twisted up into a scrunchie thing and her engagement ring glinted as she reached back and tucked away a curl or two that had escaped.

The other day he'd tried to have a talk with his brother, Joe, about the future. There was no sign of the yield from the farm getting better, and their dad's depression was making things at home pretty tense. So Conor had thought that maybe they ought to sit down as a family and discuss things. But, according to Joe, that would be counterproductive. Paddy, their dad, would think that they'd given up on him. And Orla, their mam, would think they were rocking the boat. Conor had tried to explain that he didn't want that. He'd thought that a bit of a discussion would help the lot of them get their heads round things. And he needed some idea of where his life was going, now that he was engaged. If the truth be told, it seemed to him that the best way forward might be for Joe to take over the farm altogether. Then he himself could concentrate on how to become a librarian, which, after all, he'd been thinking about for years. But he hadn't said that to Joe.

The microphone gave a sudden shriek and Conor found himself focusing on Phil. She wiggled it ineffectually, looking severely at Ferdia as if the feedback was his fault. Ferdia ignored her.

As the crowd removed its hands from its ears, Phil regained her poise. 'Now, what *is* a Winter Fest? I'm talking craft stalls, food stalls, competitions, maybe a carol concert, *lots* of local produce, and Festive Fun for the kids.'

Old Mrs Reily, who was getting rather deaf, turned to her daughter and asked loudly if the woman meant a fête. 'Because if she does, we've come a long bloody way to be told about something we do every Christmas.'

Phil removed her zebra specs and addressed the room at large. 'The exciting thing is that this provides us with a unique opportunity! If you'll start the presentation there, Ferdia, we can all see what I mean.'

A Winter Fest, as Mrs Reily remarked loudly on several occasions during the PowerPoint presentation, was indeed a class of a Christmas fête. The big difference, apparently, was that, in this case, it was also a competition.

Phil was effusive. 'It's a joint initiative between local and national tourist authorities that's happening nationwide. They've based it on the Tidy Towns idea, different places all competing to be judged the very best.' Without telling Ferdia to pause the presentation, she leapt in front of the screen and began to gesticulate with a large graphic of a holly wreath superimposed on her face. It was all about enhancing the Visitor Experience, she said, with a view to extending the season to introduce Year-round Tourist Reach. The screen shimmered and snowflakes began to drift onto the holly wreath. 'I know that Carrick is planning to enter. And Ballyfin. And I said to myself that we'd want to be in there with them. No, hang on, what am I saying? Up ahead of them!'

A woman beside Conor put her hand up. With a resigned shrug, Ferdia froze the screen. Stepping out of her holly wreath, Phil looked at the woman, who asked if she meant there'd be tourists round all year long. 'I mean what are they going to do? You can't go shoving them out the door of your B and B in this weather.'

People around her nodded emphatically, and a man at the back said you were glad of the winter months to get things ready for next year. He had a rake of jobs to do himself, he said, not to mention a shopfront to paint, and a wife who wanted a break in the sun before they were back to coping with tourists again.

People at the front began turning round

to respond, and for a moment it seemed to Conor that Phil was losing control. Actually she was way ahead of them. Changing tack sharply, she dropped the whole tourist bit and announced that they'd *really* just be enhancing a tradition that everyone loved. 'Obviously the Christmas Fête is a Lissbeg institution. But this year, if we go for the Winter Fest option, I'm hoping to be in a position to offer the perfect venue here at the Old Convent Centre. I know Father McGlynn has always provided the church hall for the fête in the past. And I'm sure he'd be only too happy to do so again . . .'

There was a significant pause during which Conor saw that you had to hand it to her.

For years Lissbeg's Christmas Fête had been dominated by the parish priest. No meeting could be held without his presence, and no decision made without his considered imprimatur, which was often withheld for weeks, during which nothing happened. Then, having finally agreed to something as trivial as the colour of the raffle tickets, he'd drop in the fact that the published date for the fête would have to be altered, or that the celebrity he'd promised to approach couldn't come and open it.

On one occasion when something vital

171

needed changing after the posters were printed, murder was nearly committed when he'd said that it didn't matter at all because he'd make an announcement at Mass. Yet each year the exhausted committee members had to grit their teeth while he was presented with a vast Christmas cake and thanked profusely for all his work and his generous loan of the hall.

Conor could see people around him exchanging glances. The Old Convent Centre had this lovely big room and the kitchen with the tea urns behind it — and the garden outside, where you could put a Christmas tree, and maybe a stall or two if the weather was good. It was bang in the middle of Broad Street, too, and had better parking than you'd get at the church hall.

Phil resumed her glasses with an air of authority. 'If we choose the Winter Fest option, I'm confident that the council will be happy for us to use the Edge of the World website to organise things effectively. And we've meeting rooms here at the centre, and access to computers, which will make everything easier.'

With her point made, she moved in for the clincher, flashing a smile at some of the crowd who rented studio space. 'Plus it'll be a great chance to showcase products, and maybe do a bit of networking. Obviously, we'd get plenty of press coverage if we happened to win the prize. Nothing wrong with that if you're growing a start-up business!'

She glanced round the room again, nodding at Aideen and Bríd and taking in Nuala Harrington, who ran the florist in Sheep Street. 'And a bit of press coverage never hurt an extant business either! Obviously, we'll have charity stalls and things like that, as usual, but I know we can achieve a great sense of professionalism and style.' Conor saw a couple of members of last year's Christmas Fête committee stiffen. Even so, you could see the decision was made. Chatting up the crowd in the centre and the local shops had done the trick.

As for the old guard, Conor suspected that just getting out from under Father McGlynn's thumb would have done it. But the idea of a newly decorated venue, complete with office support, was irresistible. As old Mrs Reily announced later at full volume over the teacups, getting away from the stink of the church hall's paraffin stove nearly bettered ditching your man the priest.

20

Mary Casey felt like a right fool. Louisa had sat down to the lunch table saying that Jazz was planning to drop by at three. And Mary had assumed it was for coffee. Well, why wouldn't she? It never struck her that the child would be coming by for anything else. So she'd slipped into her bedroom and changed out of her slippers. Then, since the shoes with the kitten heel didn't work with the blouse she was wearing, she'd put on her new cashmere jumper and her double string of pearls. Pearls, she'd assured herself, weren't over the top. You had to wear them regularly if you wanted to keep their lustre; if you left them stuck in a box they'd just dry out. But what the whole thing actually boiled down to was that Louisa had been wearing a lovely pair of ankle boots, and you wouldn't want your granddaughter sneering at your old tapestry slippers.

And then it turned out that Jazz was only

coming by to take Louisa off to some meeting. She'd breezed in on the stroke of three, looked at the bubbling percolator, and glanced up at the clock. 'Gosh, I'm sorry, Nan, we won't have time for coffee. I've got a chap booked in for twenty past.'

But, thanks be to God, Mary had had her wits about her. And, better still, she hadn't yet opened the packet of Mikado biscuits. So she'd tossed her head and carried it off with an air. 'Actually, you're right, love, there isn't time, is there? I hope it's okay to cadge a lift to Lissbeg?'

She could see Louisa wondering where that had come from. But before anything more could be said, she'd swept across the kitchen, collecting her keys and her phone. It was by the grace of God that she'd remembered Pat Fitz had a class today in the library. She could whip in there and no one would know that she hadn't planned to from the start.

Once she was settled into the back of the car, she'd opened her phone and shot off a text to Hanna:

TELL PAT 1 MORE 2DAY # U CAN
TAKE ME HOME AFTER

Mind you, sitting staring at a screen for an

175

hour was the last thing she wanted. It was a small price to pay, though, if it came to saving face.

When she pushed open the door to the library, they were all gathered round the computers. And not one man among them, which was something Mary couldn't abide. A man always brought a bit of grace to an occasion and added a bit of a challenge, but what kind of socialising could a person do in a crowd of backbiting women?

Pat Fitz raised her head when she saw her in the doorway, and Mary's eyes dared her to say a word. Hanna was sitting up at her desk but Mary paid her no attention. She crossed the room with her chin up and sat down in an empty place. A good few people turned round and smiled and said they were glad to see her. What she could see when she nodded back was that one half of them was ancient and the other was scruffily dressed.

And here was Pat now, handing out orders like Sister Benignus — you'd almost expect her to go the whole hog and give a vicious yank to your hair. The situation was ridiculous. Mind you, neither of them had been great at the lessons when they were at school, but the fact remained that Pat had always looked up to her. That was how it had been: Pat waiting for instructions and Mary leading the way. And things would be no different now if Pat hadn't gone off and taught herself to use a computer. Sure, anyone could do that. Stabbing crossly at a key marked Alt Gr, Mary told herself the whole thing was farcical.

All the same, she had an hour to spare after the class before Hanna would close the library so, since she and Pat hadn't chatted for a week, they took themselves off to the Garden Café. You had to order from the counter, so Pat went up while Mary claimed a table. It wasn't the kind of weather for sitting out in the nuns' garden. Looking through the steamy window, Mary watched a cloud of little birds fluttering round the statue in the fountain. Someone must have waded through the basin of shallow water and poured birdseed into the stone saint's outstretched hands. There was a bitter wind throwing the little birds sideways and, as far as Mary could see, half the seed was going to get blown away. Fair dos to whatever eejit had gone and put it there, though. This was no day to be trying to find your food out in the cold.

She had a neat little bird feeder herself, back at the bungalow. Johnny Hennessy from next door had hung it by the kitchen window for her the summer after Tom died. 'You'd get great company from birds,' he'd said, which Mary thought was plain stupid. She'd got used to looking for the flutter of wings, though.

And this summer, when she and Louisa would be sitting outside having breakfast, the birds got so tame that some of them came wanting pieces of toast. You couldn't have them messing on the table, of course, but if you threw a crust down for them they were cute enough to run for it. Though you'd have to sweep up afterwards for fear that you might bring rats.

Mary's mouth tightened. The lovely relaxed breakfasts with Louisa seemed to be over. And not just because the summer was gone and you couldn't go sitting on the patio. Ever since she'd started this business with Jazz, Louisa's days had changed. She was supposed to be a sleeping partner — the money behind the scenes while Jazz got on. Instead she was in and out at all hours, making calls and driving off to meetings. No time at all for a proper chat.

There were signs and portents that Mary spotted early. When the work on the bungalow was finished, a vanload of furniture arrived over from England and Louisa was inside in her rooms getting them set up. And the first thing Mary saw when she went in to look was a desk piled with papers. Mind you, it was a lovely little bit of furniture. What you'd call an escritoire. Or maybe a bureau. Nice enough but, all the same, you could see it was a statement of intent.

Louisa had got the builders to turn the window into French doors that opened into the garden. They'd installed a little sink and a work surface in one corner of the room too, so she could make herself a cup of tea without coming down to the kitchen. All the same, she'd somehow managed to make the room seem bigger than it looked before. She'd had the walls painted a warm cream colour, where Mary had had flowery wallpaper, and her pictures were all a bit plain. No story to them.

She had no side table with framed photos on it, and no little rug or cushions that would make the bed look cosy. And no dressing-table either. Mary had had a triple-mirrored, bow-fronted one in there, with gilt handles shaped like tassels. Louisa preferred to do her face in her bathroom across the hall.

Johnny Hennessy had taken Mary's old furniture off to auction for her. Though, with the amount he got and the auctioneer's fees, he might as well not have bothered. A pretty penny Tom had paid for that stuff thirty years ago but, apparently, no one had any taste for proper quality these days.

There were bookshelves on the wall by the bed now, and a panelled Japanese screen around the kettle and things in the corner. And every stitch of clothing Louisa owned was hidden by sliding doors.

And the escritoire, piled with papers and Louisa's slim silver computer, seemed to Mary to dominate the room.

She wasn't quite sure how she'd expected things to be but she knew that it wasn't this way. Louisa was still as charming and friendly as ever, and there were plenty of chats over martinis in the evenings, and meals together, and occasional walks on the beach. But the fact was that she and Jazz were wrapped up in Edge of the World Essentials. Which was a daft name for a business anyway, if you asked Mary's opinion. Not that they ever did.

The three of them had been sitting in the kitchen once, when Louisa had said that Saira Khan, whose husband was manager in the call centre, was going to help them out with research and development. 'She's very knowledgeable about the cosmetic properties of herbs.'

Now, Mrs Khan was a nice enough

woman. But she was from Pakistan. What would she know about things that grew in the nuns' garden? But when Mary asked the question, Jazz just laughed. And then Louisa explained, kind of patronisingly, that Saira's family had been making herbal cosmetics for generations. According to Jazz, they were planning to use some of Saira's mother's recipes for shampoo and hair conditioner, which sounded to Mary like a recipe for disaster. How did they know they wouldn't give people allergies and hives?

Jazz had explained that everything had to go through all classes of microbial and stability testing before you could launch it as a product. But by that stage Mary was getting bored. She'd ended the conversation by putting the kettle on, declaring that, as far as she could see, they needed to think it through better.

After that Jazz and Louisa had tended to do their talking in Louisa's flat. And now, with office space rented in the Convent Centre, they were seldom round at all. It was easy seen that while two was company three was a crowd.

Pat came back to the table with coffee and a plate of shortbread. When she moved the cups from the tray to the table coffee splashed into the saucers. That was Pat all over. She'd always been clumsy, and the way she was dabbing round now with a paper hankie would drive you mad. Still, at least she'd got hold of a jug of hot milk and asked for a proper sugar bowl.

With the table mopped, they sat down for a chat, looking out at the chilly garden. And Pat had more sense than to go asking why Mary had turned up today at her class.

21

It was surprising how quickly you got addicted to hot tea. From the moment Cassie had arrived in Ireland she'd realised that no plan could be made, or conversation had, without someone switching on the kettle. And by now she'd begun to feel that the first cup of tea in the morning was the best one of the day.

Since moving in to number eight, she'd tended not to take her morning shower till the others had got up and gone. Bríd and Aideen needed to get out of the house early, to open up the deli, and if Dan or Conor stayed over, the chances were that they'd be gone earlier still. With no need to dash off to work, Cassie was happy to take a cup of tea back to bed and wait till rush hour was over.

This morning she made it while the others were scuttling round on the landing, and returned to her warm bed with its feather duvet and lavender-scented pillows. The former dining room at number eight made a perfectly comfortable bedroom now that a row of hooks had been screwed to the back of the door, and the little chest of drawers, carefully painted by Conor, was standing under the window.

Setting her mug of tea on the floor by the bed, Cassie sat back against the plumped-up pillows and balanced an A4 notebook against her knees. Today was the first meeting of the creative-writing group in the library and you were supposed to turn up with something you'd written yourself. 'Anything at all, and any length', according to the leaflet Pat had picked up in the library. And that, as Pat said, almost made things worse.

Cassie had visited with her in the flat above the butcher's shop, and found the floor round the kitchen table strewn with balled-up pieces of paper. Seeing her in the doorway, Pat dropped her pen and made for the kettle. 'Now! Haven't you come exactly when I needed you, love. I'm demented here with the writing!'

Sitting down, Cassie had glanced sideways at Pat's copybook. Most of what she could see was scribbled out. There were a couple of doodles in the margin, one of which looked like Bugs Bunny, and at the end of the page was a series of single words.

Before Cassie could read them, Pat was back at the table, closing the book. 'Ah, there's nothing there at all, love, only old scribbles. I can't seem to write anything that makes sense.'

Over the inevitable cup of tea, Cassie had asked what she'd been trying to write about. 'That's the thing, love, I haven't a clue. I mean, what Hanna said was to write something that would tell people who you are. But who's going to turn up in Lissbeg Library that doesn't know who I am?'

'I guess she meant something personal. You know, like a window on your soul.'

Pat put her cup down in horror. 'Holy God Almighty, love, do you think so? I mean, who'd want to do that?'

'Well — writers, I guess. It's kind of what they're about.'

'Do you tell me that?'

Cassie shook her head and laughed. 'I'm the last one to ask. Honestly. And I bet you've read far more books than I have anyway.'

Pat looked thoughtful. 'Well, do you know what it is, I've always been a reader. But I wasn't thinking of writing books when I signed up for the group.'

'No?'

'Well, no.' Pat's face was screwed up with the effort of expression. 'I'm not really sure what I *was* thinking. I suppose, maybe, I thought I might write a poem.'

'Really? That's awesome!'

'No, but I don't know could I do it, now that I'm sitting here. I just like reading poems sometimes. Have you ever read Keats?'

Cassie said she hadn't.

'I used read him a lot when the lads were young. Your dad was an awful noisy baby. He'd wake up roaring at night. And Ger needed his sleep, you know, with the weight of the work in those days. So oftentimes I'd take Sonny out and let him roar himself quiet.'

'Out where?'

'Oh, just out in the street, you know, where I'd have my eye on the windows in case Frankie woke up in the house. I used to sit on the side of the horse trough in the moonlight and I'd read Keats. It was a stroke of luck that your dad was a summer baby. You wouldn't go sitting out there this time of the year.'

Cassie had tried to imagine Dad as a baby, red-faced and roaring in Pat's arms as she perched on the horse trough in Broad

186

Street, reading poems.

'I had a lot of them by heart by the time he was weaned.' With her hands wrapped around her teacup, Pat gazed across the kitchen and began to recite.

'Bright star, would I were stedfast as thou
   art —
Not in lone splendour hung aloft the night
And watching, with eternal lids apart,
Like nature's patient, sleepless
   Eremite . . .'

'Wow. What's an eremite?'

'I've no notion, love, I never found out. These days, you could google it.'

Cassie took out her phone and found it meant 'hermit'.

Pat nodded. 'Oh, right so. That makes sense.'

'So what's it about?'

'Well, the way I see it, love, he's looking up at the stars, like I was, and in one way he'd like to be like the North Star — you know, steady. Unchanging. But in another way he'd think that would be lonely. Hanging there like a hermit. Or like one of the nuns locked up behind in the convent, say. So, in the end he decides that love's the thing that matters. If you've got someone to love, you see, you'll never be left alone.'

'That's amazing.'

'Well, I liked it. I got great comfort from Keats, you know, and I sitting under the stars.'

Cassie had left her turning over a new page in her copybook. Now, sitting with her own notebook on her knees, she scribbled a couple of hundred words about celebrating her nineteenth birthday with a meal of whale blubber and dried caribou.

It was only a ten-minute walk from St Finian's Close to Broad Street so, that afternoon, Cassie walked down to pick Pat up for the writing group. When she stuck her head through the shop door, Ger's assistant was working behind the counter. Moments later, Pat came downstairs.

As they crossed the road, Cassie asked where Ger was.

Pat shrugged. 'He's away off somewhere today, love. Probably Carrick.'

Cassie linked her along the pavement, through the gate to the courtyard and into the library. Having wondered again why Pat had joined a group that seemed to daunt her, she told herself now that the answer could be simple. Perhaps Pat just liked to keep herself busy, since Ger went out a lot.

The group gathered in the reading room

off the library, and Hanna Casey, who seemed to be the facilitator, told them they were welcome. No one was to feel any pressure, she said. The purpose of the group was to share their work, swap feedback, and, if that proved helpful, maybe to workshop some ideas.

Cassie sat back and looked round the circle of chairs. There seemed to be no average age. Pat was beside her and Ferdia, the website guy, who was about her own age, was opposite. Beside him was a middle-aged woman wearing a hijab. Cassie had seen her before, in a corridor in the Old Convent Centre with Jazz Turner: they'd come out of an office, deep in conversation, and Cassie had gathered that they worked together. On the other side of Ferdia was a guy with 'retired school teacher' written all over him: he had a fountain pen, a leather-bound notebook, highly polished expensive shoes, and was wearing over-tailored smart casuals.

Hanna had just called the meeting to order and was suggesting that everyone should introduce themselves, when the door opened and a woman in her forties charged in. 'Isn't this about the height of me? I'm dreadfully sorry, Hanna. Everyone. And I *swore* I'd start off in time and wouldn't be late! Our first session too! I am *such* an idiot! Really, I couldn't be sorrier!'

Her cornrows had been braided by an amateur, and the henna that had been used on them had been left in far too long.

The woman thrust an arm into the depths of a large drawstring bag and failed loudly to find what she was looking for. Cassie, whose ear by now was attuned to the local accent, decided that, though she was Irish, she wasn't from Finfarran.

'Oh, God, this is *too* bad! I've come with nothing to write on.'

As Ferdia tore several pages out of a notebook and the woman in the hijab produced a spare biro, Cassie saw the others in the group exchange world-weary glances.

Having dropped the pages and stood on them, and then failed to get the cap off the biro, the woman took her seat again and tossed her head like a horse. 'I'm sure we've all introduced ourselves. Have we? Well, everyone knows me anyway. Oh, no, *you* don't, do you? I'm Darina Kelly! And you must be Pat's granddaughter. Welcome to Ireland, Cassandra! I can't say welcome to Finfarran because I'm just a blow-in from Dublin! You *are* Cassandra, aren't you? *Such* a lovely name!'

After that it was inevitable that Cassie was

first up to read.

'. . . there was fireweed and saxifrage for miles and miles all around and I was there on a windy day, eating whale blubber and dried caribou with strangers. And I felt completely at home. Where is my home, though, really? The indigenous people whose traditional food I was eating wouldn't call me Canadian, and I've never been to Ireland before. I wonder if I'll find the answer here in Finfarran. But maybe that's just what everyone thinks when they come home to the Land of their Fathers and wonder what "coming home" means.'

When she finished her piece everyone clapped politely and Darina proclaimed that it was smashing. Her only tiny critique, she said, was that 'Land Of My Fathers' was more properly a reference to Wales. *Mae hen wlad fy nhadau yn annwyl i mi . . .'* she began, in a shrill soprano. But Hanna stopped her.

Ferdia was up next, with six or seven lines of stuff that sounded like a computer manual. They ended in total silence, followed by a hasty round of applause. As it petered out, Ferdia explained, slightly resentfully, that he'd stuck to the letter of the instruction in Hanna's leaflet. The lines were the beginning of a sci-fi novel he'd been writing for

191

the last year or so, and he'd chosen them as typical of what he was all about. He had twelve drafts, each with a different ending, and was planning to self-publish them all as an interactive e-book, illustrated with GIFs.

Hanna's deadpan response was pretty impressive.

The focus then moved to the guy with the fountain pen, who got to his feet and announced to the room that his name was Mr Maguire. He then read ten solid pages of stuff that Cassie didn't listen to. Apparently no one else did either, because there was another long silence when he finished.

Closing his notebook, Mr Maguire sat down again. By this stage, Cassie thought she could see a gleam of annoyance in Hanna's eye. Possibly things weren't going quite as expected.

In the background, with the sound turned low, but just loud enough to be infuriating, Darina had found 'Land Of My Fathers' on her iPhone. It appeared to be a recording of a large crowd singing at a football match. Hanna cleared her throat ominously, and everyone looked elsewhere as Darina stuck the phone into her bag.

The woman in the hijab, whose name turned out to be Saira Khan, began by explaining that she'd joined the group in the hope of improving her English. She then read a short paragraph in what seemed to be perfect English, but her low, musical voice was so soft that Cassie heard hardly a word of it. It seemed to be about gardening.

She was followed by Darina Kelly who drew a large piece of paper, typed in double-spacing, out of the pocket of her tie-dye smock, and read steadily through six paragraphs of hateful glances, leaking breasts, and clotted menstrual blood. At the third expletive from the protagonist — who was a fisherman married to a wife who might have been a mermaid — Cassie heard Pat give a snort that was either hilarity or profound shock. The applause that followed the reading was effusive, though probably it was mostly an expression of relief.

In between the other readings Hanna had turned several times to Pat, who'd blushed and shaken her head. Now Hanna smiled at her again and suggested she take her turn. But, just as she'd done before, Pat shook her head emphatically. 'I won't, really, Hanna, no. Not this time anyway. It was lovely listening, though, really. Everyone's so talented. Anyway, I haven't anything done. I couldn't get round to it.'

But her hand, clenched in the fold of her skirt, was holding a piece of screwed-up paper. Later, as they left the library, Cassie jostled her affectionately. 'You did write something, didn't you? How come you didn't read it to us?'

Pat shook her head again, insisting that she hadn't.

'Oh, come on, Pat. You have it in your hand. Let me see. I'm interested.'

Pat looked away for a minute, then unscrewed the paper. It was covered with writing but every line had been heavily scored out.

22

Conor was beginning to look forward to his two days a week out driving. The thing about the mobile library van was that it raised you almost as high off the road as if you were in a tractor. Well, higher than the Vespa, anyway, or his old Ford. You could bowl along with a great view over the ditches and fences, from Carrick all the way down to Ballyfin. And once you were on the back roads you could see into every field.

It was daft the number of people who were still spreading slurry in December — you could get a wild heavy fine for that or even end up in jail. Conor could remember sneaky bits of late spreading at home, back in the past. When his dad had been fit and working, some of the rules like that weren't stuck to so carefully. But now that Paddy was fit for nothing but paperwork, everything had to be done according to the book.

That was kind of understandable. Paddy's

own state was the direct result of taking stupid risks. His accident had happened when he and Joe were inside in a pen with a cow that was in labour, and she'd turned on Joe, who was only half awake. Nine times out of ten, Paddy would have jumped the rail and been grand. But that day he'd tried to head her off while Joe got out first. Then, when he'd rolled over the rail himself, he'd landed on his back, and the insurance lads had just laughed at him when he tried to claim for the medical bills; it turned out that the cover he'd taken wasn't nearly enough.

Conor sometimes thought that half his dad's depression came from a sense of guilt. If he'd used better judgement, the accident wouldn't have happened, and if he'd paid for proper cover then at least the bills would be paid. And, in a way, poor Joe was in the same state as his father. If he hadn't been drinking the night before, and slow to move when the cow lost it, the chances were that they'd both have got out with no trouble at all.

The trouble now was that no one would talk about it. And, God knew, that was a family trait. If Conor had a bit of sense himself he'd be talking to Aideen, because the more he thought about it, the more it seemed that he'd have to give up the farm. The place would be his and Joe's eventually but, if they kept going the way they were, they'd have run it into the ground before Paddy died.

For the millionth time, Conor told himself there had to be another option. If the family sat down with a lawyer, the chances were they'd come up with some way forward that made sense and was fair. He could step back with a lump sum and go off and do the library thing, leaving Joe to take over the farm.

Or, if giving him a lump sum now would be daft, they could set it up so he knew he'd get it in the future. One way or another, if he had a game plan, he could talk to Miss Casey about getting his qualifications.

But, then, Aideen had all these romantic visions about settling down in a farmhouse. How would she feel about marrying someone with years of exams ahead, and a student loan to pay off?

The fields on either side of him still had a few cows grazing, but mostly the grass had melted away. The whole peninsula changed colour in winter, when the light was different and the growth died back, so you saw the grey stone walls. Every wall that surrounded the fields at home had been built by his father's people, and by the families of women who'd married in, bringing dowries of parcels of land. Orla, his mam, was like Aideen: she was born and raised in a town. But for generations McCarthy women had extended the family holding, and worked on it with their men.

Conor could remember his gran saying that her own mam had come with the grass of ten cows. She'd been a great poultry woman, too, and kept geese as well as hens. According to his gran, the eggs had paid for boots for the whole family. And turkeys raised by Gran herself had made the price of the old separator that used to be out in the milking parlour.

When Paddy had his health and his strength they'd been doing fine. You'd get up on a spring morning and the place would be full of life. Lambs calling, and calves needing tags, and stupid amounts of work to be done in the fields. As a young lad, Conor's favourite thing had been walking the fields with Paddy at the start of the spring. You'd be surprised by the number of years you'd find bite in the grass as early as March. They'd walk the bounds of the farm on St John's Eve, too, and Paddy would always find an excuse for lighting a bonfire. He hated being told he was superstitious, but his own dad and his dad's dad before him had never failed to light a fire on St John's Eve. It brought luck to the land.

Conor had never admitted it to Joe, but he'd done the same thing himself above on the hill last June. He'd lit it in the lee of the wall between the Broad Acre and the Lamb Field and he'd stood looking up at the stars with the flames roaring in a circle of stones that was blackened by previous bonfires. You wouldn't want to be the one who'd let the tradition go.

Up ahead he could see the pub where he planned to have a sandwich. When Miss Casey drove this route she usually stopped and ate in Knockmore. There was a drop-in centre in the church hall there, where oul ones went for their dinner, and they were always mad for a bit of diversion and chat. Miss Casey had smiled at Conor when she told him, and said she suspected he wouldn't fancy it. He didn't either, so he'd taken to grabbing a bite to eat in the pub.

There was a jeep parked outside that he recognised as Dan Cafferky's, and, when he went in, Dan and his podgy mate Dekko were sitting with a couple of pints. Dan was on his feet at once, offering to buy him a drink, but Conor said no. 'God, Dan, I'm not just driving, I'm working.'

He ordered a fizzy drink and a cheese and pickle sandwich and joined them at the table. Apparently they were waiting for Fury O'Shea who'd found Dan a load of wood to extend his shed on Couneen pier. He'd got it off the back of some building job in Carrick, so Dan was going to get it at a decent price.

'What's the extension for?'

'Just a bit of extra storage space. And I could use a ticket office for the tours.'

'I thought most of your booking happened online.'

'You'd get a bit of passing trade, too, though. In summer, like.'

There was a violent scratching at the pub door, which swung open to reveal Fury and his little Jack Russell terrier, known as The Divil. Dan got to his feet again but Fury waved him back to his seat and strolled to the bar.

'Hold your hour, we'll order first and fight about who's paying later.'

With his drink in his hand, he came back and joined them, and The Divil subsided on the floor.

Conor, who knew Fury well, gave him a nod. Dan introduced Dekko. 'Dekko's from Dublin, but we don't hold it against him.'

'Well, if that's all there's to be said against

him, I suppose he's doing all right.'

Conor glanced at Dekko, to see if he'd taken it badly. Fury was an eccentric old bugger and, if you didn't know him, you might think he was choosing to wind you up. Dekko didn't seem bothered. He winked and said he'd heard Fury was a great man to do business with.

'Ah, you wouldn't want to believe all they tell you round here.'

For as long as Conor could remember, Fury O'Shea had been the same laconic, scarecrow figure, driving round in a battered red van, with The Divil beside him on the passenger seat, barking at anything that moved. Fury was known as the best builder on the peninsula, though he didn't do estimates, let alone quotes, and he never stuck to a schedule. You wouldn't know where to find him either, because that was the way he was. He turned up when he wanted to, and he always shut off his phone and ignored messages. All the same, he wasn't called Fury for nothing. When he had his teeth in a job there was no holding him, and he wouldn't stop till it was done.

God alone knew how he coped with the state or the taxman but, whatever way he handled money, Conor had never heard anyone call him a cheat. One time he'd heard somebody call him illiterate but that was just show. It suited him when it came to filling up forms and reading regulations, and it meant he could play the gawm when he did a deal.

Now he cocked his eye at Dan and said he had the timber for him. 'I'll dump it down on the pier sometime this week.'

Dan knew better than to talk about the cost of it: it could be he'd end up paying in kind, but Fury would see him right. Dan had laboured for him in the past more than a few times, and Fury looked after his own.

Under the table, The Divil stood up and shook himself. Fury looked at Dekko and said he fancied a packet of crisps. 'Salt and vinegar. They're the ones he likes.'

Dekko looked a bit shocked and asked if he meant that the dog wanted them.

'That's the man. Don't go getting streaky bacon, now. He can't be doing with them.'

For a minute Conor wondered again if Dekko might take it badly. Instead he got up and said he'd shout for a round. 'Another pint, Dan, is it? And another 7UP, Conor? Is that a Jameson's there, Mr O'Shea?'

'It is, boy, but I've never been one to take drink from strangers. Throw The Divil his packet of crisps and that'll do fine.'

There was a queer kind of tension between

them, but that was just Fury messing.

Dekko came back from the bar with the round and bent down to throw the crisps under the table. There was a sudden snarl as the little dog's hackles rose and he showed his teeth. Startled, Dekko jerked back, banging his head on the table. Conor had his glass in his hand by then, and Dan saved his pint, but Dekko's pint tipped sideways, nearly splashing his expensive leather jacket.

Fury, who was sitting back with his glass, cocked his eyebrow. 'Maybe I'm not the only one wary of strangers.' He lounged over to the bar and got Dekko another pint. Under the table, The Divil snorted and ripped open the packet, releasing a stink of vinegar along with a shower of crisps.

When Conor left, they were still sitting there, Dekko and Dan drinking pints, and Fury swirling the last of his whiskey round and round in his glass. Dekko had put a good face on things, and was telling some long story. But Conor reckoned he felt the old man had rightly set him up.

Driving on to Knockmore, you could see the winter sun slanting sideways through the hedgerows. Miss Casey had talked to him a while back about the way she felt herself when she drove the van. For ages, she'd said, written words had carried dreams and ideas over seas and beyond mountains, which made her part of a process that stretched across distance and time. Conor kind of liked the way she'd put it.

The whole library-book thing was actually pretty amazing — like she'd said, all these novels and celebrity cookbooks were links to ancient handwritten texts from Egypt and Mesopotamia. It was a thought that made being a librarian seriously cool. Library work was about organising stuff, too, and he was fierce good at that. The thing was, though, that he'd hate to leave the farming. Basically, he was stuck between a rock and a bloody hard place.

23

Pat could remember when the first Christmas lights had appeared across Broad Street. Someone had suggested that all the businesses in the street should chip in and pay for Lissbeg's decorations, and Ger had put his foot down and said no. The rest of the town might be desperate for customers, he'd said, but no one would refuse to buy a Christmas turkey for lack of a dancing Santy over his door. He'd changed his tune after a year or two, and now he was chair of the town's decorations committee. It confirmed his status, Pat supposed, and it was a way of keeping his feet under the table at the Chamber. But that first year he'd refused to chip in a penny.

The lads were well grown then. Frankie had left school and was working behind the counter with Ger, and Sonny and Jim were wanting to go off to discos in Carrick. Pat had never seen any reason why they shouldn't. It was hardly different to Ger and herself going dancing back in the day. Or Cassie going off to a nightclub.

Ger had always been a bit ratty about the lads taking off for Carrick, though. The state might be paying for their education, he'd say, leaning on the counter and talking to Tom Casey. But didn't it all come out of his till in the end, with the weight of his damn taxes? And top marks in school were all very well, but he had still to see where it was leading. Weren't he and Miyah working on the farm when they were those lads' ages? Not sitting on their arses with a pile of books, waiting to swan off to college!

It was only old talk and a chance for Ger to keep Tom there chatting, but Pat knew how much it annoyed the lads.

Ger and herself hadn't done that much dancing. It was more a case of tagging along with Mary and Tom. And no one had gone into Carrick for dances in those days till they were well out of school: you wouldn't be let and, anyhow, it was a long way to cycle.

Back in those days you'd have no Debs or anything. Still, a lot of the kids were mad for rock 'n' roll. The place for that was Devane's dancehall, down at the end of Sheep Street. Devane got all the dance bands, so that's where you'd want to be going. At school hops you'd be expected to dance sets, like you were at a céilí, and the woeful oul music was cat.

Tom had a ducktail hairdo in the sixties, and Mary had a poodle-cut perm. Pat wore hers in a high ponytail, and Ger always claimed he had a buzz cut like Elvis Presley's. It was really just a short back and sides, though, because his father had said he'd have no Teddy Boy louts behind his counter. Pat could remember Ger spitting in the horse trough and saying his dad wouldn't know a bit of style if he saw it — the man couldn't even tell the difference between rock 'n' roll and jazz.

Pat and Mary had met in the back row at school. Everyone was supposed to look the same, in the one uniform. But the nuns knew well that half the mams couldn't afford the things you were supposed to get from Tiernan's shop in Carrick, so they turned a blind eye to the hand-knitted socks and the homemade ties. You were meant to wear shirts from Tiernan's, too, and a beret, but with the cost of the gym frock and the blazer, and the gabardine in winter, plenty of girls got sent to school in knitted tams and their mams' cut-down blouses. So long as the colours were right, nothing much was said. Differences were made, of course, but they were subtle. Clean hair and the right tie saved you from many a slap.

Pat was never short of much, but Mary, who was an only child, had everything. The nuns were always putting her up at the front when the priest came in. For First Communion she had a white handbag, and a veil with pearl beads sewn into it, and white Clark's sandals that would take the sight out of your eye. When they were all lining up to march into the church, Sister Benignus presented her with a *Life of the Little Flower,* with a gold cross on the front and a kidskin cover. The class was told it was a prize for piety and effort.

The next week Mary appeared in the *Inquirer*'s Communion Special, clasping the book, with her eyes cast up to Heaven. Afterwards she'd told Pat she was expecting Benny to take it back. They only wanted her looking holy with it, she said, so they could send the photo to the bishop. That was always the great thing about Mary. She could see right through flattery, though she lapped it up like milk.

She knew what she wanted, too, and nothing and no one had ever stopped her getting it. If there was a chicken on the table, come hell or high water Mary got the wishbone; and at Hallowe'en she always found the ring hidden in the brack. There was something restful about that, if you were a friend of hers. Things were always straightforward, and you didn't have to fight. Pat had never been one for making a fuss. And, most of the time, what Mary wanted didn't interest her anyway.

Pat's seat at the kitchen window was right beside a string of Christmas lights. For the last week, from dusk until midnight, they'd flashed on and off rhythmically, swinging in the wind between the shop's façade and the old convent's gable end. Now, looking down at the copybook in her lap, she imagined the words she'd written turning scarlet and gold, like pulsing points of light. Strung across the page, they looked ridiculous, so she scribbled them out with firm strokes of her pen. Cassie was due any minute to take her to Carrick anyway. The story was they were going in for some shopping, but Pat had a notion they might bang into that guard.

When Cassie suggested the trip she'd had a look about her Pat knew well. A kind of casual hopefulness that would almost scald your heart. Still, that was the child's business and nobody else's. Kids these days travelled the world, and picked up their own ways of dealing with life. The guard had looked decent enough the time Pat had glimpsed him. A small bit pleased with himself, maybe, but that was probably the circumstances. After all, if Cassie hadn't known what job he did, he'd have been pleased to go sailing past her in a squad car, looking smart.

And they'd seen each other since. According to Cassie, he'd taken her out to dinner in Carrick a few times, and they'd been back to the nightclub where the music was so loud people didn't talk.

Putting the copybook into her bag, Pat found herself smiling. Loud music could do wonders when you were courting. A bit of noise to cover the awkward pauses in conversation, and a chance to show off your dance moves, if you had them.

Tom had been a good dancer. She used to watch him and Mary swinging round the floor at Devane's, when she'd be sitting on a bench at the side with the bottle of red lemonade that Ger always bought her. Mary and Tom used go out round the back and be swigging from a naggin. Ger was a Pioneer, though, and he only went round the back to be smoking cigarettes.

There was a rap on the door and Cassie came in, swinging her little rucksack. 'Wow, this is so cosy. I *so* love the range!'

'Will we have a cup of tea before we go?'

Cassie slipped off her coat and hung it on the back of the chair. 'I guess we shouldn't break with tradition.'

She had an easy way in the kitchen that Pat liked. There were scones in the tin that had come out of the oven an hour ago, and Cassie found them with no fuss and put them on a couple of plates. Pat put on the kettle and poured some milk into a jug. She was looking round for the tea cosy when Cassie took out her phone. 'You know what? I'm going to call Dad and show him what's happening.'

Pat wasn't sure what she meant.

'*You* know! The flat, and the range, and Christmas lights outside. And you and me.'

'But he might be working.'

'He'll most likely be having breakfast. It's eight a.m. in Toronto.'

She was tapping away and the next thing Pat knew, Sonny's voice was answering. Cassie held the phone up and started to walk round the room. 'Hi, Dad. Guess where I am?' She brought the phone really close to the dresser. 'Recognise these tea-cups? And the plates?' Then, swinging round, she swooped in close to the scones on the table. 'And these scones? Bet you

211

sneaked a few like these when you did your homework at this table!' She moved away, tapped the phone again, and pulled Pat in beside her. 'Look at us! We're here in Gran's kitchen, cosying up by the range!'

Pat could see Sonny's face in a little box on the screen. He was looking kind of blank. She stepped away instinctively, but Cassie grabbed her hand. 'Say hi, guys!'

Pat said hello, and Sonny's face smiled. Cassie moved the phone so he could see the range behind them. 'We should totally get one of these, Dad. They're fantastic! How come you never told us that a kitchen could be so snug?'

Sonny glanced at his watch, then looked back at the screen. Pat could tell from his face he was feeling relieved. 'Sweetheart, I'm really sorry, but I've got to run. I promised I'd grab a coffee with Uncle Jim on my way to the office.'

'Cool. I'll call again in a twenty minutes or so and he can say hi as well . . . Or, no, hang on, that won't work, we're going to Carrick.'

Pat took a hold of herself and interrupted: 'Give my love to Jim, Son, won't you? And the kids. We won't go bothering you with phone calls if you're going to work. It's lovely to see your face, though. God bless, now.' She turned away from the phone and found herself holding the tea cosy, so she went to the table and put it on the pot.

Cassie followed her with the camera before turning it back to her own face, smiling and saying goodbye.

Pat had recognised the guilty note in Sonny's voice perfectly. It was how he'd sounded when they were over there and she'd wanted him and Jim to spend time with Ger. All the time they were growing up she'd watched them feeding an angry kind of resentment, and she'd never known what to do to make it stop. And it wasn't just Ger's behaviour they resented. They blamed her for not standing up more and taking their side against him. Slipping them money and trying to keep the peace hadn't been good enough. She'd known that even then.

Pouring the tea, she told herself that she'd coped the best way she could. The lads knew that, too, of course, which was why they felt bad as well as angry. It was a fierce mess, though, that she'd let the family get into. Even the sight of the kitchen just now had made poor Sonny look sick.

24

On Couneen Pier, under a rain-washed sky, Dan was working on his shed. It was chilly enough these days but, what with the exercise and his cheerful state of mind, he could hardly feel the cold.

Everything was proceeding in the right direction. Fury had come up with a load of timber and said he'd see him later for the price of it, and now Dan had finished the work, the shed was twice its former size. It had a decent heavy door, too, and new windows, set high, so messers wouldn't be peering in and thinking of stealing his gear. And, before long, there'd be plenty of new gear to put in it. Equipment that would allow him to offer really spectacular eco-tours.

It was Dekko who'd suggested extending the shed. As soon as he'd seen the pier he'd been full of enthusiasm. Screwing on the final hinge, and testing the new door, Dan could still feel the rush of relief he'd felt when they'd talked. Just the idea that he'd need to expand — even if it was only his shed space — had made him feel great.

Back in Australia, he'd described the pier and the sea coast to Dekko. The marine life around Finfarran was fabulous, he'd told him, and all he'd ever wanted was to find a way of making people appreciate it. A couple of drinks later, and he'd been confiding in Dekko as if he'd known him for years. Dekko was a great listener. He'd sat there nodding and getting another round in, while Dan talked about Couneen.

Then the next day, in a beach café, they'd banged into each other again. That was when Dan had found out that Dekko, who came from a big family on the north side of Dublin, was an investor. He wasn't the kind of guy to show off, but Dan had picked up a few hints from their conversation and, in the end, he'd asked him about it.

It turned out that Dekko's dad and his uncle were some kind of property developers. According to Dekko, they were the heart of the rowl, ordinary working-class guys who'd left school at sixteen and didn't mind getting their hands dirty. Dekko had begun working for them when he was only a kid.

Dan reckoned you could tell by the way he talked that he'd been around a bit. Not like the kind of poncy investor you'd imagine, with a posh education and a daddy who was a banker. It was bankers, he'd told Dekko, that were the ruin of poor bloody Ireland. They had the place raped and pillaged, and half the government crawling to them. Between that and the shower of penpushers, with their rules and regulations, ordinary guys like himself didn't stand a chance.

Dekko had agreed with him. It was guys like Dan that impressed investors like him and his family, he'd told him. People with passion and an idea, who just needed a leg up. People who went for their dream instead of being bogged down by bureaucracy. Decent people who never really got a fair crack of the whip. 'Because — do you know what it is, Dan? Bureaucrats are cut from the same cloth as them bloody bankers. And politicians. They sit there with their safe jobs, taking your money and making sure that you'll never get off your knees.'

That was exactly what Dan thought too.

Now, having screwed a heavy bolt to the shed door, he sat with his back to the stone wall, looking out to sea. There'd been an iffy few days a couple of weeks ago, when

Dekko went off to Dublin and stopped answering his phone. Dan hadn't let Bríd or anyone else know that had happened — he'd just said Dekko was away and that he'd be coming back soon. Watching a couple of shearwaters skimming over the waves, he told himself that his confidence must have taken a fierce knock. There was no reason at all to think that Dekko mightn't come back. But, all the same, he'd found himself getting jumpy. Especially when the phone was dead, and your man stayed away much longer than he'd said he would. Dan hadn't opened his beak to complain when he did come back, though, which was just as well, because it turned out that Dekko had got caught up doing some favour for his uncle.

Family was a big thing with him. Like he'd said himself, that was the thing about Ireland — Irish families looked after each other and had each other's backs.

In Australia Dan had stayed with cousins of his father's, who were happy to let him bunk down in their huge spare room. He'd heard you could go in on a working-holiday visa, but he hadn't realised that, for that kind, you had to be a graduate so, at the last minute, he'd taken the tourist route. Getting work turned out to be hard because he hadn't had the proper papers, and he didn't want the relations to know, in case they thought he was a gawm.

In the end he'd done a bit of backpacking, and picked up jobs on the black wherever he could. And he'd been wrestling with the idea of the complications of coming out and going back in again, with a view to staying there permanently, when he'd bumped into Dekko and everything changed. Things just came into focus. Life in Australia was great and he'd had good craic there. A few of the jobs he'd picked up were things you certainly couldn't be doing here in Finfarran. But getting your pecs sprayed with oil while you posed in designer beachwear wasn't proper work. At least, not for him. As soon as Dekko showed interest in putting money in the marine eco-tours, Dan had known for certain that he was going home. Couneen was his place, and this was his pier.

But the truth was that it wasn't his. It belonged to the bloody government. And the chances were that they'd make a fuss if they knew that he'd even built the shed. They wouldn't give a toss about the fact that he'd always kept the place clean and cared-for or that, when the path down to it had been washed away, he'd borrowed a mini digger and got it back into shape. You'd be waiting for months to get that done by the council, and they'd probably send some eejit from Carrick who hadn't a clue what to do. He'd told that to Dekko when he'd described the pier to him. The fact was, he'd said bitterly, that the pen-pushers probably didn't even know it was there.

The shearwaters skimmed across the inlet, their backs and undersides flashing like black and white traffic lights, and Dan told himself things were going to be fine. He and Dekko were going to open a proper joint business account. Then, once the money was in there, he could start buying equipment. And he wasn't a complete eejit who'd go throwing money at anything. There was plenty of good gear you could get second hand.

He wasn't daft enough to ignore health and safety regulations either. Some of their requirements were over the top but, all the same, it was better to be safe than sorry. You couldn't know the seas round here without knowing you had to be careful. And *that* was the unique thing he could bring to this business. What some bloody loan manager had called his USP. A runty little guy behind a desk who probably wouldn't know how to climb a ladder.

'What would you say your USP is, Mr

Cafferky?'

'Knowledge and experience, Dickhead.' That was what he should have said. The fact that, while he mightn't have a degree in marine biology, he knew the winds and the currents round Couneen, and could name every rock out at sea. He'd seen things in the world below the waves that that guy couldn't even dream about.

But, apparently, the fact that he knew what he was talking about didn't count as an answer. He didn't have a business plan in a folder, so that had been the end of that.

And things were getting worse, not better. If you went to a bank, these days, you wouldn't even find a runt behind a desk. Everything was automated and you couldn't find someone to talk to. You'd get letters in the *Inquirer* saying that automated banking wasn't fair to oul fellas, but no one ever said that people like himself might do with a bit of a chat.

But that didn't matter now that he'd found Dekko. Dekko was different. He didn't ask stupid questions, and he got things when you explained them. And then he just shook you by the hand and said it was time to start getting things done.

25

When Hanna arrived home Brian's car was parked in the pull-in by the gate. Walking down the narrow path between the gable end of the house and a row of leafless ash trees, she turned towards her front door and saw him sitting on the wall at the end of the field.

When she'd first come to live here, the field had been a graveyard for washing machines and old fish boxes: it seemed that half the parish had used it as a dump. Before that again, when Hanna was a child, Maggie had dug it over each year and set it to spuds. For the last year, Hanna had been turning it into a combination of flower garden and vegetable patch, with herbs and flowers close to the house and a well-drained kitchen garden dropping away towards the clifftop edge. Her potato beds looked ragged now: the last of the late crop had been lifted, and the precise edges of the ridges had crumbled under frost and fork.

Brian reached the door when she was still struggling with her latch key. The hood of his parka was pulled close around his face. 'The seagulls are going mad today. I'd say we'll have another gale tonight.'

'Well, come in before you freeze. You should have stayed in the car.'

'I did for a while, but the great outdoors called me. I've spent most of the week stuck behind a desk.'

Inside, Hanna dumped her bag and went to stir the fire. She had covered it with ashes the night before, and now, raking the poker through the embers, she exposed the glowing ends of smouldering turf. Crouching down, she built a cat's cradle of twigs on the embers. Then she set three sods of turf on end, forming a tripod shape to encourage the crackling flames to rise.

Brian, who had shed his parka, hunkered down beside her. 'Looks like you had a long week yourself.'

'I'm knackered, actually. No particular reason. Well, I did have rather a fraught first session with my creative-writing group.'

'Is that "fraught" as in "chaotic"?'

'Oh, thanks for the vote of confidence!'

'Well, you mentioned Darina Kelly had signed up.'

Hanna stood up to return the poker to its niche by the fireside. 'Actually, I think it was my fault. I sort of dropped them in at the deep end. Anyway, they now have a rigidly defined task to complete for the next session.'

'Because nothing says "creative" like "rigid definition".'

'Look, whatever it takes to keep Darina Kelly from singing the Welsh national anthem.'

'Seriously? How did you arrive at that?'

'Don't ask.' Hanna yawned. 'Would it be an awful waste of a Saturday afternoon if we just stayed in by the fire?

'Why don't you take a shower and let me organise dinner? If I hurl something together now, we can eat it later on.'

Twenty minutes later, when she came out of the shower in her dressing gown, he was chopping onions by the sink. There was a heavy shawl on the back of the fireside chair, and, as she sat down, she threw it round her shoulders over her silk kimono. Looking up, she saw Brian smiling.

'You look wonderful. A kind of exotic version of Peig Sayers.'

'What?!'

'Gold brocade chrysanthemums and creamy-brown homespun. It's very effective.'

'Easy seen you didn't suffer the hell of reading *Peig* when you were at school.'

'Mm. I'm not sure how she would have gone down in a boys' school in Sussex.' Brian's Wicklow childhood had been followed by boarding school in England because his dad had worked in the Gulf.

Hanna laughed. 'The thing is, you know, I've got three copies of the translation of *Peig* on my shelves in the library. And two in the original Irish. And they're always out. Back when it was a compulsory school text, that wouldn't have happened.'

'Well, I read it at some stage and thought it was rather wonderful. What's not to like about a memoir set on a wild, romantic Irish island?'

'Quite a lot, if it was forced down your neck by snuffling nuns.'

'They probably avoided the subliminals. I think Peig could well have had golden chrysanthemums peeking out under her shawl.'

'There's certainly a lot of nonsense talked about her generation. They weren't all rattling rosary beads and doing what they were told. Even the nuns.' Suddenly she had a vision of her great-aunt Maggie, stumping down the field with a spade in her hand.

'You know, my dad gave Maggie a silk scarf for Christmas once. A head square printed with abstract splashes of colour on a scarlet ground. I think she wore it every day from then to the day she died.'

'Summer and winter?'

'Well, when she was out of doors, yes. With an old sack thrown over it, when she'd be digging spuds in the rain.'

'Hence the homespun shawl and the silk kimono. What's bred in the bone will out in the blood.' Putting down the vegetable knife, Brian came to kneel in front of her. 'You do know I love you, don't you?'

'Yes, I do.'

'Good. Well, in that case, I'd better get on with the onions.'

As he worked, Hanna leaned back and watched the dancing flames. Saturday was always a busy shift in the library, with people turning up at the last minute, complaining about it being a half-day. Not only that, but she'd had an early start this morning because she'd had to be in before opening time to turn the next page of the psalter.

When she'd hurried into the library courtyard, Charles Aukin and Fury O'Shea were waiting on the step. Charles, it turned out, had taken a notion to come and visit the psalter; and Fury, who'd been doing some

work for him up at Castle Lancy, had offered to give him a lift into town. Fury had
worked for Hanna, too, when she'd been
doing up Maggie's house, so they knew each
other of old.

Dressed in a large overcoat and a fur-lined
lumberjack's cap, Charles had held out his
hand. 'Morning, Miss Casey. The word is,
you've decided to turn pages at random.'

For a split second Hanna had panicked,
thinking that Charles was complaining.
Then she'd noticed the glint in Fury's eye.
Standing there with their takeaway cups of
coffee, they'd obviously invented a tease
and, like a fool, she'd risen to it. Without
deigning to answer, she unlocked the door
and turned off the alarm system, hearing
them chortling behind her, like a couple of
schoolboys.

Inevitably it was Charles who'd offered an
olive branch. Fury, as Hanna knew all too
well, was made of sterner stuff. He'd
propped himself against the wall with his
hands in his pockets, as Charles, beaming
mildly through gold-rimmed spectacles, had
praised the Advent idea. 'It's exactly the sort
of thing I'd hoped for. I mean, of course
the exhibit's going to attract tourists. That
was inevitable. But I wanted it to be a Lissbeg thing as well.'

'Well, lots of people have said they'll make a point of coming by each week. I think they like the idea that it's a bit like a lucky dip.'

'See, I love that. It's how I always felt myself, whenever I flipped through the psalter.'

Suppressing her instinctive reaction to the idea of casually flipping through a medieval treasure, Hanna ushered him up to the book in its case. 'Would you like to do the page turn?'

'No, go ahead, Miss Casey. You've got the professional touch.'

Clearly her suppressed reaction hadn't gone unnoticed. In fact, she suspected that Charles might have chosen to provoke it, but his quizzical manner always made it hard to take offence.

The double-page spread she chose at random wasn't highly coloured like the last one. Here the closely written words filled almost the entire space between the margins, which were blank. But illustrations had been marvellously incorporated into the written text. Facing each other on either page were two cloaked and barefoot warriors, waving swords. On their streaming cloaks were blocks of words, following the flowing shapes enclosed by the artist's pen-strokes. It was a symphony in two colours, with the body text in black and the words incorporated into the drawings inked in rusty red, giving the warriors' cloaks the appearance of tweed.

Pushing his gold-rimmed glasses onto his forehead, Charles had leaned in to look at it. 'I don't remember this one, though I thought I'd seen them all. Psalm One Hundred and Forty-nine. And these are the guys singing God's praises with two-edged swords in their hands.' Stepping back, he resumed his glasses and turned to Fury and Hanna. 'By the look of it, whoever designed that page had seen a copy of the Qur'an. Or maybe heard someone describing one. You don't get figurative illustration in a Qur'an, but you do get blocks of text used decoratively.' He glanced back at the psalter. 'You know what? I've always wondered if each psalm had a different committee deciding how it would look.'

Fury had snorted derisively. 'I'd say that's more than likely, given it was made round here. God, you couldn't pick your nose in this place without a committee being set up to tell you how it's done.'

With dinner prepared and ready to be assembled, Brian joined Hanna by the fire. 'Look, just in case you were wondering, I'm not going to say a word.'

'About what?'

'Oh, come on, Hanna. You're going to make up your mind about where you'll spend Christmas eventually, and until then we have two logical choices. To avoid the subject or to avoid each other. I'm damned if I'm going to keep away when I could be with you. Any more than I'm going to go round treading on eggs.'

Stung by a pang of guilt, Hanna snapped at him: 'Oh, great! So you're going to play the martyr instead?' As soon as she'd spoken, she reached out her hand. 'Oh, Brian, I'm sorry. That was fatuous. I know I should be giving you an answer. I just . . . don't know what to say.'

'Which is exactly why neither of us should say anything. Leave it, Hanna. I've told you before, I'm not one of your lame ducks that needs looking after.' Suddenly he smiled. 'Or, put it another way, I'm buggered if you're going to treat me as if I'm your mother. Or Jazz. Or Conor and Aideen. I don't want to be added to your guilt-list. I want you to come if you want to come. And if you don't want to, that's fine.'

26

'So! As chair of the Winter Fest Committee, I'd like to call this meeting to order and address the first item on the agenda, which is . . .' Phil checked her paperwork conscientiously '. . . The Chair's Report!'

Bríd picked up her pencil. She'd intended to record the minutes on her phone, but her neighbour at the table had told her she was mad. 'Transcription's a mug's game, lovey. Get your action points down there next to your agenda items, and make the rest up later when you're writing up your minutes.'

Slightly shocked, Bríd had been about to argue when she realised that only a mug would be sitting here taking minutes without knowing how she'd landed the job. At the call for volunteers, everyone else had begun scrutinising their paperwork while she, who'd never been on a committee before, had looked up at the sound of Phil's voice.

The next thing she knew, Phil had fixed her with a triumphant eye and, before she could take in what had happened, everyone else was clapping. Presumably, in the interval, her appointment as secretary had been proposed and seconded, but it had all happened so quickly that she'd hardly had time to blink.

So now she'd probably do well to listen to advice from her neighbour, a large countrywoman who was explaining in a loud whisper that she'd always done decorations for the Christmas Fête. 'I wouldn't go climbing on chairs, mind. But I'd keep an eye on the paper chains and see they got rolled up right.'

Phil gathered her papers into a pile and banged it briskly on the table. 'So! The Chair's Report! Well, you'll all be glad to know that things have moved on considerably. Which means that there's good news and bad news, but isn't that always the way?'

Bríd found herself idiotically scribbling 'good news' and 'bad news', before catching her neighbour's eye and firmly putting her pencil down.

'The bad news is that Carrick and Bally-fin are going to be pretty stiff competition. Carrick's got a celebrity presenter from RTÉ for their opening ceremony, and Ballyfin are planning a Snow Queen–themed tea dance, held in the Harbour Hotel. The *good* news is that when our date came out of the hat, it turned out to be Christmas Eve!'

That didn't sound like unmixed good news to Bríd. If their event was the last in the competition, wouldn't people have spent their money at the other ones first? And hadn't most people got their Christmas presents bought by the twenty-fourth?

On the other hand, it probably wasn't a bad date for those, like herself and Aideen, who'd be selling fresh produce. No one was ever averse to an extra cake or some home-made cookies at the last minute. In fact, people seemed to go mad on Christmas Eve, when it came to food. They'd be out buying all round them, as if the fact that shops closed on Christmas Day meant they'd never open again.

Around the table lips were pursed and heads were shaking. It was clear that the people with craftwork and gifts to sell weren't impressed.

Before anyone could speak, Phil waded in again: 'So Lady Luck is on our side so far. *And* we have a unique setting here in the Old Convent Centre, and ours will be a Winter Fest *wholly focused* on what we *uniquely* provide.'

A woman at the end of the table raised her hand. 'I'm not certain that all of us know what that entails. The Christmas Fête has always been about raising money for charity.'

'It has, of course, Mrs Draper. And you yourself have chaired it with great energy down through the years. Naturally that will remain an essential focus. But the central focus of the Winter Fest will be on what makes Lissbeg uniquely great.'

The woman raised her eyebrows and said that what had made the Christmas Fête great was the amount it had raised for charity.

Various members of the redundant fête committee nodded their heads. Mrs Draper, who was now on a roll, said that this year they'd been planning to donate to the homeless refuge in Carrick.

Phil bared her teeth and said that was a brilliant idea. Perhaps it could be tweaked, though, and focused more on Lissbeg?

'Well, it could, of course, if Lissbeg *had* a homeless refuge. Or a homelessness problem. But I doubt if we'll be able to whip up either of them in a matter of weeks.'

There was a pause in which Phil visibly controlled herself and Mrs Draper pointed a commanding finger at Bríd. ' "Down

233

through the years" is not an expression that accurately describes my previous position as an elected chairwoman of Lissbeg's Christmas Fête. I served three terms but I'm not exactly Methuselah.'

As something was obviously expected of her, Bríd wrote down 'Methoosala', squinted at it uncertainly, and hastily crossed it out.

Phil adjusted her zebra-patterned specs. Mrs Draper was quite right, she said, and if apologies were in order, she'd be happy to have them recorded.

Mrs Draper inclined her head majestically. But before Bríd could record anything Phil was off again.

'Now, I understand that the Christmas Fête has always had a raffle. And I'm sure that if we add online ticket sales to our package, we can really ramp that up. In the past, I know, the committee has gone out and rustled up fabulous prizes. So that's a definite action point for today.'

Bríd's neighbour dug her in the ribs and nodded at her pencil, and one of the women beside Mrs Draper said that they always used to start by traipsing round shops and businesses. 'I'd say the crowd of us that did it before could go round do it again. You never get the same result by just making phone calls. And, God knows, by this stage, we've all developed hard necks!'

Phil waved an authoritative hand at Bríd. 'Perfect! The Christmas Fête ladies will concentrate on the raffle, then. And we'll hope to hear great things about it when next we meet!'

She swept on, listing the number of Lissbeg businesses who'd agreed to take part in the Winter Fest, and saying that everyone involved would be putting large posters in their windows and, hopefully, bumper stickers on their cars. 'By the time we meet again, our official logo will be out there. *And* the web page will be live. It'll be a special section within the Edge of the World website, so we'll encourage the judges to toggle to and fro and take in our wider picture. The subliminal message is that we're a four-season destination. *Utterly* focused on winter, in this instance, naturally. But, essentially, attractive to tourists all year round.'

The fact that not everyone was happy about that idea had obviously been dismissed.

A quiet-looking girl, who ran a graphics company, put up her hand and asked about the logo. 'I mean, do we have a working party, or an approval committee? Do we put it out to tender or . . . I dunno . . . how do we plan to generate the design?'

'I am so glad you asked that question! The *really* good news is that I've spoken to the council's Tourist Officer, and he's in *complete* agreement that getting behind the Winter Fest is a positive use of my time. So, design, posters and all related marketing issues can be handled right here in the Old Convent Centre. At no cost of anyone else's time and incurring no expense!'

A forest of hands shot up around the table but Phil kept on regardless: 'And that truly is wonderful news, isn't it? Because we certainly don't want to have to deduct vast expenses from the money we raise for those poor homeless souls.'

27

Pat mostly got her books out from the library, so there wasn't much in the way of shelves in the flat. When the lads were young they'd have schoolbooks up in their bedrooms and, after a while, Ger had a few shelves put up there. They'd come down since, though, when the rooms were done over, and now the few books in the house were kept in a glass-fronted press in the kitchen, in amongst old ornaments and boxes of bits and pieces.

She was always meaning to give the press a good clear-out, but then you'd take things down and find you'd no other place to put them. She'd given a lot of family stuff to Frankie, though she wasn't sure that he'd wanted it. And she'd sent one or two small things off to Canada over the years.

What was left in the press now probably wouldn't be wanted by anyone. Still, a lot of it belonged to Ger's people, so she didn't want to throw it away. The few times she'd asked Ger about it, he hadn't shown much interest, but some of the books, and an old photo album, had once belonged to his mam, of whom he'd been fond.

When Cassie had been over visiting, she'd eyed the press a few times, and today, as Pat was making tea, she asked if she could look inside.

'You can, of course, love, though I'd say things might be dusty.'

Cassie opened the doors and lifted down a lustre vase. It was an ugly-looking pink and purple thing, with three curly feet on it. It had arrived in the flat in a box of stuff when Frankie had cleared the farmhouse and Pat, who'd never liked it, had stuck it in the back of the press. Ger's mother used to have it on the mantelpiece back on the farm. She'd always keep a few flowers in it, next to a plaster statue of the Sacred Heart. In winter it'd be a bit of evergreen, when she couldn't get flowers, and on Palm Sunday it'd be a bit of palm, picked up after Mass.

The Sacred Heart hadn't been in the box, and Pat was glad. She'd never found the idea of a heart with big thorns stuck in it comforting; and, though she'd never said it to anyone, the hangdog look on the face always made her cross. She'd had a statue of the Infant of Prague on her own mantelpiece, but when the lads were horsing round they'd knocked the head off it, so that, too, had ended up in the press.

Cassie blew dust off the wreath of pansies round the rim of the vase. 'This is kind of cool. Where did it come from?'

'God knows, love. It would have been your great-grandmother's. Though she could have had it from her own mother, now. I don't know.'

'Was she your mom?'

'No, your grandad's. There's a photo of her there in the album up by the books.'

Pat hadn't looked at the album for ages. It was dirty enough when she took it down, so they spread an *Inquirer* out on the table to save the cloth. The album had a leather cover, with a brass clasp, and ten gilt-edged pages inside, made of thick cardboard. There was a square hole in each, and the pictures were slipped in back-to-back, so that, when you turned the pages, each photo had its own frame. They were all sepia prints, with people sitting on bamboo chairs up against painted backdrops.

'Wow. Which of these is Ger's mom?'

'I'd say she wasn't born, love, when those were taken.'

'They all look pretty prosperous.'

'I think her family had a shop inside in Carrick. Anyway, in those days, having your photo taken was a big event. You'd be wearing your best.'

At the back of the album were more modern photos, inside in a cellophane bag. Pat shook them out on the table. 'That's her now. She married around 1940, when she was in her twenties, so that one must have been taken in her teens.'

Cassie picked up the photo. 'She doesn't look much like Ger.'

'I suppose not. Though he has a kind of a look of her sometimes, round the eyes.'

'Who's this?'

It was a little black-and-white photo, with wavy edges. Pat took it and peered at the row of people standing up against a field wall. 'That'd be Ger's dad, and Ger himself, and his brother Miyah. I'd say it was taken at the farm.'

It was hard enough to recognise the people in the photo. Three of them had their faces screwed up against the sunshine, and Ger, who was beside his dad, had his head down. Pat hardly knew him from Miyah, except by the set of his shoulders. He must have been about eleven, or maybe ten.

Cassie grinned. 'I guess he never liked

having his photo taken, did he? Who's the old lady in the shawl?'

'That's Ger's Aunt Min. Well, she was his great-aunt. She wouldn't have been that old, either. All the countrywomen wore shawls then.'

'That's so cool.'

'Min the Match, they used to call her.'

Cassie's eyes widened. 'Oh. My. God. That's Min the Match! Why did they call her that?'

'She was a matchmaker.'

'No! Really? Like in *Fiddler on the Roof*?'

'Well, I don't know about that, love. She was a quiet woman, and well liked, and people could trust her. She'd take a message from one family to another. Or, if it was a case of a couple who were older, she might go to the man on behalf of the woman and give him a nudge. You'd get a lot of bachelors in a country place that might be a small bit shy of talking to women. Widowers, too, you know. Men that might be glad of a wife on a farm.'

'That doesn't sound very romantic.'

Pat laughed. 'Romance wasn't the fashion in Min's day. Marriage was more like a bargain, I suppose. Not like it is now.'

'And people liked her?'

'Well, I'd say she did a lot of good.'

241

'So were there matchmakers here in Finfarran when you were a kid?'

'There was Min all right, and I suppose I remember another few. But that'd be back in my mam's day, more than mine.'

'You didn't send someone round to give Ger a nudge?'

Pat shook her head and began to gather up the photographs. 'I didn't, no. It was Ger proposed to me.' She slipped the loose photos back into the cellophane bag and, before Cassie could say any more, turned it round to show her the torn sticker that had once sealed it. 'Look at that, now. American Tan tights. I wonder, can you still get those?'

'What are they? Oh, you mean pantyhose? What's American Tan?'

'It was a colour. I don't know, it might still be. They were sheer and shiny, and you looked like you had a great tan on your legs.'

'Oh, right. These days it's "nude".'

'Is that what they call them?'

'Well, yeah, if it's the same thing. I don't wear them. They're a bit Sarah Jessica Parker. Or the Royal Family.'

Pat laughed. 'Would you say that the Queen of England has pasty Irish legs?'

Cassie took the album back to the press and started fiddling round among the other bits and pieces. Pat stayed sitting at the table, thinking of the night on the starlit beach when Ger had proposed.

They'd all been about twenty then. She'd been working in the seed merchant's here in Lissbeg, and Ger was in the butcher's shop, working for his father. The cousin who'd brought Tom up was getting feeble, so Tom had taken over running the shop and post office in the village his people came from. And Mary was talking about going over to England to be a nurse. But everyone knew that was nonsense. She was only playing hard to get with Tom.

The four of them had made a plan to go to the pictures in Carrick, and they'd met in a pub in Lissbeg to have a drink first. If Ger wanted the use of a car then he still had to ask his dad, but Tom, who was more his own man, had driven Mary into Lissbeg and was going to take them all on to Carrick after they'd had their drink.

That night Mary and Pat were wearing new frocks that they'd made themselves. They'd gone to Carrick on the bus the week before to buy the Simplicity patterns. Mary's was a sleeveless flowery poplin with a sweetheart neckline, a gored skirt, and a self-belt. Pat's was a shirtwaist, which hadn't been easy to cut out because the fabric she'd got was tartan. It was worth the trouble because, in the end, it looked great with her wide patent-leather belt. The sleeves were elbow-length, and it had a white piqué collar, and pockets set on the slant. Mary said it would give her hips like elephant's ears. They both knew that it wouldn't, though. It was Mary herself who was a bit buxom. Though she carried it well.

The film they'd been planning to go to was a thing called *The Man Who Shot Liberty Valance.* Pat had fancied seeing *Sweet Bird of Youth* because Paul Newman was gorgeous, but the Roxy in Carrick had obviously thought they'd get more takers for John Wayne.

In the heel of the hunt it made no odds because when Mary and Tom arrived in the pub you could tell that something had happened. Mary had two pink spots on her cheeks, and her eyes were narrow and shining, and Tom was looking like he'd won the Hospital Sweep. It turned out that they'd just got engaged.

After that news they couldn't just traipse off to the pictures, so they'd had a few drinks in the pub and persuaded the barman to sell them a bottle of wine to take out. They couldn't go drinking toasts in the pub because Mary's parents didn't know yet, and half the town would be running round with the story if they'd let it out. So, they took the bottle of Blue Nun and a couple of bars of chocolate and Tom drove the car to the dunes outside town, and nearly down onto the beach.

It was a night of bright stars. They hung like jewels in an inky sky and their pale light glimmered on the waves. The boys went foraging along the shoreline for timber, while Mary and Pat went up the dunes and pulled handfuls of grass and dry seaweed, to start a fire. And the boys took off their coats and made cushions so the girls could sit down.

Pat could remember the sand sliding back under her feet as she climbed the dunes. They were so steep that she'd had to hold the hem of her skirt in her teeth, so she wouldn't walk on it. She'd pulled herself up by grabbing tufts of marram grass, and a sharp blade of it had slashed a cut right across the palm of her hand. She'd had to dab it with a paper hankie to stop the blood getting on her new frock.

The stars went kind of hazy through the smoke that rose from the bonfire, and the four of them sat there, passing the bottle round. After a while, Mary and Tom started acting the maggot. She'd take a mouthful of wine and then she'd kiss Tom, and pass it on to him that way. Ger and Pat were sitting on the opposite side of the fire, across from them, the two of them feeling a bit awkward as Tom and Mary started to snog. It didn't matter, of course, because the other two didn't notice them.

A bit after that, Mary had grabbed Tom's hand and run with him off into the dunes. They'd grabbed his coat and taken the bottle with them, so Pat and Ger just sat by the fire, looking up at the stars. Pat could hear the sea and smell the tarry smell of the burning timber. And Ger had said, without looking at her, 'Will we get married, so?'

28

The last thing Cassie had been looking for
when she came to Ireland was a relationship. But now she was beginning to wonder
if she'd found one.

Shay Doyle had been drinking at the bar
when she'd first met him in the nightclub.
She'd noticed him the moment she went in,
partly because of his good looks and partly
because, unlike most of the guys there, he
carried an air of authority. And when she
went to buy herself a drink, he hadn't tried
any of the usual guy-at-a-bar-on-his-own
pick-up lines. In fact, she hadn't realised
that he was on his own: she'd assumed that
his date must have gone to the washroom.

As she'd set off alone for her night out,
the others at number eight had looked
doubtful. It was quite sweet, actually — as
if, like Pat, they belonged to another generation. In response, Cassie had twitted Aideen
about rural Ireland not having caught up

247

with gender equality, half joking but half meaning it. And immediately Bríd had got aggressive.

'We're not bog-trotters, you know. But you're going to look pretty sad if you wander into a nightclub on your own.'

'Well, I guess anyone who thinks so won't bother to say hi.'

'Or else every weird loner in the place will assume you're looking for company.'

Aideen had leapt in at that point, eager to keep the peace. 'We could all go along for the craic, you know, why wouldn't we?'

Cassie could see Conor, who'd arrived saying he was knackered after a long day on the farm, gamely getting ready to leave the sofa. She shook her head firmly. 'Because you've got your own plans for the evening. And, besides, I'm perfectly happy being a sad loner. In my world it's called getting out and seeing life.'

Bríd snorted. 'Well, if hanging round Fly-By-Night in Carrick is your idea of seeing life, I'm sorry for you.'

Cassie had just laughed and swung her knapsack onto her shoulder. But when she'd picked her way past a couple of rough sleepers and clattered down the iron stairway to a basement entrance in a grubby side-street, she'd wondered if Bríd might be right. The

248

website had promised 'a relaxed, sophisticated environment, great music, and a convivial vibe in the heart of downtown Carrick'. The reality hadn't quite come up to the spiel.

Having got there, though, she'd decided to stay and have a drink. All that was really wrong with the place was the weird lighting. And the sound system. And the clientele, which seemed largely comprised of stag parties and stagettes.

After edging round the room, looking for a seat that wasn't directly under a speaker, she'd settled at a corner table. The atmosphere reminded her of entertainment nights on cruise ships when everyone was determined to get their money's worth and have fun. About ten minutes later, Shay had come over and smiled at her. 'I'm about to order another drink. May I get one for you as well?'

He was sober, personable, and no date had emerged from the washroom, so Cassie smiled back. 'Sure. I'll have another of these.'

When he returned with the drinks, he waited till she invited him to sit down. They didn't talk much. In fact, they hardly got beyond clarifying that, in Ireland, 'bogtrotter' meant neither a resident of New

Brunswick nor someone who loved cake. As soon as Cassie had raised the subject, she wished she hadn't bothered. The music was so deafening that Shay had had to lean in and shout at her. 'What's the New Brunswick thing?'

' "Bog-trotter" is a Canadian name for people who live there.'

'Why? Because they're culchies?'

'What's a culchie?'

'Rough around the EDGES. Not from the city.'

'Oh, right.'

'And what's with the cake?'

'*Matilda.*'

'What?'

'That Roald Dahl kids' book. *Matilda.* There's a character in it called Bruce Bogtrotter . . .' Cassie's voice was beginning to crack '. . . who STEALS CAKE.'

And that had been about it, as far as conversation went. So, when she'd said goodbye, and left without another drink, she hadn't imagined that she'd ever see him again.

Then there he'd been, cruising by in a squad car when she'd been in Carrick with Pat.

A few days after that, when he'd signalled her to stop on the motorway, she hadn't

250

recognised him. With her driving licence in her hand, and already formulating the explanation that the car belonged to Pat, Cassie had lowered the window and looked up at him. When their eyes met he'd grinned at her and winked. 'You know what it is, I thought I was never going to find you.'

'Why would you want to?'

'Because I haven't got your phone number.'

'And that's why you pulled me over?'

'Well, if I hadn't, you'd have just driven on by.'

He was wearing the same faint, agreeable aftershave she'd noticed in the nightclub.

'Do they actually let you flag people down for social reasons?'

'Well, they train us to use our initiative.'

In the end she'd laughed and given him her number, and the following day she'd had a text suggesting dinner in Carrick. Deciding not to mention it to the others in the house, Cassie had texted back and told him yes.

Unlike the nightclub, the restaurant really was relaxed and sophisticated, and Shay was good company. He'd never been to Canada but he'd spent time in the States and even taken a cruise ship from Fort Lauderdale to the Bahamas, one of those three-day trips with casinos on board.

Cassie had explained that, for her, travelling the world was about seeing life. 'That's why I chose to be a hairdresser. It's a career that can take you anywhere.'

Shay appeared to have become a guard mainly to please his parents. His dad was a retired superintendent.

'So it's not something you wanted to do yourself?'

'Well, it's a good job. Opportunities for promotion. Good pension. Good feeling that you're doing something that makes a real difference out there.'

'Aren't you a bit young to be thinking of your pension?'

'Thank you very much. I'll take that as a compliment.'

She'd guessed he was in his early thirties. Conor and Dan would look pretty gauche beside him, but not just because he was older than they were. He was city-bred, like Cassie was, and they spoke the same language in subtle ways that she felt, rather than recognised.

When the check came and she'd offered to go halves, he shook his head and raised an eyebrow at the waiter. His credit card was whipped away in a flash. So the next day she'd called him up and suggested another meal. 'My shout this time. It's only fair.'

They went to a place in Ballyfin and talked so much that they'd hardly finished eating by closing time. Cassie had half expected him to kiss her when he dropped her home, but he'd just leaned across from the driving seat and given her a hug.

The next time they met he did kiss her, standing on a wintry beach, where they'd gone for a walk.

It wasn't like they lived in each other's pockets. Shay worked long shifts — sometimes right through the weekends — and Cassie's own days were full. Spending time with Pat was fun, and having the car meant she could go off on her own exploring the peninsula. And because of her afternoons doing pensioners' hair at the Old Convent Centre, she'd picked up lots of suggestions for where to go.

If it hadn't been for Maurice, a retired baker who made special-occasion cakes to order for HabberDashery, she'd never have found the little pub in Ballyfin that served sandwiches in floury rolls called *blaas.* According to Maurice, they were traditionally made in County Waterford but, a couple of generations back, some Waterford baker had met a girl from Finfarran and 'married in' to her parents' pub in Ballyfin. Sitting in the hairdresser's chair, swathed in a towel, he'd eyed Cassie seriously in the mirror, and told her where to go. 'It's the Old Anchor, and don't go confusing it with that new place, the Anchor and Flag. You want to go round by the tackle shop and down the street beyond the pier.'

She'd followed his instructions to the letter, avoiding the shiny new pub on the corner and finding the Old Anchor at the end of a winding cobbled street. There was an open fire in the bar, and a group of elderly fishermen drinking at the counter, and when she told the barman she'd been sent by Maurice, everyone wanted to stand her a *blaa* or buy her a drink.

The floury roll filled with crabmeat was delicious, and when she exclaimed at the strength of the coffee she had with it, a man at the bar had explained that the Ballyfin fishermen had always favoured coffee, rather than tea. They'd picked up the habit from Frenchmen, who used to come round swapping coffee beans for lobsters. 'That was back in my granda's time, before they found we could make good money for lobster! But by then we'd got a taste for the black coffee with plenty of sugar. It's mighty for keeping the cold out when you're at sea.'

Another time, old Mrs Reily, whose hair she'd set the previous day, had appeared at a farm gate and waved her in. It turned out that she and her daughter, Nell, were lace-makers and they'd decided Cassie would like to see how it was done. Their home was no longer a working farm, but the big kitchen, with its scrubbed table and easy chairs by the range, was enchanting.

Nell explained that you worked the delicate bobbin lace on a cushion pinned to your lap. She and her mother used to do it just as a pastime. 'But since the psalter exhibition opened at the library, we've started selling lace initials to the exhibition gift shop. We base them on the illuminated letters in the psalter, and a young lad with a studio in the Convent Centre frames them up.' It was very interesting making a business out of it, she told Cassie, because you'd have to work out deals with the framer and the gift shop, and find out which letters sold well, and how many you'd need. 'And, of course, we'd still make lace for sales of work and the Christmas Fête. Though I don't know if they'll be wanted now that it's the Winter Fest.'

Cassie had told her that surely they would be. How could such lovely work not sell like hot cakes?

'I know, dear. And Phil's offered us a stall. But I don't know would we want to mix business with the fête.' Nell had looked worried. 'Well, I don't mean the fête, since that's not what we'll be having. But you see what I mean. Christmas is about giving, isn't it? Not promoting yourself, or networking, or whatever we're doing now.'

It struck Cassie that Phil — whom she'd thought quite reasonable when she'd heard her at the first meeting — had actually been behaving pretty badly. If the Christmas Fête was established long before the Winter Fest was even thought of, wasn't it a bit crass to come muscling in and upsetting people like Nell?

As the two ladies waved her off, Nell had pressed a little parcel into Cassie's hand. Later, in the car, she'd unwrapped it to find the initial C, beautifully worked in lace. Smiling, Cassie had folded it back into its pink tissue paper. Like the introduction to the *blaas* in Ballyfin, and the smiles on the bustling streets of Lissbeg, it was another quiet gesture of approval. And, along with the sense of warmth she felt at the thought of seeing Shay again, it was one more thing that made her feel that maybe she had come home.

29

Pat was worried. When Ger came up to the kitchen of a morning for a cup of tea and a biscuit, he'd generally bring a bit of meat for the dinner or, if they were busy below, and he didn't come up, he'd leave it on the bottom step of the stairs for her to nip down and collect. Four chops, maybe, or a couple of nice chicken breasts.

They still had their dinner at one o'clock on the days when Ger was home. If he was off somewhere, Pat would just make herself a sandwich, or slip over to the Garden Café for something light. You wouldn't want as much these days as you did when you were younger. Well, she wouldn't herself, anyway. Ger had always been a great eater.

That was one reason she was worried. Lately, he was getting fussy about his food. She'd cook the meat he'd chosen, but half the time he wouldn't want it. He'd peck at a bit of something and then just push it around his plate.

Actually, he'd been in a queer way since they'd got back from Canada. God knew he was never much of a talker, but since they'd come back you'd think he'd been trying to avoid her. It was a busy time of year, of course, so you'd expect him to be preoccupied. But half the time, these days, he was either rushing off somewhere or saying he was tired and going to bed.

The truth was that the trip to Canada might have been a mistake. And if it was, Pat told herself sadly, it was her fault entirely. She'd been so focused on the excitement of seeing the grandkids and the lads that maybe she hadn't realised that she could have been making bad worse. Somewhere in her mind she'd known that Sonny and Jim hadn't stayed away just because they were busy. But in some other part of her head, she supposed, she'd thought that things might be different if they all got together. On neutral ground, you might say. And that if the lads saw that she and Ger were getting old, they'd decide to let bygones be bygones.

But maybe, before going off to Toronto, she should have made Ger sit down and talk about a will. You could see that Sonny and Jim had done well for themselves, but the fact remained that the two of them had built themselves up over there from nothing, while Frankie had just fallen in for his house and the business over here.

Pat had always assumed that, when she and Ger went, Frankie would be done right by, but the other lads would get their share as well. But perhaps that was something that should have been stated years ago. Something she should have dealt with instead of knitting hats and sending cards.

When they came back from Canada, she'd mentioned the will to Ger, casual-like, and the way he'd looked at her, you'd think she'd hit him in the face. But that was how he'd always been about money. The one thing he was good at in life was making it, and if you questioned him, he'd think you didn't trust him to know what he was at.

Somewhere else in her mind she'd thought he might talk about the future to the lads when he was over there. Supping pints in Sonny's golf club, say. Or maybe one day over dinner, if they were all sat down. But that was only fooling herself. The fact was that Ger had always been tongue-tied. The only person he'd ever talked to was Tom.

It had begun when their desks were side by side at school in their first year at the Brothers'. Tom was already a football hero

259

and Ger was a scrawny runt. So Brother Hugh nicknamed them The Warrior and The Weasel. That was the kind of thing teachers did in those days, and they got away with it because no one would ever question the power of the Church. You were supposed to feel grateful that they'd give you an education. And you had to keep on the right side of them. Many a one would've had no chance at all of secondary schooling if it wasn't for a parish priest ringing the Brothers and putting in a good word.

At twelve years old, Ger was utterly defenceless, and he had no way to fight back. The name stuck because Brother Hugh kept egging the kids on to use it. Then, one day, when Pat and Mary were talking by the convent wall, they'd seen Ger messing about, over at the horse trough. It was still full of water then, not planted up with flowers like the council had it now. Ger was prancing along the edge of the trough, like a tightrope walker. And Nat Hughes shoved him in.

The crowd was laughing and jeering, and calling Ger a wet weasel, when Tom appeared from nowhere and grabbed Nat by the neck. Mary always said afterwards that she'd had to pull Tom off Nat before he drowned him, but that was just Mary building the story up. What really happened was that Tom held Nat's head in the trough till he had him kicking and choking, and then he hoicked him out and left him sprawling in the road.

That was Tom. There was something in him that made him want to protect people. Pat had known just how he'd felt when he'd thrown his arm round Ger's wet shoulders afterwards. Kind of daring the world to mess with him again. No one ever shouted 'Weasel' once Nat Hughes was dealt with, and from that day on, it was like Ger would trust nobody but Tom.

Pat doubted if anyone now remembered what had happened. She'd heard that Brother Hugh had died of drink, and she was glad of it. Mind you, there were still some people in town that called Ger 'Weezy Fitz'. But they meant nothing by it. It was just a name, like they called Paddy Donovan 'Horse'.

Now Ger came up from the shop with a nice cut of stewing lamb. He seemed in good enough form today, and made a bit of a joke about not wanting garlic, which was something that Pat had never fed him in his life. He was looking well, too, in the blue jumper she'd bought him in the shopping mall in Toronto.

She made the tea and they sat at the table and drank it. Ger had to go to Cork next week, he told her, so she hoped the roads would be good. You'd never know, this time of year, and you wouldn't want him driving through flood water. She had the creative-writing group to go to herself that same afternoon, though, so she was just as well pleased not to have to cook dinner before she slipped over the road.

When he went downstairs, and the stew was started, Pat thought she'd better look at the work they'd been given to do for the group. At the end of the last session you could see Hanna deciding to put smacht on them. You wouldn't blame her either, they needed a bit of control, with Darina Kelly wandering off onto the internet, and Mr Maguire boring them all to death. So they'd been given a task that, according to Hanna, was supposed to take them out of themselves.

Everyone was to close their eyes and reach into the library's lost-and-found box, and whatever object they pulled out would inspire the next thing they wrote. It was to be no more than a paragraph. 'Something that would work as the opening of a novel. It needs to be gripping, evocative, and suggestive of the genre of the book.' Hanna had gone round the circle with the box, and everyone had stuck a hand in and taken something out. Pat, who was second from last, had pulled out an old pair of specs. She hadn't had a clue at the time what you could write about them, and she hadn't come up with a single idea since.

Now, putting them on the table, it struck her that they looked like a pair worn by Ger's mam the year before she died. They were a purply-pink colour, too, the same as his mam's vase was, and the frames curled up like its curly feet. That wasn't a shape people wore at all nowadays. They must have been lying for ages in the lost-and-found. They might have been there since before Hanna took over. They could date back to the time when the library used to be the school hall.

Lifting them up, Pat squinted through them at her notebook. God, they were a fierce strong prescription, not reading glasses at all. Whoever lost them would've been half blind without them. Imagine walking out of a library when you couldn't see where you were going. If you knew you'd left your specs behind, why wouldn't you turn back?

She laid them down on the table and put on her own glasses. At the top of the page she'd jotted down Hanna's instructions.

1. Instead of looking inside yourself, you were supposed to be looking out.
2. You were to consider your object and use your imagination, and allow your paragraph to be informed by the images they provoked.

Pat frowned and wrote down 'purple specs'. God alone knew what else you could say about them.

Ever since coming home from Canada she'd had the feeling that, for years, she'd been walking round half blind herself. Taking up her biro, she drew curly harlequin frames round the words 'purple specs'.

Truth be told, life was easier when you didn't have to look at things. But the fact was that something had happened to Ger. He might have been looking fine today, holding out the bit of lamb, done up in its white wrapping paper, and wearing his blue jumper that she'd bought for him at the mall. But she'd known him all his life and she could tell when he was hiding something. She couldn't close her eyes to it but she didn't know what to do.

30

When Dan came into Phil's office, Fury O'Shea was leaning against the wall. Dan had been halfway to Carrick when a three-word text had arrived, summoning him to Lissbeg. And, as usual, when he'd tried to call back, Fury hadn't picked up.

The Divil was lying under the desk, with his paws crossed and his nose in a box of leaflets. Phil was buzzing around like a fly on speed, simultaneously talking on her phone, going through lists with Bríd, and flinging orders at Ferdia. Fury, who was perfectly at ease, had his skinny shoulders propped against a flow chart.

'You took your time, boy, didn't you?'

Dan was in the doorway when Fury spoke, and they all stopped talking and stared at him. It was bloody irritating, considering he'd turned the jeep round the moment he'd seen the text. But getting pissed off with Fury was a waste of time, so Dan didn't bother. 'What's the story?'

'Phil here has a job for you.'

Phil looked a bit startled, something that frequently happened to people when Fury arrived in their offices. Unusually for Phil, though, she said nothing.

'She's after giving me a shout about making stalls for this Winter Fest. Apparently, the committee have decided to take their theme from the Carrick Psalter.'

Two committee members, who were standing by the desk, looked indignant, and Phil leapt in at once. 'The psalter exhibition has been so attractive to tourists that I think we agreed that a medieval theme is truly emblematic of Lissbeg. And nothing says Christmas like Gothic arches and shining stained-glass windows. Warmth! Welcome! Firelight! Carol singers!' Phil planted her hands on the desk, producing a growl from The Divil. 'So what I suggested — and the committee endorsed — was a castellated front for each stall.'

One of the ladies muttered that the practice of giving chair-people casting votes was pure ridiculous.

Fury cocked an eyebrow at Dan. 'So, that's the plan. I'll make a couple of calls and source the materials, and you'll knock up a few welcoming battlements.'

266

'Why me?'

'Because I'm a builder. I don't do sets for pantomimes.'

'Well, nor do I.'

'And because Phil has money from the council to pay you for knocking up battlements.'

Phil intervened and said, actually, it was a medieval castle theme.

Fury quelled her with a look. 'Ara, for God's sake, woman, what do you think castellation was for? Giving your archers cover when they were shooting arrows at invaders. The haves up there repelling the poor have-nots.'

'Well, but —'

'Come here to me, don't be annoying me. I know well what you want. And if you think you're going to get Disneyland out of MDF and a box of screws you're kidding yourself. But if you want stalls that won't fall down, then Dan's your man.' He removed his shoulders from the flow chart and clicked his tongue at The Divil. 'I can even get you some grey paint at a decent price, if you give me a day or two. Spray-on glitter, too, if it takes your fancy.'

Dan raised his voice. 'But why *me*? How come I got mixed up in this?'

Ignoring him, Fury fixed an eye on Phil as

The Divil took his nose from the box of leaflets and pattered out from under the desk. 'I'll want cash for the materials, mind, and the same goes for Dan the Man. And don't go thinking that either of us is going to be generating invoices.'

'No. Well, no, that's fine. It'll come out of my own budget for infrastructural works here at the centre. You can just send me a note of what you've bought.'

'Name of God, woman, are you deaf, or what are you? We've agreed a price, haven't we? Well, that's the deal signed and sealed as far as I'm concerned.'

The next thing Dan knew, he was being marched down the corridor, with The Divil's claws clattering on the polished lino up ahead. Fury kept going till he had the three of them out in the garden. Then he stopped and took a roll-up from behind his ear. 'Have you got a light?'

'No, I haven't got a light. Do you want to tell me what the hell that was all about?'

Fishing a fluff-covered match from the pocket of his waxed jacket, Fury struck it on the wall. 'It's not rocket science. Phil pays me for the gear and you for the work.'

'But I don't need the work.'

'Maybe not, boy, but you need the money.'

'Look, I've got an investor. Putting money

into my own business. I don't need poxy little jobs like this.'

'Oh, right. Well, in that case you've got money to pay me for the timber I got for your shed.'

'Yes, I have.' Dan stopped suddenly, feeling stricken. 'Well — I will have. For God's sake, Fury, you've got no reason to doubt me.'

There was a pause in which The Divil made a rush at a piece of litter swirling by in the wind.

Fury exhaled a puff of smoke and looked sideways at Dan. 'It's nothing personal, boy, and I don't doubt you. I just like my money to come from a known source.'

After that there wasn't much more to be said, and Dan got away as soon as he could manage it. Because, though the joint account had been opened all right, the first tranche of Dekko's money hadn't yet turned up. And Dekko had disappeared again. He'd sent Dan a text about a week ago, saying he had a family matter to attend to but he'd be back down to Finfarran soon.

Dan had checked the account every day, hoping that the money might have gone into it. But it hadn't. Today, before hearing from Fury, he'd almost made up his mind that he ought to call Dekko. Not to put any pressure on him, just to get a sense of time-scale. But he still wasn't sure.

Now he'd hardly left Fury in the nuns' garden when his phone rang and his heart rose when he saw the name on the display. 'Dekko! How's it going, mate?'

'Not a bother on me. Everything's grand.'

'Where are you?'

'Sitting in the snug in Quinn's. Can I buy you a pint?'

Quinn's was the pub where they'd had lunch with Conor and The Divil had devoured Dekko's crisps.

'Well — yeah. I didn't know you were back in Finfarran.'

'Yeah, mate, when I arrived it was kind of late, so I didn't call.'

The signal got bad, as it always did, as Dan walked across Broad Street.

'Listen, I'll jump in the jeep now, and come over, okay?'

'No problem. I'll get your man to start your pint.'

On the motorway, Dan put his foot down, the relief still surging through his veins. They'd get some business stuff sorted out now, before everyone got distracted by Christmas parties. And Fury could take that knowing look off his face.

Actually, though, it wasn't a bad thing to

be doing some work for the Winter Fest. A decent job on the stalls would make them look classy, and Bríd would be pleased. She and Aideen reckoned that if Lissbeg won the competition it would give the deli a lift. They were up in the air about the journalists on Phil's invitation list. People who wrote about artisan food and country style and stuff. Apparently an interview or a colour piece could work wonders, and you didn't often get Dublin papers coming out into the sticks. It was a huge deal for Bríd, who never stopped worrying about her business. And Dan could understand that.

The pint was on the table in the snug when he got there, with a whiskey chaser beside it. 'Christ, Dekko, that's pushing the boat out. It isn't lunchtime yet.'

Dekko grinned and said they had something to celebrate.

'Really? What?'

'Well, I'd say you were getting a sense that I've been having a cash-flow issue.'

'Have you?' Dan put his pint down, suddenly feeling cold.

Dekko laughed at him. ' "Been having", I said, not "am having". It's all sorted.'

He'd been working with his uncle on an import deal, he said, that got kind of tricky. The red tape in this country would drive you mad. You'd think if artisan producers were trying to earn a decent living, and businesses were willing to buy and sell their goods, then people would help them. You'd think a few laws would get made up there in the Dáil that would give an ordinary man a break. But not at all: the hoops you had to jump through were wojus. And everyone all down the line had to have his cut. The excise man and the feckin' politicians, and even the bloody guard out on the beat. And there's poor guys who have goods to sell, and can't even get them to a marketplace.

Dan had a vague memory of Bríd saying the same sort of thing about biscuits and cakes. You couldn't just make them and sell them, these days, you had to put up with all sorts of inspectors coming in, poking round your kitchen.

'Well, there you are! That's what I'm saying.' Dekko knocked back his pint. 'Anyway, there's a crowd of lads I know over in Spain. Me and me uncle have dealings with them. Nicest men you'd meet in a day's walk. They make brandy for export. A little family business — grandad passing on the method to the sons, mammy inside in the kitchen doing the books. They've been at it for generations, and every bit of traditional knowledge stored away up here.' He tapped his forehead with his finger and then shook his head sadly. 'We had them set up with a few lads that would take the product here in Ireland. And it's decent stuff, you know, Dan. Not the gut-rot you'd get from some of the big corporations.'

Dan nodded. 'God, some of the things you'd read on the internet about chemicals put in commercial product would frighten you.'

'That's it. But tell that to the politicians with their snouts in the corporate trough. They don't want to know. Or, more to the point, they know damn well, but they don't care.'

'So what's going to happen to your lads in Spain? Are they banjaxed?'

'They are not. Because I'm not going to let that happen, mate.'

Dan looked at him in admiration. Here was a guy with cash-flow issues of his own, who was still out there ready to fight for the little fella. 'How will you manage it?'

'Done and dusted. Signed, sealed, and delivered. I have the buyers at this end, ready and waiting. The lads in Spain have a cousin who owns a boat. And last night we brought the first consignment of brandy over to Ireland.'

'What — just stuck it in a boat?'

'Loaded it up, brought it over, and to hell with the bloody authorities. It's safe as houses down in your shed on the pier.'

31

PAT HAS DAFT COMPU CLASS 2DAY
LUNCH G CAFE I NEVER CU COME
@1

Hanna waited for the next text. It came within seconds.

GO IN % TELL THEM2 KEEP US A
TABLE

Followed immediately by a third.

UD FREEZE BY THAT DOOR

Hanna had already bought herself a sandwich and planned to have lunch in the library. She'd seen her mother twice in the past two weeks, on one occasion obeying an instruction to invite Brian along 'so there'd be a bit of decent conversation'. Furthermore, as Mary knew perfectly well, the Garden Café didn't take reservations.

But there was no point in fighting the inevitable. Exhaling rather louder than was necessary, Hanna tapped *OK* into her phone, and glared at the thumbs up emoji that pinged back. Then, with a groan, she rang the café.

'I know I can't actually reserve a table, but if you could keep an eye on one. I mean, I know that's a bit daft, but . . . we'll be in at one o'clock, anyway. Three of us. Thanks. Thanks a million. Thanks.'

At five to one she left Conor in charge and crossed the nuns' garden to the café. This morning she'd woken to a sparkling dawn, and a crunch of frost underfoot. Now the herb beds and the fountain were washed with pale sunlight, but between the piles of crimson leaves that had drifted down from the creeper on the wall and gathered under the conifers, patches of frost still glittered on the dark earth.

Inside, the café glittered with Christmas decorations, and the wintry presence of the garden beyond the big windows made the warmth and the savoury smells more welcome than ever. Pat was there already, ensconced in a corner well away from the door. Hanna threaded her way between crowded tables, gave her a hug, and sat down. 'You got us a great table!'

Pat smiled. 'Ah, well, I came over a bit early. I had a text from Mary.'

Deciding not to go there, Hanna asked how Pat was doing. 'You're coming to the creative-writing group this afternoon, aren't you?'

'I'll be there, love, yes. Ger's off in Cork today, so I'm fancy free. Mary thinks I'm a fool to be tied by things like making his dinner but, sure, there it is. Anyway, I'll be along, but I don't think Cassie will.' Leaning across the table, Pat lowered her voice confidentially. 'You'd hate to have people talking about you when you're a young one but, do you know what it is, I'd say she's found herself a boyfriend.'

'Well, that's nice.'

'It is, and I'm delighted for her. The young ones have a great time, these days, don't they? They'd go everywhere.'

'It was good of you to lend her your car.'

'Ah, I don't mean that. I mean the way they see life, like Cassie says. God, Hanna, when your mam and I were her age we'd never have thought we could get ourselves jobs that'd take us around the world.'

'Would you have liked to?'

'D' you know what it is, I might. I don't know about Mary, though. Look at the way she was dead set against your going to

London.'

Hanna laughed. 'Well, she always said it would be a disaster — and she was proved right.'

'Not at all, child dear, it depends on how you look at it. You may be divorced, but you have a lovely daughter. And didn't you see and do all sorts of things you'd never have found in Lissbeg? And aren't you back home again now, anyway, making a new life?'

For a moment Hanna stiffened, anticipating enquiries about how things were going with Brian. But Pat had never been like that. She just smiled affectionately and, indicating a tinsel-draped blackboard, said she was thinking of having a turkey melt.

Mary arrived in a whirl of scarves and an extra cardigan that had to be taken off before she'd sit down. 'Not that I'm complaining, because it's lovely and warm in here, isn't it? But wouldn't you think they'd know that we'd all be well wrapped up on a day like this?' Settling herself beside Pat, she inspected the menu. 'I could never be doing with leek and potato soup. It costs half nothing to throw that stuff together, and they throw it into a mug, with a bit of brown bread, and charge you six ninety-five!' Dismissing the menu with a sniff, she

278

craned up at the specials on the blackboard. 'And you won't find me eating turkey three weeks before Christmas! Won't we all be sick to death of it soon enough?'

Aware that she'd told Conor she'd be back within the hour, Hanna stood up and offered to place their orders. When she returned to the table, Mary was asking Pat about Christmas hams. 'I hope, now, that Ger remembers I need one to serve four. Louisa, myself, Jazz, and Hanna. Though, come here to me, Hanna, would you think of bringing Brian? Four women round a Christmas table won't be a barrel of laughs.'

This wasn't a conversation Hanna had planned to have in public. It wasn't even one she was ready for. Though, of course, she should have been. Turkeys and hams were always ordered in good time in Lissbeg. A last-minute drive to a supermarket wasn't an option — at least, not for the likes of Mary Casey, who always declared that plastic-wrapped hams were only water and air.

Fortunately, Mary didn't wait for an answer. 'Ger said he'd pick out a nice ham and set it aside for me. And some rashers, of course, because there's no other way to keep your breast from being burned. You'll be wanting a fair-size turkey yourself this year, Pat, if you're cooking for Cassie. Or are you all going over to Frankie's for the dinner?'

Out of the corner of her eye, Hanna could see Pat looking reticent. Perhaps Cassie was planning to spend Christmas with the boyfriend. Aware of her own situation, she found her lips twitching. The last thing she'd expected at this time of her life was a stab of fellow-feeling for a twenty-year-old. Though, actually, it was more like a stab of envy. If Cassie with her feathery blue fringe missed Christmas dinner, the chances were that Pat would be sweetly forgiving. But God alone knew what Mary would do if her middle-aged daughter not only failed to turn up at the festive table but disappeared with the only available man.

A few hours later, when the creative-writing group assembled in the library, Cassie was absent. And, once again, Darina Kelly arrived ten minutes late. She eased herself into a seat beside Hanna, indicated that no one should be distracted by her, and immediately dropped her handbag on the floor. Among the objects that fell out was a man's tweed peaked cap.

As the others were scrabbling for things that had rolled under chairs, Hanna picked up the cap and handed it back to her. Darina responded with a shrill snort of laughter. 'Oh, goodness me, you don't think it's mine, do you? It's what I picked out of the box!'

Darina dressed so eccentrically that Hanna had thought just that. Or, rather, she hadn't been thinking at all because her mind was still on the question of where she'd spend Christmas.

Suddenly Darina pounced on a green notebook. 'There now! No need to search for what I've written, it's thrown itself at my feet! Will I read first, Hanna? Do you mind? Otherwise I'll probably lose it again.'

There didn't seem to be any reason why she shouldn't, so Hanna said that would be great.

Opening her notebook, Darina cleared her throat and said that, the moment she'd seen the cap, she'd thought of John McGahern. 'Such an amazing writer, isn't he? So dark, and unafraid of the rich, sexual nature of rural life. I just looked at this greasy tweed cap and I realised where it was leading me. Into truly visceral places. That's what I felt. But, in my case, one's dealing with a woman's sensibility. So I couldn't think what to do. And *then* I realised that I needed to unsex myself! I needed to reject the boundaries of my own sense of gender and explore

281

the possibilities of a penis!'

Mercifully, she'd stuck to the rules and the paragraph was short.

In the stunned silence that followed, Mr Maguire stood up and produced a tube of glue. It was still in a paper bag from the local hardware store and must have been lost by someone who'd come to the library via the shops.

Hanna gave him an encouraging smile and asked how he'd got on. This was a mistake. Apparently the exercise she'd given them wasn't one to which Mr Maguire could relate.

'Actually, Miss Casey, with all due respect, I'm not sure that it was appropriate. I mean, I'm not sure it was likely to produce the results for which you hoped.'

Repressing a desire to agree with him, Hanna suggested that he read his own paragraph.

'Oh, no, I refrained.' He gave her a disconcertingly roguish smile and announced that if he'd written about a tube of glue he'd have bored his listeners rigid. 'And no one's ever accused me of doing that!'

Fortunately, Saira Khan had produced a quirky paragraph about a pencil case, which, she explained, she'd imagined might be the opening of a detective story. 'Probably more Alexander McCall Smith than P.D. James.'

Ferdia, inevitably, had stuck to sci-fi, but his image of a Pooh Bear toy as host for an alien presence was effective. Saira, who'd never read sci-fi, wanted to know what distinguished it from horror stories. This produced a forensic response from Ferdia in which he explained that the answer lay not in the content but in the author's intended impact on the reader. 'The trouble is that mainstream publishers have drawn three genres together and confused the reading public. Horror is intended specifically to instil fear. And for me, in sci-fi, fear is just a side-effect. What I'm about is using science-oriented speculation to explore the ramifications of ideas.'

'Like J.K. Rowling?' Darina, who'd put on the tweed cap, cocked her head when she asked the question and fixed her gaze earnestly on Ferdia.

'No. Not like J.K. Rowling. Fantasy deals in magic-oriented speculation.'

'Yes, but it's the same sort of thing, isn't it?'

'No, it isn't. To begin with, fantasy's usually intended to provide a moral commentary on society.'

'Well, you could say that of all literature,

couldn't you?'

'Would you say it of Dostoevsky?'

Dostoevsky turned out to be still on Darina's bucket list. Still, by the end of the hour they'd had a lively discussion about different genres, and scene-setting — marred only by a short lecture from Mr Maguire on the opening of The Diary of a Nobody — and Hanna felt that the exercise hadn't been as lame as she'd feared.

And, apparently, she wasn't alone because, though Mr Maguire clearly hadn't changed his opinion of it, the rest of the group asked enthusiastically what they were going to do next.

She raised her voice over the bustle of departure. 'Okay. So, what I'd like you to do for our next session is to observe an animal. Just spend some time looking at movement and colour and texture, see if you can get a sense of personality — or, anyway, of something innate to the species you've chosen. Set yourself the task of describing it. Pure description. No reaction. Just write down what you've seen.'

Then, leaving them stacking their chairs and putting their coats on, she went in pursuit of Pat, who'd already left. When she caught up with her in the library doorway, Pat eyed her nervously, like a delinquent child. 'I know. I know what you're going to say, and I'm really sorry, Hanna.' Just as had happened at the last session, each time she'd been asked to read, she'd ducked her head and said no. 'Let the rest of them go ahead and you can come back to me.' And, in the end, she'd said that, in fact, she hadn't got anything down.

Now, the look on her face made Hanna feel dreadful. 'Oh, Pat! There's no need to apologise. I'm just sorry you're not having a better time, and getting more out of the group.'

'It's not the group, love, it's me. Honestly. I don't know how it is, but I think I've got no imagination. Or powers of analysis, or something, I don't know what. Do you know what it is, I'd say I looked at those purple specs for a good half hour. And, to tell the truth, I don't think my mind led me anywhere at all.'

32

Half the conversation in number eight, these days, was about how Phil was hustling things past the committee without getting proper approval. Still, you had to admit that the woman got results.

Each time Dan went in to work on the stalls in the Old Convent Centre, there were more lists and announcements up on a board in Phil's office, and more updates and instructions being churned out. The latest thing she'd been on about was 'kerb appeal', and the next one, according to Ferdia, was going to be 'subliminal flow'.

As far as Dan could tell, this meant fairy lights. The council already had the town's Christmas tree set up by the horse trough in Broad Street, but Phil had managed to get sponsorship for a red carpet flanked by lanterns, and little lights in all the trees around the nuns' garden. The plan was to have food and drink stalls out by the fountain, and the craft and gift stalls and other stuff inside.

The stalls were basically just trestle tables with cut-out painted castle bits screwed to the front. Bríd said they were going to look like rows of Punch and Judy theatres, but Dan reckoned she was wrong. Of course, at the moment they were just bits of MDF with a stone effect painted on them, but with glittery patches sprayed on, and holly and ivy draped round the castellation, they'd look the part. He had only a few more to finish, so it was pretty late for Phil to be presenting designs to the committee. But even if they kicked off, it made no difference. He was getting paid anyway. And, actually, it might be a bit of a laugh to see Phil under fire.

The main thing was that Bríd had said she was up for a drink afterwards. Well, she hadn't exactly said so, but she was going to be at the meeting, so there was a good chance that that was how it would pan out. There were times when Dan wished he and Bríd could be more like Conor and Aideen. Having a laidback relationship was great, but it did have its drawbacks. For one thing, you never quite knew where you stood.

He hadn't expected Cassie to be at the meeting. Nor, by the look of her, had Bríd, who was sitting by Phil when Dan arrived. Most people had taken their seats by the time Cassie came in with Nell Reily. The old biddies were all mouthing compliments about Nell's hair, which was looking different. Cassie, who had a mug of coffee in her hand, slipped into a seat and gave a big wave.

Dan could see it going down seriously badly with Bríd. He'd never quite worked out what her problem was with Cassie, and the only time he'd mentioned it she'd given him the evil eye. It was probably just female stuff anyway, and he had enough problems of his own without getting into all of that.

Phil tapped her pen against her water glass, and called the meeting to order. 'Once again, it's wonderful to see a full table! The energy and commitment that's going into this project is remarkable. And I know that the whole town will see dividends when we get our hands on that trophy. Now, as is customary, we'll begin with my Chair's Report.' She took off her zebra specs and looked round the table. 'You'll see from your agenda that we have several reports this evening. The ladies from the raffle working party. Dan Cafferky, who'll tell us about the designs for our themed stalls. And Cassie Fitzgerald, who's generously offered to provide an addition to our programme. We'll also hear from Ann Flood — not about over-the-counter cures for our winter coughs and colds, but on behalf of the Lissbeg Choristers, who'll be joining us at the Winter Fest, as medieval carollers.'

People turned and looked at Ann Flood, who was sitting with Dan on a bench at the side of the room. Dan's attention was still on Bríd. He hadn't told her he'd be at the meeting and he wondered now if he should have done. She was always going on about keeping private space in her life.

'*How*ever . . .' Phil beamed round the table '. . . we won't keep any non-committee members beyond their agenda item. And, as you see, the reports have all been grouped together at the top.'

She nodded across at Cassie and put her specs back on. 'As far as my own report is concerned, I've pretty much said what I need to. So I'll call on Cassie Fitzgerald to start us off.'

There was a round of applause, led by a couple of pensioners, and Cassie got up looking totally relaxed. 'You only clap because you're scared of what I might do with my tongs if you didn't!'

Everyone laughed, except Bríd.

Cassie smiled round the table. 'Look, it's

no big deal. I just suggested that the Winter Fest could make use of the room set up for my hairdressing. There's a chair and a mirror, so why not do face-painting for kids? It'll feel grown-up and exciting, like taking a trip to a beauty parlour. We can call it "Santa's Salon".'

Phil tapped for attention again. 'Cassie, very kindly, has offered to man it. And, as she's trained as a beautician, I think we're fortunate indeed.'

'Well, I'm a hairdresser, not a beautician. Or a makeup artist. But, hey, it can't be that hard to make a kid look like a cat. Anyway, if you think it's a good idea, I'm happy to do it.' Then she swung her bag onto her shoulder and said she'd leave them to it.

By the time the door closed behind her, Phil was asking Bríd to minute the committee's thanks to Cassandra Fitzgerald. Bríd looked round, as if she was waiting for more comments or objections, but everyone was nodding, so she made the note.

Riding on the wave of approval, Phil tapped on her glass again. 'Now I'd like to ask Dan Cafferky to speak to his progress with the stalls. You'll see the drawings there among your papers and, before Dan speaks, I think we should give him a well-deserved round of applause.'

You could tell that half of the crowd round the table hadn't even looked at the papers. And now they were stuck deciding whether they should have a quick shufti at the designs or do the polite thing and applaud. Not wanting to look either ill-prepared or unsupportive, most of them clapped.

The main thing in Dan's mind was that he shouldn't go mentioning Fury. 'Least said, soonest mended' had always been Fury's motto, and he wouldn't want his name turning up in the minutes of a meeting.

Anyway, Phil cut in before he'd said much. She did right, too, because a couple of people were squinting at the drawings, and you knew that, if they started talking, they'd have the whole lot redesigned. 'I must say that the involvement of so many young people is impressive. Could we make sure that our thanks appear in the record?'

She didn't mention that Dan was being paid and nobody asked any questions.

Bríd, who knew what he was getting and where it was going, crossed her eyes at him. It was the kind of look that made Dan think she'd be okay for tonight.

Outside in the hall, he found Cassie talking on her iPhone. She finished the call as he came out, and asked if he fancied a beer.

It seemed as good a way as any of passing the time, so Dan sent a text to Bríd to say he'd be round in Moran's.

They got their drinks and found a table and, for something to say, Dan told Cassie that the face-painting thing sounded good.

'One of my pensioners thought of it. I'm not really sure that I ought to have gone along.'

'Why not?'

'It's all a bit over the top, don't you think? The competitive element? I just feel sorry for whoever's in there now, reporting on the raffle.'

Apparently the old biddies that normally rounded up prizes for the raffle had hit a brick wall. Cassie explained that they'd normally squeeze a big prize out of a local business. Two nights at a hotel, say, or a flat-screen TV. 'And to get that you have to go to Ballyfin or Carrick, right? I mean, there's no big hotel or anything here in Lissbeg. So they did. And they were told to forget it. Carrick and Ballyfin aren't going to help this year because they want to win the trophy themselves.'

It made sense to Dan, who shrugged, and took a pull of his pint.

Cassie ran her hand through her fringe. 'How come winning is such a big deal?'

'It's easy seen you're not from a place that depends so much on tourism.'

'So — what? You win a trophy and the whole world decides to visit?'

'Kind of. Well, it gives you the edge, maybe.'

'I just think it's crap that the raffle ladies can't rustle up a decent prize. It's for a homeless shelter in Carrick, for God's sake.'

Dan frowned. 'But won't all the money that's made go to the shelter?'

'You think? The stalls are going to be selling produce by people like Bríd and Aideen. Not buns and baby clothes made by little old dears, who give them for free. If you ask me, the charity shtick is just like your medieval cutouts.'

'How d'you mean?'

'Stuck on to a commercial venture to give it a fuzzy Christmas feel.' Cassie stood up and edged out from behind the table. 'Phil's shifting money around from one budget to another and I'll lay odds that, when the accounts are done, there won't be much left to give to the homeless. Well, there certainly won't if it all comes down to the proceeds of a titchy little raffle. That hasn't even got a decent prize.'

She disappeared off to the loo and Dan sat back with his pint. Gunther, a guy from back his way who made and sold goat's cheese, had told him he'd been hoping for a great return from the Winter Fest. Bríd had been talking about doing mince pies up in special Christmas packaging and getting decent money for them too. Because, of course, none of the artisan-food crowd could afford to go giving stuff away.

The same went for the arty-crafty lot, renting space in the Convent Centre. They were all just start-up businesses — weavers and potters and people, trying to make ends meet. And, now that he thought about it, Phil's posters did just say 'Charity Raffle'. Nothing about the homeless shelter in Carrick getting the full whack. He wondered if he ought to talk to Bríd about it. But the chances were that she'd tell him to butt out. Especially as she knew he was taking cash himself for doing the work on the stalls.

Taking a deep pull of his pint, Dan wished he could talk to Bríd as easily as he could sit down and talk to Cassie. A bit of advice would be useful. Because Dekko had just put another consignment of stuff in his shed on the pier.

33

Peering out of the window, Cassie could see that the sky was slate grey. But the temperature was nowhere near freezing, and last night the forecast had shown what had seemed to her no more than a sprinkling of snow.

Irish people were weird about the weather. This morning Conor, who'd stayed overnight, had left number eight early, to move stock that was grazing on the hills to fields closer to the farmhouse. And when Bríd and Aideen had gone out later, they were bundled up as if they expected a blizzard.

After breakfast Cassie shrugged on her coat, hitched her knapsack over her shoulder, and set out for Ballyfin. It was no fun just shooting down the motorway, so she planned to take the back roads and see if she could skirt the edge of the forest and find her way to the high mountain pass at the southern side of Knockinver.

Soon she was driving down a one-track road towards trees that disappeared and re-appeared as she navigated dog-leg bends. Up ahead, the sky steadily darkened to a pewter colour. Then, out of nowhere, a gust of wind hurled a shower of hail against her windshield. Switching on the wipers, she leaned forward. Beyond the windshield, the road seemed almost in darkness, so she hit the fog lights. Flying hailstones were hitting the road like bullets, and leaping back into the air. Fiddling with the controls, Cassie tried to work out if she'd do better relying on the headlamps without the fog lights, or whether she might see more with no lights at all.

As she inched on down the road, the weight of the hailstones seemed to be too much for the wipers, so she pushed their speed up to max. Briefly, it made a difference. Until the arm passing in front of her suddenly stopped at upright, then floated randomly left and right, doing no good at all.

Up ahead was a T-junction. Turning onto it, she realised there was a passing place about ten yards away, where she could pull in by the forest edge. But now, to see anything at all, she had to lean over and peer through the passenger side of the windshield, where the single wiper was still working. So, even travelling the short distance to the passing place was horrible, with her right foot stretching for the accelerator, and the frightening awareness that her instinctive responses belonged in a left-hand drive car.

As soon as she pulled in, and the wipers were off, the windshield caked up altogether. Opening the door, she stepped out into the bitterly cold wind in order to squint at the sky. The heavy clouds were still as dark as pewter and the hailstones blown sideways against her face felt like tiny shards of glass. She was about to get back into the car to call a garage when a battered red van appeared, coming towards her. It pulled up as it drew alongside, and Fury O'Shea leaned over to shout out of the window.

'Are you having trouble?'

'One of my wiper blades broke.'

Fury climbed down from the cab and strolled over to her car. 'You're Ger and Pat Fitzgerald's granddaughter, aren't you?'

'That's me. Cassie. The car's Pat's but I guess she didn't fit winter wipers.'

Fury was scraping at the coat of hailstones on the windshield. 'You never know what to expect of the weather round these parts, girl — we don't do seasonal.'

He was wearing the same oversized waxed jacket she'd seen him in previously, and the ends of his corduroy trousers were stuffed into wellington boots. Rubbing his hands together to warm them, he jerked his head towards the van. 'I'd say I might have a fix for that wiper in the shed. The house is just down the road. I'll give you a cup of tea till the hail clears, and then we can drive back and set you right.'

He ordered his little Jack Russell terrier into the back of the van, and Cassie climbed into the passenger seat. The heater in the cab was going full blast and there was a smell of linseed oil, sawdust, and extra-strong mints.

As they rattled away, Cassie tried to thank him.

'Well, I couldn't go leaving you at the side of the road, could I? You wouldn't have frozen to death, mind, but, even with that grand tinfoil coat, you would have got nippy.'

'I was on my way to Ballyfin. Pat said I could take the old road over the mountain pass if I skirted the forest.'

'Well, if you were navigating by eye, you weren't making a bad fist of it.' He swung the wheel and the van crunched down the gravel drive of a house that backed onto the forest. It was set at an angle to the road, so that trees were on three sides of it, and Cassie could see a dog kennel and a group of sheds at the rear.

The big room that Fury led her into had a kitchen at one end, a table and chairs in the middle, and an easy chair angled to face a TV that stood on a large fridge-freezer.

'This is really kind. I'm sorry to have troubled you.'

Fury grunted and went to fill the electric kettle. The Divil, who had pattered in behind them, jumped on one of the chairs and settled his chin on the table.

'Is this where you grew up?'

Fury shook his head. 'Not in this house, no. I built it. The place I grew up in has fallen to bits now. It was down the road.' He assembled mugs, milk, and sugar on a corner of the table, most of which was taken up by something covered with a cotton dust sheet. There were curls of wood shavings scattered on the floor beneath The Divil's chair.

'Are you a wood-carver?'

Fury cocked an eyebrow at her. 'Aren't you the inquisitive one?'

'Well, I just wondered.'

'I was raised a forester, if you must know.'

'That's what your dad did?'

'And his father before him. Back for generations. The forest got sold off, though.'

As he went to put water in the teapot, Cassie sat down by The Divil. When Fury handed her a steaming mug she wrapped her cold hands around it gratefully. 'Who sold off the forest?'

Dipping his beaky nose into his own mug, he gave her a sharp look. 'What do you do for a living yourself?'

'I'm a hairdresser.'

'Oh, right. I thought you might be an investigative journalist.'

He didn't seem particularly cross, though. Cassie ran her hand through her fringe and shook it back into place. 'I guess Irish people don't like straight questions.'

'You've noticed that, have you?'

'Well, yeah. Since I've been here.'

'Bet you grew up thinking you were Irish yourself, though.'

Cassie laughed. 'Well, half Irish. My mom's from Québec.'

'Will you be wanting biscuits?'

'Because my mom's from Québec?'

'Because I've never known a woman who didn't want a biscuit with her tea.'

'Oh. Okay. Well, I won't say no.'

'I wouldn't doubt you.' He produced a tin of fig rolls from a cupboard and looked severely at The Divil. 'Yer man there is the same, of course, and now he'll want his saucer as well.'

With The Divil sitting beside her lapping tea and crumbled fig roll from a saucer, Cassie tried another angle. 'How come you wanted to be a builder, not a forester?'

'I didn't say that's what I wanted.'

Feeling repressed, she returned to her tea. Fury said nothing for a minute. Then he laughed. 'Well, if you want the story it's no secret, and I suppose you may as well have it from the horse's mouth. I went away, like your dad and your uncle Jim. To England, in my case, to work on the sites. My older brother fell in for the house and the land here at home. And by the time he died of drink he'd let the house go to ruin and sold off most of the forest.'

This was rather more information than Cassie had bargained for. Glancing up, she found Fury looking amused.

'There you have it. A straight answer to a straight question. Will we change the subject?' He reached forward and lifted the dust sheet from the table. On sheets of newspaper, among more shavings, was a range of chisels, several pieces of wood, and a group of carved figures.

Cassie gasped in delight. 'You *are* a wood-carver!'

'Well, I know my trees, I can tell you that.'

She picked up one of the figures. It was a donkey. You could see every hair in his coarse, bristly mane. Grouped together on the table were three half-carved sheep. They were made of paler wood than the donkey. Beside them was a man leaning on a stick. He was wearing a rough jacket and trousers and his feet were bare.

Cassie picked up another figure, similarly dressed, but with a sheepskin tied round his shoulders over his jacket. He had a close-fitting cap on his head and held a little lamb in his arms.

The men were about four or maybe six inches high. On the table, propped against a little pile of sawdust, was the half-carved figure of a baby wrapped in a blanket. You could see that the fabric was thick and tightly wrapped, and that the baby was deeply asleep.

Putting the shepherd back on the table, Cassie lifted another carving. 'You're making a Nativity scene.'

'You'd call it a crib round here.'

'And this is the ox.' She turned the piece in her hands, admiring the curved horns. You could see how the marks of different tools had defined the folds of its dewlaps and the curly hair on its poll. 'Are you going to paint them?'

'Name of God, girl, are you thick or what are you?' Fury slammed his mug on the table and, troubled by disturbed sawdust, The Divil sneezed. 'Why do you think a carver chooses different kinds of wood?'

Cassie hadn't thought about it at all. 'Because they're easy to work? Or they're what you've got?'

Fury sopped up his spilled tea with a corner of the cotton dust-sheet. 'Well, that too. But because they give you different colours. You don't want to clog up your work with layers of paint. Different trees give different colours. Sapwood or heartwood makes a difference too. If you know your trees you'll make your choice.'

'Do you get it all from the forest?'

Fury shook his head. 'The little fellow is cherry sapwood. So are the lambs. I know a fella that has an orchard. But there's pine and ash there from the forest. And the ox is red oak.'

'How do you know what animals looked like back then? Wouldn't they have been different? I mean, like, different breeds?'

'I wouldn't know, girl. Chances are you're right.' Fury pointed to a little piece so dark

303

it was nearly black. It was a border collie, with a thick ruff of shaggy hair and a pointed face. 'You probably wouldn't get herd dogs like yer man there over in Bethlehem either. But he's what you'd see round here.'

Yesterday Conor had told Cassie that Hanna was turning a new page of the psalter each week in the run-up to Christmas and, since she'd never seen the exhibition, she'd gone in to take a look. She hadn't waited to check out the meaning of the text, but she'd been fascinated by a little illustration in the margin of the left-hand page. It was of a flock of sheep strung out across a green field, with the sun setting behind distant mountains, and it looked exactly like a photograph she'd taken last week.

Now, looking at Fury's carvings, she realised it had never occurred to her that visual artists expressed images in what amounted to a language, and that the artist could choose to make it foreign or native, or to weave one into the other, to create a conscious effect.

When she said so, Fury nodded at her. 'Ay, well, if you've noticed that you've noticed more than most people. And I'll tell you something else, girl. Most people stand still the whole of their lives and see things from one point of view.'

34

Sitting at the kitchen window with her note-book, Pat told herself this was another task that she wouldn't be able for. Concentrate on looking at an animal and write about what you see. An 'exercise', Hanna called it, which was a funny word when you thought about it, because nowadays you'd think of exercise as kicking up your legs.

Pat had grown up in a house like a little English villa on the outskirts of Ballyfin, with a garden in front and behind and a few apple trees. Nothing like a farm, and they'd never had pets either. Not even a dog. When she'd married Ger they'd always had a couple of yard cats. In those days Ger wouldn't let her feed them, so they'd keep down the rats.

Fuzzy, the cat they had now, was more of a pet. He was a handsome cat but he wouldn't be indoors. Mostly you'd hardly see him, unless he was sunning himself on the shed. Pat had gone into the lads' old bedroom, which looked out on the yard, to concentrate on him, like Hanna said. It was a cold day, though, so he wasn't there.

Sister Benignus used to call copybooks 'exercises'. They had pictures of round towers and wolfhounds on the back cover. Or maybe it was the front. Anyway, the wolfhound was a big, tall dog, with long feathery legs on him that would make you think of Cassie's feathery fringe. But Hanna's exercise was about looking at a real animal, not a picture. Time was, you could look out in the street and see all classes of animals. Back before the new mart was built in the 1960s, there used to be fair days here in Lissbeg. Broad Street would be crowded with stock, and farmers and dealers, and every beast was driven to town on foot. Pat's mam used to take her to the fair.

She could remember groups of cattle and sheep standing on street corners, and the shaggy dogs with watchful eyes that minded them. You'd see the dogs running low to the ground with their ears pricked if a beast broke away. They'd snake to and fro between other men's cattle till they'd cut out their own bullock or cow, and turn it back down the street. You'd almost think the cattle were grateful, too, when the dog found them. As a child, she'd felt the same way herself, when she'd let go of her mam's hand one day, and got lost among legs and swishing tails.

Nowadays, the only memory of the fair was the horse trough in Broad Street, and you'd hardly see a dog in the street that wasn't on a lead.

Ger's dad used to drive his stock fifteen miles to a fair in the days when he was farming. She'd never asked Ger if he'd been brought along. You'd see little lads in the streets all right, running messages for their fathers, or holding a horse or a donkey for a few pence.

Back then, Pat had been slightly afraid of her mam's cousins from the country. The women would smell of turf smoke and clove rock, and the men would spit in the street. Some of the boys holding the horses were probably her own relations but, at the time, she'd kept away from them because she wouldn't be used to a farm.

That changed after she was married, of course. But because Ger had the shop and Miyah had the farm, she'd really only gone out there to visit his mam. The women would rear the poultry then, but they wouldn't have much to do with the farm animals. Ger would go off to the mart with

Miyah and their dad — like he still went now on his own — and Pat would take Frankie and the other lads to sit in the farm kitchen. Oftentimes they'd spend the afternoon washing eggs with Ger's mam.

Sitting at her own kitchen window, looking out at Broad Street, Pat laid her notebook and biro down on the sill. She wished she hadn't said a word to Frankie the other day about Ger. You couldn't get a better son than Frankie. He was always looking out for her, like the way he'd bought her the car. Ger had never been happy about her driving but he hadn't made a fuss at all because the gift had come from Frankie, who'd always been able to twist him round his thumb.

The only reason she'd said a word to Frankie was that, for the last while, she'd been getting more and more worried about Ger. Lately he'd moved into Sonny and Jim's old bedroom. And, before that, she'd woken once or twice and found him standing at the window, leaning out. That was when he told her he'd change bedrooms. He'd been sleeping badly, he said, and he didn't want to be waking her up all hours. You could see it was still going on, even in the lads' room, because, when she'd go in to make his bed, he'd have three pillows up in a heap, like he'd been sitting up half the night.

It had struck Pat that maybe he'd been worried about the business. So, when she'd bumped into Frankie in the street the other day she'd asked him to come for a coffee. Ger had got up at the crack of dawn, and spruced himself up in his good suit, and gone off again to Cork. Frankie was in town picking something up for his wife. He'd time for a coffee, though, he'd said, and he'd taken Pat into a pub.

They'd sat in the lounge bar where the coffee you got was a Rombouts that came with its own filter sitting on your cup. The filters were fierce fiddly things, and she'd been so distracted that she'd hardly managed a sip. In the end she'd just come straight out with it, and told Frankie she was worried about his father. Was there anything going on, she'd said, that would have Ger in a state? But the way Frankie responded had left her none the wiser. He'd offered her a cream cake, as if she was a child, and came out with a lot of platitudes, with half an eye on his watch.

Besides he might not have been the right person to ask. To begin with, if he did know something was wrong, he probably wouldn't tell her, because he wouldn't want her worried. And, then again, he might just be embarrassed by the question. As far as the rest of the town was concerned, Frankie was his father's partner, but she'd often thought that he might know no more about Ger's business deals than herself.

Anyway, she'd got no good from that conversation, and she hoped to God that Frankie wouldn't go telling Ger that she'd asked. The chances were that he wouldn't, though, because Frankie was never one to go stirring up trouble. From the time he was a toddler Pat had watched him learn that the way to keep in with Ger was to start no battles. He was cute, too, like his dad, when it came to money. Another man might resent the fact that his father wouldn't step down and let him take over, but so long as Ger was in harness, that was a manager's salary saved. And that'd be game ball by Frankie. He always had an eye to the main chance, which was why he hadn't minded at all when Sonny and Jim had had to go off, because there'd been no work for them, while he'd drawn the long straw and had a cushy life at home.

She'd often wondered why Ger had been the one who'd ended up as a butcher. He hated blood. When he was a child he used to run away when his father would be slaughtering. You had no legal slaughter on farms, these days, but back then every family with a bit of land would be killing their own meat.

Pat supposed that many a child had been scared by the blood and the screaming, but it sounded like Ger had had a worse time than most, because his father had seen him as a coward. One day, when Ger was about seven, he'd dragged him in when a pig was being killed, and made him hold a bucket for the blood. Pat only knew because Ger's mother had told her. He'd run to his mam, roaring, and she'd cleaned the blood off his face and his clothes under the yard tap.

You could tell by the way she'd told the story that his mam had worried ever since that she should have stopped his dad. But how could she? And maybe the poor man thought he was doing it for the best.

You'd wonder, too, if Ger had been given the shop as the least worst option. Handling carcasses might not be as bad as coping with beasts in pain. Pat knew that Ger always hated being on the farm when the vet came. Even the sound of a bawling cow upset him. And, according to Miyah, who'd thought it was hilarious, he'd got sick on his boots years ago when he'd had to stick a screwdriver in a sheep that had bloat.

At two o'clock, Cassie came by, and they went over the road for Hanna's creative-writing group. Pat got her own bit out of the way quickly — a few lines describing Fuzzy that she'd made up out of her head. The rest of the crowd clapped like mad because it was the first thing she'd read to them, and Hanna said she must have worked real hard on it, which made Pat feel ashamed.

Then Saira Khan did a bit about a squirrel she'd seen in the nuns' garden; and Mr Maguire turned out to keep hens, and read out a list of differences between Dorkings and Araucanas.

Ferdia and the others had pieces, too, but Pat didn't really hear them. She was remembering the day she'd let go of her mam's hand and got lost at the fair.

It had been raining and Broad Street was crowded. The cobbles were covered in muck and her shoes were in a state. She couldn't have been more than seven or so because the cows' haunches were way above her. The swinging tails were slapping her cheeks when a dog came up and circled behind her, cutting her off from the cows. He had a pointy black face, with white spots on it, like eyebrows, and white fur on his muzzle, with black bristly whiskers on either side.

You could see the insides of his ears, that were grey, like pussy willow. He didn't bark or jump up. Instead, he circled round her again, pushing her back from the cows. His legs were dirty with muck, and he had tags of matted, rusty hair, like a coat thrown round his shoulders. He didn't really come near her, he just pushed her with his eyes.

In a minute or two he'd got her away from the cattle, but he didn't just leave her crying there in the street. There were animals calling, and shouts and whistles and curses going on all around them, and she saw the dog's ears move forwards and back. Then his nose turned, and she looked round and heard her mam calling. And he waited till Pat ran across to her before he went back to his cows.

35

The seagull turned his head and looked straight into Cassie's lens, his grey and white feathers and pale gold beak echoing the colours of the creamy-yellow lichen on the grey clifftop rock. Cassie was about to press the shutter when a violent gust of wind hit her on the shoulder, bowling her sideways and sweeping the bird off its perch.

'Damn!' She checked her camera, which had been jerked from her hand and was dangling from its strap on her wrist. It was fine, but she decided to take no more risks and, tucking it safely into its case, she made her way back to the car. She'd drive on to the internet café in Couneen and upload the shots she'd taken in the last few days. The family at home hadn't shown much interest in the stuff she put on Instagram, but the friends she'd made on the cruise ships seemed to think that Ireland was cool.

When she walked into the shop in

Couneen, it looked like the café was closed. There was no one behind the counter either. But as she hesitated in the doorway, Dan clattered down the stairs. 'Hi, can I help — Oh, hi, Cassie.'

'I wanted to go online with a coffee but . . .'

Dan waved her in. 'No problem. I can stick a kettle on.'

'But if you're not open . . .'

'That's always a moot point at this time of year. Honestly, it's no hassle. I'll make you a cup and you can work away.'

By the time she'd uploaded the photos, he'd brought her a coffee with a cookie on the side.

'You weren't out with a camera in this weather?'

'Well, yeah.'

He looked at her screen and chuckled. 'You might do better to switch to interiors.'

'I think I'll give up. I usually do. What are you up to today?'

'The parents are off on a skite, so I'm minding the place. Serving the odd customer. Dragging bags of nuts up to the sheep.'

'So your folks have a farm?'

'I wouldn't say that. Just a few sheep, and my mum keeps hens. This was always a place for fishing, not farming.'

'And your family's always lived here?'

'Yup. Time immemorial. The place that's a shed now behind the shop was my grandparents' house. It's hard to tell with old houses round here, but it could've been built a few hundred years before that.'

'Awesome!'

'Tell you what,' Dan turned away from the table and went to put on a jacket, 'do you want to come up and I'll show you a proper interior? The fireplace in my grandad's house is practically a museum piece.'

He locked the shop and they climbed a steep path to the old house, which had whitewashed walls and a corrugated-iron roof. The windows were roughly boarded up, with wide gaps between the boards; and the door, which was white uPVC, had obviously started life in a suburban terrace. One panel was badly dented but it still had a little inset fanlight and an imitation Georgian knocker.

'The original half door gave up a few years ago. The place doesn't really need one, but this keeps the hens out. I found it in a skip.'

Dan led Cassie into the single room, which was piled with tools and sacks of animal feed. Sunlight falling through the boarded windows made broad stripes on the floor, but the ends of the room were in shadow. He pursed his lips. 'Not sure you'll get much of a shot with this lighting.'

But, forgetting photography, Cassie was already at the hearth. The fireplace was in the gable wall of the house, a high chimneypiece with spaces left between the stones to make little niches for storage. There was a tarnished tin tea caddy in one, and a decaying box of matches in another. An iron crane festooned with pothooks still stood by the hearth, and rusting beneath it was a wheel that had once worked a bellows. The proportions of the tapering chimneypiece were beautiful, and over the stone lintel above the opening, a wooden shelf held a candlestick, and a faded picture in a frame. 'This is so amazing. They cooked on an open fire?'

'I'd say if my nan had lived there'd have been a range installed, and electricity and running water. But she died young and Grandad was happy to leave things be. He ate below in the shop with us, and most evenings he'd be down the pub with his mates. Anyway, half the time he'd be out fishing at sea.'

'Did you know him well?'

'I sure did. I was always out in a boat with him. He was a great teacher.'

Cassie sighed, lifting down the tea caddy and brushing dirt from the lid. 'You see, that makes me really envious. I bet he told you all sorts of stories about how life was when he was young. Stuff that makes you feel rooted here yourself.'

'I suppose that's it. I've never wanted to live anywhere else, anyway.'

'But you went to Australia.'

'That was just for the craic. Or maybe I had a notion of making my fortune.' Dan shrugged. 'It wouldn't have worked out anyway because this is where I belong.'

Cassie crouched down by the fireplace to peer up the chimney. The stone walls were furred with burned-on soot and she could see straight up to the sky overhead.

Dan hunkered beside her. 'At night you could look up from beside the fire and see stars.'

Cassie pulled a face. 'My dad grew up in the flat where Pat and Ger are living now. I guess he and my uncle Jim went to Canada to make their fortune. But they never came back, and they never talk about the past.'

'They never even came on a visit?'

'Nope. I'm the only one of my family who seems to have had the urge.'

'But, shur, you're a great traveller, aren't you?'

'Yeah, I like to travel. But this trip is different. I'm not like you. I don't know where I belong. But I guess I've always wondered if it might be here.'

'Is it?'

Cassie laughed. 'I dunno. I just wish I could be here with my dad and have him teach me stuff. Like your grandad and you.'

'Was your dad raised a farmer?'

'See, I don't even know that!' Cassie stood up crossly, wiping the dust from her hands.

'Can't you ask your gran?'

'I don't think so. She's a pet but she's . . . kind of emotionally frail. It's like there are no-go areas? And, as far as I can see, my grandad never talks at all.'

Catching sight of Dan's face, she wondered if this was way too much information. After all, she hardly knew him. The thought prompted the realisation that she'd never talked like this to Shay. That was strange. Everything she'd just articulated seemed to have crystallised since she'd come here to Ireland, and Shay was a big part of her new sense of feeling at home. Yet somehow Dan seemed more likely to understand.

He was looking slightly awkward but she could feel he was sympathetic. Then he stood up, moved away from her and began to heave a sack of feed towards the door. 'Ger would rap out the orders all right, but he's no conversationalist. His customers hardly get a word out of him when he's serving inside in the shop.'

Cassie went to place the tin candlestick on the windowsill. Taking out her camera, she tried to frame a shot that took in the lines of light falling through the boards.

Dan leaned on the doorframe and looked across at her. 'How about your mum's family? Are you close to them?'

Cassie shook her head. Her mom was an only child, whose parents were both dead and, though Gran'ma had lived to be quite old, she'd had Alzheimer's for ages. There had been a few visits to the care home for seniors where she'd lived but mostly they'd been half embarrassing, half distressful, and after a while Cassie and her sisters weren't taken along.

She looked through the lens at the candlestick on the windowsill, focusing on the stump of a candle that was almost burned down to the quick. But the shot she took didn't look like much of anything, so she deleted it.

Then, glancing up, she realised that Dan was waiting to go. 'Oh, God, I'm sorry. You need to get up to your sheep.'

'They won't starve.' He came over to join her at the window and, turning the candle-stick, began chipping pieces of wax off it, using his fingernail.

Cassie had a feeling that, given half a chance, he'd start sharing confidences himself. And she wasn't sure that she was up for it. Dan was nice, and undoubtedly attractive, but he wasn't her problem. And, if he needed someone to talk to, surely he had Bríd?

Looking up, she saw a strange expression in his eyes. For a moment she thought he was about to make a move on her. But instead he turned away, running his hand through his hair. It was an oddly despairing gesture, and before she could decide what to make of it, he'd gone back to the thresh-old and heaved the sack onto his shoulder.

His car was round the side of the building with a trailer hitched to the back and, as she walked down to her own car, he waved as he drove off.

On her way back to Lissbeg Cassie won-dered if the Fitzgeralds too had a tumble-down house that had once been the family homestead. Uncle Frankie's fancy home had been built near the old farmhouse. The home that Ger had grown up in wouldn't have been like Dan's grandad's place,

322

which, as Dan had said, was pretty much a museum piece. But she wondered what it *was* like.

Dad and the uncles must have visited there when they were kids. Maybe they'd hung out in the kitchen with their grandma. Maybe they'd carried animal feed up to the fields, like Dan. She wondered if the house had had a range, like Pat's, in the kitchen, and whether it was still standing, with windows boarded up, like the Cafferky place, and empty rooms full of dust and memories, and slanting sunlight.

And, if such a house existed, who would it belong to? Was it standing there waiting for Dad and Uncle Jim to come home? According to Jazz Turner, Hanna had inherited the house where she lived from some ancient auntie. It was left to her when she was only a kid and she'd grown up and emigrated to England. And, when she came back to Ireland, it had almost gone to ruin. But Hanna had done it up and settled in.

Cassie had a vision of herself in another fifty years. A voyager with her travelling done, coming home to a craggy niche in some green mountainy field. Would she be a warm presence in the community, like Min the Match or Pat? Or crabby and totally taciturn, like Ger? You could never tell what would happen next in life, though — look at poor Gran'ma with her Alzheimer's. So maybe it was best to live for today and let the future look after itself.

36

Bríd was beginning to feel claustrophobic. Oddly enough, it wasn't Cassie's presence in the house that had bothered her lately. It was Dan. He was turning up at number eight far more than he used to and, since he'd begun the work at the Old Convent Centre, he'd taken to nipping across the road for a lunchtime sandwich from the deli. There was nothing wrong with that, of course, but the last few times he'd come in he'd seemed to be looking for a conversation and, with the length of the queue at lunchtime, that was just daft.

She still fancied him. Big-time. Though lately she'd wondered if it was a bit crass to keep leaping into bed with him and afterwards to hold him at arm's length. The bottom line, though, was that they weren't a couple. And he knew that because they'd said so often enough. When you bought in to commitment, like Aideen and Conor, most of your own life seemed to disappear. Dan would be worse than Conor too. There was a vulnerable streak underneath all that aggression, and the unfortunate woman who got him would spend half her life propping him up.

So Bríd wasn't going to be rushed. She had a business to build in the medium and long term, and in the short term she and Aideen were up to their eyes preparing for the Winter Fest. As well as keeping up their ordinary routine, they'd been planning seasonal products — Christmas cookies, mini plum puddings, and chocolate Yule logs. If the press was going to be there in force, then things didn't just have to taste good, they needed to look spectacular. She'd been in touch with their local suppliers, lots of whom had taken stalls as well. You didn't want to double up on what you'd be selling, but you could flag the fact that HabberDashery used local cheeses and other produce.

It all took time to organise, though, so, to tell the truth, it was great to have Cassie at home to cook dinner.

Now as she opened the door of number eight Bríd could see down the hall and into the kitchen, where Aideen was laying the table and Cassie, wearing an apron, was working at the stove. Cassie leaned back and waved. 'Meatballs and pasta again. But this time I got inspired and added aubergine.'

Chucking her coat on the rack behind the door, Bríd asked if there was time to grab a shower.

'No problem. This'll be fine for ten minutes. Will we pour you a drink?'

Fifteen minutes later, wearing her PJs and dressing gown, she gratefully took the first sip of wine and joined them at the kitchen table, happy to relax.

Aideen took a tinfoil parcel from the oven and unwrapped a fragrant loaf of garlic bread. 'Carb overload — but Cassie reckons we deserve it.'

'Well, you do. You've been working like demons.'

Bríd felt a flicker of irritation. Not everyone could go round taking months off work, like Cassie. And people who worked hard didn't necessarily need cosseting. Pulling a piece of bread off the loaf, she told herself not to get ratty. It was just that Cassie's thing about hanging loose always got up her nose.

Anyway, the pasta was gorgeous. The balance of oregano and thyme was perfect, and there was a hint of paprika that made a huge difference. Bríd was about to ask for the proportions when Aideen spoke first.

'You know that saying about being careful what you wish for? Well, I never really thought about it till tonight.'

'So how come you did now?'

'Well, Cassie and I were talking. You know, about making money, and work, and Conor and me saving up.'

'And?'

'And, well, I dunno, I suppose I've had this fantasy about working like mad and saving for a huge big wedding. And then Conor focusing on farming and me being a farmer's wife.'

Cassie was sitting back, smiling. She had a sort of relaxed assurance about her that probably came from a long day doing nothing at all.

Aideen took a forkful of pasta and planted her elbows on the table. 'But, you know, Cassie was saying that maybe I'm putting too much pressure on Conor to be a farmer. Not overt, you know. Kind of implicit.'

It was exactly what Bríd herself had thought, so the wave of annoyance that possessed her made no sense. But how dare Cassie barge in and offer advice to Aideen? Cassie, who'd turned up out of nowhere and would, no doubt, disappear again at the drop of a hat. How well she hadn't thought about who'd have to cope if it turned out that she was wrong!

But it wouldn't do to make a fuss at the dinner table. Especially since, in an argument, she'd end up on Cassie's side. Which was pretty bloody ironic. Determined to suppress her reaction, Bríd took another gulp of wine while Aideen rattled on.

'I need to get on to Conor and tell him I'm fine with him being a librarian. I mean, the thing that matters is that we're happy. And you can't have a marriage where one partner is stressing the other one out.'

Cassie nodded. 'I know it's got nothing to do with me but, if I were you, I'd give myself time to think. Get my head round the options. Be really sure what I wanted myself before sitting down to talk.'

Aideen looked at her earnestly. 'You're absolutely right. I need to take my time and choose my moment. God, Cassie, I'm really, *really* grateful. Wine, pasta, and life lessons all on the same night!'

Bríd could feel her back teeth clench in exasperation while, at the same time, a bit of her mind was amused. But, though irony was all very well, it was important not to let the others in on the joke. Being able to laugh at herself was one thing. Handing Cassie a laugh at her expense was something else again.

And for the rest of the meal she managed. The conversation moved on to other things, though every so often Aideen would reiterate her gratitude. At one point, she announced that Cassie ought to be a relationship counsellor. 'You really do see through the crap to what matters!'

Cassie laughed and quoted some stylist who'd said that a hairdresser's chair was the same as a therapist's couch. 'Anyway, I've always been a meddler. I've got matchmaking in my genes!'

Bríd, whose back teeth were still almost welded together, said nothing.

After they'd eaten, Aideen decided she'd go upstairs, shower and put on a dressing-gown. She might as well be as comfortable as Bríd, she said, if they were going to have to go through more lists for the Winter Fest.

Cassie, who had plans to go out, said she'd do the washing-up, if Bríd would dry. The last thing Bríd wanted was a girly chat at the sink, but Cassie was already stacking plates and rattling knives and forks.

'It's no problem, I've half an hour to kill. And, anyway, if there's two of us, we'll whip through it at speed.'

With no option, Bríd smiled, and went to get a tea towel from the drawer.

To begin with, it all went fine. She told Cassie again how great the pasta had been, and asked about the paprika and herbs. That got the plates washed and dried and the cutlery dripping on the drainer. Then, as they moved on to the pots and pans, Cassie mentioned the drink she'd had the other night with Dan. 'That time he and I went to Moran's, after the committee meeting?'

As soon as Bríd had come in, Dan had jumped up to get her a drink. Earlier on, at the meeting, their eyes had met across the table. It was one of those secret looks that made her long to be alone with him, and she'd known that he'd go home with her that night. Having exchanged it under the eyes of all those po-faced committee members had made it kind of funny and extra sexy, so she'd turned up at the pub in a great mood.

And they'd had a good time. She'd even been glad that Cassie was there, because that kept the conversation general. It had been an easy, relaxed evening followed by a great night's sex, and none of the intense emotional stuff that she'd carefully been fending off.

Now Cassie pushed her fringe out of her eyes with a soapy forearm. 'Is Dan okay?'

Bríd's eyes narrowed. 'How d'you mean?'

'Well, I just thought he might be bothered about something. He didn't *say* he was but I wonder if he is? It wasn't just that night in Moran's either. I met him again yesterday and he still seemed kind of troubled.'

At that moment something snapped inside Bríd. To her horror she heard her voice sounding over-loud and pompous. 'You know something, Cassie? You really need to mind your own business.'

'What?'

'You heard. You may not have noticed, but you're not a relationship counsellor. You're a hairdresser. And you don't belong here, you're just passing through. So don't imagine we've all been sitting waiting for someone to come and fix us. We're just fine. I don't need your advice, and nor does Aideen. And nor does Dan — just in case you've been making any plans.'

Cassie looked more amused than angry. 'Making plans? What does that mean?'

'Take it any way you please. I'm just warning you. Back off.'

'Oh, my God, you think I fancy him!'

'I never said that.'

'It's what you mean.'

Actually it wasn't. Bríd was just furious with Dan. What was he at, making strangers feel she was neglecting him? Because that was what it amounted to. He'd said something to Cassie — or, okay, he hadn't said anything, but he'd been going round with that hangdog look he kept wearing lately — and now Cassie was accusing her of being unsympathetic. Or insensitive. Or both. And she *knew* she was being unsympathetic. She didn't need a cocky Canadian hairdresser pointing it out.

Slamming the wet tea towel down on the work surface, Bríd suddenly realised she was eaten up with guilt. And she'd been so busy resenting it that she hadn't asked herself why. The fact was that she probably did love bloody Dan Cafferky. And now she'd have to deal with what that meant.

Still, better for Cassie to think she was suspicious than to know that she'd hit a nerve.

'Well, I can tell you this anyway — you're wasting your time if you fancy your chances with Dan.'

Cool as a cucumber, Cassie glanced round to check on the kitchen, before turning back and meeting her eyes. 'You know what, Bríd? You're right. That *would* be a waste of time. Because, as it happens, I'm perfectly fine with my own guy. He's a grown-up.'

37

IM AFTER MAKING SCONES U CD BRI%G A POT OF JAM

Sitting at her kitchen table, Mary Casey pinged her text into the ether and immediately typed another:

NOT RHUBARB

Laying the phone down, she looked at the scones that were cooling on her wire rack. You'd think, after baking scones all these years, she'd remember how many her recipe would yield. Yet here she was again, with nine of them needing to be eaten. Louisa liked a nice fruit scone with a cup of tea of an afternoon, but Louisa was slim as a sally and never came back for seconds.

Still, having Pat over for morning coffee would put paid to a fair few of them anyway. Pat had never been much good at the baking. She made a decent jar of jam, though, so long as it wasn't rhubarb. The way that Pat added ginger to rhubarb jam was only woeful. And the way she wouldn't be told was far worse.

Mind you, if she was no hand at scones, Pat had always been good at dressmaking. Better than Mary herself, though it wouldn't do to admit it, because if you gave Pat an inch she'd take a mile. Of course, she'd never had the figure that Mary had and, back at school, she'd been flat as a board, right up till they'd done their Leaving. She was good at running up frocks that made the best of what she had, though. Not that it made much difference in the end. She'd got no great catch in Ger Fitzgerald.

Back when they were girls, she and Pat used to spend whole weekends cutting out and sewing. Mary had had a treadle sewing machine. It had a wooden stand, and a base made of curly ironwork. There was a long box at the side, where you kept the bobbins, and the bits and pieces you fixed to the foot to do things she'd never quite got a grasp of. It had come with a book that would tell you what they were. Pat had the whole thing mastered, of course, but that was no great wonder if you had to dress as carefully as she did.

Standing up from the table, Mary went to

get a cloth from the sink. No matter what way you put your scones on a rack, you always got crumbs falling onto the table beneath it. Lifting the rack by its wire rim, she gingerly swiped the crumbs aside and folded them into her J Cloth. Then, having set the rack down again, she shook the crumbs into the sink and ran the tap to dismiss them.

Tom had never cared for a fruit scone. The day that she'd first seen him, she'd known that they'd be married, and he'd always said he'd felt the same way about her. She and Pat had gone to a match and he'd been centre-forward. She'd seen him before in Crossarra, where an old, bad-tempered cousin of his had kept the post office; but he wouldn't be round Lissbeg, except after school.

The day after the match, he was hanging round the horse trough with a crowd of other fellows from the Brothers'. Pat didn't want to cross the road from the convent gate, in case they'd be seen. But Mary didn't give a hoot for old Benignus. There was no harm in talking to a fellow bang in the middle of Broad Street. Anyway, she'd always been the nuns' pet, and the bishop was her mam's uncle.

Tom was going out with Nuala Devane at

the time. They weren't doing a steady line — or, if they were, it ended pretty quickly. Nuala's dad had the dancehall in Sheep Street and her mam sold tickets at the door. You'd see Nuala herself selling red lemonade through a hatch at the end of the hall. Her eyes were always on Tom when he and Mary were dancing. All the girls used to be looking at Tom, though he never seemed to notice. It never bothered Mary, not even when she spotted Pat was one of them. What else would they do but look at him and envy what was hers?

Tom was different to the other fellows, the way he'd be quiet and gentle. He was always off doing jobs for his aunt Maggie — setting her spuds, and doing her shopping, and keeping her company round in her shed of a house. That house in its sloping field gave Mary the shivers. It was wild old-fashioned, and Maggie Casey was an old besom with hardly a penny to bless herself. So Tom wasn't there by her fire for what he could get. He said she was lonely.

The first time Mary complained about the time he spent round in Maggie's place, she'd thought she'd have him toeing the line at once. It was the shock of her life when she'd found that he wouldn't budge. But, having lost a battle, she'd known better than to start fighting a war. Instead she'd bided her time and, when Hanna was old enough, she'd taken to sending her round to give Maggie a hand. That was how Maggie had ended up leaving the house and the field to Hanna, and people probably thought that had been Mary's plan from the start. The truth was that she'd no interest in an old *bothán* on a cliff or who'd fall in for it. But if Tom didn't need to go fussing round Maggie he'd stay at home minding his wife.

It was the same thing with Ger Fitz.

Tom had loads of friends. There were the lads in the GAA, and the crowd he'd hung round in school with. And Mary had always loved the way he was popular. People didn't just envy her because of how he looked, or how he treated her: he was a good man, and everyone knew it, and Mary was proud to think that she'd been his choice. She'd told him so before he died, because she'd wanted him to know it. But that had been in the ambulance, on the dreadful rush to the hospital, and she wasn't sure that he'd heard her because he'd been in so much pain.

Anyway, Ger Fitz was the one friend that she hadn't been sure about. The fact was that he was another Maggie Casey, needing care and taking up Tom's time. Most of the time he'd never utter a word but he'd always

be talking to Tom. You'd see his face sometimes, when Tom wasn't looking, and you'd
know how much he depended on him
because he had no one else.

She could see from the start how that
would go on after she and Tom were married. Ger would be turning up all the time,
wanting a hand or looking for Tom's advice.
And, to make things worse, she knew that
Ger had kind of fallen for herself. The thing
was that she and Pat and Ger and Tom used
to be a foursome. And, though they'd had
great craic together, things had got tricky at
the end.

Mary straightened the wire rack that she'd
put down slightly crooked. Moving it caused
a couple of spots of flour to fall onto the
table, so she licked her finger, picked them
up and rubbed them away on her hand.

Having found Tom, she'd known that
she'd never want another fellow but, back
then, it had felt strange to think that her
bed was made. She hadn't set out to chat
up Ger Fitzgerald. She'd hardly looked at
him, really. But she'd known he was looking
at her. And what harm was there in that?

What she didn't know was whether Tom
or Pat had ever noticed. But what if they
had? Mary had always had lads looking at
her. Even now, if she put her mind to it, she

knew she could turn heads. Not that she'd be running round at her time of life like she needed a man. That would be pure indecent. These days she'd settle for a bit of companionship from the likes of Louisa and Pat. And, anyway, no one on earth could replace Tom.

Still, she hoped to God that Tom hadn't noticed the way Ger used to look at her. It was the sort of thing she thought about now and she lying alone in the bed.

It was good, in a way, though, that Ger had got fond because, otherwise, he'd never have married Pat. Mary hadn't fixed it, of course. How could she? But she'd known that that was what would happen as soon as she'd accepted Tom. And she was glad of it. It was a case of killing two birds with one stone. You wouldn't want poor Pat left on the shelf when she and Tom were married. And with Ger married there was less chance he'd be hanging around poor Tom.

And that was how it had worked out. Mind you, it seemed to have driven Ger right back into himself. No one could call him a bad husband, but Pat can't have had much fun in her life with him sitting there like a block.

Still, what would Ger Fitz have to say for himself that you'd want to be listening to anyway? And wasn't she herself there, like always, if Pat wanted to talk?

38

Because everything in Carrick was on a scale that was smaller than Cassie was used to, she found it charming. Shay took her to some really cool restaurants, and a couple of his friends from work played Irish traditional music and knew all the pubs where the landlords were happy for people to start up a session. When Cassie mentioned that in number eight Bríd dismissed the music as ghastly stuff that was only played in tourist traps. Cassie liked it, though. One of Shay's friends was seriously good and played a mean accordion. The other had explained to Cassie that all you needed to play a bodhrán was an inherent sense of rhythm. It became pretty evident that that wasn't so but, if you got the right seat and enough players were crowded round the table, laughing and talking and playing, you could have a fun night.

And it hardly mattered where they went

because everything was fun with Shay. They saw a play that turned out to be deeply boring, but the jokes he'd whispered under his breath had nearly made her laugh out loud. He'd found her an app she hadn't even thought of looking for, which gave her masses of facts about Finfarran's history. He took her to the cinema in the Omniplex, and to the Aquadome, and taught her a showy butterfly stroke that she hadn't known before.

A couple of times they drove for miles on the long roads east of Carrick, where flocks of grey Canada geese grazed in the marshy fields. The first time they went that way they found a pub that looked like it hadn't had an update since the 1950s. There was a roaring fire in a back parlour, where there were chintz armchairs and a round oak table; and Shay ordered hot whiskeys with brown sugar, lemon, and cloves.

The next time they went there it was lunchtime, and they sat in the same parlour, eating bacon and cabbage. Cassie had wrinkled her nose when Shay ordered it, but it turned out to be piles of wafer-thin slices of delicious ham interleaved with tender, buttery cabbage, and served with roast potatoes so good that they kept asking for more. In the end, the landlady had laughed at them, and said they'd better leave room for a bit of pudding. It was lemon cake, served with thick cream as well as homemade custard, and afterwards they'd tramped for miles on the chilly, windswept marshes, and driven back to Carrick actually feeling hungry for tea.

Shay always seemed to get the best table in a restaurant, and complimentary drinks would often appear at the end of a meal. He laughed when Cassie mentioned it, and said that being a guard never hurt. People got to know you, even if you didn't belong to a place, and, yeah, there might be perks involved, but the bottom line was that good policing meant knowing your community.

'So you're not from round here?'

'We moved a lot when I was a kid because of my dad's job. My parents live in Limerick now.'

He had no great plans for where he'd end up physically but he'd worked out a proper career plan because that was the only way to get ahead.

'Is it hard to get promotion?'

'Competitive as hell. The trick is to drive the interviews yourself by getting the right stuff down on your application.'

'And how do you know what that is?'

'I ask my dad.' Shay grinned. 'No, that's

not true. It's pretty straightforward. But I won't bore you with it.'

But actually he'd gone on about it a lot. According to his dad, the key to a successful application was to focus on Context, Action, and Result. 'Summarise a problem you've faced in your current job. How you proceeded. What was the outcome. Get it down. Keep it concise. Stick to your plan when you're interviewed. Make sure to sell them what they want.'

'Wow. Talk about focused. You're going to end up as a chief superintendent or something.'

'Not me. I'm no careerist. Just a guy who wants to get on.'

Cassie liked that. He had his future planned, but he wasn't driven. And he didn't talk about the minutiae of his work. The bodhrán guy had cornered her in the pub once and given her a list of the most common incidences of rural Irish crime. Fortunately, Shay had rescued her. Blowing on the nape of her neck, he'd kissed her tattoo and told his mate to shut up. 'Cassie isn't interested in thefts of farm equipment and diesel. She doesn't want to hear the story of our boring, plodding lives.'

But the next time that they'd been alone, he'd told her something pretty exciting.

He'd been working as part of a team that was keeping an eye on a criminal gang.

'Why not just arrest them?'

'Because now's not the time.'

'You're just trying to sound mysterious.'

'Okay. If that's what you want to believe.' Shay flashed his eyebrows at her. 'It's a big deal, though. The right stuff to be involved in if you want to make your mark.'

Cassie had frowned. 'And should you be telling me about it?'

'Nope. Which is why I know you're not going to pass it on.'

She'd liked that, too, because it showed she was trusted. Though, later on, she'd realised that what she'd really liked was the fact that he'd wanted to impress her.

Later still, she wondered why she hadn't found it pathetic that a man his age and in his position would go round showing off. But that was after he'd taken her to the Royal Victoria Hotel.

It was late afternoon and she'd driven to Carrick and left her car parked by the county library. Walking into town, she'd seen Shay coming towards her. They'd arranged to meet in a café when his shift was over, but now he took her by the shoulders instead and pointed across the street. 'Have you ever been into the Royal Vic?' Steering her through the traffic, he led her up shallow steps to a hotel entrance where double doors opened into a perfect Victorian reception hall, full of velvet upholstery and dark, carved chairs.

The lounge bar was dark, too, with half-drawn blinds and huge brass ceiling fans. There were brass vases of holly on tall mahogany stands, wreathed in garlands, and immensely discreet fairy lights twinkling among the bottles on mirror-backed shelves. As Cassie and Shay walked between the heavy crimson curtains that were looped back in the doorway, a barman appeared and ushered them to a table.

Cassie sat down and looked around, half laughing and half impressed. 'Is this for real?'

'Totally. I thought you'd like it.'

'Well, yeah, it's certainly — quaint.'

'They do a great gin and tonic.'

'At this time of day? I don't think so.'

'Oh, come on. It's nearly Christmas. It's not about the drink, anyway. PJ, the barman, does an amazing dance.'

He raised his hand and the barman, who'd been hovering, re-approached the table. Shay introduced them, and ordered two gin and tonics with ice.

PJ, who was wearing a white coat and a

natty tartan bow tie, had an oiled comb-over that made Cassie's fingers itch for her scissors, but his watery blue eyes were very kind. At the back of her mind, she wished Shay wasn't being quite so hearty. There was a patronising note in his voice when he made the introductions, and it seemed to her that PJ was aware of it. Though, maybe, hanging round pensioners was making her over-sensitive. Anyway, if PJ *was* upset, he certainly didn't show it. Instead, as Shay had said he would, he went into a sort of dance.

The spotless white napkin that hung on his arm was flicked deftly over the surface of the table. Olives and salted almonds in little bowls appeared, as if by magic, and PJ glided away to mix the drinks behind the bar.

Ice, gin, tonic, and limes were produced, measured, poured, and cut, as precisely as if his every move was choreographed, and when he reappeared at the table, the tray with its two highball glasses was poised, shoulder high, on the splayed fingers of one hand.

Restraining an urge to applaud, Cassie thanked him. Then, as he flitted off again, she turned back to Shay. 'Well, that was impressive.'

'I know.' He raised his glass. 'Here's to us.'

'I'll drink to that.'

Sipping her perfect gin and tonic, Cassie leaned back and relaxed. Despite its décor, the Royal Victoria had succumbed to piped music and, in the background, she could hear Shane MacGowan and Kirsty MacColl singing 'Fairytale Of New York', which, judging by the number of times she'd heard it on the car radio, appeared, despite its raucous lyrics, to be Ireland's favourite Christmas song. Irish radio didn't seem big on Rudolph and 'Happy Holiday'. It was more about missing your silver-haired granny and crying into your beer.

Ever since she'd talked to Fury O'Shea she'd been thinking about Dad and Uncle Jim growing up over the butcher's shop, then taking off to Canada. How come Uncle Frankie hadn't left as well? It wasn't her business, really, but ever since she'd arrived, Ireland had felt more and more like home. Didn't Dad miss it? And, if so, how come he never visited?

She looked at Shay. 'Did you ever think of emigrating?'

'Not me. I'm an only son. They'd never let me go!' He took her hand. 'You know what I like best about you? That you're footloose and fancy-free and you take life exactly as it comes.'

Cassie knocked back her gin and tonic. 'Actually, I've been thinking how much I feel at home in Finfarran.'

She was about to pursue the conversation when Shay looked into her eyes. 'So, here's a thought. How about ordering some more of these, taking a room for a couple of hours, and saying our goodbyes in style?'

Cassie blinked, unsure that she'd heard him right. 'Goodbyes?'

'Well, I'm going to be out of here for Christmas, and you did say you'd only be round for another couple of weeks.'

She pulled back to look at him properly. 'I said that's what I thought. I haven't actually planned when I'm leaving.' She hadn't actually taken in the fact that he'd be away for Christmas either. But of course he would. He'd go home to his parents for Christmas Day. Still, she'd assumed that he'd spend time with her afterwards. When they might go to bed, which they hadn't done yet. Maybe he'd even invite her down to Limerick, say for New Year's. Or for what people here in Ireland called Stephens's Day.

She'd never thought they were going to spend their lives together. But the idea that he'd take her to a hotel room, and then disappear, was a bit much. 'So that's what you can do in the Royal Victoria? Book a room and shag for a couple of hours?'

'Oh, come on, Cassie. No, it's not. It's just that I happen to know the duty manager.' He reached over and lifted her chin with his forefinger. 'I wouldn't take someone like you somewhere like that. Give me credit for a bit of style.'

Cassie jerked away from him. 'Oh? Okay. Top marks for style, Shay. Zero for class. Falling into bed together isn't how I normally choose to say goodbye to someone. Mostly, I settle for a handshake.'

She saw him flush slightly as he set his glass on the table, and the shrug he gave was petulant. 'Fine. Okay. Forgive me for picking up the wrong signals.'

'And exactly how did I signal that I was up for this?'

'Travelling to see life. That's what you told me.'

He'd regained his composure now, and was sitting back again. A hundred replies surged into Cassie's mind but, out of the corner of her eye, she could see that the barman was watching them unobtrusively.

Standing up, she reached for her coat. 'Well, I've seen all I want of you, so I think I'll be leaving.' Shay didn't move a muscle, and she'd almost left the table when she stopped and looked back at him. 'You're married, aren't you?'

It had only struck her at that moment, dozens of small clues coalescing as she'd shrugged herself into her coat.

'No.'

Shay met her accusing stare blandly, and for a moment Cassie was about to apologise. Then he raised his glass to her. 'There is a fiancée in Limerick, though. Well detected.'

She walked away, consciously trying to move casually. When she reached the looped-back curtains at the entrance to the lounge, PJ appeared beside her. 'Is everything all right, Miss?'

'Fine, PJ. Thank you. The drinks were perfect.'

'I hope we'll see you here on another occasion. We're an old-fashioned place, you know, and we value our guests highly.'

To her surprise, Cassie found herself welling up. She blinked, hoping PJ hadn't noticed. 'Thanks. Yes. Maybe I will come by another time. You can make me an Old Fashioned.'

'I'd be glad of your opinion of it. I always favour Canadian whiskey because of that touch of rye.'

'It's my dad's favourite.'

PJ permitted himself a smile. 'Well, I hope I'll have the opportunity of making him one, too, if he comes home for a visit.' Seeing her surprise, he inclined his comb-over and lowered his voice discreetly. 'You're Pat and Ger Fitzgerald's granddaughter, aren't you?'

Cassie kept a straight face till she reached the pavement. Then, as she dabbed her eyes and blew her nose, she found herself giggling. Carrick might be bigger than Lissbeg but, obviously, that made no difference to the reach of the Finfarran grapevine. What would PJ have done, she wondered, if Shay had tried to take Pat and Ger Fitzgerald's granddaughter up to a hotel bedroom? Gone for him in a rugby tackle and wrestled him to the ground?

Swinging her knapsack onto her shoulder, she made her way to the car park. Right now, she was still feeling shocked and a bit upset, but she could imagine that, in time, she'd be telling the whole story as a joke against herself. Not yet, though. And definitely not if Bríd was in the audience.

39

Conor used to wonder why the Christmas book display was always so predictable. Each year he'd be sent to lift down the box of decorations from the top shelf in the kitchenette, and Miss Casey would set up a stand near the desk with an array of books under a sign that said 'CHRISTMAS TITLES'. She'd put the books on the stand, he'd wreathe it round with chains of silver beads and, once again, people would be greeted by Dickens's *A Christmas Carol*, Louisa May Alcott's *Little Women*, and a range of what Miss Casey called Golden Age detective stories, with names like *Tied Up in Tinsel* and *Murder for Christmas*.

Over in Children's Corner there'd be another stand — this time without chains of beads, in case anybody swallowed one — with copies of *The Polar Express*, *The Tailor of Gloucester*, and *How the Grinch Stole Christmas!*

He understood the predictability now, though. According to Miss Casey, there was no point in going for other titles. People liked rereading old favourites at Christmas, and that was that. You got overspill, so *Pickwick Papers* could be slipped in on the adult stand; or maybe the Puffin Classics edition of Alcott's *Eight Cousins,* that had a picture of a girl ice-skating on the cover. But, otherwise, it was same old same old.

One year Miss Casey had put up a book called *Christmas at Candleshoe,* which had nothing to do with the festive season but had a character whose name was Gerard Christmas. And, by the sound of it, all hell had broken loose. Apparently, things were made worse by the fact that the author, a guy called Michael Innes, wrote detective stories which many people in Lissbeg quite liked. But the *Candleshoe* book didn't feature his famous Inspector John Appleby, and even though the following year Miss Casey put up another one, called *There Came Both Mist and Snow,* which *was* set at Christmas and *did* have Inspector Appleby, she swore that several readers hadn't forgotten, or forgiven her.

As time passed, Conor realised that Christmas reading really was kind of sacred. Particularly when it came to kids' books.

Today, as he drove the mobile library along the southern side of the peninsula, he was carrying three copies of *How the Grinch Stole Christmas!*, four of Roddy Doyle's *Rover Saves Christmas,* and several of Hans Christian Andersen's *The Snow Queen* in the children's section, and a bunch of Agatha Christies that included *Hercule Poirot's Christmas, Star Over Bethlehem,* and *The Adventure of the Christmas Pudding.* And he seemed to have put through a hell of a lot of requests for celebrity Christmas cookbooks, and lifestyle titles about designing your own festive wrapping paper, and turning your boring old year-round home into a world of magic and sparkle.

The world beyond his windscreen today was grey and nondescript. Plenty of thin mist and no sign of snow. Even so, there was a crowd of kids playing in the school-yard as he cruised down towards a seaside village. Beyond the yard was a little pier and a narrow cove where gulls and gannets were floating above choppy grey waves. As Conor pulled in by the school gate, the children formed a straggling queue, and the classroom assistant, who'd been supervising their play, came to greet him.

It was a two-room national school, exactly

like the one he'd been to himself, and it had two entrances to the lobby, with 'Girls' carved on the lintel over one and 'Boys' over the other. According to his mam, the boys' doors used to be on the right because the Church said that a man's place was at the right hand of God, while women hung round on his left. By his day, though, anyone could go through either door, and the second one here, which had two wheelie bins pushed up against it, was clearly never used.

Conor dealt briskly with the queue, handing out loans and taking returns from gloved or mittened hands, and then helped Marian, the classroom assistant, to carry a box of copies of *The Night before Christmas* through to the lobby. Several of the kids ran alongside, explaining that their last week of term was going to be an orgy of art and craftwork, drama and writing, based around Clement Clarke Moore's poem.

One small girl with a drip on her nose solemnly explained to Conor that it was really called *A Visit from St Nicholas* because that was a name for Santa Claus in the old days. Each springy curl of her red hair was touched by a droplet of mist, and the blue eyes in her freckled face were tightly screwed up with the effort of communication. Conor squatted down and nodded in encouragement, thinking that, when Aideen was at school, she must have looked exactly like this.

'And Santa Claus is a name that *comes* from St Nicholas because, in the old days, they didn't know how to pronounce it. And the people in the book have a mouse in their house, and I'm going to put it in a picture.'

He left Marian unpacking the box of books, surrounded by excited kids, and returned to the van, where a new queue had gathered, this time composed of adults. One asked if he'd seen the preparations for Ballyfin's Winter Fest. The Harbour Hotel there had a glassed-in Winter Garden, overlooking the ocean, and the manager had arranged for decorations to be sent down from Dublin. 'They're going to do the whole thing in silver and white, and have a 1920s jazz band.'

Conor couldn't see what a 1920s jazz band had to do with Christmas but, according to the queue, Ballyfin was going for a speakeasy theme. Their Snow Queen was going to be dressed as a flapper entirely covered in swansdown.

One of the women, to whom he was handing an Agatha Christie, shrugged dismissively. 'It's bound to be synthetic and she'll probably end up scratching. But, sure, Ballyfin would put its granny out in a G-string if it meant they'd get their mitts round that trophy.' Did Conor know, she asked, that the hotel was going to be giving out free cocktails? 'They're calling them Ballyfin Icebreakers, and, basically, they're just masses of sugar whooshed up with blue Curaçao.' She knew, she said, because her nephew, who worked at the Harbour Hotel, had had to invent them.

As Conor drove away from the seaside village, he told himself it was no wonder the Lissbeg crowd were failing to get a big prize donated for their raffle. The entire peninsula seemed to be losing the run of itself, and no one was going to give anyone else a hand up the Winter Fest ladder.

For the last few weeks, on mobile days, he'd been bringing a packed lunch to eat in the van. There was a pendant he wanted to buy for Aideen for Christmas, and he'd calculated that not having pub food would pretty much save him the price of it. Up beyond Finnegan's Bar, where he'd normally take his lunch break, there was a lay-by where tourists were supposed to stop and take photographs: it was a good place to park the van so, with his mind on his peanut-butter sandwiches, Conor whizzed past Finnegan's and bowled on down the road till he came to it.

He'd hardly opened his sandwich box when there was a thump on the van door, and a face appeared at the window. 'Name of God, Conor, you're treating this yoke like a race-car!' His brother Joe stumped round to the passenger side, and climbed into the cab beside him. 'I was waiting for you back in Finnegan's car park.'

'Why?'

'Because I wanted a word.'

'And you couldn't have a word with me at home?'

Joe looked shifty, and nicked a sandwich. 'Well, no. I wanted to run something past you before talking to the folks. I think we're going to need a family conference.'

This was rich, coming from Mr Say-Nothing-You'll-Only-Upset-the-Parents, but Conor contained himself.

Having nicked another sandwich, it took Joe about ten minutes to explain himself, and Conor, who by that time had moved on to a KitKat, was left kind of gobsmacked. 'You're getting *married*?'

'Yeah.'

'To Eileen Dawson?'

'Yeah.'

'I've never even seen you out with her.'

'Yeah. Well, I don't go round jumping on desks, proclaiming my feelings like you do.'

Conor hadn't actually intended to jump on a desk to propose to Aideen in the library. It had just happened, and it was only later that he'd realised he'd never hear the end of it. Especially from Joe. Staring at his brother, he bit into his KitKat. Eileen Dawson's dad owned a big business that sold farm machinery, with branches in three counties. 'And Dawson's offered you a job?'

'Full-time, with a serious salary. But he wants to base me in Cork.'

'But . . .'

'No, hang on. I've told him it isn't going to work unless you're on board. And you're not to feel pressured. But . . . if you *could* commit to the farm, I'd chip in a labourer's wage. So you wouldn't be working on your own. And I could see about a bit of investment.'

'Like, in farm machinery?'

'Well, yeah. Dawson would be up for that. And, the thing is, Conor, this wouldn't necessarily be forever.'

'What — your marriage to Eileen?'

Joe reached over and clipped him round the head. 'No, you plank! The farm arrangement. I mean, at some point, if you wanted to do your librarian thing, we could always

361

put in a manager.'

Conor folded the chocolate wrapper carefully against his knee. His toes were curling with excitement. This could work.

Joe looked at him anxiously. 'Honestly, Conor, I don't want you feeling pressured.'

'God, no. It would actually do the opposite. I mean it would give me breathing space. Like, if Aideen and I got married next year, say. And I stuck with the farm for a few years after that. If I had a man with me, and I went for it full-time, and you bunged in some investment . . .'

'Eileen was talking about next year too. We could have a double wedding.'

'Seriously?'

'I don't see why not. And if she's up for it, her old man will be. He's a decent codger, old Dawson. I'd say he'd splash out on a really boss wedding.'

Conor blinked. 'I don't know what Aideen would think.'

'Well, no. We'd have to take it step by step and see how the girls feel. But I know Eileen will love her and I bet she'll get on with Eileen. At least, I hope to God she will, if they're going to end up sisters-in-law.'

This was all happening a bit too fast for Conor. Two things were clear, though. With him working full-time, and Joe helping with the money, the farm could get back on track, and so might Paddy. And even if it did mean parking the librarian thing, he'd be able to fulfil Aideen's dream of being a farmer's wife.

40

Hanna looked up as Jazz walked in, bringing a breath of chilly air with her. Her dark
hair was pulled back in a ponytail and the
furry collar of her coat was turned up
around her ears. Hanna moved to kiss her,
exclaiming at the touch of her cold cheek.
'You didn't walk here, did you?'

'No, but the wind is freezing. It's lovely to
see your fire.'

'Come and sit down.' She hung the coat
up and drew Jazz over to a chair. 'I'm burning driftwood. Brian and I picked up a sack-
ful down on the beach last week.' She had
left it to dry in the shed before bringing it
indoors, and now grains of sea salt embed-
ded in the wood were throwing up blue
flames among the leaping gold.

Jazz sank into the fireside chair, stretching
luxuriously. 'Do you remember the cottage
in Norfolk in winter? I think this is twice as
nice.'

Hanna laughed. 'Well, it's about five times smaller. Maybe more.'

'I don't know why we called it a cottage. It was more like a mansion.'

'It's an English thing, I suppose. At least, it is in your dad's world. A country retreat is always a cottage, regardless of size.'

'And you've always called this place a house.'

'That's what Maggie called it. And how I think of it. Practical and fit for purpose. Spuds out in the field and no roses round the door.'

'Heaven, though, compared to a shoebox in Lissbeg.'

'Oh, sweetheart, aren't you comfortable?' Hanna looked troubled. 'I've worried that I haven't a spare room for you.'

'For goodness' sake, Mum, I'm perfectly comfortable! It's a bog-standard studio apartment with everything I need. And, more to the point, it's a spit away from work.' Jazz laughed at her. 'Anyway, you should know more than anyone that living in your mum's spare room is a bad move.'

'There's a *slight* difference between me and your nan!'

Jazz giggled. 'You know, it's amazing how she and Granny Lou are getting on.'

'She can be charming when she wants to.'

'Louisa?'

'No, idiot. Mary.'

'Well, it looks like they've achieved the perfect arrangement in terms of living space. I'm not sure Nan's all that happy about Edge of the World Essentials, though.'

'Why not?'

'Oh, just because she's not the one who's running it! Or even involved.' Jazz pulled off her ankle boots and wriggled her toes in front of the fire. 'I reckon she thinks we swan around all day, having power lunches. Actually, it's more like endless hard slog.'

'Aren't you enjoying it?'

'I totally love it! It's all coming together so fast, and Saira Khan's R and D work is amazing. We made the perfect choice for our managers. And Louisa's there in the middle, like a rock. Everything's good!'

You could see that Jazz meant it: though she looked tired, her animation was real. Still, Hanna found herself worrying again about Christmas. It was clear that Louisa and Jazz had formed a unit and Mary was feeling left out. So it was likely that Christmas dinner would be served with a barrage of barbed remarks. Mary Casey's tongue was sharp anywhere, but on her own territory, where she was in charge, it could be lethal. Was it fair to leave Jazz and Louisa to

366

put up with her alone?

Nervously plaiting the fringe of the shawl that she'd drawn around her shoulders, Hanna remembered that the festive season was notorious for family squabbles. What if Jazz were to have a wretched Christmas? What if, only months after Louisa had moved in, she and Mary were to quarrel?

'I found biscuits, is that okay?' Jazz pulled out the low box that served both as a table and a footstool, and set down a tray before going back for the teapot. As she placed the pot on the hearth she noticed Hanna's face. 'What's up?'

'Nothing at all. Let's have tea.'

Sitting back on her heels, Jazz looked at her ruefully. 'Oh, *Mum*! Have you any idea how annoying it is that I can't say a word without you starting to panic?'

'I'm not —'

'Yes, you are. I mentioned that Nan was being huffy and now you're sitting there imagining World War Three.'

'Well — I've been wondering about Christmas.'

Jazz eyed her severely. 'And?'

'Nothing. Only that it's just as well that I'll be there at the bungalow, if Mary's building up to one of her strops.'

Having poured two cups of tea, Jazz

milked and sugared them deliberately. She handed one to Hanna, then went and resumed her own seat. 'You were planning something else, weren't you? You were going to go somewhere and spend Christmas with Brian.'

'Well, we did think about it. But —'

'And now you're thinking of backing out because of me.'

'Not just you. There's Louisa —'

'Who is going to be absolutely fine. She likes Nan. I think she's actually a bit sorry for her. And, unlike you, she's well able to deal with her being a prat. So am I, incidentally.' Jazz sat back, the picture of assurance. 'I'm Dad's daughter as well as yours, you know. It comes in handy sometimes.'

Hanna wasn't sure whether to laugh or cry. Just now, with her narrow face and level eyes — and her suddenly reacquired English accent — Jazz was indeed the image of Malcolm.

'Look, Mum, I adore Nan, you know I do. But I'm not you, and she's not going to dominate my life. The fact is that she's a monster, and the more someone gives her, the more she tries to take. Which isn't good for anyone involved. Even her. And the sad thing is that she knows it but she just can't help herself. Or maybe she lacks the courage to face what she does. *Any*way, the point is that it doesn't help to encourage her.'

Jazz's eyes suddenly danced, and she laughed out loud. 'Shall I tell you my own plans for Christmas Day? A lazy morning in my perfectly comfortable shoebox. Lunch with Nan and Louisa at the bungalow — which is going to be delicious because Nan's cooking always is. And then Saira Khan and I are spending the afternoon in Carrick.'

'In Carrick?'

'Volunteering at the homeless centre. We're bagging up cosmetic products as gifts for the rough sleepers. The twenty-fifth is just an ordinary day for Saira because she's Muslim but she's part of an Islamic outreach group in Carrick that helps the homeless. So that's why she's going. And, you know why I'm going, Mum? Because I want to.'

'But won't Louisa feel —'

'Obliged to entertain Nan? No, she won't. Louisa's the one that Dad and I got our genes from. I've watched her in action at business meetings. I know.'

Hanna decided the time had come to reassert her own authority. Letting the shawl slip from her shoulders, she picked up her teacup. 'Well, you've certainly organised your own day, but that doesn't mean you can organise mine.'

'But what about Brian?'

'Brian? Now you're suggesting I arrange my Christmas round him?'

Seeing Jazz's appreciative grin, Hanna smiled back at her. 'This is only a suggestion, of course, but you might consider that your egoism could well have derived from your nan's side of the family.'

'And skipped a generation when it came to you?'

'I'll have you know that I can be just as determined as any Turner if I choose.'

Jazz shrugged. Then her eyes narrowed as she looked across the hearthstone. 'Seriously, Mum, this can't go on all your life.'

For a moment there was an impasse and then, by tacit agreement, they changed the subject.

But later, as Hanna helped her into her coat and turned up the furry collar, Jazz hugged her fiercely. 'Think about what I was saying. Promise? And, honestly, Mum, there's no need to worry about Louisa. She'll probably spend Christmas afternoon on Nan's sofa, drinking martinis and wearing a party hat.'

The chill that entered the house as Jazz left was sharper than it had been earlier.

Hanna closed the door quickly, and stirred the fire to a blaze before doing the washing-up. The room, with its drawn curtains and two-foot-thick walls, was soon warm again and, as she tidied up and prepared for bed, it seemed to her that the house fitted around her as snugly as a snail's shell.

In a way it had become a totem, a certain sanctuary: the place where, without exactly planning it, she'd imagined she'd live in increasing self-sufficiency and find increasing contentment as time went on. But now, as she slipped off her kimono and curled up under the duvet, she wondered if the snail shell might have become too tight. Was fear of moving forward making her cling to what she'd created?

Reaching over to turn off the light, she suddenly wondered how Mary had felt before she'd divided the bungalow. Jazz was right when she'd said that Mary lacked the courage for honest introspection. But there were other challenges, equally requiring of courage, that Jazz was far too young to understand.

The next morning Hanna overslept, having lain awake worrying. As she frowned at the bathroom mirror, reflecting on the great truths contained in Nora Ephron's *I Feel Bad About My Neck,* she realised that today was the day of the last psalter page-turn before Christmas. Groaning, she abandoned all thought of breakfast, and settled for coffee instead.

Still, she made it to Lissbeg well before she needed to open up the library and, with the outer door secured, she unlocked the psalter's display case.

As usual, the wonder of the little book set all her worries aside. Closing her eyes, she opened a page at random, and found herself looking at an illustration that, except for a lozenge of text in the centre of each, filled a double-page spread. Facing each other across the text were four jagged icebergs, their vast size suggested by groups of tiny figures looking amazed. The background was deep indigo, pricked with green stars, and the icebergs, which were pale blue, had been touched with gleaming silver. Filling the outer margins was a flowing design that looked like streams of water cascading down the pages to form a golden lake.

The gold, silver, and coloured paints were startling in their brilliance. If — as Charles Aukin had imagined — one of the monks who had made the psalter had seen, or heard of, a copy of the Qur'an, whoever had created this illustration must have seen, or heard stories of, glaciers. And even the

Northern Lights.

But why not? One of the most popular books in European libraries in the Middle Ages was the *Voyage of the Abbot Brendan,* an Irish story which, translated into several languages, had amounted to a medieval bestseller. Some of the adventures it chronicled were obviously fantasy, but Hanna knew that Irish monks really had made long ocean voyages in shallow skin boats, consciously testing their faith and courage by choosing to risk the unknown. Some, she remembered, were said to have reached Newfoundland, and there were ruins of beehive huts they'd constructed on Iceland's Heimaey Island.

Each lozenge of text contained a single verse of the psalm. The illustration and her rudimentary knowledge of Latin recalled them to Hanna, dragged out of her memory from a concert she and Malcolm had gone to in London. *He sendeth snow like wool. He scatters hoarfrost . . . He casteth forth his ice like morsels . . .* Then there was a bit about the wind dispelling the cold. And then . . . *He maketh the ice to melt and spring water to flow . . .*

For a moment Hanna stared at the book intently, her mind focused on the beauty of the spreading golden lake. Then she noticed a little image framed in the illuminated capital letter at the beginning of the text. Sitting astride giant snails that were saddled and bridled, like horses, two cats, wearing armour and carrying lances, were locked in a frozen stand-off with their shoulders grotesquely hunched.

Stepping away from the book, she reached for her phone.

'It's me, Hanna.'

'I can see that. I've still got caller ID.'

'Jazz says we should take our relationship on to the next level.'

'Does she? What a foul expression.'

'I know. Isn't it? Revolting. But the thing is, Brian, we should.'

'Okay.'

'I think I've been scared to death. But that's just foolish.'

'Yup.'

'Because, actually, being independent means being able to face change.'

'True.'

'So, let's do this. Let's spend Christmas together in an ice hotel.'

After what seemed like an age, he spoke again. 'Was that an ice hotel or a nice hotel?'

'Oh, shut *up,* Brian.'

'Right, so.'

'And stop being monosyllabic or I might have to murder you instead.'

41

Though she'd never said so, Pat had always thought Mary and Ger were similar. He had the same bullying manner about him that Mary had. And they were both sort of pathetic, the way they could never be content. The difference was that Mary always felt entitled, while Ger felt he wasn't and it left him angry inside.

When Mary had made a move on him Pat had known it at once. With anyone else, Mary would have flirted openly but with Ger it had had to be covert. Because, though Tom would have known that she meant nothing by it, he would have been angry if he'd seen Ger hurt.

Ger had always fancied Mary. Pat knew that from the start. He'd even have risked losing Tom's friendship if he'd thought he might get her. You'd think Mary herself would have known that if she wasn't open, like she always was, Ger might have thought she was serious. You'd think she wouldn't let him tear himself apart when he hadn't an earthly chance. If you did, you'd be wasting your time, though. What would a cat do but kill a mouse?

Sometimes Pat wondered how things might have turned out if she'd not married Ger at all, but had got on a train the day Tom was wed and left Lissbeg for good. What would poor Ger have done then, though, with Mary trying to cut him out, and Tom torn between them? And what would she herself have done without Mary as her best friend?

Because, underneath all the flounce and flightiness, Mary was a rock. Pat remembered the night she'd been in labour with Frankie. Mary had marched up to the flat and told Ger not to bother with the midwife. They'd need an ambulance fast and he wasn't to wait. Later on, the doctor told Pat that, if she hadn't been got to the hospital, she could have lost the baby. All Mary said was that any bloody fool could see that she needed help.

It was the same way after Jim was born, when Pat had gone into depression. They'd told her she couldn't have another baby because they'd had to do a hysterectomy. She'd signed the paper beforehand, of course, but they hadn't asked her to read it, and she'd never thought they'd do that to her while she was asleep.

Afterwards, everyone kept saying she was lucky to have three grand lads. It was Mary who'd known how much she'd wanted a daughter. Pat had never said a word but Mary knew. She'd arrived next day with a box of chocolates, and tipped them out all over the hospital bed. Then she'd forced Pat to eat all the orange creams.

'Don't tell me you hate them, because I know you do. But you can get them down without gagging, girl, which is more than I can. Here, I'll have the strawberry ones, and they're just as bad. Then, when that lot's out of the way, we'll eat the decent ones.'

'Why can't we just leave the soft centres?'

'Holy God, Pat Fitz, have you not seen that sour-faced sister? Sitting there waiting for leavings, with the tongue hanging out of her mouth. Sure, I wouldn't leave that one the wrapping papers.'

'Well, can't you take the orange ones home?'

'What do you think I am? A bloody pack-horse? Get that lot down, and don't argue. Come here to me, now, we'll have a race.'

Forcing down chocolate creams under the sister's frosty stare had got Pat giggling. It was like being back at school, acting the eejit in the back row. Then, when they'd moved on to the rest of the chocolates, Mary had taken an envelope out of her bag. 'Hanna's after drawing you a picture.' Hanna had only been six or so, but the colouring-in was lovely. As soon as Mary saw the tears in Pat's eyes, she handed her a hazelnut whirl. 'She's a lucky girl, you know, to have you for her godmother. Because, God knows, I'm no hand at the mothering job meself.'

They just kept eating after that, and didn't talk much. But when Mary discovered that the nurses had told Pat she couldn't breast-feed, she hit the roof. Pat had a perfect right to turn herself into a cow if she wanted to, and no hospital Hitler could go round telling her what to do. It was exhausting to lie there in bed with Mary raging and calling for the registrar. But, afterwards, when the nurses helped Pat to breastfeed Jim, she was glad.

Later that night, when the lights were down, she'd opened a package that Mary had left on the locker. It was a knitting pattern for a little girl's jacket, and some needles and pink wool. In one way, that was Mary Casey, who could never knit, getting a job done for her. And if she'd thought that

Pat was going to be sitting up knitting any time soon, she'd missed her mark. But, actually, the fooling round, and feeding Jim, and remembering Hanna had made a difference. And no one but Mary could have known how they would.

So wasn't it a terrible thing that she couldn't talk to Mary now, when she needed her most?

Ger had disappeared off somewhere again, and now Pat was really worried. She'd closed her eyes to the signs for weeks. She'd told herself there was no reason he shouldn't go to Cork wearing his new blue jumper. It had a V-neck and striped cuffs, too, which weren't his style at all.

The bottom line was that she couldn't keep fooling herself. It wasn't just the jumper. Normally he'd only go down to a mart in Cork once a month. Now and again he might have a meeting there, too, but never this time of year. He'd always be below in the shop. There was no end to the work in the week before Christmas, and only the other night, he'd come up the stairs and he looking dead tired. Yet he'd disappeared off again today, and said he'd be back late.

He'd been losing weight too. Pat had noticed it. And she'd seen him checking his appearance in the glass. And then, of course, there was the bed thing. He was still spending the nights in Sonny and Jim's old room.

She was sitting at the kitchen table when the truth suddenly struck her. Ger must have met a young one down in Cork.

No sooner had she worked it out than she was dying to talk to Mary. There wasn't anyone else to talk to, for starters. But, more than that, Mary would keep her calm. You couldn't trust her not to make a drama out of nothing, yet if something was really wrong, she'd always talk sense.

But not this time. Not about Ger. Not now that Tom was dead. Mary had never forgiven Fate, or God, or whoever made the decisions, for leaving Ger to Pat and taking Tom. So now she'd feel nothing but triumph. She'd try to hide it, of course, but Pat would know.

But that was how Mary was and Pat didn't blame her. There was no point in asking someone for more than they could give. All that ever happened was that both of you got hurt. Besides, she knew that once Ger was gone Mary would be her rock again. And that would be the time she'd have need of her most.

And he would go, too. Because any young one who wanted him would want him for his money, so the plan would be to marry him and dance him into his grave. You might think that sounded daft, but it wasn't. Pat had sat over in Canada watching hours and hours of *Judge Judy.* Weren't one half of the cases on that programme about old fellows making fools of themselves? And the other half about wives who hadn't seen what was going on?

42

Most of the peninsula's pensioners seemed to have decided to adopt new hairstyles for Christmas. Cassie, who had dyed her own hair green and tipped her fringe with silver to be festive, had great difficulty dissuading Ann Flood from trying the same effect. The rest of her clients were sniffy about Ann having her hair cut at the Old Convent Centre anyway. According to the hardliners, she didn't qualify because she was still in full-time work. Still, it was the opinion of the town that the only way she'd be got out of her shop was in her coffin, and if age was the determining criterion, she certainly counted as a pensioner. So some people were willing to give her the benefit of the doubt. Everyone agreed, though, that she'd do better to keep a low profile and not be taking up Cassie's time with ridiculous requests.

Cassie had added a morning session to

her usual afternoon one. Even so, she was beginning to feel she was working on a conveyor-belt, with far too much to do and not enough time to chat. The main subject of the week was coming through loud and clear, though. Everyone was fed up because they still hadn't found a big prize for the raffle. And Phil didn't seem to notice, or even care.

Sitting in Cassie's chair, swathed in a towel, Nell Reily looked at her anxiously in the mirror. 'Most years we'd have half the tickets sold before the event, Cassie. But how can you do that when you can't say what the prize is? I've had people coming up in the streets, asking me about it, and I'm there making faces, not knowing what to say. It's a shame for us.'

Cassie nodded sympathetically. She'd heard the same complaint half a dozen times and, along with it, a dawning re-alisation among the pensioners that nowhere in Phil's publicity was there any mention of the homeless shelter in Carrick.

Maurice, the retired baker, had lowered his voice and told her that Phil thought homelessness wasn't sexy. 'She's afraid the notion of rough sleepers would put the tour-ist authorities off. You know, the crowd judging the Winter Fest.'

As it happened, Cassie knew that he was right. According to Bríd, the matter had come up after the last committee meeting, at what Phil called her post-mortem session with Ferdia, where Bríd was in attendance to take notes. Phil's decision was to play down the homeless shelter. Why, she'd asked, would Lissbeg want to link itself with one of their strongest competitor's worst negative aspects? It was Carrick's problem and Carrick could keep it. Then she'd told Bríd that, since action wasn't required, it wasn't a point to be noted.

But it wasn't Cassie's place to tell that to Maurice, or anyone else. Bríd wouldn't want her to repeat something she'd happened to overhear in number eight, and in Cassie's first job her boss had said that a stylist's chair was the equivalent of a Catholic priest's confessional — you listened, gave no opinions, and never passed anything on. It had struck her at the time as a good rule, even though it came from a guy who was known as the world's worst gossip.

Maurice got up from her chair shaking his neatly cut head sadly. 'God knows, maybe Phil's right, if that's what she thinks. But you can't go turning your back on people in trouble. If the problem's there, it's up to us all to try and do something about it.'

When her morning clients were dealt with, Cassie decided to have a sandwich in the café before going over to pick Pat up for the afternoon's creative-writing group. On her way out, she met Dan emerging from Phil's office. He had a scarlet smudge on his forehead, where he'd pushed back his hair with a painty hand. Having fallen completely into the vernacular by now, Cassie asked him what the story was.

Dan gave her the thumbs-up. 'The stalls are done and dusted, anyway. Phil's just paid me for them.'

'Good job. So the drinks are on you, then?'

'In more senses than one.'

He was looking so pleased with what was obviously a joke that she asked him what he meant.

'Well, you know the Ballyfin crowd went over the top and gave out free cocktails?'

'Complimentary, is what they called them. Though somebody said they'd spelled it "complementary" on the programmes.'

'Yeah? Well, by the sound of it, their event last weekend was a humdinger. So Phil's been going round like the Antichrist, trying to find some way to top them. And you know what happened this morning?'

'What?'

'Dekko's only after donating us a case of

brandy. So Phil's planning spiced punch, served in medieval-looking beakers.'

Cassie blinked. 'What's a medieval-looking beaker?'

'I dunno. Lumpy pottery yokes, I suppose. Or maybe just ordinary cardboard cups with something stuck around them. Anyway, Lissbeg's going to be giving out Winter Warmers.'

'What happens if the crowd's so big that the punch runs out?'

'Phil says it won't matter. She lurked round the back in Carrick and Ballyfin — the judges turn up about half an hour in, and they only stay twenty minutes. So we'll ration the punch till they're gone, and then the devil can take the hindmost.'

'But aren't the hindmost going to feel a bit cheated?'

'Maybe. But here's the genius bit. Phil's going to put a "free for all" sign over the drinks stand. And if we end up with a different kind of free for all, no one can say that we lied.'

The last bit sounded unlikely to Cassie. Probably Phil had been joking. Or maybe Dan was. Anyway, the mounting competitiveness had long since started to bore her.

She smiled at Dan and said it was really generous of Dekko to make a donation. Dan nodded enthusiastically and said it just showed, didn't it, that ordinary, hard-working businessmen were far less greedy than the high-ups? More honest, too, when it came down to it. It was brilliant knowing you were backed by someone like that.

Cassie left him with another smile, and went into the nuns' garden. The temperature had risen after a frosty snap in the weather, and it was a grey day, cold but very dry. Phil's fairy lights had already been twisted round the bare branches of the trees that bordered the herb beds, and strung between the firs by the old convent wall. The herb beds themselves were mostly covered with a dressing of leaf mould, in preparation for next year's planting, but the low hedges of rosemary and bay still had their matte grey and polished dark green leaves, and winter savory and chervil flourished in sheltered corners.

Each plant was marked by the labels on little stakes that Cassie had noticed the first day she'd come to the garden with Pat. Now, as she walked along the gravel path, she saw Saira Khan kneeling on a plastic cushion, straightening a label and removing a piece of rubbish that was entangled in some thyme.

Cassie stopped and hunkered down beside

her, holding open the mouth of the sack into which Saira was gathering litter. Saira dropped a handful of chewing-gum wrappers and cigarette butts into the sack and smiled her thanks.

'There's not a lot to do outdoors in a herb garden in winter. But they say we're due for another change in the weather, so it's best to get out and tidy up while you can.'

Cassie glanced round. 'It's looking good.'

In summer the flowering herbs probably softened the lines of the garden, but now you could see how the beds and paths were laid out. Everything radiated from St Francis in the centre of the fountain. The statue faced the stained-glass windows in the high wall against which the rows of headstones in the nuns' graveyard were enclosed by cast-iron railings. In the wintry garden, where Phil's fairy lights had still to be lit, the stained glass above the graves offered tall streaks of dull colour, the lead tracery echoing the interlaced pattern of vines and twigs from which the crimson Virginia creeper leaves had fallen and drifted in heaps.

At first it seemed to Cassie that the coloured glass and fallen leaves were the only vibrant splashes in the grey-green setting. Then her eye was caught by a glint of metal where a brass plaque on the back of a bench caught the afternoon sunlight. 'Is that the bench they put up for the nun that used to work in the garden? The one who's buried over there?'

Saira nodded. 'Sister Michael. I never knew her. But I use her herb book. The one Hanna has in the library.'

'Did Sister Michael write it?'

'I don't think so. She just worked in the garden and the kitchen. They gave it to her, I think, so she'd know how to use the herbs.' Saira shook the rubbish down to the bottom of the sack. 'Are you coming to the writing group this afternoon?'

Since it was the last session before Christmas, Hanna had asked them each to bring a book they were fond of, and to read their favourite paragraph to the group. Cassie had pushed a copy of Dervla Murphy's *The Waiting Land* into her knapsack that morning: she'd found it last week on a shelf in number eight, with Aideen's Aunt Bridge's name written inside. As it was a travel book, she'd started it, and now she was hooked. She'd only got halfway through yet, but it was full of amazing descriptions so it shouldn't be hard to pick a paragraph. Taking it out, she showed it to Saira, and told her that Pat had chosen something too.

'Maybe she's happier reading someone else's words than writing her own.'

Cassie nodded, wondering if they were going to find themselves listening to Keats.

Saira said she'd decided on a passage from Sister Michael's herb book. 'The names of the flowers and plants are like a poem.'

That sounded strange but, later, as they all sat in a circle in the reading room, Cassie realised she'd been right.

'Blackberry, calendula, chamomile, cleavers, comfrey, dandelion, elder . . .' Saira glanced round the circle and then looked back at the book '. . . fennel, goldenseal, gumweed, hawthorn, mugwort, marshmallow, nettle, peppermint, Skullcap, valerian. Willow bark. Yarrow. Yellow dock.' She looked pleased as everyone clapped, and the book was examined and exclaimed over. Her low voice with its singsong inflections had made poetry out of what was hardly more than an instruction manual.

Then, when Ferdia had read from a second-century Greek satire, which he claimed was the earliest sci-fi book, Mr Maguire came out with an unexpectedly intense paragraph from a book called *Madame Bovary,* in which the newly-wed heroine finds her husband's dead wife's dried bridal bouquet in their bedroom.

Darina was absent, having gone to Carrick to buy Christmas presents. So, since Cassie had read already, Hanna turned to Pat.

When Cassie had picked her up, after lunch, Pat had seemed a bit down. But now she looked like a kid expecting a treat. She produced a book bristling with bookmarks, and looked earnestly at Hanna. 'I didn't choose a paragraph. I picked out short little bits that I like all the way through the book.'

You could see Mr Maguire about to point out that that wasn't the exercise, but Hanna jumped in and said it was a fine plan.

It sounded like a kids' book. Pat began on the first page with a description of a house so low, and with thatch so covered in grass, that no one would have seen it if it wasn't whitewashed. Then there were bits about ballad singers at a fair, gold coins hidden in a teapot, and a gypsy camp. Between each few sentences she turned the pages to her next bookmark, and another little series of images emerged, as if painted on postage stamps. As she came towards the end, she explained that, at one point in the story, there was a magic cauldron that produced any food at all that a person could wish for.

'And what does Eileen, the little girl, choose? Only white pudding and tomatoes.'

Pat smiled across at Cassie. 'I thought that bit was great.' She flipped to the next marker and read a description of the house on Christmas Eve, with a candle burning in the uncurtained window, the pictures framed in holly, and the smell of spices and herbs. 'And the child gets a book for a present, and it makes a big impression on her. It draws her away on adventures but, then, in the end, it draws her back. And that's the point. The children know that their mam and dad would be desperate if they never came home.'

Pat sat back, a little breathless, and Saira said that the book sounded beautiful. 'What's it called?'

Pat turned to Cassie. 'Well, Cassie knows the answer to that, don't you?'

Cassie shook her head. 'Not me. I've never read it. You tell us.'

There was a weird pause in which Pat pressed the book to her chest. For a moment her face twisted. Then it went blank. Cassie wasn't sure if anyone else was aware of what had just happened. All she could see was the book's title, visible now between Pat's clutching fingers. It was *The Turf-Cutter's Donkey.*

With a sickening jolt, she remembered the conversation they'd had in Toronto. This was the book Pat had lovingly sent for her thirteenth birthday. The book she'd lied about and said she loved though, in fact, she'd never opened it. And now Pat was looking at her as though she'd struck her in the face.

43

It snowed overnight. When Cassie got up to take her first mug of tea back to bed, white flakes were still whirling past the kitchen window. Later, having had breakfast, she was tempted to crawl back under the duvet. But she'd promised to gather holly and ivy for the Winter Fest and, though she'd grown increasingly disenchanted by the idea of the event, she couldn't very well back out.

The weather had cleared by the time she left the house. Although it had been nothing like a proper Canadian snowfall, the snow on the ground was a good four inches thick, with an icy crust that crunched beneath her feet.

As soon as she reached the back roads, she hardly recognised the landscape. The snow-capped peaks of Knockinver were silver against the sky. The ditches that lined the roads were white and sparkling, and the footprints of birds and small animals made tracks in the empty fields. In a few places, cattle were huddled round a field gate but, for the most part, the only farm animals Cassie could see were sheep, gathered under hedges, their fleece grey-white against the snow.

During the night, she'd woken repeatedly, racked with remorse for what she'd done to Pat. Finding it impossible to go back to sleep, she'd turned on her bedside lamp and read another chapter of *The Waiting Land*. At least when you were reading you weren't thinking, and each time, after a while, she'd manage to drop off for an hour or two, before waking up again feeling wretched. Then, thumping her pillow for what had felt like the millionth time, she'd remembered her own sense of rejection and humiliation when Mom had failed to appreciate the pendant she'd brought from Barbados. How had poor Pat coped year after year when each of her carefully chosen gifts had appeared to go unheeded?

Immediately after the session in the library, Pat had slipped out ahead of her and, giving her a few minutes, so they wouldn't look foolish, Cassie had run across the road in pursuit. What she'd wanted to do was to run away but, since moral cowardice had caused this mess, she knew she mustn't indulge in it again.

Pat was standing with her back to the kitchen door, putting the kettle on. *The Turf-Cutter's Donkey* was lying on the table. Cassie could see that it was a library copy in a plastic cover with a catalogue number pasted across its spine. Because, of course, Pat's own copy was thousands of miles away, probably thrust to the back of a cupboard or, worse still, thrown in the trash and buried in landfill.

And the awful thing was that Pat had been so forgiving. Stammering and feeling terrible, Cassie had tried to explain, but Pat had told her gently that it was fine. 'You're not to worry, love, because I know what happened. You were only trying to make me feel good — and you did. Anyway, it was my fault in the first place. You were probably far too old for the book when I sent it to you.'

'But I lied to you, Pat, and I'm so sorry. I shouldn't have.'

'Well, no, but you're not to make a thing of it. I get things wrong.'

'I did love the Christmas card. I kept it for years.'

Pat smiled wanly and Cassie nearly burst into tears. 'Truly. I did. It's why I'm here now. Honestly, Pat. If you hadn't sent it, I'd never have found my way here. And now that I'm here, I feel like I've come home. And that's because of you.'

Pat had made tea, which Cassie was glad of because she still felt shaky and close to tears. They'd sat on either side of the kitchen table, holding onto the hot mugs as if they were lifelines, and talking themselves back to some kind of normality.

After a while Cassie said she'd love to read *The Turf-Cutter's Donkey* and Pat smiled and told her she'd have to borrow it from the library. 'Or you could read it over Christmas. It doesn't need to go back for another ten days.'

Still clutching the mug, Cassie had stretched out a hand. 'I've been wanting to ask, would it be okay if I came and spent Christmas Day here?'

Pat went pink with pleasure. 'Really? Don't you know you'd be more than welcome? I'd thought maybe you'd be off somewhere with Shay.'

With an obscure sense that exposing her own bad judgement would amount to doing penance for her lie, Cassie explained that she'd thought so, too, but that Shay had turned out to be a cheat.

Pat put down her own mug of tea and grasped Cassie's hand tightly. 'Oh, Holy

God, love, aren't women awful eejits? The way we can't see what's there in front of our eyes!'

Surprised by her vehemence, Cassie had tried to play things down. 'Well, it's not like my life was invested in the guy. I'll be far happier here with you and Ger. We'll have a proper family Christmas, and raise our glasses to real relationships.'

Pat nodded emphatically. But her lips had trembled and, for a moment, she'd looked so old and frail that Cassie cursed herself mentally for having upset her.

Now, driving through the snowy landscape, she told herself that at least she'd had the sense not to demand reassurance of her forgiveness. Instead she'd taken *The Turf-Cutter's Donkey* to the press, and placed it on the shelf beside the lustre vase, saying she'd save it to read beside the range on Christmas Day.

There were access trails from the road into the forest. Conor had told her that, a few years ago, lads from Carrick used to come in vans to strip the trees and sell the holly, but Fury and The Divil had caught them and seen them off. It sounded like Fury still took a proprietary interest in the forest, even though his family no longer owned it. According to Conor, it belonged to some guy who now lived abroad.

Gingerly navigating the packed snow, Cassie turned off the tarmac road, and bumped down a trail. The surface here was hard as iron and ice crystals sparkled in the ruts. As you went farther into the forest, the pointed firs and pines gave way to oaks, interspersed with smaller deciduous trees. Every so often a jay or a starling would swoop past with its feathers puffed out against the cold.

Before long, peering between the frosted trunks and branches by the trail, Cassie saw a flash of scarlet. There was a group of three branching holly trees, close together in a little clearing, where the light had encouraged their growth. Two were laden with berries, and the third had only gleaming spiny leaves. She had brought a long-handled hedge-cutter, found for her by Aideen in the shed at number eight, and a large plastic tarpaulin, which she hefted onto her shoulder when she got out of the car.

It wasn't far to wade through the undergrowth to the hollies and, hanging from the branches of another tree nearby, she saw long tendrils of ivy. Some were almost as fine as yarn, and others had clusters of black berries among their green, gold-tipped leaves. Spreading out the tarpaulin, she set to work methodically, piling bright-berried holly branches onto the plastic, and adding the longest trails of ivy she could reach. When it seemed she had as much as she could carry, she made a bag by turning the four corners of the tarpaulin to the centre, wincing as the sharp leaves pricked her wrists.

She was about to heave the load onto her back when a small, short-haired terrier shot into the clearing, barking and showing its teeth. Before she could react, a fallen branch cracked like a pistol-shot and Fury O'Shea appeared from behind a tree. He clicked his teeth as he strode towards her, but the dog had already rolled over at her feet.

'He's been known to bite intruders.' Fury looked down in disgust at The Divil's ingratiating wriggling.

Cassie scratched The Divil's chest with the toe of her boot. 'Maybe he thinks I'm intruding in a good cause.'

'Are you?'

'I'm not sure, actually.' She hoisted the bulging tarpaulin onto her back. 'This lot's for the Winter Fest.'

Fury put his gloved hand under the load to secure it, and together they made their way back to her car.

Once the load was in the trunk, Cassie realised that her own hands were freezing. Blowing on them ineffectually, she said she'd better get on. Fury clicked his fingers at The Divil, who was conscientiously peeing on all four wheels of the car. 'Would you say that a cup of tea would help restore the circulation?'

She looked around, wondering if he meant they were near a tea shop, and Fury chortled. 'What's happened to your bump for locality? My place is over there beyond the trees.'

Leaving the car parked by the trail, Cassie followed his unerring path through the wintry forest, treading in his footsteps, as if she were St Wenceslas's page. Behind them, The Divil bounced like a rubber ball, avoiding ruts and roots and clinging briars, and sneezing in outrage when his muzzle dipped in the snow.

The big room was as she remembered it, with the addition of a blazing log fire on the hearth. Fury removed the fireguard and hung his socks on the fender, shuffling into an old pair of carpet slippers and going to make the tea.

Cassie hung her coat on the back of a chair and asked if his boots were leaking.

'Why?'

'Well, because you're drying your socks.'

'Holy God, woman, if you must be inquisitive, you might avoid jumping to conclusions. I'm warming them, not drying them. Is that all right with you?'

'But don't your feet get cold with no socks on?'

'They do not.' He nodded at the table, at which The Divil was already seated, looking expectant. 'What do you think of the finished article?'

The crib figures were set out in rows on the newspaper. Each had been completed and, apparently, buffed with a piece of rag dipped in oil. The buffing had brought out the grain and the colours of the various woods, and the Infant now lay in a manger on which wisps of hay, spilling over the sides, had been carved in intricate detail.

When Cassie picked it up, Fury jerked his head at it. 'That's holly wood. Beautiful to work.'

Cassie looked at the figure of St Joseph: it was a young man, squatting with his forehead on his crossed arms, which rested on his raised knees. The carved Virgin was lying on her side with a blanket drawn over her body, one elbow bent and her head propped on her hand. The folds of the blanket and her dishevelled hair were as delicately carved as the hay spilling out of

403

the manger, but you could see that the fabric was rough, like the blanket that swaddled the Infant. 'Aren't these two usually shown kneeling, worshipping the child?'

Fury placed a saucer of tea in front of The Divil. 'Ay, well, you'd be pretty knackered if you'd been wandering the streets for hours with a pregnant wife, looking for shelter. And you probably wouldn't be kneeling in adoration if you'd just given birth.'

Cassie set the two figures on either side of the Infant in the manger. The red oak ox and the dark dog were ranged behind them, along with the sheep, the ass and the shepherds, and the wise men in their flowing robes, with a sleigh piled with gifts and furs. Accepting a mug of tea from Fury, she looked up at him. 'You know when you were away in England? Why didn't you want to come home?'

He leaned forward to pour milk into The Divil's tea. 'I take it you've been hearing stories about your own family?'

'No, I haven't, that's the point. My dad and my uncle Jim went away and they haven't come home to visit. Ever. I never thought about it till I got here myself, but it's weird.'

'Ay, well, maybe it's their business, not yours.'

Cassie wrinkled her nose, feeling repressed again. She turned back to the crib figures, thinking that, in a shop, they'd cost a fortune. Then she had an idea. 'Are you going to use these as a Christmas decoration?'

Fury snorted again. 'Not at all, girl. Stick 'em at the back of the shed, probably. I only did them for pastime when there was nothing on TV.'

'Can I have them?'

She blushed as he raised an eyebrow at her.

'Sorry. I don't mean to be pushy. And it's not for myself. It's just the Lissbeg lot haven't found a prize for their raffle. And the old dears are really upset. I mean, the pensioners . . .' She stopped, realising that Fury must be a pensioner himself. He didn't seem offended, though, so she hurried on. '. . . and the raffle's in aid of a homeless shelter, so this would be kind of appropriate. You know, people wandering the streets with nowhere to stay.'

By way of reply, he went and took a pile of old newspapers from a box beside the hearth. 'Wrap them up properly, mind, and you might as well take the rag with you, and give them a buff up when you set them out.'

As she stood up and walked to the door, he took her by the elbow. 'My dad left everything to my brother, Paudie, because Paudie was the eldest. I don't suppose I thought he'd made the right choice. Well, I knew he hadn't, because Paudie was a bloody wastrel. My mother, who might have talked a bit of sense into my father, was dead, and he was a man who talked to no one, so the way it was left only emerged when he died.'

He paused for a moment and shrugged before going on. 'I don't think I blamed Paudie but it took a long time for me to forgive my father, who hadn't the guts to question the stupid rules he'd grown up with. It's an old story, and I'd say it's messed up many a family the world over.'

The Divil, who'd insinuated his nose between Fury and the doorjamb, tried to wriggle past into the snow. Fury hooked a foot under his belly and scooped him back into the house. Then he let go of Cassie's elbow. 'I'll tell you two things I've learned, girl, since I came back to Finfarran. First, that you do best to make your peace with the past while the people you left are still in the land of the living. And, secondly, that it's never too late to come home.'

44

It was hardly a week since Joe had dropped his bombshell, and Conor couldn't believe how fast things had moved.

Joe had gone home that night and talked to Paddy, and the next evening the four of them had sat down together in the kitchen and a five-year plan had got mapped out. You'd think, by the way Paddy responded, that he'd been dying for the chance to start the conversation, and for the first while, Conor had felt kind of miffed. How well Joe had kept his heels dug in when he'd no reason of his own to get things moving. Now that it was his wedding, not Conor's, in the balance, he was moving at the speed of light.

It was all good, though. Conor could see that. And, judging by his mam's face, it was a big relief to her. In fairness, though, her first instinct was to turn round to him. 'You've no doubts now, Conor, have you?

This has to work for you as well. It's not all about Joe.'

Joe hadn't liked that much but Orla wasn't going to let him make the running at Conor's expense. Paddy was the same, fair dos to him. Though, when he asked the same question, it was perfectly clear what answer he wanted. 'You're sure, boy? Because we can't start out half cocked.'

Orla had put a hand on his arm. 'There's Aideen to think of too.'

Paddy looked aggrieved. 'Nobody's saying she can't have whatever damn wedding she likes.'

'Ah, it's not just the wedding, Paddy, and you know it. If Conor decides to commit to the farm it'll make a difference to Aideen, as well as to him.'

You could see that one not computing with Paddy, who stuck his jaw out, not liking to be crossed. But Conor wasn't worried because, if he knew nothing else, he knew that Aideen would be all for Joe's plan.

The family spent ages talking that night, looking at ways and means and getting out maps of the farm. They'd been to a solicitor since then, and discussed how to organise deeds and settle money, and how to be cost-effective when it came to tax. A couple of times Orla had asked if he'd talked yet to

Aideen, but Conor had decided to hold back until he was sure of his ground. Because of his depression, Paddy had been known to get bullish, and you'd want to be sure he was really okay with all the solicitor said. And there was Orla herself to be thought about too. She might well have her own ideas about Aideen moving in.

He cornered Orla one evening when she was shutting in the hens. Bid, the sheepdog, was circling round behind her, as if the hens weren't well used to putting themselves to bed at dusk. Conor shot the bolt on the shed door, and clicked his fingers to bring the dog to heel. His mam put her back against the wall and smiled at him. 'Well, what is it?'

You could never fool Orla, even though she didn't say much. Conor put his own shoulders against the wall beside her. 'I was only wondering — how are you going to feel with Aideen in the house? I mean, she can get a bit carried away. She's not used to a farm.'

Orla bumped him with her shoulder. 'Well, there won't be blood on the hearth-stone, if that's what you're worried about! Aideen's a dote, Conor. And I know what you mean. But it won't be a problem. We'll get on fine. And won't she have her own business to go out to every day?'

'Well, I don't know . . .'

'No. And you won't know till you talk to her. I understand why you've held back, but you do need to sit down with her. She ought to be part of this planning process, if things are going to work.'

So today Conor had decided that that was what he would do. As soon as he'd got the cows fed, and himself cleaned up, he'd fix to meet Aideen and talk the whole thing through.

The snow was still white on the top fields but lower down, where the cattle were, it was just a patchy slick. Heaving the last bale of silage off the tractor, Conor slit the plastic with his knife. The freezing ground around the galvanised-iron feeder was already churned into muck, through which the eager cows pushed their way to the food.

Sloshing through mud to the icy trough, Conor wriggled the frozen rubber pipe to release the flow of water from the well in the field above. You had to be up and down to the cows all the time in this weather — if it wasn't feeding them, it was making sure they had water: and, if you didn't keep a hawk's eye on the pipes they'd be backing up or bursting, and the council would be out complaining about the roads getting covered in ice.

The farm work done, he decided to take the Vespa to Lissbeg, rather than the car, which would have been the warmer option. With only three days to Christmas, the motorway was crowded with people off to do their shopping in Carrick, so being able to weave in and out through the traffic would save him a good half-hour.

He left the bike in the car park on Broad Street and nipped through the library courtyard, which was the quickest way to the café. Today was the last day before Miss Casey's Christmas break, and he hoped she wouldn't grab him with more instructions for keeping the place from burning down, blowing up, or being broken into. He'd borne them cheerfully enough yesterday, but he didn't want a second session now, with Aideen waiting for him. No voice summoned him, though, so he went through to the nuns' garden, where a couple of guys from the council were manhandling Christmas trees, planted in barrels, onto the walks.

Phil had decided at the last moment that the garden didn't look festive enough and, at the rate she was going, it looked to Conor like she'd soon add a bouncy castle and neon penguins. Yesterday she'd rushed into the library saying it'd be awfully medieval

411

to have the carols round the psalter when the judges came through. When Miss Casey asked what carols she had in mind, she'd said it'd have to be whatever they'd already practised, but, since 'Feliz Navidad' was in Latin, it ought to be fine.

Afterwards Miss Casey had gone round in conniptions for hours because, apparently, 'Feliz Navidad' had been written in Spanish in 1970.

The Garden Café now had a plywood arch surmounting its doorway with 'Cakes and Ale' painted on a scroll held by two cartoon monks. When Conor got inside, Aideen was sitting at a corner table. As usual, his heart lurched when he saw her. She was wearing a wine-coloured Puffa jacket that looked great with her red hair.

When he sat down at the table, she seemed anxious. 'How come you're texting me at eleven in the morning? Is everything okay?'

'Everything's grand. I just wanted us to talk.'

He was taking a deep breath when Aideen nodded and started to gabble. 'I've been thinking that too. And I keep trying to find the right moment. But it isn't easy. Cassie and Bríd keep telling me that I ought to say it out straight. Well, Cassie does . . . Well, no, she doesn't, actually, because she says I have to be *really* sure in my own mind first . . .' She leaned forward, looking intense. 'But I *am* sure, Conor. I've thought it all through, and I know it's the right thing. For both of us. In the long run. And it's not you. Honestly. It's me.'

Conor's jaw dropped. You didn't have to spend your life reading chick-lit to know what 'it's not you, it's me' meant. Here he was, full of plans for the future. And here was Aideen, dumping him. In the middle of the Garden Café.

He could hear his voice going funny. He could hear her interrupting him, too, but the big thing was to keep going and not to let her finish. Because, if once she said it out loud, then it would be said.

'Listen to me, Aideen, no, shut up, I just want to tell you —'

'Look, I really want to say this —'

'No, but the thing is —'

'— I know I've been really selfish, not coming out straight.'

'I could have said this a week ago, but I was holding back to make sure things were perfect —'

'I just want you to follow your heart and go and become a librarian.'

'I want to chuck the librarian thing and really commit to the farm.'

They both stopped, having spoken in chorus. Then Conor's phone suddenly buzzed and he nearly hit the roof. 'Holy shit!' Dragging the phone from his back pocket, he glared at a text from Joe: *Is she up4 the dbl wedding?*

At the far side of the table, Aideen's eyes were out on stalks. 'Did you just say you want to commit to the farm?'

'Did *you* just say you want me to be a librarian?'

'Yes. But I don't.'

'Then why, in the name of God?'

Aideen's blue eyes filled with tears. 'Conor, I just want us to be *happy.*'

'Right. Hold that thought.'

Sticking his phone back in his pocket, Conor shot over to the counter and came back with two cups of tea. The thing to do was to start again, and go at this methodically. If Bríd wanted Aideen back at the deli, she could damn well wait for her. And if Joe wanted answers, he could bloody well join the queue.

Half an hour later he was back on the Vespa, in a state of bliss. It had snowed while he was indoors and the roads, which, earlier, had been grey with freezing slush, had a new layer of sparkling white on them, like icing on a cake. A few feather-light

414

snowflakes still whirled down on the icy wind, but the sun hung in the sky like a pale gold disc.

Everything was settled. Aideen was coming to the farm for her Christmas dinner, and Joe's Eileen had been invited along for the tea. They'd have plenty of time for talk, and to get the measure of each other, and they'd all start down a new track in the New Year.

As he whizzed along between high ditches, a car swung onto the road from a turning up ahead, and sped past him. The driver was Dekko, Dan Cafferky's mate, but it was too late to salute him and, anyway, he'd been going so fast that Conor had instinctively tightened his grip on the handlebars. The turning was one that he needed to take himself so, leaning over, he swung to the left, consciously avoiding Dekko's tyre tracks for the pleasure of tracing his own single curve on the gleaming snow.

As he straightened up and sped on, he saw what looked like a log or a bag of rubbish up ahead of him. Then, squinting through his goggles as he came closer, he realised it wasn't a log or a bin bag. It was a body in a dark coat, huddled at the side of the road.

Braking so hard that the bike skidded, he jumped off, pushed up his goggles and ran towards what he could now see was an elderly woman. He knelt down beside her and it was Nell Reily. There was colour in her face and, though her lips were pale, she didn't seem to be freezing. So she couldn't have been there too long.

Conor got his arm under her shoulders and half lifted her. But before he could move her further, she caught hold of his hand. 'Take it easy, there. I'd say my ankle's broken. Maybe the wrist on that side as well.'

'Jesus, Nell, were you knocked down or what happened?'

'It was only a car went past me too fast and I lost my balance.' Laughing weakly, she gestured at a couple of envelopes beside her on the snow. 'Wouldn't Christmas cards drive you mad, Conor, all the same? We had two arrive in the post today from people I hadn't sent one to. So I told my mother I'd walk down to the box below at the cross. And didn't I know well that they'd never have got there in time for Christmas anyway!'

She was beginning to shiver violently, and Conor looked round, feeling frantic. He couldn't put an old woman with broken bones up on the Vespa behind him, and even if he got his jacket round her, she mustn't lie here in the cold while he called for help. Then, with a gasp of relief, he saw a car edge round the corner. When it pulled up beside them, Cassie leaned out and asked what was wrong.

45

The A and E Department at Carrick's Mary
Mother of God Hospital was crowded, but
Nell, who had been a nurse there in the
past, was philosophical. Once you were tri-
aged, you were on a list, she told Cassie,
and you'd get dealt with eventually. 'I'd say
I'm in a queue for X-ray and, by the look of
the lot that's got here before me, I'll be here
a while.'

Among the groups and individuals sitting
waiting for attention were numbers of
people who appeared to be the worse for
drink imbibed at Christmas parties. Others,
like Nell, were victims of the unusual icy
weather conditions. Interspersed between
them, subdued kids were attended by anxious mothers, and a large man in a reindeer
suit sat with his head between his knees and
his antlers dangling from his hand.

Nell was eager for Cassie to go home and
leave her. Conor, she said, had called her

nephew Paul in Ballyfin, who would come and pick her up, once they knew how things stood. He'd be back in the house now, keeping an eye on her mother, and Nell would give him a shout, as and when.

Not wanting to abandon her, Cassie hung on for an hour or so, fetching one coffee after another from a machine in the corner. And Nell got more and more concerned by the thought of her driving home through the snow. 'It gets dark awful early, these days, and I wouldn't like to be the cause of you coping on the motorway and you not used to the left-hand car.'

It was hardly mid-afternoon, yet the lights in the waiting area had been turned on, and beyond the plate-glass windows, the low, scurrying clouds loomed dark as lead. So, with one eye on the window and the other on the weather forecast on a TV screen above the reception desk, Cassie decided Nell was probably right.

As soon as the decision was made, Nell relaxed, and before Cassie left, she asked her to fetch her a magazine, saying she supposed she'd better get used to reading, as she wouldn't be doing any lacemaking for a good while to come. 'And it'll be Christmas at the nephew's this year, I suppose, but what matter when I didn't break my neck!'

Leaving her ensconced with a copy of *Woman's Way,* Cassie left the crowded reception area and went to find a washroom before going back to the car. She emerged having dried her hands on the most powerful air-drier imaginable, and told herself wryly that, if the X-ray department was equally ultra-tech, Nell would be fine.

There was an overhead sign just outside the washroom, showing the way to the hospital's coffee shop. With luck, they'd serve something better there than the ghastly stuff from the drinks machine and, now that Cassie thought of it, she discovered she was starving. It should be at least an hour before dusk fell properly so, following the colour-coded lines on the floor, she set off down a corridor to grab a coffee and a snack.

Pretty soon, the lines became obliterated by scuff marks caused by trolley wheels, and Cassie realised she'd turned the wrong way. Irritated, she retraced her steps, glancing occasionally through open doorways, where rows of bored or worried-looking people sat slumped uncomfortably on plastic chairs or struggled hurriedly to their feet when their names were called.

The signs over these doors read 'MCATTS', 'Walk-In Sex Health' and 'Orthopaedic Outpatients'. As she passed, it struck Cassie that everyone waiting looked extremely dapper.

With a grin, she remembered hearing of kids who were warned not to go out with holey vests on, lest they'd find themselves in a hospital where their iniquity would be revealed. Clearly the same principle applied here in the outpatients' clinics where, unlike the A and E patients, people had known when they'd set off this morning that they'd end up stripped to their underwear, or with some supercilious stranger peering at their feet.

She was speeding up, thinking she'd found her way again, when, out of the corner of her eye, she saw a familiar shade of blue. There, to her amazement, was Ger, emerging from a clinic, carrying a piece of paper in his hand. He looked very small and wizened under the hospital's harsh strip lighting, and he was wearing the blue V-neck sweater that she and Pat had bought him in the mall.

The first thing that occurred to Cassie was that this was none of her business. She hadn't expected to encounter her grandad here, but that wasn't surprising. After all, she'd hardly seen anything of him since she'd arrived in Ireland, so she couldn't expect to know where he'd be on any given day.

But, having seen her, Ger stopped dead and appeared to panic. At first it seemed that he would bolt. Then he shoved the piece of paper into his pocket, scuttled across the corridor and edged her into a corner, as if trying to make sure that they weren't seen. And then, once he'd got her there, he seemed unable to speak.

Feeling that she could be stuck for life between her grandad and a fire extinguisher, Cassie asked if he fancied a sit-down. There was no reason to think he would, but she had to come up with something. After a moment, in which he seemed to be trying to make up his mind, he nodded, and led the way unerringly to the coffee shop she'd been searching for.

As she sat opposite him with what proved to be yet another cup of horrible brown liquid, Cassie had no idea what to say next. Then, as if producing evidence in court, Ger pulled out the piece of paper and flattened it on the table. He didn't have long to talk, he said, because he had to go for a blood test.

Cassie registered suitably polite interest. Ger folded the paper again, and thrust it back into his pocket. 'They give you the form in the clinic and you take it up to Bloods.'

'Right. Well, I suppose they have to have a system.'

'Oh, they're fierce organised, all right. You couldn't better them.'

There was a pause in which Cassie tried to visualise the sign over the door from which he'd emerged. But either she hadn't seen it or she hadn't been paying attention. Taking a deep breath, and feeling fairly certain it hadn't been Walk-In Sex Health, she asked him which clinic he attended.

'Just a heart place.'

'Oh.'

'It's my age, really. They diagnosed a kind of a heart-failing problem.'

'Wow. I'm sorry.'

'Yes. Well, that's all it is. After we came back from Canada I had to go down for tests in Cork. One thing and another, you know, till they worked out what was the problem. And now I have to come here to the clinic, till they fix on the medication.'

'And that's — okay, is it?'

'God, yes. Not a bother on me. They balance it out, you see, till they'd have the formula right. Optimisation, they call it. Two of the pink pills and three of the yellow ones, say. Morning times or evenings, whichever works best. Then that's what they'll stick to. But they'll keep an eye on it. To make sure it's all game ball.'

As Cassie had spoken hardly six words to him on any previous occasion, it felt weird to be sitting there discussing his medication.

Ger tapped the pocket into which he'd pushed the form. 'You mightn't like the syringes, or the fella in there with the needle, but you'd have to admit they do a grand job in Bloods.' Then, leaning forward, he lowered his voice conspiratorially. 'The thing is, though, that I haven't mentioned the old heart to your granny. I wouldn't want to worry her.'

Cassie was nodding sympathetically when, suddenly, she remembered a conversation with Pat. It was after the *Turf-Cutter's Donkey* disaster. They'd been sitting at the table. She'd just told Pat that Shay was a cheater. And Pat had said that women never saw what was right in front of their eyes. Cassie's eyes widened. Pat had been so vehement. And so sad . . . She blinked in horror, but Ger didn't seem to notice.

Instead he lowered his voice even further. 'No, you see, I wouldn't want Pat troubled. Not before Christmas. She'd only get upset.'

Choosing her words carefully, Cassie

asked him if *not* telling Pat might be worse. 'I mean, if she doesn't know where you've been going, she could be imagining all sorts.'

Ger frowned. 'Like what?'

'Well, I dunno. That you had some other reason for disappearing off to Cork.' Then — seeing his puzzled expression — she threw caution to the winds. 'Look, okay, you might as well know this. I reckon she thinks you're having an affair.'

There was an astonished silence in which Ger looked completely blank.

Out of the corner of her eye, Cassie saw that a woman at the next table was trying to eavesdrop. Lowering her own voice, she leaned forward. Inevitably, the woman strained harder to hear them, and Cassie found herself cupping her mouth with her hand. 'I'm not just making it up. Really. The other day, we were talking and . . . Honestly, Ger, I know I'm right.'

For a moment Ger's face expressed nothing but outrage. Then, as he stared at Cassie, she saw dismay dawn in his eyes. 'But why would she think that, for God's sake?'

It seemed a bit mad to mention *Judge Judy.* Anyway, it couldn't just be about that. There must be some other reason, to do with Ger and Pat's relationship. Perhaps

Ger had a history of cheating, and Pat had spent half her life ignoring the truth. But, curious though Cassie was by nature, she wasn't about to interrogate her grandad about his marriage. Anyway, the point was that, whatever might have happened in the past, he certainly hadn't got up this morning and put on his blue sweater to go philandering. This was about what was going on right now.

Casting a cold glance at the inquisitive woman, she reached out and grasped Ger's hand. 'I don't know why Pat should think so. But she does, Ger. And you have to reassure her. You have to tell her what's really going on.'

46

Christmas Eve in Phil's office started on a note of hysteria. The pottery that had promised to provide beakers for the vital Winter Warmers had failed to deliver.

When Bríd looked into the office to pick up some labels she found Phil shouting blue murder on the phone, and Ferdia in the background, looking resigned. 'Should I come back later?'

He threw her a deadpan look. 'It's the Pretty Pots crowd, miles out beyond Carrick. Their van's had a flat.'

The original plan had been to get beakers from a potter who worked in the Convent Centre but as she hadn't had anything deemed suitable Phil had gone further afield.

She finished the call and clutched her head. 'What can you *do* when people won't keep their *word*?'

'Look, leave it to Aideen and me. We'll

427

sort something. Aideen's going to be handing the punch out anyway. We're leaving it till the last minute to make it up.'

Phil ran a hand through her hair and adjusted her zebra specs. 'Would you, Bríd? Thank you! And, yes, don't go putting it out till you see the judges coming.' The journalists and reporters, she said, would be arriving simultaneously, and Ferdia would corral them, and present them with press packs, before turning them loose. 'Actually, hold back on putting on the punch until I give you the signal. I don't want the stall mobbed before they get a drink.'

The idea of the stall being mobbed had sounded way over the top until Bríd went out to the garden and found that the Winter Warmers were now the star of the show. The stall was the first thing the press and the judges would see when they walked down the red carpet and, as she told Aideen later, it was just as well that it wouldn't feature pottery beakers made more than thirty miles away, given that the carpet itself was sponsored by a firm Phil knew in Cork. 'I dunno if she thinks she'll get the judges so pissed that they won't notice, but it's crazy to greet them with stuff that hasn't the slightest connection to Lissbeg.'

'Well, Dekko provided the brandy for the punch.'

'And that's the point, isn't it? The brandy's Spanish and Dekko's a Dub who doesn't even live here.'

'Still, it was nice of him to donate it.'

'Um.' Bríd looked at the raffle display, which had been relegated to a corner of the garden when the punch stall was set up. 'What about the crib that Fury O'Shea donated?'

She could see Aideen about to enthuse about how it was Cassie who'd asked for it, and stopping, in case she might say the wrong thing. Bríd made a face at her. 'I *can* give credit where credit's due, you know. It's a brilliant raffle prize. But it's not exactly featured, is it? And I know they've hardly sold any tickets yet.'

The garden was looking lovely, though. The trees and the herb beds were glistening white, and the gravel paths had been cleared of snow, so people could walk round in comfort. The other outdoor stalls, surmounted by Dan's castellations, were festooned with holly and trails of ivy, and already being set up with food and drink. And, according to the weather forecast, the day was due to be chilly, but bright and dry, with no danger of more snow before night-fall.

Inside the Old Convent Centre, all the offices and studio spaces were decorated with holly and ivy too. Several of the designers and artists had resisted Phil's medieval theming. Instead they'd produced their own sumptuous Christmas effects, featuring winter landscapes, polished wood, and handcrafted jewellery displayed on frosted mirrors. Rich scents of wax and honey drifted from a candle-maker's workshop, and bars of rosemary and lavender soap were piled up in the Edge of the World Essentials' reception area, where the Turners' R and D team were preparing to ask for feedback on their prototype package design.

Other stalls were set up in the old refectory, where the Lissbeg Choristers were due to sing carols during the afternoon. They, too, had dug their heels in, and monks' habits, sourced by Phil, had been quietly dumped in favor of their usual black trousers and wined-red shirts. Most of the other volunteer helpers had followed suit and worn ordinary clothes with the addition of official badges, the occasional pair of elf's ears and sparkly reindeer antlers.

Cassie's face-painting was just one of the activities organised for children up and down the corridors and, in the end, to everyone's surprise, Charles Aukin had offered himself as Santa Claus, complete with vast polished boots and a long silver beard.

In fact, there seemed to be two separate events happening simultaneously — Phil's competition entry, demanding immediate attention, and a less obvious, slightly-higher-tech-than-usual version of the normal Christmas Fête.

And in the midst of it all, Cassie seemed to be everywhere, providing answers to multiple last-minute problems.

The fact that Bríd appreciated the raffle prize didn't mean she'd changed her opinion of Cassie. If anything, she'd been finding her even more irritating lately. Take the raffle, for example. When you came to think of it, marching into someone's home and demanding a prize was just about the height of her. It was hard to imagine why Fury had been so accommodating.

The truth was that Fury was a bit like Cassie, the way he was so sure of himself. So maybe that was why the two of them had ended up in cahoots. They were certainly thick as thieves today, with Fury whistling at Dan to produce a hammer and nails and a stepladder, and herself holding it steady and giving orders about decorations. It was like there was nothing and nobody that Cassie didn't want to organise.

Fury had turned up with The Divil at his heels and a sack of mistletoe. As soon as Phil spotted it, she'd rushed up, full of excitement, and practically kissed him on both cheeks. 'You are such a star! And this is so medieval! Well, ancient, really. Druidic. Mistletoe from the dark depths of our own forest. Grown on the gnarled branch of an ancestral oak.'

Fury snorted. 'Holy God, is there no end to your ignorance? It's not a forest plant at all, it grows best in the open. What it wants is a man-made habitat and a host like a hazel or an apple. That whole druidic oak story was invented by some chancer who knew feck-all about druids or trees.' Then he'd lounged away before Phil could say another word.

Midday was the official opening time and, based on Phil's sleuthing, the ETA for the judges was somewhere round half past twelve. But you couldn't be sure: by the time they'd arrived in Carrick, for example, the TV celebrity who'd charged a fortune to cut the ribbon had gone home.

So Phil had avoided an opening ceremony. Instead, the Lissbeg event was to be in full swing by twelve thirty, apparently uncon-

432

cerned by the judges' arrival. In the background, armed with a walkie-talkie, she'd be working to a schedule. But everyone else had been urged to assume an easy, nonchalant air.

Mrs Draper, the former chairwoman of the Christmas Fête, privately told Bríd that she couldn't be doing with it. Phil would want to cop onto herself before she had the whole town laughing at her. Not that it wasn't already, because it was.

Bríd, who was arranging Christmas cookies and pots of relish on the HabberDashery stall, was about to agree when Phil appeared beside them. 'It's ten minutes to kick-off, and you won't believe what's happened! The priest's produced a whole new order of carols. And half the choristers don't know half the tunes, and the others don't know any of the words!'

'Can't they just say no, and stick to what they've practised?'

'Well, you'd *think,* wouldn't you? But they're in there like hares caught in the headlights. And now he's saying they've grouped themselves wrong and they'll all have to swap places.'

Mrs Draper, perceiving that her moment had come, removed her shoulder from the side of the stall and, ignoring Phil, turned majestically to Bríd. 'I suppose I'd better go inside and put manners on him. Stick a dozen mince pies in under the stall for me, Bríd, and a chocolate Yule log. I'll pick them up when I've got things back on track.'

Ten minutes later, crowds were beginning to gather in the nuns' garden, though most of them had had to come in through the courtyard gate. Phil had decreed that the red carpet should remain roped off until Ferdia — strategically placed on the roof — should signal the approach of the judges.

Aideen had begun to heat up the first batch of punch and Dan, with his hammer still stuck in his belt, was poised by the Winter Warmers stall. There was a board in front, saying 'OPENING SHORTLY', which Phil had instructed him to whip away as soon as she gave the word.

The HabberDashery stall was at the other side of the garden, with the stained-glass windows behind it, and the light from the refectory throwing coloured shapes on the snow. Bríd's Christmas produce was already selling hand over fist. She was doing a great trade in pots of cranberry jelly, tied up in gauze with gold ribbons, and oat biscuits, in hand-painted boxes, for serving with cheese. Everyone began by saying they had their presents got already, and then decided that some aunt or cousin could do with a salmon roulade or a mini Christmas pudding.

The pale winter sunlight was almost lost in the riot of festive lighting. All around the perimeter of the garden the trees were sparkling, light streamed from the café windows and, on either side of the red carpet, the rows of lanterns were lit. The crowds on the gravel paths were beginning to move indoors, and more people were arriving every minute.

Behind her, Bríd could hear the choristers bursting into song in the refectory. Everyone seemed to be singing the same carol, with great confidence. So, apparently, Mrs Draper had put manners on the priest.

With no one to help her, because Aideen was on the other stall, Bríd had hardly had a moment to raise her head. But as she handed over a customer's change, she noticed a group of figures clustered on the red carpet. Phil was in the middle, looking pretty frantic, and, to Bríd's annoyance, Cassie was there as well. Wasn't it just like her to get herself front and centre for the judges' arrival? Not that it mattered a damn, but it was irritating as hell.

Then, seconds after the thought crossed her mind, the group on the red carpet shifted, and Bríd realised that it couldn't be the judges' arrival after all. Not unless they'd come with a police escort.

Her eyes widened. The two figures beyond Phil and Cassie were a couple of guards in uniform. They weren't looking the least bit festive. And one of them, with his notebook out, seemed to be questioning Dan.

47

Cassie was on her way to begin her face-painting when she saw Phil summon Dan. Then, as a woman with a toddler on her shoulders moved out of the way, she saw the police uniforms. The older guard, who was short and a bit portly, she knew by sight as a sergeant stationed in Lissbeg. The taller, younger one, holding a notebook, was Shay.

Her first instinct was to cross the garden and find out what was wrong. Then she wondered if she ought to find Bríd first. As she dithered, Shay, looking very assured and threatening in his uniform, stepped in closer to Dan. Moving back instinctively, Dan found his way blocked by the sergeant, whose rocklike placidity looked to Cassie to be even more forbidding. On a thick leather leash, he was holding a quivering dog.

All of a sudden, Cassie knew exactly what was happening. As she stood there in dismay, Fury and The Divil appeared beside her. Apparently intent on lighting a roll-up, Fury eyed her slantways. 'What's the story?'

'I think it's Customs. It must be Dan's brandy. I know they've been waiting to make arrests.'

'And how exactly would you know that? No, wait, you can tell me later.' Fury flicked his match into a herb bed, where it sizzled in the snow. 'Get over there now and keep them talking. I'll get rid of the brandy.'

'What? Hang on. Wait a minute. What'll I talk about?'

But he was gone, with The Divil close behind him, and she crossed the garden with no idea of what she was going to say.

On the red carpet, Phil appeared to be about to go into hysterics. Cassie decided that her own best course was to be a dumb foreigner. So she tapped Phil on the shoulder and demanded to know where the face-paints had gone.

'What?'

'The paints. For my face-painting.' She turned to Dan, as if she hadn't noticed the guards. 'You haven't seen them, have you, Dan?'

Then she rounded querulously on Phil again. 'I ordered them specially from the internet. And I know I'm a volunteer, and that all this is for charity, but I *did* pay for them myself, Phil, and now they've disappeared.'

Phil goggled at her. Shay, who couldn't have expected Cassie to appear, looked simultaneously angry and wooden. The sergeant, who, Cassie suddenly remembered, was called Mossy Connor, took her elbow. 'If you wouldn't mind, Miss, we're asking a few questions.'

'Oh, I'm sorry. Of course. It's just that my sign says that the face-painting starts at twelve thirty. It's in the programme too. And we can't disappoint the kids, can we? Not at Christmas.'

She could see Shay beginning to look suspicious.

Beside her, Phil peered wildly at her watch. 'Oh, my God, is that the time? The judges . . .'

Cassie beamed at the sergeant. 'Not real judges, you know. Just the Winter Fest ones. They'll be here in a moment. We're all very excited.' Catching sight of the dog, she bent down to pat it. 'What a gorgeous fellow! What's his name?'

The dog, a silky-haired spaniel, looked at her severely.

'Oh, I shouldn't pat him, should I? Not when he's on duty. Or is that just guide dogs? I'm never sure.'

The sergeant said that the spaniel's name was Bullseye. 'It's a kind of a literary joke, you see, Miss. Bullseye in Dickens's *Oliver Twist* was a dog belonging to a criminal. While Bullseye here is a serving member of the Force. Mind you, we had other literary options. Elizabeth Barrett Browning's spaniel, Flush, for example. Or Montmorency, from *Three Men in a Boat*.'

Cassie had no idea what he was talking about but, catching the word 'literary', she asked madly if he'd ever considered joining a creative-writing group. 'They have one here at the library and it's really vibrant. I mean, it releases so much hidden talent and potential. Not to mention being a wonderful chance to make new and interesting friends.'

Shay cut across her, turning to Phil. 'Right, Mr Cafferky will have to come with us. And we'll need to search the premises.'

'The premises?'

'The whole area. Garden. Buildings. Outbuildings, if you have them.'

'But you can't. We've got the judges coming. And — oh, my God! — the press. Journalists. Television! I can't have the place overrun by sniffer dogs and guards.'

'I'm afraid you don't have a choice.'

440

Shay put his hand on Dan's shoulder, and Cassie was groping for something else to say when she heard Fury's voice. Looking round, she saw him approaching, the pinched-out rollup behind his ear and The Divil at his heels. 'How're you doing, Mossy? Ready for the Christmas?'

The sergeant nodded placidly. 'Sound out, Fury. How's things with you?'

Spotting the spaniel, The Divil bared his teeth ferociously. Fury hitched him firmly onto his hip. 'Never better, Moss, boy. What's the story?'

The sergeant jerked his head at Shay. 'We've had word from our colleagues that a stash of contraband was found down on Couneen pier.'

'Go to God!'

'In young Cafferky's shed.'

'Would you look at that!' Fury turned to Dan. 'Someone must have broken in and used it while you were away.'

Bullseye looked at The Divil and the sergeant looked at Dan. 'You've been off somewhere, have you?'

'Not at all, man. He's been here day and night, working for me. Well, I tell a lie. For Phil. But you haven't been down to the pier, have you, Dan?'

Cassie saw Dan's eyelashes drop, but he

441

looked up again immediately, taking Fury's cue. 'No.'

Fury shook his head. 'God, Mossy, you couldn't be up to them. To break into a poor lad's shed and use it like that.'

The sergeant nodded placidly again, but Shay squared his shoulders and flipped his notebook shut. 'This isn't getting you anywhere, Mr Cafferky. We've arrested Declan Donovan. And his uncle. And his Spanish associates. Mr Donovan who, I believe, is a business partner of yours?'

'No. Well, I mean . . .'

'Do you intend to give in evidence that he's not your business partner? Because you do share a business account.'

'But there's nothing in it!' Dan turned to Fury. 'He kept saying he'd put money in, but he never did. And I don't have any money. We didn't *do* any business.'

He stopped suddenly, his jaw dropping. 'Ah, shit. There is money in it. But it's what Phil paid me for the work I've been doing here.' He looked desperately at the sergeant. 'Your man said he'd be my investor. But I haven't seen a red cent of his, honest.'

Fury controlled The Divil, who was scrabbling to get down.

'Well, there you are, Mossy. He spots a gobdaw with a shed on a lonely pier. And he's in like Flynn, making a right fool of him.'

Quelled by a flicker of a glance from Fury, Dan visibly restrained himself, while the sergeant nodded lugubriously, as if despairing of the evils of the world.

For a moment it seemed to Cassie that the police might buy Fury's story, but Shay turned menacingly on Phil. 'Right. Well, I think we'll begin by tasting these Winter Warmers. After which, Madam, you might like to explain where you sourced the ingredients.'

Cassie realised that, ever since Fury had arrived, he'd been easing the group counter-clockwise, so that Shay and Mossy, with Dan between them, were facing the Broad Street entrance, and she and the others were looking towards the Winter Warmers stand. Behind it, unseen by the guards, Bríd and Aideen had been working like demons, and by now the 'OPENING SHORTLY' sign had been taken down, and a queue of people was forming.

Marching down the red carpet, with the others in his wake, Shay thrust himself to the front of the queue, demanding a drink. Aideen smiled at him politely and, dipping a ladle into the steaming pot, filled a cup with a dark brown liquid, adding a shaving of orange zest and a couple of liberal shakes of cinnamon and nutmeg.

Out of the corner of her eye, Cassie saw a man and his wife, who had just bought drinks, pulling faces. As she watched, the woman discreetly tipped the contents of her cup into a herb bed.

Shay, who was intent on the stall itself, seized the cup from Aideen and knocked back a mouthful. Immediately his face went scarlet and he choked. 'Jesus Christ, what is *in* that?'

The sergeant sniffed the cup. 'I'd say the base is probably Rooibos. Maybe a dash of hibiscus. Cayenne? Chilli? Something with a kick. No brandy anyway.'

Fury snorted. 'Ah, for God's sake, man, have a bit of sense. Would she be handing out Spanish brandy in cardboard cups?'

Shay swung round and eyeballed him. 'Who said the brandy was Spanish?'

Everyone else's eyes swivelled towards Fury, who cocked his head at Shay. 'Well, *you* did, didn't you? At least that's what I gathered. When you said your man's associates came from Spain.' He winked at the sergeant. 'Mind you, I thought that was the kind of detail you lads weren't supposed to blab about.'

The sergeant made an appreciative noise

444

and Shay jabbed his finger at the stall. 'Your advertising says drinks free for all.'

'And drinks free for all is what's gettin' gev out. Hot, spiced, nonalcoholic tisanes.'

'The posters say punch.'

'God, for a man of your trade, you're not very observant. There's a sign over there says "Cakes and Ale" and they're serving quiches and lattes. Have you not noticed Phil's medieval theme?'

Sticking his jaw out, Shay rounded on Phil. 'Right, we're combing the premises.'

Before Phil could answer him, her walkie-talkie squawked. 'Oh, my God, it's Ferdia. The press are coming!' She flicked a switch and listened for a minute, the colour draining from her face. 'And he's sighted the judges!'

Fury looked at the sergeant. 'What's wanted here, Mossy, is a bit of discretion. There's no call to go letting Lissbeg down. I'll keep an eye on Dan the Man, and you two go on inside with Phil and get searching. Though you won't find a sniff of any brandy. You can take my word for that.'

The sergeant nodded and said he'd suspected that would be the way of it.

'Ay, well, you were right, but, shur, you'd better earn your pay.'

Phil pivoted on her heels, looking frantic.

'But the greetings, the press packs . . .'

Fury gave her a shove. 'You can leave that to Cassie and me. Just keep the guards out of sight.'

The next twenty minutes felt like a circus. Propelled by Fury, Cassie galloped down the red carpet to where the group of judges seemed slightly perplexed to be greeted by a scarecrow figure in a torn waxed jacket, the indignant Divil, and a snub-nosed, effusive Canadian with green and silver hair. Smiling, shaking hands and handing out press packs, she could see Bríd scuttling back to the HabberDashery stall, and Aideen continuing to ladle out drinks to people who grimaced and spat as soon as they tasted them.

With the introductions performed, Fury and The Divil melted away, leaving Cassie to lead her group around the garden. Dredging up a disjointed assemblage of facts culled from half-remembered conversations, she outlined the Old Convent Centre's genesis in the discovery of Sister Michael's herbal, and explained how Lissbeg's determination to hang on to its local library had impacted on the town's regeneration. 'It's really amazing, the difference that one book made . . .'

Ushering them along a path towards the

open door to the old convent building, she saw Bullseye dragging Shay along a corridor, with Mossy and Phil bringing up the rear. Immediately she swerved to the left and led her own group towards the library courtyard. '. . . and not just one book, either. You've heard, of course, of the famous Carrick Psalter . . .'

As she bustled them up the library steps, she could see an elderly judge panting for breath. One of the others, a tourism official in fake Manolos, had ricked her ankle at the sudden left turn, and was now hobbling slightly. A photographer, with a better turn of speed, asked if they were going to have time to take pictures.

'Of course. Definitely. There's a photo-op arranged.'

With no idea whether there was or not, Cassie swept them through to the exhibition space.

'The layout here, of course, is state-of-the-art. And the psalter, which is, er, medieval, is one-of-a-kind and definitely local. Locally made. Definitely. Artisan painters were involved. And it was gifted to the town, of course . . .'

The elderly judge, who had got his breath back, looked impressed. 'My goodness, that's remarkable. Who was the donor?'

Cassie panicked, unable to remember the name. 'Er, well, he's rather a reclusive old gentleman. A philanthropist. I'm not sure that he'd necessarily want me to say . . .'

At that moment the judges and the press gaped collectively, as a figure appeared from behind the psalter case, extending a genial hand. He had a long silver beard, highly polished black boots, a scarlet suit trimmed with ermine, and a scarlet cap with a white bobble perched on the side of his head. 'No, no, I'm very happy to meet you all, and more than happy to speak about it. In fact . . .' he beamed round at them expansively '. . . the giving of this particular gift may have been the greatest pleasure of my life.'

48

Phil didn't stay to supervise the clear-up. By the time the judges, the press, and the public had left, she'd developed a massive migraine so Cassie and Bríd had told her to go home.

The surreal sense of two separate events happening concurrently had continued right through to the end of the day. As Cassie led the press and the judges down the corridors and in and out of the studios, Phil had hustled Shay, Bullseye, and the sergeant ahead of them, while Fury dodged nimbly between the two groups. Each time Cassie turned a corner, his stork-like figure would signal to her discreetly, and her hasty U-turns in response had bewildered her charges. At one point she'd whipped them into a room off the kitchen, where Maurice, the retired baker, was sitting with Mr Maguire, gorging on mince pies, and her hasty improvisations about quality control had baffled Maurice as much as the judges.

In the meantime, the stallholders, the crowds, and the volunteers had variously continued their sales and shopping, explained the centre's facilities, and piled into the old refectory, where the Lissbeg Choristers were belting out carols.

There was a tense moment in the middle of 'O Little Town of Bethlehem' when Bullseye became agitated and Darina Kelly was asked to open her bag. But it turned out he'd been alerted by a bottle of Bach Rescue Remedy, and Darina was restored to the alto section without need for further questioning.

That was one of several stories that Cassie heard afterwards, as they sat about, having got rid of Phil with the promise that they'd lock up. The perishable waste had been disposed of, and the garden stalls dismantled and stacked in the refectory. Cassie, Conor, and Aideen were recovering in the pensioners' day-care facility, with Dan and Bríd.

Aideen, who'd had to cope with the press reaction to the nonalcoholic Winter Warmers, was lying flat on her back on a pile of yoga mats.

Cassie had arrived after the others, having waved off the volunteers, including Pat.

Conor was slumped in a chair, wondering what Miss Casey was going to say about the headline he'd seen a reporter tap into his tablet: 'NATIONAL TREASURE PRESENTED TO LIBRARY BY SANTY' probably wasn't the story she'd hoped to come home to. Still, with any luck, the paper might run it before she got back.

Dan and Bríd were sitting side by side on a tabletop, looking shell-shocked. When Cassie joined them, Bríd slipped off the table and said she'd make tea. 'Or it might have to be cocoa. We used up the pensioners' entire supply of teabags on Fury's tisanes.'

Cassie followed her into the kitchen, which looked like a bomb site. 'How many boxes did you get through?'

'I dunno. Dozens. There seemed to be a helluva lot of peppermint and chamomile, and then we chucked in the Irish Breakfast, which may have been a step too far.'

'I thought that was the genius bit. The colour led Shay right up the garden path.'

She had seen him again as he'd marched out, looking furious. In the background, the sergeant was chatting amiably with Fury, and The Divil was taking it upon himself to see Bullseye off the premises. Shay was six feet ahead of them when Cassie had stepped into his path. 'I guess you'll have a report to write now before you get off to Limerick. Probably not one you'll want to allude to next time you go up for promotion, though? Shame about that.'

Now, remembering the look in his eye, she hugged herself happily. Adding insult to injury probably wasn't the most mature course to have taken. But it felt really good.

Bríd, who was stuffing empty cartons into a bin, looked up suddenly. 'Listen, I want to say this. I owe you one. Thanks.'

'No problem.' Cassie leaned into the bin, putting her weight on the cartons, so they'd collapse and make room for more. 'So, does this mean what I think it means?'

'What?'

'That you and Dan are a couple?'

Bríd stiffened, like The Divil seeing Bullseye. Then she laughed and shrugged. 'I guess. Well, yes, I suppose so. God knows he needs somebody to keep him out of jail.' She and Dan had talked, she said, and in January she was going to sit down with him and look at his business plan. 'And when I say "look at" I probably mean "draft". I don't think he's ever put anything down on paper. And he hasn't a clue about getting advice or grants.'

'Okay. That's logical. But it's not what I meant.'

Bríd threw her a baleful look and slammed the lid onto the rubbish bin. 'You're still not a relationship counsellor, Cassie, okay? So back off.'

Cassie grinned. 'Sorry, I can't seem to help it. I guess it's the matchmaker gene.'

Crossing to where the kettle was boiling, Bríd took a tray down for the mugs. 'I could do with some help with this cocoa, though, if you're up for it.'

'Okay.'

'Thanks.'

'You're welcome.'

They carried it through to the others and found Fury perched on the table next to Dan. The Divil, who was lying on Aideen's stomach on the yoga mats, leapt up and joined them, lapping cocoa from a saucer with his forepaws on the table: the fact that there was no milk, and that all the sugar had gone the way of the teabags, didn't seem to bother him.

Fury reached into the poacher's pocket of his jacket and produced a squat brown bottle.

Dan's eyes rounded. 'God, Fury, I thought you'd got rid.'

'So I did. The full case, bar the one.' He

453

removed the cork and tipped a slug of brandy into each mug, adding a splash to The Divil's saucer.

Cassie took a sip and felt the warmth slip down her throat. The slightly shaky chill she'd felt since they'd carried the stalls in from the garden left her, and her sense of exhaustion began to ebb.

Dan swallowed his mugful in one gulp. 'Where's the rest of it?'

'What kind of an eejit do you take me for? You may be a free man now, but they could whip you in for questioning after Christmas. I only got Mossy to back off because someone higher up had put a freeze on your joint bank account. He took my point when I said you hadn't the cash to do a runner.'

Bríd glared at Fury. 'Even if they do pull him in, they haven't got anything on him.'

'And as long as he's got nothing to tell them, they won't have anything on me.' He winked at Dan. 'Not that I'm saying you'd open your beak on purpose, mind. Or that Mossy Connor would ever try to finger me. It's the crowd inside in Carrick that I'd be wary of. So, no offence, Dan, but I'll keep the fate of the brandy to myself.' He buried his nose in his mug again before emerging to ask who had won the raffle.

Cassie, who'd locked the takings into the

office, on Phil's instructions, said that old Mrs Reily had had the winning ticket. 'And she's decided to give it to the day-care facility, here at the centre.'

'Fair enough. Did it make a few euros?'

Cassie looked remorsefully at Fury. 'Nothing like it should have done. I'm really sorry. And you'd have got a good price if you'd sold it instead of donating it to us.' Phil had stuck it in a corner of the garden, where you'd hardly see it, she said. And, of course, they'd sold almost no tickets in advance.

Downing the last of his cocoa, Fury reached into the pocket of his disreputable corduroy trousers and produced a large wad of euro notes. 'Well, we'd better get up to Phil's office and put that right.'

Dan found his voice before the others did. 'Holy God, you went and sold the brandy!'

'I told you before, boy, that you don't need to know what I did.'

Then, relenting, he dug Dan in the ribs. 'Anyway, by this time, the evidence should be a couple of hundred miles away, under a load of timber in the back of some fella's van.' Flicking the notes with his finger and thumb, Fury winked at Cassie. 'I suppose it's only rough justice that this lot should go to the homeless shelter in Carrick. So let's get it up to the office before I change my mind.'

They climbed the stairs in a bunch, with The Divil pattering behind them, and Fury added three hundred euro to the box that Cassie had labelled 'Raffle Takings'.

Seeing the sum, Cassie looked at him sharply. 'You can't have got that much for a case of black-market brandy, minus a bottle.'

'Yeah? Well, your man mightn't have known there was a bottle missing.'

'Even so.'

Poking a finger into the small of her back, Fury pushed her towards the doorway. 'Holy God, do you never stop sticking your nose in? If I made a bit extra on the timber deal, what's that got to do with you?'

'Well, I hope that raffle money cheers Phil up when she sees it, because it sounds like there isn't the slightest chance of Lissbeg winning the trophy.'

She explained to Fury that a barman in Moran's had texted to say he'd overheard the judges talking. The whole thing was a stitch-up. Apparently some high-up in government had a nephew who'd organised a Winter Fest in Dublin, and that had been earmarked as the winner from the start.

Fury snorted appreciatively. Then, as soon

as Cassie had locked the office, he hustled her down the corridor, announcing that they'd all go up on the roof and say 'Happy Christmas' to the moon.

She hadn't realised that the roof was accessible but, after a long trek down corridors, up staircases, and through eerie, empty rooms in the upper, undeveloped part of the old convent, they emerged from a pointed doorway into the night air. Darkness had fully fallen while they'd been doing the clear-up. High above, snow-filled clouds had billowed in from the ocean, driven by a wind from the northeast. Among them, the crescent moon was a sliver of silver and a blue-black sky was studded with bright stars.

There was a leaded space behind a parapet all around the rooftop and, walking carefully, Cassie crossed it and looked down on Lissbeg. Below her was a bird's-eye view of the little shops on the far side of Broad Street, with their shining snow-covered roofs. And there, in the centre of the street, was the long stone horse trough, where Pat had once sat nursing a baby, looking up at the stars. Single strings of coloured Christmas lights swung between the convent building and the shops and businesses opposite, receding as Broad Street narrowed and curved away beyond the marketplace.

She could see frost shining on windowsills and doorsteps, like the glitter sprinkled on the Christmas card she'd kept as a bookmark for years. She could feel the chill of the parapet under her elbows, and see the square of golden light in the window above the butcher's shop.

And, except for the Christmas lights and the lighted window, everything was composed of different shades of silver and blue. The starlight on the steep slate roofs with their dormer windows; and the pale, icy blue of the fallen snow; the curved shapes of the mountains in the distance; and the huge sky, like a dark, glimmering bowl. As she watched, snowflakes began to drift from the driven clouds. Leaning on the freezing parapet, Cassie laughed out loud. It was the Christmas card come to life and, just as she'd imagined when she'd first thought of coming here, she'd walked straight into it, mistletoe, glitter, and all.

49

As Pat had left the Old Convent Centre Cassie had caught up with her, carrying a paper bag. It was just some leftover mince pies, she'd said, made by the girls from HabberDashery. Then she'd given Pat a hug and rushed away.

Ger had never been a great one for sweet stuff and, lately, Pat hadn't had much of an appetite. She had a grand Christmas dinner all prepared, though, because Cassie was coming to eat with them. Still, even if the mince pies weren't eaten tomorrow, they could always be taken to Frankie's place for tea on Stephens's Day.

As Pat had crossed the road from the centre she'd seen that Ger had already shut the shop. Time was when the two of them used to be working till all hours on Christmas Eve, dealing with people who'd forgotten the rashers for the turkey, or the sausage meat for the stuffing, or the crock of goose fat for roasting the Christmas spuds. These days, people picked up all those bits and pieces in the supermarkets in Carrick when they rushed in to get last-minute batteries for toys they'd bought for the kids. Despite all her plans, this was the first year that Pat herself hadn't sent presents to Canada. She'd only have got them wrong and, besides, the heart had gone out of her. Instead she'd sent each of the lads a money order and told them to get themselves something they'd like, and gifts for the grandkids as well. After the last date for posting had passed she'd felt bad and wished she'd bought presents as usual. But it was too late then to change her mind.

When she let herself in, the shop was dark and very neat. Ger never left the displays or the counter anything less than spotless; and because he never had decorations up, the place looked the same on Christmas Eve as after any other working day.

Before going upstairs with the mince pies, Pat sat down on the straight-backed chair that stood next the door. Ger's was about the only shop in Lissbeg that kept up the old custom, and the same chair had been there since his father's time. It had a curly rail across the back, that was worn with polishing, and turned-out front feet that

460

were carved like lion's paws. Older customers were still glad of it, though young people
hardly noticed it at all. They moved so fast
nowadays you could hardly keep track of
them.

She'd already decided that if Ger was
planning to leave her she'd have to get him
to sit down and make a will first. That way,
whatever else happened, the lads would get
their rights. Ger would never willingly cheat
his own flesh and blood, but if some young
one from Cork had her claws stuck into
him, you couldn't be sure that he'd keep
thinking straight.

It could be that he'd fixed to leave as soon
as he'd got Christmas over, so a bit of Pat's
mind felt that she ought to confront him at
once. But that might spoil tomorrow for
Cassie. Still, she couldn't keep sitting here
in the dark with the Christmas lights out in
the street flashing. So, carrying the bag of
mince pies, she climbed the steps to the flat.

The first thing she saw was that Ger had
the range roaring, and the door at the front
of it open so you could see the leaping
flames. The lamp on the dresser was turned
on and the one that hung over the kitchen
table wasn't. And his mam's lustre vase was
up on the mantelpiece stuffed full of holly,
the bright berries clashing with the pink and

purple glaze.

Ger was sitting by the range with a cup of tea, wearing his blue jumper. He had a look on his face that told Pat he was working up to something, so maybe he'd decided to speak out now, and not wait till later.

There was a hollow feeling in her stomach as she put the paper bag on the table, and took off her coat and hat.

'Holy God Almighty, woman, what have you done to yourself?'

Ger's roar startled her because, with all the rush of the Winter Fest, and the fact that she'd been worrying, she'd completely forgotten that Cassie had cut her hair. They'd passed each other in a corridor just before the Winter Fest opened and, before she could argue, Cassie had badgered her into her hairdresser's gown — and, as a matter of fact, when she'd looked in the mirror afterwards, she'd thought the result was pretty good.

Now she pulled down the little, short, choppy bits at the front, like Cassie had showed her, and tucked the side bits back behind her ears. 'Do you not like it?'

Ger said nothing, but he poured her a cup of tea and Pat sat down.

'Do you like the holly I put in the vase?'

He must have decided to deck the place

out for Cassie, and that was nice. 'I do, of course. Where did you get it?'

'Cassie dropped it over. She said she had it spare.' Ger leaned forward. 'She said something else to me, too, the other day, when I met her in Carrick.'

Cassie had said nothing about meeting Ger in Carrick, so this was the last thing Pat had expected to hear. It took several minutes for her to realise what he was trying to tell her. And when it sank in, she was lost for words.

Ger, who had his hands jammed between his knees, looked across at her anxiously. 'You see why I said nothing, don't you? I didn't want you to worry. I never thought you'd get daft notions like you did.'

'So there isn't some young one in Cork?'

'Ah, listen, girl, would you have a bit of sense? Who'd want me?'

Pat said nothing again, till her brow creased. 'So the hospital says you've got some kind of heart thing?'

'Heart failure. They've done all the tests and they're optimising medication.'

'And that'll cure it?'

'Well, no.' Ger half held one of his hands out. Then he stuck it back between his knees, and shook his head. 'That's what I told Cassie all right. But no.'

'There's no cure?'

'No. And the way my heart is . . . At my age, it's complex. Like, there's things they can do for some people. But not me.'

She put her own two hands over her mouth and sat there looking at him. After a while, she stood up and went to put the kettle on. Then she turned round and asked him how long they'd said he'd got.

'Months. Maybe a year. Sure, I'm tough out, Pat, you'd never know. Aren't we all living on borrowed time anyway? You might well be gone yourself before this gets me.'

It was true enough, and just like Ger to say so.

He looked at her sideways and said that her hair looked grand.

Pat moved back and forth across the kitchen, making tea and automatically reaching for the mince pies. When she opened the bag, they were there inside, packed in a Tupperware box. On top of the box was a branching sprig of mistletoe.

Turning her face, Pat crossed the room and went to lower the blind. Years ago, before people got double-glazing, windows used to get starred all over with frost. She remembered her mother heating a thimble and letting her make patterns, little circles on the frosty glass through which you could see the shining world beyond. Now, outside her kitchen window, the Christmas lights were pulsing and splashes of green and crimson joined the golden firelight flickering on the walls.

Out of nowhere, she remembered the feel of the sliding sand underfoot the night she and Mary had climbed the dunes, looking for fuel for the fire. The sound of the sea had been loud in her ears and she'd held the hem of her skirt in her teeth as she'd scrambled upwards, knowing that Tom was below on the beach behind her. And the blade of grass had slashed her palm and the blood had tasted of salt when she'd tried to staunch it.

Leaving the blind where it was, and the room full of pulsing light, she turned back to Ger with the tea. He was looking awfully white and anxious in his blue jumper, and the hand he held out had a smudge of soot on it, from when he'd struggled with the range. He saw the smudge and rubbed at it ineffectually before taking his cup.

Pat sat down opposite him, glad of the warmth of the fire. She had a terrible urge to go and ring Mary, but that would be daft. She looked down at her own fingers, locked around her teacup. Suddenly she heard herself say she was sorry that Tom was dead.

'Why so?'

Her fingers tightened round the cup till the knuckles were white. 'Don't you know well that if he was alive you'd be round there talking to him?'

Ger set his tea on the range and leaned towards her. 'Haven't I got you here to talk to?'

That stopped Pat in her tracks and she looked up at him.

His face twisted into a kind of rueful grin. 'And, according to Cassie, I should have done it sooner. But how was I to know you were such a fool?'

Pat set her own teacup down beside his. She didn't feel like crying. It was more like she was choking. All those years when she'd turned to Mary and he'd turned to Tom. All kinds of memories they could have made that were never made at all. At this stage it didn't matter why or how it had happened: what mattered now was that they still had time.

Ger stood up and crossed the room to the window. Then, with his back to her, he asked what was in the paper bag.

Pat looked round bewildered till she saw what he meant. 'Mince pies. Cassie gave them to me. I thought we might take them to Frankie's on Stephens's Day.'

'Couldn't you and I have one here now by the fire?'

Pat's forehead creased. 'Do you think you should?'

'Name of God, woman, I've a heart condition, I'm not dying of obesity! It's Christmas Eve, can I not have a mince pie?'

Pat couldn't remember a single year when they'd sat by the fire on Christmas Eve with mince pies. But that was the point, she told herself, and wasn't it strange that Ger should see it? Now was the time to start making new memories . . . together.

She went to the table and opened the box of mince pies. The golden rounds were sprinkled with icing sugar and, here and there, the dark delicious filling had bubbled up from under the pastry lids. Only a few moments ago her throat had been dry and aching, but now she found she was hungry for their sweetness, in the same way that she felt a new hunger for every last crumb of life she and Ger would share.

As she piled the mince pies onto a plate, her eye was caught by Cassie's sprig of mistletoe. Each pair of pale green tear-shaped leaves made a shape that looked like a wishbone. And each veined berry was so translucent you could see the hopeful seed nestling at its heart.

Ger had gone back to his seat by the fire. With the mistletoe in one hand and the plate in the other, Pat crossed the room and set the mince pies down on the range to warm. Then she held the mistletoe over his head and bent down to kiss him.

EPILOGUE

Behind her, Cassie could hear the others laughing and drinking the brandy, and The Divil's shrill bark as he struggled in Fury's arms. Then the individual voices were lost as they drifted away to find new viewpoints from the roof. Staying where she was, Cassie reached into her pocket and pulled out her phone. When Dad answered, she could see that he was sitting in his den.

'Hi, sweetheart, what's happening?'

'Just calling to say hi because it's Christmas Eve.' She held up her phone to show him the falling snowflakes. 'Look!'

'It never snows in Ireland at Christmas time!'

'Well, that's what it's doing right now.' Moving the phone, she showed him the view of Broad Street. 'See? Just like a proper Christmas card.'

'Oh, my God! Where are you standing?'

'On the roof of the old convent.'

'*Where?*'

'A lot of things have changed here, Dad. You need to come and see for yourself.' She moved the phone so he could see Broad Street curving off into the distance. 'Remember PJ the barman in the Royal Vic in Carrick?'

'PJ? Is he still alive? What about him?'

'He says he'll make you an Old Fashioned when you come home to visit. Proper Canadian whisky with a touch of rye.'

She heard him laugh and, turning the phone, she brought it back to take in the butcher's shop. 'See that lighted window? That's where I'm going to be tomorrow. Having turkey and ham and Christmas pudding with Grandad and Gran. Will you call us? Honestly, Dad, I'm not being Min the Match. I know they'd love it.'

Watching his face, she found herself almost holding her breath and praying. She didn't know what had gone wrong in the past, and probably Fury was right that, in a way, it was none of her business. But she'd seen how Dad had reacted the time she'd called him from the flat. Pat had thought she hadn't, but it was obvious that he'd hated the sight of the home he'd grown up in. Maybe since then, though, he'd come to see things as Fury did — that it's best to

470

make your peace with the past while the people you love are still here. Anyway, he gave her a crooked smile and said okay, that he'd call.

'You will?'

'If you really want me to.'

'I really do.'

'Then I will.'

'Good. We'll be waiting.'

From the far side of the rooftop, Cassie could hear the others' voices, shouting 'Happy Christmas' to the moon. When she ended the call, she put her elbows back on the icy parapet and stared down across the street at the golden square of light.

ACKNOWLEDGEMENTS

My thanks to my brilliant editor, Hannah Robinson, and to everyone at Harper Perennial New York, who has worked so meticulously on this edition of *The Mistletoe Matchmaker,* and to Markus Hoffmann at Regal Hoffmann & Associates.

I also remain very grateful to all at Hachette Books Ireland, and, as ever, to my agent, Gaia Banks, at Sheil Land Associates, UK.

ABOUT THE AUTHOR

Felicity Hayes-McCoy was born in Dublin, Ireland, and graduated in English and Irish from UCD in the 1970s. She then built a successful UK-based career as an actress and writer, working in theatre, music theatre, radio, TV, and digital media. In addition to her successful Finfarran Peninsula series of novels, she is the author of two memoirs, *The House on an Irish Hillside* (UK: Hodder & Stoughton, 2012) and *A Woven Silence: Memory, History & Remembrance,* and of *Enough Is Plenty: The Year on the Dingle Peninsula,* a lifestyle book illustrated with her own photographs (Ireland: The Collins Press, 2015). She and her husband, Wilf Judd, divide their time between London and Ireland. With him she wrote *Dingle and Its Hinterland: People, Places and Heritage* (Ireland: The Collins Press, 2017).

The employees of Thorndike Press hope you have enjoyed this Large Print book. All our Thorndike, Wheeler, and Kennebec Large Print titles are designed for easy reading, and all our books are made to last. Other Thorndike Press Large Print books are available at your library, through selected bookstores, or directly from us.

For information about titles, please call:
(800) 223-1244

or visit our website at:
gale.com/thorndike

To share your comments, please write:
Publisher
Thorndike Press
10 Water St., Suite 310
Waterville, ME 04901

11/19

DATE DUE